FUTURE**SHOCKS**

FUTURESHOCKS

EDITED BY
LOU ANDERS

A ROC BOOK

Roc
Published by New American Library, a division of
Penguin Group (USA) Inc., 375 Hudson Street,
New York, New York 10014, USA
Penguin Group (Canada), 90 Eglinton Avenue East, Suite 700, Toronto,
Ontario M4P 2Y3, Canada (a division of Pearson Penguin Canada Inc.)
Penguin Books Ltd., 80 Strand, London WC2R 0RL, England
Penguin Ireland, 25 St. Stephen's Green, Dublin 2,
Ireland (a division of Penguin Books Ltd.)
Penguin Group (Australia), 250 Camberwell Road, Camberwell, Victoria 3124,
Australia (a division of Pearson Australia Group Pty. Ltd.)
Penguin Books India Pvt. Ltd., 11 Community Centre, Panchsheel Park,
New Delhi - 110 017, India
Penguin Group (NZ), cnr Airborne and Rosedale Roads, Albany,
Auckland 1310, New Zealand (a division of Pearson New Zealand Ltd.)
Penguin Books (South Africa) (Pty.) Ltd., 24 Sturdee Avenue,
Rosebank, Johannesburg 2196, South Africa

Penguin Books Ltd., Registered Offices:
80 Strand, London WC2R 0RL, England

First published by Roc, an imprint of New American Library,
a division of Penguin Group (USA) Inc.

First Printing, January 2006
10 9 8 7 6 5 4 3 2 1

Copyright © Lou Anders, 2006
Please see p. 309 for additional copyright notices.
All rights reserved.

Roc REGISTERED TRADEMARK—MARCA REGISTRADA

LIBRARY OF CONGRESS CATALOGING-IN-PUBLICATION DATA:

Futureshocks / edited by Lou Anders.
    p. cm.
  ISBN 0-451-46065-0
  1. Science fiction, American. 2. Culture shock—Fiction. 3. Forecasting—Fiction. I. Anders,
  Lou.
  PS648.S3F94 2006
  813'.6—dc22   2005026775

Set in Fairfield
Designed by Elke Sigal

Printed in the United States of America

For my wife, Xin,
who insures that the shocks in my own future
are all of a delightful nature.

And for my son, Arthur,
to whom the future truly belongs.

ACKNOWLEDGMENTS

*Thanks and then some are due to many people,
but chief among them are Alan Beatts, Cory Doctorow,
Gardner Dozois, Jen Heddle, Graham Joyce, Tom and Pam Kanik,
John Picacio, Robert J. Sawyer, and Liz Scheier.*

CONTENTS

INTRODUCTION:
THE BUSINESS OF LYING

"The oldest and strongest emotion of mankind is fear,
and the oldest and strongest kind of fear is fear of the unknown."
—H. P. LOVECRAFT, "Supernatural Horror in Literature"

"Science fiction, essentially the literature of altered circumstances,
is the obvious place to seek a language for the unprecedented,
especially since it offers as many anxious images as utopian ones."
—COLIN GREENLAND, *The Entropy Exhibition*

Once upon a time, it was impossible to fear nuclear annihilation. Only the invention of the nuclear bomb gave rise to the nuclear phobias of the sixties and seventies. What other phobias might there be, just waiting to be discovered? What shocks lie in store for us, untapped for now, but of which it will be possible to be afraid *one day*? Surely there are undreamed-of dark linings surrounding the silver clouds of artificial intelligence, space and cyberspace exploration, increased globalization, the coming transhumanism and unchecked bioengineering? The dystopian tradition has long been a strong thread within science-fiction literature, and not every potential future gleams so bright as to require mirrorshades.

There are those who feel that science fiction's significance lies elsewhere than in its prognostications. In the introduction to her classic work *The Left Hand of Darkness*, Ursula K. Le Guin writes, "Science fiction is not predictive; it is descriptive. . . . Prediction is the business of prophets, clairvoyants, and futurologists. It is not the business of novelists. A novelist's business is lying." Or, to express it another way, as Howard V. Hendrix stated at a recent conference, "No matter how often we're zapped with the shock of the new, we still won't be cured of the future." Simply put, the purpose of George Orwell's landmark novel *1984* was not to prevent the rise of a totalitarian government in 1984 but to describe unnerving trends he observed around him in 1948. Science fiction's primary relevance is not in its prognostic capabilities but rather in the insights it provides when its extrapolations of the future are used as a lens through which to examine the human condition in all its ramifications.

On the other hand, sometimes science fiction gets it right, as in 1946, when Murray Leinster published "A Logic Named Joe" in the pages of *Astounding Science Fiction*, making him the sole science-fiction writer to predict the personal computer and the Internet. In 1944, Cleve Cartmill described the chain reaction of a nuclear bomb so accurately in his story "Deadline" that the author was investigated by the FBI, the agency being concerned over a potential breach of security on the Manhattan Project. The very idea of a nuclear bomb was first introduced in H. G. Wells's 1914 novel *The World Set Free*. Physicist Leo Szilard read the novel in 1932, and by 1934, he had filed for patents on the idea. Then, of course, the paragon of our genre, Sir Arthur C. Clarke, is generally credited with having created the notion of the communications satellite. The term *robotics* was coined by Isaac Asimov, and the word *cyberspace* derives from the fiction of William Gibson.

But whether science fiction's predictions emerge as being accurate portrayals of tomorrow or merely fanciful metaphors of today is immaterial. As the only literary genre that even acknowledges the impact of technological development, its importance to the Information Age is paramount. It has often been said that change is the only constant, and indeed, the rate of change is accelerating exponentially. This is a phenomenon that causes some people tremendous excitement and others a great deal of anxiety.

Outside of the science-fiction field, perhaps the most prominent acknowledgment of this occurrence was made by futurologist Alvin Toffler, who proposed a new psychological disorder for our evolving world. In his 1970 work of the same name, Toffler described "future shock" as "the dizzying disorientation brought on by the premature arrival of the future . . . a time phenomenon, a product of the greatly accelerated rate of change in society. It arises from the superimposition of a new culture on an old one. It is culture shock in one's own society." Toffler went so far as to suggest the formation of special groups exclusively dedicated to examining the future, to determine the effects, pro and con, of each new technological development before its implementation into society. Whether Toffler would recognize this or not, such a group already exists and, in fact, has accrued quite a distinguished history. Many of its celebrated members are gathered in these very pages.

What follows is an anthology of science-fiction stories that envision the dangers lying in wait for us on the road ahead, or lurking just around the corner of history. Each of the writers has been asked to provide an examination of new fears arising out of sociological, biological, or technological change. There may be no cure for the future, but some ingenious folks are rushing to meet the future head-on. What they find in these journeys of the imagination may be enlightening, terrifying, even amusing, or simply . . . shocking!

—*Lou Anders, May 2005*

Paul Di Filippo is one of the most imaginative individuals working the field today. A highly prolific writer, he has published seventeen books since his first, *The Steampunk Trilogy*, appeared in 1995. However, as Paul points out, if you start counting from his first appearance in a professional magazine in 1985, his totals do not yet average out to one book per year. By 2010, the twenty-fifth anniversary of that debut, he hopes to have twenty-five books to his credit. Meanwhile, he continues to live in Providence, Rhode Island, with his mate, Deborah Newton, two cats named Penny Century and Mab, and a cocker spaniel named Ginger.

SHUTEYE FOR THE TIMEBROKER
Paul Di Filippo

Three A.M. in the middle of May, six bells in the midwatch, and Cedric Swann, timebroker, was just sitting down to nocturne at his favorite café, the Glialto. He had found an empty table toward the back, where he would be left alone to watch the game.

The game on which his whole future depended.

He took a rolled-up Palimpsest flatscreen from his pocket, snapped it open, and the baby freethinker within the screen, knowing Cedric's preferences, tuned to a live feed from Pac Bell Park. Shots of the stands showed that the brilliantly illuminated park was full, and that was good news, since Cedric had brokered the event. A timebroker was nothing if he couldn't deliver warm bodies. But the box score displayed in a corner of the screen held less happy tidings.

The Giants were losing 4–6 against Oakland, with only one more inning to go.

Cedric winced and crumpled, as if pitchforked from within. He had fifty thousand dollars riding on the Giants.

The bet had been a sure thing, intended to offset some of his debts from a recent string of gambling losses. But just prior to the game the fucking Giants had been forced to bench their best pitcher with injuries. The lanky Afghani newbie had been moved up from the Kabul farm team to boost the fortunes of the San Francisco team after their disastrous '36 season, and he had indeed done so. But now his absence was killing Cedric. And the club's remaining players were stumbling around like a bunch of fucking sleepers!

The failure of his home team was most disappointing.

Especially since Cedric didn't have the fifty thousand dollars he had wagered.

A window opened in Cedric's Palimpsest, showing the facial of the Glialto's resident freethinker. As usual, the restaurant's freethinker wore the likeness of Jack Kerouac. On the occasion of the one-hundredth anniversary of Kerouac's birth, there had been a big Beat revival nationwide—but nowhere more fervently than in San Francisco—and the Glialto freethinker had adopted its avatar then, although the café's personality was decidedly less bohemian than old Jack.

"Happy six bells, Cedric. What'll you have this hour?"

"Uh, I don't know. Jesus, I'm not even hungry—"

"C'mon now, you know what your mom would say. 'Skip caloric nocturne, risk metabolic downturn.'"

"Yeah, right, if my mom was the fucking NIH or FDA. Oh, all right, then, make it something simple. Give me a plate of fish tacos. And an Anchor Steam."

"Coming right up, Cedric."

The little window closed just in time to afford Cedric a complete panoramic view of an A's player slamming a home run out of the park.

"Christ! I am so drowsily boned!"

Bobo Spampinato was not going to be happy when he or his tetraploid muscle came to collect his fifty thousand. Cedric's boss, Tom Fintzy, of Fintzy, Beech, and Bunshaft, Timebrokers, was not going to be receptive to another loan request, and in fact would quail at Cedric's firm-tainting misbehavior, if he should learn of it. Cedric already owed a couple of years' projected commissions to FB&B, loans taken out ostensibly to take advantage of some hot IPOs, and the boy-wonder timebroker had been indulged thus far only because of his exceptional past performance.

And Caresse. Caresse was going to be extremely disappointed in Cedric, to say the least, especially after financing her boyfriend's most recent expensive course of therapy.

Cedric moaned loud enough for nearby patrons to hear him and gaze sympathetically or disapprovingly. He buried his head in his hands to escape their stares. The café in San Francisco's North Beach neighborhood was not as packed as it would've been at midnight, when many people ate nocturne. But there was still a good-sized crowd of witnesses to Cedric's despair and shame.

Noise from the happy, busy throngs on Columbus Avenue pulsed in as the café's door opened and closed. People going to work, to clubs, to parks, to movies, to happy homes. Why couldn't Cedric be one of them, moving easily through the brightly lit city at six bells in the midwatch? But he was completely isolated, and all because of his stupid gambling addiction.

The rumble of a small kibe's wheels approaching caused Cedric to look up. Here came his meal. The kibe deposited the dish and drink before Cedric, then rolled off. The smell of the fish tacos made Cedric nauseous, and he pushed the plate away. But he downed the beer in one long swallow and ordered another.

Going back to work drunk could hardly complicate his life any further, and it might blunt the pain.

The fourth generation of antisomnolence drugs after Provigil, released in 2022, completely eliminated the need to sleep.

With the simple ingestion of a single daily pill, humanity was forever freed from the immemorial shackles of nightly unconsciousness.

As easily as that, people increased their effective life spans by a third.

Dreaming and whatever function it fulfilled were pushed way down below liminal awareness. Scientists were not quite sure if such drugs as Eternalert, ZeroBlink, Carpenoct, and Sunshine Superman even permitted dreaming at any stratum of the mind's operation. But in any case, no one seemed to suffer from the banishment of these ancient nightly hallucinations.

The issue of physical tiredness, the cyclical buildup of somatic fatigue poisons, was remedied by dietary nutraceuticals, intervals of sedentary activities, and bouts of physical therapy.

In a few short years after the introduction of these drugs, enormous changes in global society were already institutionalized.

Developed countries who could afford the pricey proprietary drugs now operated on twenty-four/seven time. (The poorer nations remained zones of sleep infiltrated by rich elites of the perpetually wakeful.) The vast majority of the citizens of America, for instance, made no distinction among any of the hours in any given twenty-four-hour period. Work and play, study and travel, might occur at any time of the day. The old navy system of watches and bells, suited for perpetual alertness, was commonly adopted. All the old distinctions between hours when the sun was up and the hours when it was down disappeared. Before too long, hyperflextime reigned, with duties and pleasures being dynamically apportioned among the available hours.

Strange synergies of R & D began to accumulate, as single-minded researchers were able to doggedly follow paths of experimentation without downtime, and could coordinate their efforts globally without the impediments of operating in incompatible time zones. New products flooded forth at unprecedented rates.

But most important, time became fungible, a commodity to be traded.

And whenever there was something to be traded, brokers arose.

A timebroker mediated between individuals and institutions, citizens and the government. Individuals registered their shifting schedules hour by hour with a timebroker of their choice. During such and such hours, they would be willing to work; during other hours, they were interested in attending a concert, a ball game, a university class, a gym. Contrarily, institutions registered their needs. The symphony wants a thousand listeners at four A.M. on Sunday. Can you provide them?

Institutions paid the timebrokers large fees for delivering guaranteed numbers of people—customers or workers or jury pools. Citizens received discounts on the face value of tickets or tuition, or bonuses from employers, or tax breaks from the state and federal governments, for being willing to commit blocks of time via their timebroker. Timebrokers lured institutional customers away from their competitors by exhibiting superior reliability and offering sliding fees. Individual citizens jumped from broker to broker based on offers of better incentives. Brokers could refuse to service individuals based on a record of noncompliance with promises.

Timebrokers operated globally, facilitating trade among all the hyperactive countries no longer in thrall to sleep.

In America, fifteen years after the release of fourth-generation a-som drugs and on the verge of seventh-generation versions, unemployment had effectively disappeared as the economy expanded by a third. Everyone who wanted a job had one. Timebrokers were especially in demand.

Except those unlucky enough to fall afoul of their own bad habits.

Like Cedric Swann.

Bobo Spampinato and his goons came for Cedric during the dogwatch after the game. Cedric would have preferred, of course, to deal with the bookie at his home, a luxurious condo in the Presidio with killer views of the Golden Gate Bridge. In the privacy of his quarters, Cedric could have kept his indiscretions quiet, begged for mercy without shame, and generally made a pitiful spectacle of himself, thus possibly earning leniency. But perhaps knowing this, and being a man of no mercy, Bobo accosted Cedric at work.

"Mr. Swann, there are some, uh, people here to see you. They claim it's about a debt of yours." The voice of Cedric's executive assistant, Delma Spicer, normally firm and assured, emerged from Cedric's Palimpsest in quavering tones. Her pixie face, maculated with active tribal tags, gleamed with a sudden exudation of flop sweat.

Cedric looked frantically about his office for a miraculous exit he knew wasn't there. Behind the framed Todd Schorr print? No such luck. At last he caved in. What else could he do? Time to take his medicine. How bad, after all, could it be?

"Send them in, Delma."

Rising to his feet, Cedric managed to come around to the front of his work surface just as Bobo and friends entered.

Bobo Spampinato was a short, scrawny Laotian man of boyish appearance. He had been adopted as an infant by a childless Italian couple. Bobo's new father chanced to be responsible for half of the illegal gambling in California. Upon the old man's death, Bobo took over the family business. He was normally quite busy directing matters at a high level, and a field call such as today's was something of a perverse honor.

As usual, Bobo wore ErgoActive sandals, a pair of linen dress shorts, and a tie-dyed T-shirt whose living swirls reconfigured themselves stochastically based on a continuous feed of the Vegas line. His bowl-cut black hair fringed a pair of hard dark eyes. His unsmiling lips betokened the seriousness of the occasion. Despite the stylishness of his own fashionable suit, Cedric felt like a child next to Bobo's grim, informal cool.

Bobo was flanked by his muscle: two enormous humans wearing only leather chest harnesses and thongs, whose genome, judging by the brow lines, hirsuteness, and musculature on display, plainly included snippets of gorilla.

Cedric gulped. "Um, hello, Bobo. Good to see you. I was just going to call—"

"You owe me close to two hundred grand now, Swann. What are you going to do about it?"

"Well—pay it back, of course. Little by little . . ."

The larger of the gorilla-men grunted discontentedly, and Cedric wondered if they could even speak.

"Not good enough, Swann. I'm not a bank that makes loans. I need that money now. All of it."

"But, Bobo, please, that's impossible. I don't have that kind of liquidity. My condo's mortgaged to the hilt. Even if I sold everything I own, I couldn't raise two hundred Gs."

"That's not quite true. I understand that your loving parents were quite generous when you graduated from college a few years ago. You have a forty-year a-som rider on your health insurance, all paid up."

When fourth-generation antisomnolence pills hit the marketplace, most health insurers refused to cover them, deeming them lifestyle drugs, choices, not necessary to combat any disease. But as the drugs became ubiquitous and essential for any full-fledged citizen to serve as a fully functioning member of society, the insurers relented to the extent of writing riders to their policies that would allow people to buy the drugs at a discount. A discount that still allowed immense profits for the pharmaceutical firms. Such clauses made the difference between being able to afford a-som and devoting half of one's income just to maintaining wakefulness parity with the Joneses.

Cedric almost could not comprehend what Bobo was demanding. In hock already to his employer, there was no way Cedric could afford a-som payments out of his weekly salary without his insurance policy.

And without a-som, one might as well not exist.

Stuttering, Cedric said, "It . . . You . . . That's unthinkable."

"But obviously I am thinking about it, Swann. And you have about ten seconds to do the same."

The smaller of the gorilla-men snorted through gaping nostrils while the other cracked knuckles the size of walnuts. Cedric blanched.

"Time's up. What'll it be, Swann?"

With shaking hands, Cedric used his Palimpsest to transfer his prepaid a-som coverage to Bobo.

Rolling up his own flatscreen with a satisfied grin, Bobo said, "That squares us, Swann. You know how to reach me for your next bet. But I'll have to get the money up front from now on."

Bobo and company departed. Cedric collapsed against his work surface. But he was not permitted any time to collect his wits or assess his future.

Tom Fintzy, head of FB&B, offered a stern patrician mien to the world at the best of times. White-haired yet virile—his hair color a disarming cosmetic shuck, his virility the result of regular telomere maintenance and resveratrol patches—the chief timebroker had held many lucrative, high-status jobs prior to the a-som era: CEO of this and president of that. Cedric had heard all the boring tales endlessly. But upon coming out of early retirement, Fintzy had truly carved his niche in the timebrokering field, showing a superior talent for collating huge masses of individuals with the needs of corporations, NGOs, and government agencies. Now, standing in Cedric's office, Fintzy looked even more unforgiving and decisive than ever.

"Please pay attention, Cedric. I believe you know that according to your employment contract, our firm's freethinker is allowed to monitor your office space and all media traffic in and out of same."

Cedric's Palimpsest, still unrolled, now displayed the facial of FB&B's freethinker, an image of a smiling, grandmotherly matron.

"Hello, Mr. Swann," said the freethinker. "I'm afraid you've been a bit naughty."

"During the time you were entertaining your latest guests," Fintzy continued, "our freethinker deduced the illegal nature of your past activities, assembled proof of all your illicit transactions, including the records of the loans from FB&B you obtained under false pretenses, wrote a report on your case, synopsized it, outlined the range of recommended disciplinary actions and subsequent cost-benefit analysis, and submitted the whole to me. I have tried to act in a similarly timely fashion. Mr. Swann, you will not be turned over to any law-enforcement agency by us, due to the embarrassing nature of your crimes and the way it would reflect poorly on the character of FB&B. However, your contract with us is hereby terminated and any future salary you might earn will be garnished by us until your loans are repaid. Moreover, you will have a black flag attached to your Universal CV. You have ten minutes to clear the building before security arrives."

Cedric, of course, could make no palliating reply to such a comprehensive and clearly stated case of malfeasance. Nor could he find it in himself to rage or bluster or revile. So he simply gathered the personal contents of his office—everything fit in a small trash basket—and left.

Dressed in the living jelly slippers known as Gooey Gumshoes, her denim Daisy Dukes revealing generous crescents of butt cheek, and a bandeau top straining across her ample chest, the attractive black woman carried what appeared to be a small shallow suitcase. She stepped into the living room of Cedric's condo and said, "Just a minute, honey, and I'll make you feel all better." She set the suitcase down in the middle of the open floor space, stepped back, and sent a command via her Palimpsest.

Cedric watched grimly from his seat on the couch. He doubted that anything could make him feel better.

Unfolding its cleverly hinged sections, extruding carbon-fiber struts, cantilevering, snicking together in LEGO-block fashion, tapping compressed air cylinders and flexing plastic muscles, the suitcase bloomed like a newborn foal struggling to its feet. In under thirty seconds, a padded massage table—fairylike, but capable of supporting the heaviest client—stood waist-high where the suitcase had rested.

"Oh, no, Caresse, I'm not in any mood for a massage—"

Caresse Gadbois advanced toward the professional stage where she relieved the daily somatic tensions of her eternally on-the-go clientele—in a resolutely nonsexual manner. Licensed and bonded, Caresse had attended school for two years and apprenticed for an equal period before establishing her own practice. She was one of tens of thousands of traveling masseuses who helped the a-som society function.

"The hell with that shit, boyfriend! That's your toxins talking. I don't know what's bothering you, but whatever it is, it won't seem quite so bad after a massage. Strip, pal, and get on the table. What's the point of having a masseuse for a girlfriend if you can't get a nice backrub for free anytime you need one?"

Caresse's mildly accented voice—her family hailed from Haiti, having legally emigrated to America during Caresse's youth, when their island nation became a USA protectorate—worked its usual voodoo magic on Cedric. He undressed down to his boxers as Caresse removed various lotions and balms from her large professional satchel.

On the table, Cedric relaxed under Caresse's expert touch. His consciousness descended a notch, into that slightly hypnagogic microsleep which scientists theorized helped to permit continuous awareness. Still able to maintain an undemanding conversation, Cedric listened to an account of Caresse's day, the various people she had helped, interjecting suitable affirmatory comments at regular intervals.

Admittedly, Caresse's ministrations did help to relieve some of the tension in Cedric's frame. When she had finished, he arose from the table feeling that perhaps he was not totally doomed after all. As he dressed, while Caresse convinced her massage table to resume its suitcase disguise, he said, "Caresse, honey, I have something to tell you. Unfortunately, it's pretty bad news."

Caresse's typically cheerful attitude dissolved in a sober frown. "What is it, Cedric? You're not sick, are you?"

Cedric winced at Caresse's genuine concern. Her first thought had been for his health. What a selfish jerk he had been—still was! Telling her the truth would not be easy. Might as well just plow painfully ahead.

Sitting on the couch with Caresse, Cedric revealed everything, from his final unwise wager on the Giants—damn their shitty playing!—through the surrender of his a-som coverage to Bobo, down to his firing and black-flagging.

When he had finished, Caresse said nothing for an excruciating time. Then she said, "The therapy didn't take then. I just threw my money away on quacks. I'm lodging a complaint!"

Cedric hung his head. "No, Caresse, don't. I was on tropeagonists the whole time I was at the clinic. I smuggled them in. Caresse—I just couldn't bring myself to give up gambling! But I've hit bottom now. Really, I have! I'm lower than coffee futures. Honest!"

Silence. Cedric focused on his palms folded in his lap, waiting for Caresse to render judgment on him, experiencing each second as a hellish eternity. He stole a glance at her face, and saw that she was silently crying. He felt like shit.

At last she said, "I was right. You *were* sick. Really sick. Your addiction was totally stronger than you could deal with. But if you think you've changed now—"

"I am, I am! Totally changed!"

"Well, then, I guess I can forgive you."

Now they were both crying. Through the tears, they kissed, and the kissing soon passed into more frenetic activity, utilizing the substantial couch as platform. There was no bedroom to retreat to. People didn't have bedrooms any longer. They had a variety of couches and recliners used for relaxing. This furniture supported sex as well. If someone was a real hedonist, they might have a room devoted just to screwing, but such an excess was generally thought déclassé. Most people happily used their ex-bedrooms for media centers or home offices or rec rooms, gaining extra functional apartment space at no additional cost.

At one point early on in the lovemaking, Caresse kicked off her Gooey Gumshoes and the footware obediently humped themselves across the floor and out of the way beneath the couch, moving like certain ambulatory mycotic ancestors.

The makeup sex was spectacular. But Cedric emerged depressed anyhow. The full consequences of his fall now weighed heavily on him. Cuddling Caresse, he generously shared his anxiety with her.

"I'm going to have to give up this place. I'll lose all my equity. Not that it's much. And I've only got a little more than a week's worth of a-som on hand. I *would* have to get fired right near the end of the month! So I'll have to find a job right away. But I can't work as a timebroker. Fintzy's fucking black flag sees to that! But I don't have any experience that would bag me a job that pays as much. And with the garnish on any future salary, how am I going to make ends meet? It looks like I'm going to have to choose between becoming homeless, or becoming a . . . a sleeper!"

Cedric waited for Caresse to offer him an invitation to live with her. But he waited in vain. Had he pushed her affection and charity too far? When she finally spoke, her comment was noncommittal and only vaguely comforting.

"Don't worry, Cedric; it'll all work out."

Cedric tried to be macho about his plight. But his fear leaked out. "Right, sure, it all will. But I'm just a little scared, is all."

Like most of the developed, a-som world, the United States of America now boasted a birthrate which fell well below replacement levels, the culmination of long-term historical trends that had begun a century ago, and which a-som tech had only accelerated. Had immigration not kept the melting pot full, the country would have become radically depopulated in a few generations.

Children could not take antisomnolence drugs until puberty, a condition which nowadays statistically occured on the average around age twelve. Their juvenile neurological development required sleep, periods in which the maturing brain bootstrapped itself into its final state. This process had proven to be one of the few vital, irreplaceable functions of sleep. (And even if infants and toddlers had been able to take a-som drugs, no sane parent would have wanted them awake twenty-four/seven.)

Consequently, parenting had acquired another massive disincentive. The hours when children had to sleep had formerly been shared by their parents in the same unconscious state. No particular sacrifice had been required on the part of the adults. But now, staying home with archaically dormant children constituted cruel and unusual punishment, robbing adults of all the possibilities that a-som opened up. More than ever, adults concerned with careers or intent on socializing and indulging their interests regarded child raising as a jail term.

The child-care industry had adapted and boomed in response. Battalions of nannies specializing in the guardianship of sleeping children now circulated throughout the country, supporting the flexible lifestyles of absent mothers and fathers. Amateur babysitters had gone the way of paperboys. But the job, while essential, was still regarded as unskilled labor, a view reflected in its low pay.

Sinking down through the vocation sphere, the black flag on his UCV denying him employment everywhere he turned, Cedric Swann had finally found employment as one of these rug-rat guardians.

Ironically, the intermediary between Cedric and his employer, TotWatch, Inc., were the timebrokers Fintzy, Beech, and Bunshaft.

Cedric had reluctantly continued his registration with his ex-employer, acknowledging that FB&B did offer the best deals. And apparently, the firm's ire at Cedric did not impede its greed for another warm body to meet the quotas of its clients—if any client would have him.

Desperate for money, Cedric had specified an open-ended availability as a nanny. Children were asleep at all bells of all watches. Their schooling was just as free-form as their parents' lives. Class time—a small fraction of total learning hours dispersed across various modalities of instruction—was brokered out to public and private schools that operated around the clock.

Today, Cedric had a gig over in his old neighborhood. The contrast with his own new residence couldn't have been greater, and the irony was not lost on him.

After selling his condo and most of his furniture and possessions, Cedric had found a cheap apartment in Chinatown, above a dank, smelly business that biocultured shark fins for the restaurant trade. Now all his clothes smelled of brine and exotic nutrient feedstuffs, and his view was not of the Golden Gate Bridge, but rather the facade of a martial-arts academy, where a giant hardlight sign endlessly illustrated deadly drunken-master moves.

As for his a-som doses, Cedric had managed to stay supplied. But only by abandoning the brand-name sixth-generation pills he had been taking and switching to a generic fifth-generation prescription. The lesser drugs maintained his awareness fairly well. At least he couldn't detect any changes in his diurnal/nocturnal consciousness; but then again, that was like trying to measure a potentially warped ruler with itself. Although occasionally his limbs did feel as if they were wrapped in cotton batting, and his tongue would stick to the roof of his mouth.

Leaving his apartment at first bell of the first watch, Cedric used his Palimpsest to find the location of the nearest Yellow Car. One of the ubiquitous miniature rental buggies was parked just a block away, and Cedric was grateful for small miracles. He could have taken a crosstown bus, or even have walked to save money, but he felt that his spirits would benefit from a small indulgence.

Cedric missed so many things that had vanished from his life. Naturally he missed his luxurious home and lifestyle. The sensations engendered by those material losses had been expected. But more surprisingly, Cedric missed being a timebroker, the buzz he had gotten from collating supply and demand, from filling a San Diego trope-fab with eager workers or making the San Jose Burning Man a success. Now he felt powerless, isolated, unproductive. Watching sleeping *larvae!* How had he fallen so far?

But if not for Caresse's continued affection and support, Cedric would've felt a lot worse. Having her as his girlfriend had been his mainstay. Caresse continually reminded him that the black flag on his UCV would expire at the end of five years or at the repayment of all his debts, whichever came first, and that all he had to do was stick it out that long. Her optimistic outlook was invaluable. And the free body rubs and the sex didn't hurt either. They were supposed to hook up after Cedric's gig later, in fact, and Cedric was counting the minutes till then.

Climbing into the Yellow Car, Cedric started it with his Palimpsest. He noticed with irritation the low-fuel reading on the car's tank, due to an inconsiderate prior driver, and swore at the necessity of stopping at a refueling station. But then again, he could top off his Palimpsest with butane as well.

The dusk-tinged streets of San Francisco on this lovely late-spring evening were moderately thronged with busy citizens. There were no such phenomena as "rush hours" or "off-hours" any longer. The unsynchronized mass impulses of the citizenry, mediated by the timebrokers, resulted in a statistically even distribution of activity across all watches. No longer did one find long queues at restaurants at "dinnertime" or lines at the DMV. With every hour interchangeable, and everything functioning continuously, humanity had finally been freed from the tyranny of the clock.

After hitting the pumps, Cedric made good time to his destination. The large glass-walled house where Cedric was to babysit commanded a fine view of the bay, and Cedric felt a flare of jealousy and regret.

Alex and Brian Holland-Nancarrow greeted Cedric pleasantly. Both of the slim, modishly accoutred men shared an expensively groomed appearance that bespoke plenty of surplus cash—as if the house weren't proof enough of that.

"We're in a bit of a hurry, Cedric. But let us show you a few things you'll need while you're here. As you know from TotWatch, we have two children, Xiomara and Tupac. They're both asleep already. Here's their bedroom."

Reverently, the fathers opened the bedroom door a crack to allow Cedric to peer within. The unnaturally darkened chamber, the smell of children's breath and farts, the sound of comalike breathing—these all induced in Cedric a faint but distinct nausea. It was like looking into a morgue or zombie nest, or a monkey cage at the midnight zoo. He could barely recall his own youthful sleeping habits, and the prospect of ever again sleeping himself made him want to vomit.

"We have a security kibe, and you'll have to give it a cell sample. Just put your finger there—perfect! We're heading up to a wine tasting in Sonoma, and we should be back by four bells of the midwatch. Feel free to have nocturne with whatever you find in the fridge. There's some really superior pesto we just whipped up, and baby red potatoes already boiled."

"Fine, thanks, have a great time."

The Holland-Nancarrows departed in a crimson Wuhan Peony, and Cedric thumbed his nose at them once they were safely out of sight.

Back inside, he looked for ways to amuse himself. He watched a few minutes of a Giants game on his Palimpsest, but the experience was boring when he didn't have any money riding on the contest. He prolonged the meditative drinking of a single boutique beer from the house's copious stock, but eventually the bottle gurgled its last. He made a dutiful trip to the bedroom and witnessed the children—shadowy lumps—sleeping as monotonously as before. Cedric shuddered.

Eventually, Cedric found himself poking around the family flatscreen. The display device occupied a whole wall, and somehow even vapid entertainment was more entrancing at that size.

And that's when he found that the Holland-Nancarrows had departed so hurriedly that they had left their system wide-open. They had never logged off.

After hesitating a moment, Cedric decided to go exploring. He paged through their mail, but discovered only bland trivia about people he didn't know. He discovered what Alex and Brian did for a living: They designed facials for freethinkers. In effect, they were cyberbeauticians.

Then Cedric stumbled across a bookmark for a Cuban casino. Apparently, his hosts had recently placed a few amateur bets.

Cedric hesitated. In the pit of his stomach and down to his loins, a familiar beast was awaking and growling and stretching its limbs.

Just a small visit, to taste the excitement. He could lurk without playing.

Yeah. And the Mars colony would find life someday.

Under Cedric's touch, the screen filled with a first-person-shooter image of the casino floor. Cedric was telefactoring a kibe, whose manipulators would emerge into his field of vision when he reached for something. Cedric wheeled the kibe toward the blackjack tables, his favorite game.

Cedric started betting small at first. The wagers came, of course, from the cyberpurse of the Holland-Nancarrows. If he drained the purse of too much money, they'd spot the loss and track down the bets to a time when they weren't home. But if he won, he'd leave the purse at its original value and transfer the excess to his own pockets. They'd never have occasion to check.

And of course, he *would* win. And win *big*!

The hours sped by as Cedric played with feverish intensity. His skills had not left him, and he was really in the zone. The cards favored him as well. Lady Luck had her hands down his pants. Pretty soon, he had racked up ten thousand dollars of the casino's money. Only a drop toward lifting his debts, but certainly the best-paying babysitting gig he had ever had.

Cedric left the casino and squirted the funds to his account. No one would ever be the wiser.

He was opening a second celebratory beer when the police arrived.

"Cedric Swann, we have a warrant for your arrest. Please come with us."

"But . . . but I didn't do anything—"

"The Holland-Nancarrow freethinker swears otherwise."

On the big wallscreen appeared the facial of the house's freethinker: an image of ex-President Streisand. "That's the man, Officers."

The house's freethinker! But who would set a freethinker to monitor legitimate transactions originating in-house?

Paranoid parents, obviously.

Who the hell could think as deviously as a breeder?

Cedric's possessions now amounted to a single scuffed biomer suitcase of clothing and his Palimpsest. Cedric and his suitcase called a single room in a flophouse in the Mission District their home. The flophouse was a rhizome-diatom hybrid, taking form as a soil-rooted siliceous warren of chambers, threaded with arteries and nerves that served in place of utilities, all grown in place on a large lot where several older structures had stood until a terrorist attack demolished them. The site had been officially decontaminated, but Cedric wasn't sure he believed that. Why had no one snapped up the valuable midtown real estate, leaving the lot for such a low-rent usage? In any case, Cedric felt like a bacteria living inside a sponge.

He supposed that such a lowly status was merely consonant with society's regard for him, after his latest fuckup.

Instead of meeting Caresse at a restaurant as they had planned, Cedric met her on the night of his arrest at the jailhouse where he had been taken by the cops. She came to bail him out, and he accepted her charity wordlessly, realizing there was nothing he could say to exculpate himself. He had been caught red-handed while submitting to his implacable vice.

Caresse had been silent also, except for formalities with the police. Cedric fully expected her to explode with anger and recriminations when he got into her car. But the calm disdain she unloaded on him was even more painful.

"You obviously have no regard for yourself, and none for me. I've tried to be understanding, Cedric, really, I have. I don't think any woman could have cut you more slack, or tried harder to help you reform. But this is the absolute end. I've put up your bail money so that you could be free to plan your defense—as if you have any— and so that you wouldn't have to be humiliated by being in prison. But that's the end of the road for you and me. I can't have anything else to do with you in the future. Whatever existed between us is gone, thanks to your weak-willed selfishness."

Cedric looked imploringly at Caresse's beautiful profile with its gracefully sculpted jawline. She did not turn to spare him a glance, but kept her eyes resolutely on the busy midnight city street. He knew then that he had truly lost her forever, realized he had never fully appreciated her love. But he had neither the energy nor hope to contest her death sentence on their relationship.

"I'm sorry, Caresse. I never meant to hurt you. Can you drop me off at my place?"

"Of course. I've got just enough time before my yoga class."

The Holland-Nancarrows declined to press for any jail time for

Cedric, considering that they had not actually lost any money, nor had their precious children been harmed by the bad man. (The casino took back Cedric's winnings on the basis of identity misrepresentation by the player.) But that did not stop the judge hearing Cedric's case from imposing on Cedric a huge fine and five years' probation. Cedric's own court-appointed freethinker lawyer had not been receptive to the notion of an appeal.

Worst of all the repercussions of his crime, however, was that Cedric was double black-flagged, denied employment even as a nanny.

He had no choice but to go on welfare.

The welfare rolls of the sleeplessly booming USA economy had been pared to historic lows. Only the most vocationally intransigent or helpless indigents lived off the government dole.

And now Cedric was one of this caste. Unclean. Unseen.

And a sleeper as well. A living atavism.

The dole didn't cover a-som drugs. Not even the fourth-generation, expired-shelf-date stuff shipped to Third World countries.

Being a sleeper was hell. It wasn't that sleepers were persecuted against, legally or in a covert manner. Nor were they held in contempt. No, sleepers were just simply ignored by the unsleeping. They were deemed irrelevant because they couldn't keep up. They were living their lives a third slower than the general populace. After a night's unconsciousness, a sleeper would awake to discover that he had a new congressional representative, or that the clothes he had worn yesterday were outmoded. New buzzwords were minted while he slept, new celebrities crowned, new political crises defused. The changes were not always so radical, but even on a slow Tuesday night they were incremental. Day by day, sleepers fell further and further behind the wavefront of the culture, until at last they were living fossils.

Cedric could hardly believe that such was now his fate.

After his sentencing and his removal to the flophouse, once he had consumed the last of his a-som scrip, Cedric had managed to stay desperately awake for a little over forty-eight hours, thanks to massive coffee intake, some Mexican amphetamines purchased on a street corner, and a cheap kibe massage that left him reeking of machine lubricant from a leaky gasket on the kibe.

The ancient sensations flooding his mind and body exerted at first a kind of grim and perverse fascination. The whole experience was like watching the tide reclaim a sand castle. Sitting in his tiny room, on an actual *bed*, he monitored his helpless degeneration. His concentration wavered and faded, his limbs grew unwieldy, his speech confused. Despite raging against his loss, Cedric ultimately had no choice but to succumb.

And then he dreamed.

He had forgotten dreaming, the nightly activity of his childhood.

Forgotten that some dreams were nightmares.

He awoke from that initial sleep shaking and drenched with sweat, the night terrors mercifully fading from memory. He retained only vague images of teeth and crushing weights, falling through space and scrabbling for handholds.

Cedric got up from bed, dressed, and went out into the streets.

Kibes running errands or patrolling for lawbreakers mingled with the many humans. The Mission District was not populated entirely by charity-case sleepers. Many of the people on the street were citizens in fine standing. Here was a colorful clique of tawny Polynesian immigrants, adapting to life away from their sea-swamped island homes. Their happy, bright-eyed faces seemed to mock him. From Cedric's new vantage point down in the underbelly of the a-som society, everyone looked wired and jazzed up, restlessly active, spinning their wheels in a perpetual drag race toward an ever-receding finish line.

But having this vision didn't mean he still wouldn't rejoin his ex-peers in a second.

Cedric was convinced that everyone could smell the sleep-stench rising from him, spot his saggy eyelids from a block away. Eating in a cheap diner that allowed him to stretch his monthly money as far as possible, Cedric resolved to kill himself rather than go on like this.

But he didn't. In a week, a month, he relearned how to function with a third of his life stolen by sleep, and became resigned to an indefinitely prolonged future of this vapid existence.

As role models for his new lifestyle, Cedric had the other inhabitants of his flophouse. He had expected his fellow sleepers to be vicious father-rapers or congenitally brain-damaged droolers or polycaine addicts. But to Cedric's surprise, his fellow sleepers represented a wide range of intelligence and character, as extensive a spectrum of personalities as could be found anywhere else. In the short and desultory conversations Cedric allowed himself with them, he learned that some were deliberate holdouts against the a-som culture, while some were ex-members of the majority, like Cedric himself, professionals who had somehow lost their hold on the a-som pinnacle.

And then you had Doug Clearmountain.

Doug was the happiest person Cedric had ever met. Short, rugged, bald-crowned but with a fringe of long hair, Doug resembled a time-battered troll of indeterminate years.

The first time Doug made contact with Cedric, in the grottolike lobby of the flophouse, the older man introduced himself by saying, "Hey, there, chum, I'm Morpheus. You want the red pill or the blue?"

"Huh?"

"Not a film buff, I see. Doug Clearmountain. And you are?"

"Cedric Swann."

"Cedric, it's a pleasure to meet you. Let's grab a coffee."

"Uh, sure."

Over coffee Cedric learned that, before settling in San Francisco, Doug had been an elder of a religious community that featured, among other tenets of its creed, the renunciation of a-som drugs. The community—a syncretic mix of Sufism, Theravada Buddhism and TM—had struggled in the wilds of Oregon for approximately fifteen years before bleeding away all its members to the siren call of twenty-four/seven wakefulness. Doug had been the last adherent to remain. Then one day, when he finally admitted no one was coming back, he just walked away from the empty community.

"Decided it was time to do a little preaching amidst the unconverted."

Cedric took a swig of coffee, desperate to wake up, to dispel the funk engendered by his nightly bad dreams. "Uh, yeah, how's that working for you? You convinced many people to nod out?"

Undaunted by Cedric's evident disinterest, Doug radiated a serene confidence. "Not at all. Haven't made one convert yet. But I've found something even more important to keep me busy."

The coffee was giving Cedric a headache. A tic was tugging at the corner of his right eye. He had no patience for any messianic guff from this loony. "Sure, right, I bet you're really busy working to engineer a rebellion that nobody in their right mind wants. Down with the timebrokers, right?"

"Hardly, Cedric, hardly. I'm actually doing essential work helping to prop our incessant society up. It can't survive much longer on its own, you know. It's like a spinning flywheel without a brake. But this is the course that the bulk of our species has chosen, so me and some others are just trying to shepherd them through it. But I can see that you have no interest in hearing about my mission at the moment. You're too busy adjusting to your new life. We'll talk more when you're ready."

Doug Clearmountain left then, having paid for both their coffees.

At least the nut wasn't a cheapskate.

For the most part, Cedric resisted the impulse to reconnect with his old life, the glamorous satisfying round of timebrokering, gambling, and leisure pursuits. He spent his time giving mandatory Palimpsest interviews to his freethinker probation officer (whose federally approved facial was that of a sweater-wearing kiddie-show host who had retired before Cedric was born). He roamed the hilly streets of the city, seeking to exhaust his body and hopefully gain a solid night's sleep. (Useless. The nightmares persisted.) He watched sports. He tried to calculate how long it would be before all his debts were paid off with the court-mandated pittance being deducted from his welfare stipend. (Approximately eleven hundred years.)

Once he tried to get in touch with Caresse. She couldn't talk because she was in the middle of a massage, but she promised to call back.

She actually did.

But Cedric was asleep.

He took that as a sign not to try again.

Six months passed, and Cedric resembled a haunted, scarecrow model of his old self.

That's when Doug Clearmountain approached him again, jovial and optimistic as ever.

"Congratulations on the fine job you're doing, Cedric."

Cedric had taken to hanging out at Fisherman's Wharf, cadging spare change from the tourists via Palimpsest transactions. He was surprised to see Doug there when he raised his dirty bearded face up from contemplating the ground.

"Go fuck yourself."

Doug remained unfazed. "I'm not being sarcastic, son. I was just congratulating you on half a year as a sleeper. Do you realize how much of our planet's finite resources you've saved?"

"What do you mean?"

"You're using a third less energy, a third less food than your erstwhile compatriots. I'm sure Gaia appreciates your sacrifice. When the a-som society came fully online globally, it was like adding another America to the planetary eco-burden. Ouch! Despite all the fancy new inventions, our planet is heading toward catastrophe faster than ever. All we're doing lately is staving off the inevitable."

"Big whoop. So I'm a tiny positive line item in the carbon budget."

"Well, yes, your sacrifice is negligible, regarded in that light.

But there's another way you can be of more help. And that's by dreaming."

Cedric shuddered. "Dreams! Don't say that word to me. I haven't had a pleasant dream since I went cold turkey."

Doug's perpetual grin gave way to a look of sober concern. "I know that, Cedric. That's because you're not doing it right. You're trying to go it alone. Would you like some help with your dreams?"

"What've you got? A-som? How much?"

"No, not a-som. Something better. Why not come with me and see for yourself?"

What did Cedric have to lose? He let Doug lead him away.

The authorities had marked the small waterfront building for eventual demolition, as they continually enhanced the system of dikes protecting the city's shoreline from rising sea levels. For now, though, the structure was still high and dry. Doug pried back a suspiciously hinged panel of plywood covering a door frame and conducted Cedric inside.

The place smelled like chocolate. Perhaps the Ghirardelli company had once stored product here. But now the the large, open twilit room was full of sleepers. Arrayed on obsolete military cots, two dozen men and women, covered by blankets, snored peacefully while cranially wired to a central machine the size of a dorm fridge.

"What . . . what the hell is this? What's going on?"

"This is a little project I and my friends like to call 'Manhole 69.' Ring any bells? No? Ah, a shame, the lack of classical education you youngsters receive. Well, no matter. The apparatus you see is a REM-sleep modulator. Invented shortly before the introduction of a-som tech, and then abandoned. Ironically unusable by the very people who needed it the most. Basically, this device provides guided dream experiences within broad parameters. The individual's creativity is shaped into desired forms. Nonsurgical neuronal magnetic induction, and all that. Everyone you see here, Cedric, is dreaming of a better world. Here, take a look."

Doug borrowed Cedric's Palimpsest and called up a control channel to the dream machine. A host of windows filled the flatscreen. Cedric witnessed pastoral landscapes populated by shining godlings, superscience metropoli, alien worlds receiving human visitors, and other fanciful scenes.

"Are you totally demented, man? So you can give people pretty dreams. So what? Don't get me wrong, I'll take a few hours under your brain probe, just to get some relief. But as far as helping the world become a better place, you're only kidding yourself."

"Oh, really? Would you care to discuss this over some coffee?"

"Coffee? What're you talking about?"

Doug didn't answer. He was too busy sending instructions to the dream machine. All the flatscreen windows formerly revealing the variegated dreams of the sleepers changed at once to the same real-time image: the interior of the very building Cedric and Doug stood in, captured by Palimpsest cam. But the screen views held a difference from reality: a steaming paper cup stood atop the dream machine cabinet.

"This should only take a second or two."

"What should take—"

Cedric smelled the coffee before he saw it. There it rested, just where the dreamers had envisioned it.

Cedric walked in a daze to the cabinet, picked the coffee up. The cup and its contents warmed his fingers.

Doug's manner altered to the serious affect of an expert in his field with something to sell.

"Two dozen people programmed to dream the same thing can instantiate objects massing up to ten ounces. I expect that the phenomenon scales up predictably. Something to do with altering probabilities and shifting our quantum selves onto alternate time lines, rather than producing matter ex nihilo. Or so certain sleeper scientists among us theorize. But we're not interested in such parlor tricks. Instead, we want to shallowly engrave a variety of desirable futures into our local brane, thereby increasing the likelihood that one of them will become real. We're shifting the rails that society is following. And as Thoreau once ironically observed, rails rest on sleepers. There are places like this around the globe, Cedric. And the more sleepers we enlist, the greater our chances of success. Are you on board, son?"

Cedric regarded Doug dubiously. Had the manifestation of the coffee been a trick? Maybe that cabinet was hollow, with a false top, the coffee concealed inside. Should he ask for another demonstration, or take the old man on faith? Why would anyone bother to try to hoax him into simply going to sleep? And what else was he going to do with his life?

"Here," said Cedric, offering the coffee to Doug. "You take this.

"I guess I'm finally ready for a little shut-eye."

John Meaney has a degree in physics and computer science. He holds a black belt in Shotokan karate. He can do the splits between two chairs when properly cajoled. Somehow, all of these facts seem at play in his excellent novels, *To Hold Infinity*, *Paradox*, *Context*, and *Resolution*. John has been short-listed for the British Science Fiction Association Award multiple times. On this side of the pond, his novella "The Whisper of Disks" was included in the 2003 *Year's Best Science Fiction: Twentieth Annual Collection*. The *Times* called Meaney "the first important new SF writer of the twenty-first century." I could not agree more. In my opinion, he could not write a bad story if he tried.

LOOKING THROUGH MOTHER'S EYES

John Meaney

I can't wait until I'm born. To live!

Not long now.

Such a gift!

"Three days," I hear Mother say, as she lies upon the bed. "Perhaps four, my sweet Druggan. Then our daughter will be here."

"So soon?"

My father's words wash like distant surf, but I can make them out. That, too, is a sign of my impending arrival. Mother pulls him toward her—such strength in our arms, the strength of warm passion—and when she kisses him, hard and deep, I swear I sense the electric touch of his masculine lips through hers.

For sure, I feel the tears that come flooding afterward, when Father goes outside to draw water from the well.

"Oh, my sweet love," she whispers, wrapping her hands around herself. Ourself. "Not long. By the Worldmaker, not long now."

Does she say these words to Father or to me? I cannot tell.

I love you, Mother.

I wish that she could hear me before she dies.

While she is still mobile, Mother takes herself—ourself—to the Budding Grove. We walk slowly, stopping to catch our breath every twenty paces. Two women neighbors help her, but their conversation is distant from me; I understand little of what they say. On entering the sacred area, their voices assume the lilt of solemn prayer.

I know from what Mother has said, from her conversations with Father, that he has important work nearby. With his three crew members, deep in the Bendtree Woods, he is training an entire grove to form itself into a new fishing vessel. Every day when he does not take his current boat out upon the Maximal Lake, he visits the growing vessel, checks its growth and form, sprinkles Vat-blessed fluids across the curved, living wood to enhance its health and strength. When it reaches full growth, they will ax it from the roots and roll it to down to the shore. There, it will slide out onto the silver waters of the Lake: a body of water so wide that the far shore may not be seen.

I find it hard to imagine any of these things.

Mother, I'm sorry. I want to see it all.

"Let us pray," she murmurs, adding: "I'm too gravid to kneel, but the Worldmaker understands."

Yet I'm afraid. So afraid.

Mother leans back against a tree for support. Through her thin robe, the bark is rough against us. She joins in the chant for a time, rocking slightly, lulling me almost to sleep. Her hands are enfolded across her middle, our middle, in a gesture I find incredibly comforting. She continues in a soft musical tone, and it is a moment before I realize the truth: She has stopped praying now, and is talking directly to me.

"Druggan's work-brother, called Jilfar"—she speaks with such sadness that I want to weep—"perished in the last great storm. The village, and Druggan's boat, remain shorthanded for now . . . but the budding proceeds well." A pause, then: "We pray for the new man, not knowing what he will be like. What else can we do?"

I wish I could answer her, somehow.

Not long now.

Slowly, Mother pushes ourself upright, away from the supporting tree. "Time we laid back down, my girl."

The walk home is a painstaking, painful affair. But at the end lies our cottage, fragrant with herbs, and the joy of preparing a succulent dinner. Afterward, tonight as on other nights, Mother (and therefore I) will recline on the long cot sweetened with grasses, and she will say:

"What of your day, Druggan? Tell me, sweet husband."

My father will pause, quaff some honeybeer, then relate what he has seen and done.

Druggan worked hard today, alongside old Harbin.

"Ah, but the dock . . ." he would say later to his wife. "You should've smelled it."

At dawn, they found a whitish putrescent mess on the jetty: nine-armed squill, dead and already beginning to rot, so close to the life-giving silver liquids of the Maximal Lake. They had almost escaped.

Set back from the dock proper, a row of hardy crane trees supports big plump bulbs formed of stringvine and membrane. Inside them, kept fresh, the catches of all three village boats hang waiting until the cook-pots are ready. But squill have sharp barbs on their flexible limbs, and if they are insufficiently stunned by the storage sacs' anesthetizing exudate, they sometimes cut their way free and slip to the ground, then pull themselves mindlessly toward the near-est open body of aqua argenta.

"If I'd realized," said old Harbin, "I'd have given them a helping kick."

A slime trail led all the way to the jetty's end. One or two squill must have managed the whole length and dropped off the edge, into freedom. But most of the batch had been close to birthing; three of the bodies were an exploded mess. The white/lilac/transparent remains stank as they dried out.

But one was still whole, and trembling.

"Worldmaker's spit!" said Harbin.

He strode back to a hard-shell storage pod and grabbed a pair of long brooms. By the time he returned, the squill had split apart. The squill-nymphs, the whole batch, were scuttling on their tiny needle-legs toward the jetty's end.

"No, let them grow"—Druggan caught Harbin's tunic sleeve—"for when they're grown, maybe one or two of them will be back inside our nets."

"Right." Harbin spit onto the jetty. "When you and I are long gone."

"No matter." Druggan shrugged, looked back up the slope, beyond the crane trees. "The village continues, doesn't it?"

Harbin turned away, scowling, yet Druggan understood. Harbin's hair was graying, yet he had shown no signs of continuance. It was beginning to look as though he was sterile.

Another job for the Budding Grove, once Harbin is gone.

This is what Elder Likana (herself now close to term) taught: that babies could not be born early or small, for the very air would cause their skins to redden and bubble. "They burn," she would say, "because their skin area is large compared to their volume. They haven't had time to grow an outer membrane." And Alken, on one of his selling trips to Minkal Province, had witnessed a premature girl squealing with pain all of her first day, and perishing that night when the temperature plummeted. Not even burning torches, held close, could help her.

But Druggan watched the tiny squill-nymph drop into the lake—plop, plop—and wondered why things had to be the way they were. Had the Worldmaker no compassion?

Druggan let out a breath, gripped his broom, and began to push the adult squills' remains across a jetty slick with salty ichor, lique-fying flesh, and slime. The frosts had already evaporated, and his tunic was dark with sweat: Today was going to be a scorcher.

Do I catch a glimmer? My first true sight of the world?

There have been nearly-hues since the beginning: a mist of maybe-colors that envelop me, sometimes with orange warmth, other times gray and cool. Beyond my beloved Mother, boundary of my universe, something now moves and I almost see it. Then I hear Druggan, my father, speaking.

"I love you, my sweet." His words are clearer than ever.

"Yes." Mother's voice is hoarse, a whisper. "I know."

I feel the diminishing blanket of her surrounding me.

Mother. I love you, too.

How I wish I could tell her! Father's fingers clasp hers, the fingers of her left hand, and I feel—

By the Worldmaker!

—yes, I feel her right arm move, but it is different from anything I have experienced before because I *willed it* to move. Mother gasps—we gasp—and we are suddenly, in that moment, closer than we have ever been.

"Try it again, my sweet." Mother's voice is a whisper for me only; I wonder what Father makes of it. "Try it. See what happens."

I strain.

No . . .

I strain mightily.

Come on . . .

But nothing occurs, and Mother murmurs: "Too soon."

My time is not yet, but neither is it distant. Faint weeping, the saddened sound of it, reaches me, and I know it is my father. He does, after all, understand.

Today, they sailed far out into the Maximal Lake. The village and the hills beyond grew small in the distance, were gone. The four-strong crew (including Harbin, who was unusually quiet) worked hard, sinking their nets deep, for they knew that Druggan's daughter was due soon. Still, catches had been good recently, and they could afford to lose a day's work or more.

"A daughter," Druggan muttered, standing at the bowsprit. "A daughter."

They turned back late. The sky was already pale gray and violet; breathtaking streamers of light slid across the shining water. Faint wisps of pink acidic mist, tingling to the touch, gathered near the vessel as the purple shadows of coastline grew larger. In those cool shadows, the small orange flames of beacons shone, guiding them toward the waiting village.

Then something massive moved beneath the boat.

"Spitting Worldm—" Harbin stopped.

Everyone held their breath.

The blessing. Druggan closed his eyes briefly. Did the blessing work?

They waited for the rearing jaws, for the huge bite that could snap their vessel in half. All of them prayed in silence; though whether from personal fear or concern for the village, who could say? For sure, the loss of an entire boat and crew would be a disaster for everybody.

Beneath them, the shadow arced again.

"Look." Young Vilkro pointed. "It's diving."

The great serpent sank from sight.

"Don't count on it." Druggan waited for the count of a thousand heartbeats, then let out a long breath. "All right . . . We're safe. I guess it didn't like us."

It was twenty days since the last dry dock, when all four of them had slathered Vat-blessed gel across the hull's underside and keel. Everyone knew that it was potent stuff. Still, Druggan and Harbin had knelt all night long in the Blessing Glade, praying to the Holy Processor for extra protection, hoping to magnify the repelling spell.

"It'll be better," piped up Vilkro, "when we get our new crew-man. I'm right, aren't I, Druggan? We won't need to sail out so far."

"Jilfar's replacement, aye." Druggan patted Vilkro's shoulder. "He'll be needing someone to show him the ropes."

"Yes, sir!" Vilkro straightened, his eyes gleaming. "I'll do my best."

Druggan nodded, watching Harbin work his way aft, checking nets for tears. Druggan wondered what Harbin was thinking. Perhaps talk of the Budding Grove cut deep inside, shaming him.

Not fair, my friend. You're a good worker.

For sterility cast its affliction without regard to character or moral upbringing, whatever Elder Likana might say. In olden times, so the tales told, many people had been barren, far more than nowadays. Yet Druggan had no reason to suppose that modern folk were saintlier than their forebears.

"Crew, hoy!" called a voice from the looming jetty.

Vilkro threw a line.

Home, thought Druggan, and safe.

"Are you sure, my love, that you want to walk?" Father's voice is taut with concern that even I can hear. "Why not just sit here, by the window? I'll pull the curtain and you can—"

"I want to see it . . . properly. To smell the mist."

"Oh, my sweet. Of course."

He helps us stand. Indirectly, I feel how strongly muscled he is, how iron-hard his grip. I find this fact reassuring.

"No rush," he says now. "Just take it slowly. That's it."

"Thank you, my dearest Druggan."

"I love you."

"Yes. And . . ." We give a sharp intake of breath, then: "Me too, my fine husband. I have always loved you."

I'm sorry, I want to cry.

Because I have no right to spoil their perfect union. They should go on forever as they are now, and so they would in any universe that was based on justice and the happiness of those who live within it. But I already know . . . such is not the way of the world. Harshness is all.

Except when moments of heartbreaking love relieve the emptiness.

"It's wonderful."

"You always adored the lilac mist."

"And you don't, Druggan?"

"When you're with me, I see beauty everywhere."

They embrace, and I withdraw inside as much as I can. This is their moment, not mine. My own time is coming soon enough, regardless of whether they or I deserve it.

Dawn painted rose and peach across the eastern sky, and its reflection in the silver lake was breathtaking. It looked like two skies, merged and shining as one.

Druggan stopped halfway up the steep path to the Budding Grove, and looked toward the dawn. I'm so lucky to see this, he decided, even though sunrise also marked the flow of time, the passage of days he and his beloved wife could never revisit.

Then he continued his climb until the slope flattened, and he passed through a natural archway formed by two iridescent trees. A stream trickled across the ground before him; an arc of pink stepping-stones, long ago worn smooth, spanned the stream. Druggan crossed quickly.

Passing through a stand of reflective mirrortrees, he came to the Budding Grove proper, where he went down on one knee and made formal obeisance to the Holy Processor, making the Sign of the Ship with both hands.

He looked up.

The central tree was white and strong, and from it depended seven amber sacs. In one, a human-shaped shadow lay still; in the others, the smaller shadows of budding nightcats and guardowls, destined for the village aeries, were quiescent, slowly growing.

* * *

I honor you all.

Kneeling, he bowed.

Druggan rose and began to turn away, but suddenly the human shadow moved an arm, almost as if it were waving, then hung still once more. Yet a sign of movement, so early in its development, must be a good omen. Even as Druggan thought this, a flock of pteragulls rose beyond the grove and clattered and screeched their way into the air, accompanied by a soft mewling sound from the shadows inside the Budding Tree.

Druggan bowed once more.

He took a last look around the grove—the lesser trees bore empty, flaccid sacs—then made his way back through the mirrortrees to the sacred arch, where the small stream tinkled and flowed. The eastern sky was beautiful enough to weep over, but Druggan was moving quickly now, with no time to stop and wonder. His crew would be waiting, and a day's work lay ahead.

Another day to experience in full, for it would never come again.

Sometime in the night, Father's grip tightens on our hand.

"My love," he whispers. "I have felt the spark."

"Oh, my husband!" Mother is astounded with sudden joy. "My sweet, sweet husband . . . Are you . . . ?"

"I'm sure," he says, taking her hand (and I understand that this is too important to lie about). His grip feels strong. "Today, in the Grove, I prayed. And tonight . . . I know. Suddenly, I just know. It's a son."

"Ah, Druggan . . ."

Her tears, my tears, are born of pain, but they are also joyful.

"Wait for me," says Father, "in the afterlife. My spirit will not be long in joining yours."

She tries to answer, but my muscles contract involuntarily, and our throat cannot make a sound.

"Everything will be fine, my darling." Father kisses us. Her. "Everything is fine."

* * *

Nekmol, the quietest of the crew, guessed Druggan's secret. When Druggan confirmed it, young Vilkro punched the air in triumph as though it were his own good news, not another's. Harbin, in contrast, was solemn, placing the calloused palm of one hand over Druggan's abdomen and, with his other hand, forming the Sign of the Ship.

"May life continue"—his rough voice thickened—"forever."

"Thank you, Harbin, my oldest and closest friend."

That evening, back in the village, Harbin presented Druggan with a folded tapestry from Silgen Province, depicting the Landing Times. Druggan unfolded it.

Stitched silver threads formed the Sky Parents' vessel, while the Fall from Heaven was heavy with red and orange, showing the flames which engulfed their shattered sky-boat. Sinners of those early days were shown with burning skin, grotesque expressions on their faces—bulging eyes, tongues extended—as they clutched their throats.

Then the holiest of them were shown kneeling before the Vat, their new brothers growing in the sacs of the first Budding Tree, and the path of salvation was clear for humankind to follow. That was the last panel in the tapestry.

Druggan folded it back up.

"It's beautiful."

"Aye, my captain."

The two of them nodded, leaving all of their years of friendship unspoken—each knew what the other was thinking—then turned away and headed for their separate homes. Druggan had not even smiled; the gift had been offered with deep affection and respect, not with a glib surface pleasantry, and he had accepted it in the same solemn spirit.

It marked their long years sailing together, and it marked the changes overtaking their lives. The time of innocence was gone.

* * *

"It's our last night together." Mother's voice is a little slurred. "I'm almost sure of it."

"I love you, sweetheart."

Cramp catches us, and for a moment she cannot move. Then she reaches out and strokes his face. "I love you, Druggan."

"I have a little present. Here."

I can feel beads, held in our hand.

"Amber," says Mother. "My favorite. Always my—"

She stiffens. I stiffen.

Worldmaker!

It is fire, this marvelous, magical color. Spots of bright burning fire, and I know this is what Mother means by "amber." My first, my very first . . . No. They are gone again.

But I saw them.

"My love?"

"Everything went black, Druggan. I think . . . I'm fine."

They are kissing now, but I no longer worry about withdrawing from their experience. I'm too wrapped up in the joy of what just happened, of what it means for me.

For I have glimpsed the world, and it is beautiful.

Druggan is saved the burden. His three crew members are joined by brawny Reltim, who is Elder Likana's husband and a decent man. Each takes one corner of the bier and lifts, and the woman whimpers with pain. Then they move off, with Druggan walking alongside, holding his wife's hand as she writhes, trying not to cry out.

Villagers watch solemnly as they pass the pentagonal well, the open-sided meeting hut, the nightcat pens and the guardowl aeries, and stop before Elder Likana's cabin. She is waiting, and makes the Sign of the Ship at their approach, before intoning the sacred words that begin the ceremony. Then the four men continue, carrying their burden, and Likana joins them, walking on the opposite side from Druggan. She continues to pray; Druggan continues to hold his wife's hand.

It is wet and slippery in his grip.

". . . and may the Sky Parents descend, accept your soul into the Sacred Airlock, and bear your eternal essence to the starfields of Heaven, now and until the end of . . ."

He is oblivious to the prayers. Druggan knows only that this is his wife, the woman he loves, has always loved. He tells her this once again, but the pain is upon her now and surely she cannot hear.

Now they are stopping before the squat stone pedestal which is called the Birthing Pillar.

". . . ever and ever, endit."

"Endit," murmur the four bearers.

Then, straining, they lift the bier higher and carry it forward—carefully, carefully—and lower it atop the Birthing Pillar, and let it rest. They release their grips, step back, and bow.

Druggan kisses his wife's hand, tears trickling down his face.

And then she screams.

Oh, by the Worldmaker! It is now. The moment is now-now-now because I am here and I'm ready for life and I cannot stop what is happening. It burns, it hurts, and it is lovely. So lovely.

Mother. I love you.

Surely she knows this, that I love her as she must have loved her own fine mother, but I want to tell it to her, just once while we have the chance, and suddenly I feel cool air in my throat and I yell the words:

"I love you, Mother!"

Just for a moment, her nerves regain control and she gives a miraculous reply: "Love you . . . Daughter."

It is the most perfect moment.

A crack follows, a solid sound inside my skull, and then a wet ripping as the neurumbilical tears off and I will never be a part of

Mother again. Her brain, her flesh, her skin reduce to a slick veneer that covers me, no more.

Oh, my wonderful mother.

I want to call to her again, but it is too late.

I love you.

Her liquefying flesh is degrading now, exposing me to the cold bite of wonderful, life-giving air, as she splits—all around me, she splits apart—to become wet gobbets sliding off my own true skin.

Mother . . .

She is no more.

Blood-slick, flesh-slick, remnants of her body slide from me, sloppy and juicy, falling to the ground with a liquid splat. I reach, with fingers which are mine, are mine for real, to scrape clots of brain tissue from my hair . . . hair which is already sticky with her drying juices. (And I suppose I'll have to wash it soon. Is that too prosaic?)

This is life.

And as I rise, standing shakily on my newborn legs for the first time, I look down and see the tear-streaked face of my father, the bearer of my future brother. Druggan stares up at me, then bows his head, in reverence and in thankfulness.

I raise my hands, look up to the sky—so blue, so beautiful—and cry out:

"My name is Leera!"

I am born into the world.

Since his first sale to August Dereleth's biannual magazine *The Arkham Collector* in 1968, **Alan Dean Foster** has gone on to produce something on the order of a hundred novels, while his short fiction has appeared in all the major SF magazines, numerous "Best of the Year" compendiums, and six collections of short fiction. He is well-known for having novelized the original *Star Wars* movie, as well as the first three *Alien* films and the television series *Alien Nation*, and receives story credit for the script of *Star Trek: The Motion Picture*. Perhaps best-known to SF readers for his stories of Flinx and the Commonwealth, it is his Spellsinger series (particularly *The Paths of the Perambulator*) that holds a special place in my heart.

THE MAN WHO KNEW TOO MUCH
Alan Dean Foster

"**P**ssst . . . wanna buy some real *hard* stuff?"

Charlie Fellows paused. It was late, he was on his way home, and the alcove from which the voice emerged was very dark. Still, he hesitated. Buying stuff on the street was always chancy. You didn't know if what you were getting was pure and undiluted or just a cheap knockoff from Taipei or Shanghai. The latter might consist of nothing more than a couple of cursory introductions and a table of contents followed by hours of listings scanned from the local telephone books.

Night damp wafting in off the Pacific teased his lips with a chill burning. He clutched the collar of his coat tighter around his neck. It was cold. The familiar throbbing had already started at the back of his head, demanding attention. Demanding to be fed. A quick glance left and then right revealed that the narrow side street off University was deserted. Not surprising, at this hour. He licked slightly chapped lips and gave in. "What . . . what've you got?"

A thin crescent of Cheshire cat ivory, the ghost of a grin, appeared in the darkness. Nimble fingers brought forth and manipulated a flat, rectangular, maroon-tinged plastic container that resembled a woman's oversize compact. A single internal LEP illuminated half a dozen rows of neatly aligned chipsets. Each was no bigger than his little fingernail. Charlie eyed them hungrily.

"What did I tell you? All uncontaminated, newly pressed, and unabridged. Straight from the relevant authorized sources."

Charlie's eyes widened slightly as he leaned forward to inspect the glistening array. They glittered like miniature Christmas ornaments. He could not conceal his eagerness. "Looks good. Where'd you get 'em?"

It was the wrong thing to say, and he knew it as soon as he said it. The case snapped shut with a soft airtight *pop*. "Sorry, man, I guess I had you scoped wrong. You take care now, and—"

Charlie put out an anxious hand to forestall the younger man's departure. "No, wait—I'm sorry. That was a dumb thing to say."

"Yeah, it was." One hand on the alcove's dark door, the sallow-faced pusher paused.

"It just slipped out." Desperately, Charlie mustered his most ingratiating smile. "Let me . . . Can I see the stuff again?"

Still hugging the shadows, the pusher performed his own swift street survey. A quick flick of one fingertip and the case reopened. "What's your pleasure, citizen? What fires your interest?" Despite the tension inherent in the moment, his words floated on an undertone of mild amusement.

Charlie's response didn't disappoint. "Everything."

Nodding, the pusher's finger traced the air over the shimmering chipsets, as if by so doing he could command them to rise from their holding sockets and perform a tempting little dance in midair. He was deliberately making Charlie wait, enjoying the other man's impatience. "Well, now, I got here some natural science, some high-energy physics, a little general geology—but I prefer to specialize, you know? Mostly soft stuff tonight: American Lit, some archetypical anthropological Australian dreamtime studies, collections of arcane Melanesian oral traditions. Also a couple odds and ends." His hovering finger drifted over one corner of the case. "Maintenance manuals for Harley-Davidson models 1945 to 2005, the Complete Julia Childs's French Chef, Frescoes of the Northern Italian Renaissance." His gaze bored into Charlie. "That last one's discontinued."

Charlie nodded eagerly, unable to take his eyes off the magical, gleaming little squares. No gem dealer in a back-alley Jaipur bazaar ever gazed with greater avarice upon an open handkerchief laden with jewels. "You said American Lit. You got Twain, Melville, Hawthorne?"

"Irving, Ferber, Poe—all the biggies. They're all here." Withdrawing specialized nonferrous tweezers from a shirt pocket, he delicately plucked one chip from among the dozens, held it out toward his potential customer. "Have a look. First-class manufacture. Exactly what an authorized prof would use for broadcast."

Extracting the folding loupe he carried in one pocket, Charlie examined the chipset as best he could in the dim light. The minuscule factory identification markings looked genuine, but could he trust the provenance? His head throbbed. He'd been paid two days ago. He decided to take a chance.

Commerce concluded, the pusher vanished into the night. Charlie made no effort to see which way he went. Already, the freshly minted chipset was burning a hole in his pocket. Fired with expectation, he brushed past a few startled pedestrians on his way home, hardly seeing them. Had they taken the time to study his face, they might have recognized the eager, focused stare of an addict.

Once inside his apartment, the door safely bolted against the outside world, he changed into the terry-cloth bathrobe rendered smooth by endless washings, made coffee, and readied himself. Out from its hidden compartment in the wall behind the Vienna

Kunstmuseum poster came the brainet. Working carefully, sensuously, he eased the lightweight plastic helmet with its embedded network of wires and transducers over his head, meticulously fine-tuning the fit. Worn too loose and he might miss whole short stories. Fastened too tight and it would squeeze his ears.

Though the illegal chipset was immediately accepted by the receptacle in the handset controller, he didn't relax until the familiar warmth began to steal over his thoughts. The pounding at the back of his head eased. The pusher had been as good as his word, as good as Charlie's money. This was the real thing. Snugging down into the crushed depths of the easy chair, sipping coffee by rote, Charlie lapsed easily and effortlessly into the contented semicoma of someone soaking up hundreds of mental units via direct induction.

He didn't quit, he couldn't quit, until four in the morning, by which time he had absorbed the complete works of every great and numerous minor American fiction writer of the eighteenth and nineteenth centuries. Sated, exhausted, he wrestled his head out of the brainet, staggered to the bedroom, and slept right through until suppertime. It cost him a day at work, but he didn't care. When queried by his superior, he would claim that illness had laid him low—which was not entirely untrue. It had been a near-perfect assimilation, smooth and virtually painless except for a persistent cramping in his right thigh. He felt the usual exhilaration, the classic thrill, the unmatchable mental high. Of becoming smarter, more erudite.

He had Gained Knowledge.

At work the following day his boss bawled him out good. Illness or no illness, he was told, he should have called in so his division could at least have brought in a temp for the day. Adrift in remembrances of works as diverse yet enthralling as *A Voyage to the South Seas*, *The Headless Horseman*, *Omoo*, and much, much more, Charlie didn't care. He took note of the stern tongue-lashing with half a mind. The remainder was still luxuriating in the memory of the effortless absorption of knowledge. The glow lasted all week.

By Saturday he needed another hit, and went looking for the pusher.

The chipsets that university professors used to distribute material to their students contained enormous quantities of information that were supposed to be doled out gradually, by experts and specialists, in measured doses of information, properly footnoted and annotated. Their contents were not intended even for experienced instructors to absorb all at once. There was real danger involved in doing so; the threat of overloading the cerebral cortex, of swamping the brain's ability to process raw data.

But because it shouldn't be done, didn't mean it couldn't be.

Soft-spoken and polite, well educated, a reliable toiler in Menlo Park's silicon alleys, Charlie Fellows was a knowledge addict. Ever since he had been exposed at a college party to the brainet and the chipsets it broadcast, the nonworking portion of his adult life had been given over to learning, finding out, spending time in the acquisition of lore. When the ability to do so only slightly less than instantly, to suck up whole reams of learning overnight, had become scientifically possible if physically dangerous and culturally frowned upon, a small but thriving subculture had sprung up in its wake. Charlie had become an active member of that subculture very early on. It was an obsession he had in common with his closest friends, with Cheryl Chakula and Wayne Moorhead and C.K. Wang and Winona Gibson. Some of them he saw regularly at work; others he knew socially.

Like all of them, he was a knowledge junkie.

If the acquisition of erudition was your be-all and end-all, if it was your grail, your heart's desire, then no faster way had ever been devised to achieve it than through the use of the brainet and the chipsets with which it was fueled. Like information acquired by reading or viewing, once stored in the mind, data derived via inducted chipset contents stayed put. Charlie's brain was stuffed, swollen, crammed full of wondrous esoterica gleaned from night after night of reposing in his favorite chair while the brainet pumped fact after fact through the neurons hiding under his hair. He knew more about saltwater aquarium maintenance than any pet store manager. His ability to delineate the formulae for common sugars and proteins was the equal of innumerable highly paid chemists on the payroll of Betty Crocker and Duncan Hines. He could recite quatrains whole and entire from medieval French poetry and discourse learnedly on the mechanics of moon rockets as well as bicycles. Only two dilemmas marred his artificially acquired scholarly bliss.

It wasn't enough. Ever.

And when he wasn't learning, his head began to hurt.

It was not as if no warnings existed. Every chipset manufactured for industrial or university use carried imprinted upon it in microscopic font the standard caveat. "The Surgeon General has warned that the assimilation of too much knowledge too quickly can be hazardous to your health." At least once a week one of the major newscasts carried the story of some poor soul dead of an overdose on Proust or Hawking, African agricultural statistics or an attempt to digest the entire *Mahabharata* in one evening's sitting. What was news to the uncurious was not news to Charlie. He knew the risks from personal experience.

Just last year, his friend and company coworker Dexter Ashburn had OD'd right on his florid and floral living room couch halfway through Manley's *Guide to the Echinoderms of the Western Pacific*. Sheree LeMars was still in rehab, recovering from an ill-conceived attempt to mainline *The Complete Fashions of the English Court: 1600–2000*. And then there was the sad, bad case of little Chesley Waycross. He was still recovering from the beating he'd received from a disgruntled customer. Ches had tried to trade straight up for a copy of *Barrington's Ornithology of Brazil and Venezuela* with an unperused bootleg of *The Complete Literature of Sixteenth-century Tibet*. Unfortunately, the chipset Chesley had offered in exchange had been bogus: There was no literature in sixteenth-century Tibet. His enraged client had netted nothing but a standard pornset compilation; common, cheap, and useless. He'd taken out his anger and frustration on the unknowing Waycross.

One had to tread carefully on the street of knowledge.

Why not stop? he had once been challenged by an ex-girlfriend. Stop learning? he had replied. One might as well stop breathing. Hadn't Erasmus (whose complete writings Charlie had inhaled one night on a beautiful day in May) said that "To stop learning is to start to die"? Sure it was so, she had agreed, but with the brainet and enough chipsets, wasn't the reverse true?

Charlie didn't care. He only knew that from the time he had been old enough to read, the pursuit of knowledge had been the principal driving force in his life. If only we lived for a thousand years or so there might be no need to try to cram so much information into so little time, he knew. But humans did not live for a thousand years. If you wanted to learn a little bit, a minimally respectable amount, really learn, then direct induction was the only way. Ignorance could not be borne. It was unthinkable. Like his friends and fellow addicts, it wasn't simply that Charlie *wanted* to know. He *had* to know. *Needed* to know. Needed knowledge as urgently as he needed food, or water, or air. Otherwise, what was the meaning of life? Gobbling hamburgers and watching football? Mindless reproduction and the acquisition of false wealth? Far better to grasp the intricacies of diatom skeletons, the taxonomy of Southeast Asian flowers, the workings of the aurora or the mysteries of zydeco music. So what if it killed you, eventually, by overloading your cranial capacity?

At least you would die knowing *something*.

They caught up with him eventually. If he'd moved away, he very likely would have escaped arrest, trial, incarceration, and imprisonment. But he loved where he lived, he liked his job, and besides, the best stuff was always to be found in the vicinity of major universities. Stanford was no exception. Given the scope of his personal chipset inventory and the extent of his addiction, the judge threw the book at him. This was not necessary, since he had long since inducted the complete civil code of the State of California. It did not help his defense, however.

He was sent to the Northern California Center for the Treatment of the Data Addicted, in Monterey. There, when he wasn't in lockdown and forced to watch endless hours of mind-purifying daytime television, he wandered the halls in the company of fellow compulsives: lapsed physicists from the heavily addicted part of Pasadena that bordered Caltech, dour-faced recreational users caught hiding out with volumes of Balzac and African healer texts up in Humboldt County, softly mumbling immigrant programmers from Uttar Pradesh and Canton and Singapore. Shared verbalized snatches of Rabelais and Einstein and Cosell filled the hallways, repeated by the desperate inmates as self-sustaining mantras, but it wasn't enough, not nearly enough, to satisfy the information-starved like himself.

It was almost as tough as being forced to go cold turkey. In addition to television, the presence of daily newspapers, weekly magazines, and broadband Internet access provided the merest dribble of data, the feeblest kind of mental methadone. To someone used to ingesting the complete works of Shakespeare or *Mammals of Eastern Russia* or *Statistical Digest of Nebraska* in a few hours, it was the cerebral equivalent of providing nothing but distilled water for months on end to a community comprised of seventy-year-old Scotsmen.

Charlie pleaded. He wept, he raged, he implored. It was no use. Newspapers, magazines, TV, Internet were all that was supplied. Information presented in the traditional manner: to the brain via the eyes, slowly, oh, so slowly.

He got better. Withdrawal was painful, but he got better. Gradually he relearned how to read a magazine: how to skip the advertisements, block out the irrelevant, and concentrate on the articles only. How to handle a newspaper again without avidly devouring the obituaries or the columns of sports statistics or the innumerable but still educational want ads. How to watch and enjoy television without . . . well, without doing much of anything. Slowly, he could feel his brain softening to something like normal. The process of re-habilitation was made easier because during it all he retained every-thing he had absorbed through the use of his now-confiscated brainet and precious, priceless, irreplaceable chipsets. He did not lose information already acquired; at least, no more than was typi-cal. In data rehab, some leakage was inevitable.

When they felt he was sufficiently cured, they returned him to society. He was welcomed back at his job, for despite his boss's occasional outbursts, Charlie was regarded as a fine, competent worker who excelled at his craft and would willingly work long hours. Besides, everyone now knew that he had been sick. He went about his daily activities with a new serenity, the result of the best treatment the State could provide. He went about them for weeks, and then for months, without a relapse. Went about them until he was sure he was no longer being monitored by the local police data division of Narcotics.

Only then did he once more begin to venture out to his old, fa-miliar haunts in response to the lure of pure, undiluted, concen-trated knowledge. His first buy since getting out of rehab was a wondrous compilation of the lives of the Mughals, translated from the original Sanskrit. Nestling back in his chair, the newly pur-chased, battered, but still serviceable secondhand brainet resting awkwardly but satisfactorily on his head, he let himself lapse all over again into the sumptuous, sensuous sensation of effortlessly absorbing erudition. Of learning far faster than he ever could by the ancient eye-scan method called reading. Of becoming more know-ing. It might kill him, but he didn't care. We all die eventually any-way. Only some of us die knowing more than others.

In a way, he felt bad for the authorities. All the courses of treat-ment they had devised, all the expensive programs and curriculum that had been developed with an eye toward curing the afflicted, couldn't really treat the root causes of the problem. Once one has be-come truly, madly, deeply addicted to the acquisition of knowledge, nothing else really satisfies. It was like any true craving: The more you have, the more you want. For the first time, where knowledge was concerned, the brainet made it possible to completely indulge that compulsion.

It was midmorning when old Aurangzeb, the last of the Mughals, finally passed into history and into the repository of Charlie Fellows's memory. With a languid sigh of complete satisfaction that bordered on the prurient, Charlie blinked and tenderly removed the plasticized network of chips and induction contacts from his head. A glance at the clock showed that he had missed another day of work. He didn't care. He now knew all about Akbar and Shah Jahan and their most interesting ilk, and felt much the better for it. The more *knowledgeable*. The pounding at the back of his head was no worse than tolerable. He felt fine. Infused. Educated. There was only one problem. As always. As there ever would be.

He was still thirsty.

Sean McMullen is one of Australia's leading SF and fantasy authors. He is the winner of over a dozen awards for SF and fantasy and has had twelve books and fifty stories published. His works have appeared in Australia, the USA, Britain, France, Poland, and Japan. In addition to his writing, Sean works in scientific computing, and has played in rock and folk bands, early music groups, and the State Opera. He has done armored and traditional fencing, and has been a karate instructor in the university club for twenty years. He is currently studying for a Ph.D. in medieval literature at the University of Melbourne. Of his contribution here, he says, "The idea grew out of a TV interview I did about growing our own aliens, and it certainly strikes me as a future shock. The rather pretty backdrop is from my Ph.D.!"

THE ENGINES OF ARCADIA
Sean McMullen

I am a refugee. I built my engine to escape the drab and stifling age into which I was born, and suffice to say that it worked, and I am free. I am a criminal, too. My engine makes use of energies that could leave a crater the size of a large city if liberated all at once. I had built unauthorized devices and studied prohibited fields, with a view to endangering myself and abusing the public health system. If I used them my life insurance would become invalid. So too would my health care scheme, and I would be fated to the public hospital system should I be injured. Misuse of private resources for dangerous recreational pastimes would get my property confiscated and my savings allocated to me in an allowance.

I was, of course, no stranger to the legal system, having convictions for intimidating language, coarse language, sexually abusive language, cashier rage, and expressing views conducive to inciting destructive emotions. Add this to the fact that my engine was effectively a thermonuclear bomb being used to power a prohibited experiment with a seat bolted to it, and I could have spent a dozen lifetimes in a rehabilitation clinic without completing my sentence. On the other hand, I escaped, so what did it matter?

My departure was without ceremony or announcement, for reasons that are probably clear by now. My tests with models and mice had been completed, and my full-size engine stood ready for use. My first jump was through a single day. Having verified that the door to my cage lay open, I deleted my records, splashed petrol around my workshop, set the place afire, then vanished. The sensation of traveling on the engine is like a journey in a passenger jet with the window shutters down, because one is totally cut off from the universe outside, yet moving at great speed. My instruments registered the speed, however, and for a long time I just sat there, mesmerized by the flicker of centuries passing faster than seconds.

At first I felt grim triumph, knowing that all of the people, laws, organizations and creeds that had stifled me for so long were passing into oblivion, and this transmuted into relief at being free. Finally I felt trepidation, as I began to wonder what I would find when I stopped. I had brought no weapons, food, or water; all that I had was a solid-state recorder, a solar-powered torch, and the clothes that I wore. Finally I began to ease the power back, and the bubble of nothingness that had surrounded the engine and myself faded into bright sunshine as I came to temporal rest.

Glancing about, I saw that the engine was standing within the grounds of a vast park. The grass was short and dense, there were a half dozen statues and fountains visible from where I sat, and the garden beds were lush with flowers. The figure of a winged woman carved from white stone was standing nearby. It was perhaps twelve feet high, and it faced the time engine, arms outstretched as if welcoming me. The air was warm and balmy, and there was no wind. Off to my right and towering above the trees was a medieval castle.

I stared at the structure in disbelief for perhaps half a minute. It had turrets, crenellations, arrow slits, and towers, but it was no ruin. The walls gleamed white in the bright sunlight, great colourful banners hung on either side of the gate, and gaudy pennants flew from the flagpoles. Astounded, I glanced down to the control console, wondering if I had somehow managed to defy the causality asymptote and go backward. The display assured me that I was in the year two hundred and forty seven thousand, six hundred and twelve. I looked back to the castle, now noticing details that I had missed earlier. The towers were exceedingly slender, the white walls were unblemished, and no guards patrolled behind the crenellations. Somehow there was nothing really military about this castle, even though castles are by their very nature fortified mansions.

Nevertheless, the sight of a building out of an earlier, more violent period made me uneasy. I had brought no weapons, after all. Still, the look of the garden around me spoke of nothing but peace and tranquillity, and this reassured me. I closed down the power generators and converters, set a combination on the control panel's lock, and disarmed the power cells. Satisfied that the vehicle was secure, I set off to get a better view of the castle.

I soon found that I was on the summit of a hill, and once I moved clear of the glade I was presented with a vista stretching from due north to southwest that extended all the way to the horizon. Even in that first glance I counted over a dozen other castles dotted across the forests and fields, and here and there I could see smoke rising from villages. The large number of castles immediately suggested that there was danger in this deceptively tranquil countryside, so I was now faced with a dilemma. Should I go back to my time engine and travel on to some safer era, or should I seek a welcome in the nearest of the castles? The debate with myself did not last long. I had fled my time to escape overweening, state-sponsored safety, so why should I look for it now? I set off down the hill, trying to be cautious as I walked, while not seeming stealthy.

The first people that I encountered were a group of children picking bright yellow fruit from a low, wide tree, and singing in a strangely familiar yet incomprehensible language. With them was a white Shetland pony hitched to a tiny cart. At the sight of me they cried out in amazement and pointed, then came running over and crowded around me. Their total lack of fear of strangers astonished me; then I was even more astonished to realize that they were not children. The diminutive men had downy beards, while the even smaller women had tiny but fully developed breasts. Not one of the men could have been above five feet in height, and the women were ten or twelve inches shorter.

As they felt my hands, arms, and leather jacket, I noticed that they were all dressed in tunics and sandals, and had the look of prosperous peasants. None of their clothing was patched, torn, or ragged, or showed any signs of grime or stains. Both sexes had flowers in their hair, and from this I assumed that I had arrived in the middle of some festival.

I did not understand the words of the one who appeared to be their leader, but he clearly suggested that I be escorted somewhere. The group formed into a little procession, and I was decorated with flowers as we walked the quarter mile or so through orchards and parklands to a village at the base of the hill. It consisted of two or three dozen cottages, a little market, and a handful of artisans' shops. Here the interest in me was so great that we were stopped by the crowd, and I had a chance to look around over the heads of my hosts.

The houses were all solidly built and in perfect repair. Every window had a sill box planted with herbs and flowers, neatly hung laundry fluttered above weed-free vegetable plots, and there was not one broken shingle on any roof. I was surprised to see no church, chapel, or indeed any place of worship; in fact, the village did not even have a meeting hall. There was the scent of cooking on the air, everything from bread baking to pies and stews. Not at any time during my stay did I see any indication that shortages or starvation had ever been known in this place.

Presently I noticed that riders were approaching from the castle. By now I was not surprised to see that they were riding the tiny white ponies, or that each pony had a little man at the reins, and an even smaller woman riding sidesaddle behind him. All were dressed gaudily, in finely tailored robes, and the villagers bowed down as they arrived. I made a point of bowing graciously, while not seeming servile. They responded with bows of their own, and after a long and involved series of gestures I found myself walking with the riders to the castle.

The castle's drawbridge was not a drawbridge. There was a wide stone bridge over the moat, and beyond this there was an archway with no gates. Trumpeters on the archway played a fanfare as we entered; then I was escorted into a vast hall that was set out for the midday meal. This was a meal such as the original Middle Ages would never have seen, however, because not a trace of meat appeared on the tables at any time. It was all fruit, vegetables, pastries, and cheeses.

Presiding over the feast was a couple who seemed to be the local ruler and his consort. Some very confused gestures and questioning established that the rulers were named Aral and Linsey. I was seated between these two, and the meal was conducted with a great deal of formality. I counted thirty-seven courses, ranging from the very first platter of candied nuts that arrived at noon, to the sugar dates that were set before me when it was nearly evening. Each course was preceded by a trumpet fanfare and declaration by a herald; then a procession of servery maids would bring out the actual food. There was no alcoholic drink, and the portions were so moderate that I felt no more than merely satisfied by the time Aral stood up to indicate that the meal was at an end.

The entire company now paraded behind Aral into another hall. Here a consort of woodwinds played as the courtiers stepped, bowed, flourished, and gestured their way through a series of stately dances. It was during the dancing that I first noticed that relations between Aral and Linsey were less than cordial. She was exceedingly suspicious of any other woman who came anywhere near him, and the music was often punctuated by a shrill outburst from her if even a serving maid approached them.

By the end of the dancing the sun was near the horizon, and I now became an audience of one as the dancers paired off with one another in an elaborate series of courtship rituals that rivaled the dances in complexity. Again, Linsey made it plain in a loud and shrill voice that no other woman was welcome anywhere near her partner. The company gradually dispersed in pairs, but not one of them matched the pairs that had been seated together at the meal. No amorous advances were made upon me, but this was understandable. I did not speak the language, and was two feet taller than any woman present.

Going out into the cloisters, I passed several couples who sat or stood fondling each other, looked up to see a suitor climbing a rope to a second-floor window, and surprised a handmaid as she opened a side gate to a tiny man in a dark cloak. Aral must have eluded Linsey in search of other company, because her sharp voice echoed through the castle as she searched for him. For the next few minutes any number of masked and cloaked figures hurried to and fro among the gathering shadows on silent, slippered feet.

To my surprise Linsey now appeared out of the shadows. She was grim and unsmiling as she came striding up to my bench, sat stiffly on the edge, snatched up my hand and slapped it down on the velvety cloth covering her thigh. She then proceeded to deliver a diatribe, of which I understood nothing, but which I assumed involved Aral. My hand being placed upon her thigh appeared to constitute some type of symbolic sexual encounter, which was a means of saving face because of Aral's alliance elsewhere. With face saved and honour satisfied, Linsey now stood up and marched away. For a time I pondered my curious new status as sex object as other individuals and couples darted to and fro.

As dusk faded into night the castle became still and silent. Nobody had thought to give me a place to sleep, but the air was warm and the night windless, so I stretched out on one of the padded benches in the cloisters and draped the backrest cloth over myself.

Aside from Linsey, I was probably the only person in that castle who did not sleep with someone else that night. I awoke with dawn's light streaming in from the east, then set off to find breakfast in whatever form it came. I soon learned that nobody was up and about at that hour: not a servant, not a peasant, and certainly not a noble. I drank from a fountain in the gardens, and picked some fruit from the trees for my meal, then began to explore the place.

The castle was devoid of anything military. The coats of arms on the shields in the feasting hall mostly featured flowers, with occasional birds or animals. The shields were merely painted canvas stretched over wicker frames. Nobody seemed to own anything more offensive than an eating knife, there were no dungeons, and I saw no suits of armour or chain mail. Down in the stables a dozen or so little white ponies munched their chaff, while two pairs of intertwined legs protruded from the hayloft. One pair of feet was grubby and bare, the other wore richly embroidered slippers.

It was no different in the village; clearly, nobody rose with the sun. A brisk walk up the hill took me to my engine, which had been garlanded with flowers but not interfered with in any other way. I sat on a stone bench, looking out over the landscape and playing files from the twenty-first century on my memory vault. A keyword search under *medieval* and *utopia* produced several articles and papers on medievalist arcadianism, and I put one of these on speech-play.

The author argued that the Middle Ages had a status in literature akin to a utopia or even a paradise, and that this was partly due to the real nobles and knights trying to live up to standards set in the chivalric romances of the day. Much of the literature of later centuries treated the chivalric fiction as if it were real, and this dream vision of the Middle Ages had eventually swamped actual history in popular consciousness. There was romance, adventure, feasting, and general revelry, and as long as the rule of the monarch was benevolent there was justice and prosperity. I wondered what the author would have made of what I had found, but he had ceased caring a quarter of a million years earlier. In this new medieval arcadia the world had been tamed and transformed into one vast estate garden. Violence had vanished, and adventure of a sexual nature was now the only outlet for people's energies. They courted, fell in love, slept with their lovers, cheated upon their lovers, fell out of love, then moved on to new lovers—all in the space of a night, from what I had seen.

There appeared to be no money in circulation. People merely did what required doing because it was their place to do it, or bartered what they had for what they wanted. War, commerce, and scholarship had ceased to exist, while courtship, fine arts, and hospitality trades had flourished. As lives go, those of these people seemed futile to me, yet I had to admit that it was philosophically difficult to pass judgement on them.

The buildings were old, and while the repairs to some wooden fittings appeared recent, the core structures seemed designed to survive for geologically great lengths of time. The stones of the walls were some type of ceramic, while the roof beams seemed to be a type of plastic with the properties of metal. The villagers knew enough masonry and carpentry to perform minor repairs to buildings, but no more. Who, then, had built the castles?

When I returned to my hosts, the business of the morning was being organized between the village and castle, and this turned out to be a tournament. Stands and a tilting race were set up by both villagers and castle servants. A fanfare signaled that the stands were ready, and they were quickly filled by courtiers and lesser nobles.

The servants and villagers watched from the surrounding fields. My expectations of seeing something martial quickly came to an end. Two little knights faced each other, both on white ponies, and wearing just their courtly robes under surcoats. Both carried a canvas shield and a large ball of flowers. They rode at each other, flinging the balls of flowers as they closed. I soon worked out that if the flowers burst upon one's opponent, he was considered to be vanquished. If both were vanquished, it was considered a draw. Each knight wore an elaborately embroidered favor on his right arm, and after each bout there was a great show of emotion from the diminutive ladies who had fashioned them. It was not the stuff that great deeds of arms are made of, and I must admit to becoming bored very quickly.

For the next few days I made the castle my base while I explored everything within a half-day's walk. The three other castles that I visited were of almost precisely the same mold. Apart from the ponies, there were no domestic animals larger than a sheep. Wildlife appeared to be mainly birds, although once I caught sight of a wolflike animal about the size of a spaniel.

Linsey spent time with me whenever Aral managed to elude her, which was fairly often. Through her I learned enough of their language to hold a coherent conversation, and I was astonished to find that it was a form of English. The English of Chaucer had become incomprehensible to all but scholars after a mere six hundred years, so it was remarkable that all traces had not been lost after a half million. The survival of a somewhat evolved English led me to think that the medieval arcadia in which I now roamed had been set up not long after my time, and that its basis might be genetic.

This pleased me not at all. I had journeyed into the future to escape the venal restrictions of an overprotective world coalition of security, and to discover what glorious destiny humankind had eventually achieved. Finding that the nanny state had triumphed, and that humanity's achievements had been discarded for a quarter of a million years of hey nonny no and amorous hanky-panky had come as a very unpleasant shock.

On the evening of my ninth day in the arcadia I sat on what had become my bench in the cloisters, wondering whether to explore the place further, or to journey on in search of some better future. Linsey was with me, sitting rigidly upright and unsmiling, but holding one of my hands firmly against her right breast to let passersby know that she was not alone, even though Aral had eluded her. By now I had learned that they were count and countess, or corrn and cornniss, as she pronounced it.

My thoughts were interrupted when the count strolled through the gate arm in arm with a barefoot peasant girl. Linsey immediately bounded up from the bench and dashed for them, shrieking what was probably abuse and waving her hands in the air. The peasant girl ran back the way she had come, while Aral dashed for his apartment tower. Even though she was the most disagreeable of these living automata of the future, I could not help but like the countess. She at least had some spirit about her, and I fancied that her descendants would one day liberate the world from this living tapestry.

During the dancing of that evening I was called upon to perform various feats of strength, such as taking two of the women by the hands and lifting them a yard from the ground. I was developing a role for myself akin to that of a jester or juggler, and while this was hardly my idea of a career path, it did at least give me a role and identity. That night I retired to my bench early.

I awoke with the moon high. The castle was in absolute silence, and I was not at all sure what had roused me. I fancied that I had dreamed of a shriek of terror echoing through the corridors and cloisters of the palace, something absolutely out of place in this perfect world. Could it have been something else? Some woman having an orgasm, perhaps? With the amount of copulation that was going on, I thought it a wonder that I had not heard evidence of more orgasms. I was settling down to get back to sleep when I caught sight of half a dozen shadows hurrying past in the distance, carrying something between them. All going to the same orgy, I thought, and soon I began to doze again.

The following morning I set off into the woods, thinking to explore some ruins that I had seen from the castle's towers. After following a well-worn path for a mile or so, I came to a clearing that was scattered with bones. All of them were of the little people, by the look of their size. All had been gnawed thoroughly, and many had been cracked open. Here and there I saw the paw prints of what might have been spaniel-sized wolves. This immediately explained the lack of graveyards. When people died, they were carried out into the forest and literally thrown to the wolves. I had learned that religion and ideas of an afterlife had gone the way of war, violence, and politically incorrect jokes, so unceremonious disposal of the dead in this facile future of diminutive and gentle knights and ladies came as no surprise. A few scraps of fine cloth confirmed my theory, and I was about to walk on when a whimper from above drew my attention. Ten feet from the ground, clinging to a tree trunk and sitting on a branch, was Countess Linsey.

It was the work of moments to climb up beside her, but it took a lot longer to persuade her to release the tree trunk and allow me to help her down. Her left temple featured a large and ugly wound, and there was blood matted in her hair and on her bedrobe. Her feet were bare, but did not show the dirt and scratches that walking such a distance would have caused. She had been carried here.

Because the countess weighed no more than a child, it was no effort to carry her out of the woods. I stopped at a fountain so that she could drink, and I washed the blood from her hair and cleaned her up as best as I could. At the castle we were greeted with both joy and dismay, and even as I laid her in her own bedchamber the place had begun to fill up with maidservants and well-wishers. There was no longer a trace of the sharp-tongued antagonism that Countess Linsey had displayed since my arrival.

By now I had realized that these people had virtually no medical skills beyond bandaging up cuts and scratches, and I suspected that the killer diseases had been long conquered. Victims of serious accidents were just left to die, however. As far as I could tell from her single injury, Linsey had fallen and hit her head, probably during a late-night pursuit of the count. She had been carried out into the woods for disposal by the wolves, but here she had revived. She probably had a mild concussion, but would recover with rest.

The sun was an hour from the horizon as I left the afternoon feast, and I carried with me a selection from the courses to feed to the countess. I looked to her tower as I walked across the courtyard to see whether a light was burning behind the leadlight windows, and was gratified to see her standing on the balcony, looking west to the setting sun. Then, quite without warning, she flung herself over the railing and plunged to the cobbled courtyard below.

By the time I reached Linsey she was dead. A crowd quickly gathered, but the concept of death did not sit easily with these people. It was not that they feared it; they did not understand it at all. I carried her body to a nearby bench, and draped a hanging over it. The onlookers drifted away, and presently I was the only one left sitting vigil. I concluded that Linsey had attempted suicide the night before, as well. Why? Possibly there was a genetic trigger, some internal euthanasia mechanism that caused individuals who did not fit in to remove themselves from both society and the gene pool. The countess exhibited jealousy, which did not fit in, so rather than let the trait spread like a cancer, her genes had sacrificed her. The undertakers of this future had carried her away for disposal by the wolves, yet she had not been dead. Later she had revived and climbed into the tree to escape the wolves. Logically that did not really follow, but perhaps the terror of being torn apart outweighed the fear of a quick, clean death from a fall.

I cannot say how long I sat by the body of my only real friend in that world. Night fell, and presently the moon was high, so the gardens were well lit. I remember thinking how quiet the castle had become, because all the secretive scurryings of lovers going to assignations had ceased. Then I noticed them, a cluster of small, pale figures that kept to the shadows as they approached. I assumed that these were the undertakers, come to remove the body of the countess again. They spread out to encircle the bench— and then I saw the shadow of a club go up.

I raised my arms to stop the blow, then leaped from the bench as the others closed around me. I seized the nearest thing to hand as sharp, stinging blows began to rain down on me, and that thing happened to be my first attacker. Held by one leg and swung like a club, he proved very effective against the others. No more than a dozen blows had six bodies laid out on the flagstones of the cloisters. The others scattered into the darkness, and I took my solar torch from the clasp on my belt and played the beam on those lying at my feet. All were naked, and armed with the tools of trade used by the village artisans. My club turned out to be Aral. Glancing over myself, I realized that the little axes and chisels had cut me here and there. Blood was seeping through my clothes, but none of my injuries were serious.

It was at that very moment that I resolved to leave. Monsters of the night had been all around me in the daylight, laughing, singing, feasting, and playing. This was unpleasant enough, but part of my decision was also based on fear of what they might do to my engine. A concerted attack by a dozen of them wielding axes, or a bonfire built up around it, would certainly damage the key mechanisms and power sources beyond repair. I armed myself with a hatchet-sized ax and made my way out of the castle by torchlight. As I walked, I began to think about the real society of that remote and distant time.

There were no police in this future, so what happened when someone transgressed their laws and protocols? Countess Linsey had clearly been such a transgressor, and her fate had certainly removed her from the gene pool. Her first bruise had not been from a suicide attempt; it had been from an attack by those around her. By night the little folk indulged in their facile adulteries or slept, but from time to time those who were most normal—in terms of what passed for normal—hunted down and killed those who did not conform.

Perhaps it was genetically programmed schizophrenia. At some time in the distant past some scientific institute's experimental animals had demonstrated that a totally pacifistic population would inevitably throw up occasional violent mutants. A scientist could remove disruptive individuals, but the idea behind this particular project was that an ideal humanity was to be engineered, a humanity that was absolutely politically correct and totally nonviolent. Initiative was to be purged as strictly as indolence, and everyone was to have a place. At some stage old humanity must have allowed itself to cease reproducing, thinking of the entire new species as its children. The problem of mutations had remained, however. The more aggressive, domineering individuals would tend to be more successful, and to reproduce more. Eventually the traits of dominance and competition would creep back into the population, because there would be no scientist overseer to remove them. It was then that someone must have thought of schizophrenia as a survival trait.

The entire population had been engineered to become genetic vigilantes on the nights following the full moon. Doubtlessly they would not have remembered that they had killed some of their playmates during the night, and the values of the group would always average out to maintain the norm. The act of culling is intrinsically an act of power, but how can there be an act of power in a world without power? The solution had been to enshrine the role of executioner in the genes of humanity, because decisions on what is perfect cannot be made by those who *are* perfect. The mind of some reformist politician of the very distant past had been imprinted upon humanity, and it was a mind that hated those who did not conform to its idea of nonviolent tolerance and perfection. Like mice in a cage, the imperfect were identified, and for the greater good they were weeded out. Violence and intolerance were made part of the politically correct and socially perfect arcadia that had settled over the world.

The fleeting shapes of white bodies in the moonlight warned that the genetic constables had not given up on me. Rather than confront an entire crowd of them, I skirted the village and made my way up the hillside to the glade where I had arrived. Somewhere in the darkness came the thin howl of a little wolf, but this enemy from the past held no terrors for me.

The first rock very nearly knocked me senseless, but although I staggered, I did not go down. Without stopping, I raised my coat over my head to blunt the force of any further missiles. The skill to fling rocks had been kept alive in the game of flinging flowers from horseback. Luckily I was seen as the threat, and not my time engine. When I reached it at last, the device was hung with flowers, some wilting and others fresh, but it had not been damaged. As I got closer, however, I saw that stakes had been driven into the soil, and been used to secure ropes tied to the skids that it rested on.

Chuckling smugly to myself, I began to power up and configure the engine for my escape. I was in the middle of the clearing, and my attackers could not heave rocks far enough to reach me unless they left the shelter of the trees. I was so busy that I did not notice what had arrived from between the trees.

A tiny, naked warrior sat astride a white pony, holding a long, white lance high in the moonlight. This lance had a very sharp point. As I watched, more riders appeared from among the trees. I glanced to the engine's console, noting that the power was building but was not yet at an operational level. The first rider lowered his lance and charged, bearing down on me. The tip of his lance was absolutely steady, as I took the ax from my belt. I flung it more to distract him than with the intention of causing any harm, but the head buried itself in his chest, and he tumbled from the pony only feet from the time engine.

Already a second rider was charging, but this time I shone my torch in his face. The dazzle was enough to put him off his aim, and he rode harmlessly past. Now two riders charged together. With a sudden qualm I realized that the vigilante personalities of these creatures were more intelligent than the daylight personas. They had deduced that I could not dazzle two of them at once. The metal tips of the approaching lances glinted in the moonlight. I looked down and pattered codes into the keypad, oblivious to whether there was as yet power to operate the circuits; then, with my eyes on the lance points again, I pushed the throttle lever over as far as it would go while praying that the power level had risen far enough to sustain a temporal resonance.

The ghosts of lance points passed through my body as I slipped away into their future.

I put myself a thousand years into the future of my attackers, but although the memories of me had vanished, the medieval arcadia had not changed in the slightest. The village and castle were identical, while the feasting, courting, and flinging of flowers went on as before. In this time I appropriated a backpack, waterskin, ax, and knife, along with as much food as I could carry. Then I traveled on.

No arcadia is perfect. Catastrophes in the form of giant meteorite strikes, explosive caldera eruptions, ice ages, newly evolved plagues, or simple drought are beyond the control of any planner, and every few hundred thousand years an event big enough to bring down a simple civilization takes place. Sooner or later something would plunge the world into darkness that would be simply too disruptive to withstand. I traveled on, stopping time and again. I have now traveled eleven million years, yet both the village and castle are still there, and the little people are no different.

I can only conclude that something is maintaining the arcadia, something so vast and powerful that it can cope with even an ice age or meteor strike. What I call homo arcadiensis are the engines of this arcadia; they power a collective mind that rules and maintains the world. The medieval arcadia is merely a proven, stable setting to keep them healthy and contented.

Prejudice, violence, and inequality cannot exist if only a single intelligence exists on the earth, yet a second intelligence does exist. Me. The temporal range of my time engine is not much more than eleven million years, and I shall soon have to make a decision about when to stop and settle. My time engine travels only in one direction, yet my future is absolutely unchanging. When I do stop for long enough, the living engines that maintain and preserve arcadia will discover, and attempt to purge me.

Should I be a cancer cell, and establish a colony of misfits? I look across at a castle eleven million years old, and ponder ethics that have not been relevant for all of that time.

Writing from out of a renovated 1907 schoolhouse in Atlanta, Georgia, **Caitlín R. Kiernan's** self-styled "gothnoir" tales of dark fantasy have garnered her three International Horror Guild awards, a Barnes and Noble Maiden Voyage award, and Bram Stoker award and British Fantasy award nominations. She is the author of five novels—*The Five of Cups, Silk, Threshold, Low Red Moon,* and *Murder of Angels*—and her short fiction has been collected in *Tales of Pain and Wonder, From Weird and Distant Shores,* and *To Charles Fort, With Love.* She also scripted *The Dreaming* series for DC Comics/Vertigo, as well as two miniseries, *The Girl Who Would Be Death* and *Bast: Eternity Game.* When it came time to sound the call for *FutureShocks,* she was top of my list.

THE PEARL DIVER
Caitlín R. Kiernan

Farasha Kim opens her eyes at precisely six thirty-four, exactly one minute before the wake-up prompt woven into her pillow begins to bleat like an injured sheep. She's been lying awake since at least three, lying in bed listening to the constant, gentle hum of the thermaspan and watching the darkness trapped behind her eyelids. It's better than watching the lesser, more meaningful darkness of her tiny bedroom, the lights from the unsleeping city outside, the solid corner shadows that mercury-vapor streetlights and the headlights of passing trucks and cars never even touch. Her insomnia, the wide-awakeness that always follows the dreams, renders the pillow app superfluous, but she's afraid that muting it might tempt sleep, that in the absence of its threat she might actually fall *back* to sleep and end up being late for work. She's already been black-cited twice in the last five years—once for failing to report another employee's illegal use of noncorp software and once more for missing the start of an intradepartmental meeting on waste and oversight—so it's better safe than sorry. Farasha tells the bed that she's awake, thank you, and a moment later it ceases to bleat.

It's Tuesday, so she has a single slice of toast with a smear of marmalade, a hard-boiled egg, a red twenty-five milligram stimugel, and an eight-ounce glass of soy milk for breakfast, just like every other Tuesday. She leaves the dishes in the sink for later, because the trains have been running a little early the past week or so. She dresses quickly, deciding that she can get by one more day without a shower, deciding to wear black stockings instead of navy. And she's out the door and waiting for the elevator by seven twenty-two, her head already sizzling from the stimu-gel.

On the train, she stares out at the winter-gray landscape, Manhattan in mid-January, and listens to the CNN2 *Firstlight* report over the train's tinny speakers: the war in Turkey, the war in North Africa, the war in India, an ecoterrorist attack in Uruguay, Senate hearings on California's state-funded "suicide camps," the weather, the stock-market report, the untimely death of an actor she's never seen. The train races the clock across the Hudson and into Jersey, and, because it's Tuesday morning, the *Firstlight* anchorwoman reminds everyone that there will be no private operation of gasoline-powered motor vehicles until Thursday morning at ten o'clock Eastern, ten o'clock Pacific.

The day unfolds around her in no way that is noticeably different from any other Tuesday.

Farasha eats her lunch (a chocolate-flavored protein bar and an apple from the vending machines) and is back at her desk three minutes before anyone else. At one nineteen, the network burps, and everyone in datatrak and receiving is advised to crossfile and reboot. At one minute past three, the fat guy five desks over from her laughs aloud to himself and is duly docked twelve points plus five percent for inattentive behavior. He glances nervously at the nearest observer, risking another citation, risking unemployment, and then goes back to work. At four thirty-eight, the lights on the fourth floor dim themselves for seven minutes, because it is Tuesday, and even the corporations are willing to make these inconvenient, necessary sacrifices in the interest of energy conservation. Good examples are set at the top, after all.

At six P.M., as a light snow begins to fall, she walks alone with all the others to the Palisades station and takes the lev back across the river, back to the city. On the train, she watches the snow and the lights dotting the gathering night and listens indifferently to the CNN2 *WindDown* broadcast. The stimu-gel capsule is wearing off early, and she reminds herself to mention it to her physician next month. It wouldn't be the first time she's needed her dosage adjusted.

Farasha is home by seven thirty, and she changes clothes, trading the black stockings for bare legs, then eats her dinner—a spongy slice of vegetarian meat loaf with a few spoonfuls of green peas and carrots on the side, a stale wheat roll, and a cup of hot, sweetened mint tea. The tea is good, at least, and she sips the last of it in front of the television, two black-and-white *Popeye the Sailor* cartoons and one with Tom and Jerry. Her company therapist recommended cartoons in the evening, and she enjoys them, though they don't seem to do anything for her insomnia or the nightmares. Her insurance would cover sleep mods and rem reconditioning, but she knows it's best not to make too much of the bad dreams. It's not something she wants on her record, not something she wants her supervisors getting curious about.

She shuts off the television at nine o'clock, does the dishes, takes the short, cold shower she's been putting off for three days, and then checks her mail before bed. There's something wordy and unimportant from her half sister in Montreal, an ad for breast enhancement that slipped through the spamblock, a reminder that city elections are only a month away and she's required by company policy to vote GOP, and something else that's probably only more spam.

Farasha reads the vague header on the fourth item—INVITATION TRANSCEND—then tells the computer to empty the in box. She touches the upper left-hand corner of the screen, an index finger pressed against and then into the phosphor triangle, and it vanishes. The wall above the kitchen counter is only a wall again.

She brushes her teeth, flosses, takes a piss, then washes her hands and is in bed by nine forty-six. She falls asleep ten or twenty minutes later, trying not to think about the dreams, or the next day, concentrating on the steady roar of a water sweeper moving slowly, methodically along Mercer Street.

Farasha Kim was born in Trenton, the year before the beginning of the Pan-American/European Birth Lottery, to a Saudi mother and a Korean father. She was one of the last "freeborn" children in the U.S., though she doesn't see this as a point of pride. Farasha has never bothered with the lottery, not with the birth-defect rate what it is these days, and not when there are already more than ten billion people in the world, most of them living in conditions she prefers not contemplate. Her father, a molecular biochemist at Columbia University, has told her more than once that her own birth was an "accident" and "ill-timed," and she has no wish to repeat any of the mistakes of her parents.

She grew up in Lower Manhattan, suffering the impeccably programmed attentions of the nanny mechs that did the work her mother and father couldn't be bothered with. Sometimes in the uncomfortable dreams that wake her every night, Farasha is a child again. She's five, or eight, or even eleven, and there's usually a nagging sense of loss, of disappointment and sadness, when she wakes to discover herself aged to thirty-seven years.

In one recurring dream, repeated at least twice a month, she's eight and on a school field trip to the Museum of Modern Art. She stands with the edu-mechs and other children, all nameless in the fickle memory of her unconsciousness, gazing up at an enormous canvas hung on a wide white wall. There are no other paintings on the wall. A towering rectangle of pigment and cold-pressed linseed oil, sweeping arcs of color, a riot of blues and greens and pinks and violets. Sea foam and rising bubbles, the sandy, sun-dappled floor of a tropical lagoon, coral and giant clams and the teardrop bodies of fish. Positioned near the center is the figure of a woman, a *naked* woman, her skin almost the same shade of brown as Farasha's own, swimming towards the shimmering mirror surface. Her arms outstretched, air streaming from her wide nostrils and open mouth, her strong legs driving her up and up and up. And near the bottom of the painting, lurking in lower left-hand shadows, there's a shark with snow-tipped caudal and dorsal fins. It isn't clear whether or not the shark poses an immediate danger to the swimmer, but the *threat* is plain to see.

There's a label fixed to the wall beneath the painting, black lettering stark against all that white, so she knows it's titled *The Pearl Diver*. No such painting has ever hung at MoMA; she's inquired more than once. She's also searched online databases and library hard copies, but has found no evidence that the painting is anything but a fabrication of her dreaming mind. She's never mentioned it to her therapist, or to anyone else, for that matter.

In her dream, one of the children (never precisely the same child twice) asks one of the edu-mechs what the woman in the painting is doing, and the droid answers patiently, first explaining what pearls are, in case some of its students might not know.

"A natural pearl," the mech says, "forms by secretions from the epithelial cells in the mantle of some mollusks, such as oysters, deposited in successive layers about an irritating foreign object, often a parasitic organism. Layers of aragonite or calcite, the crystalline forms of calcium carbonate, accumulate. . . ."

But the eight-year-old Farasha is always more interested in the painting itself, the brushstroke movement and color of the painting, than in the mere facts behind its subject matter, and she concentrates on the canvas while the mech talks. She tunes it out, and the other children, too, and the walls of the museum, and the marble floor beneath her feet.

She tastes the impossibly clean saltwater getting into her mouth, and her oxygen-starved lungs ache for air. Beneath her, the shark moves silently forward, a silver-blue-gray ghost propelled by the powerful side-to-side sweeps of its tall, heterocercal tail. It knows things that she can only guess, things that she will never see, even in dreams.

Eventually, the droid finishes with all the twists and turns of its encyclopedia reply and ushers the other children towards the next painting in the gallery. But Farasha is left behind, unnoticed, forgotten, abandoned because she can no longer separate herself from *The Pearl Diver*. Her face and hands are stained with paint, and she's still rising, struggling for the glistening surface that seems to be getting father away instead of nearer. She wonders if people can drown in paintings and kicks her legs again, going nowhere at all.

The shark's dull eyes roll back like the eyes of something dead or dying, and its jaws gape open wide to reveal the abyss waiting for her past the rows and rows of ragged teeth. Eternity in there, all the eternity she might ever have imagined or feared.

And the canvas pulls her in.

And sometimes she wakes up, and sometimes she drifts down through frost and darkness filled with anxious, whispering voices, and sometimes the dream architecture collapses and becomes another dream entirely.

There's a small plastic box on Farasha's bedroom dressing table, polyethylene terephthalate molded and colored to look like carved ivory, and inside are three perfect antique pearls from a broken strand that once belonged to one of her Arab great-grandmothers. Her mother gave her the pearls as a birthday present many years ago, and she's been told that they're worth a lot of money. The oyster species that produced them has been extinct for almost a hundred years. Sometimes, she goes to the dressing table after the dream and opens the plastic box, takes out one or two or all three of the pearls and carries them back to bed with her. In her sweating, sleepless palms, they feel very heavy, as good as stone or lead, and she can't imagine how anyone could have ever worn an entire necklace of them strung about her neck.

On those mornings after *The Pearl Diver*, when it's finally six thirty-five, and the pillow has begun to bleat at her, Farasha gets up and returns the heirloom pearls to their box, which they share with the few inexpensive, unremarkable pieces of jewelry that she owns. She never takes the pearls out any other time, and she tries not to think about them. She would gladly forget them, would sell them off for whatever she could get, if the dream would stop.

And after Tuesday, there is Wednesday and then Thursday and Friday, each inevitable in its turn and each distinguishable from the other only by its own specific monotony. Farasha works Saturday, because her department fell behind last month by twelve and three-quarters over the previous month and because she has nothing else to do. She dreads her days off and avoids them when she can. However, her employer does not encourage voluntary overtime, as clinical studies have shown, repeatedly, that it decreases the value of overtime as an effective deterrent to the myriad transgressions that must be guarded against at every turn. She takes her extra days and hours on campus whenever she can get them and wishes for more.

On Sunday, there is no work, and she isn't religious, so she doesn't go to church, either. Instead, she sits alone in her two-room apartment on Canal Street. The intermittent snow showers of the last four days have been replaced by a torrential rain which drums loudly against her window. For lunch, she has a can of cheese ravioli and a few slices of dried pear, then tries again to get interested in a romance fic she downloaded the weekend before. She sits in the comfortable chair beside her bed, the lines of text scrolling tediously by on her portable, hidden sensors reading the motion of her eyes from word to word, sentence to sentence. When the computer detects her growing disinterest, it asks if she would prefer the fic be read aloud to her, and Farasha declines. She's never liked being read to by machines, though she can't recall ever having been read to by a human.

"My mail, please," she says, and the fic dissolves, becoming instead the in box of her corporate account. There's a reminder for a planning meeting on Monday morning, a catalog from a pharmaceutical spa in Nevada, and another mail with the subject line INVITATION TRANSCEND. She starts to tell the computer to delete all three, even though it would probably mean a warning from interdept comms for failing to read an official memorandum. Instead, she taps the screen with the nail of her left index finger, tapping INVITATION TRANSCEND before she can think better of it. The portable advises her that all unsolicited mail, if read, is immediately noted and filed with the Homeland Bureau of Casual Correspondence and the Federal Bureau of Investigation and asks her if she still wishes to open the file. She tells it yes, and the blue and white HBCC/FBI notice is promptly replaced with the body of the message. She notes at once that the sender's address is not displayed, even though the portable is running the corporation's own custom version of Microsoft Panoptic 8. Farasha shifts in the chair, and its legs squeak loudly against the tile floor, squeaking like the sleek, quick rats that infest the building's basement.

The message reads simply:

INVITATION TRANSCEND
Final [2nd] outreach imminent. Your presence is requested. Delivery complete and confidential [guaranteed]. There is meaning in you and Outside, still. You shall see that. Wholeness regained through communion with the immaculate appetite. One way. Sonepur. Baudh. Mahanadi. This overture will NOT be repeated. Open doors do not remain open forever, Ms. Kim. Please expect contact. Merciful closure. Shantih. Amen. Off.

"Bullshit," Farasha mutters, scanning the message once more and finding it even more opaque and ridiculous the second time through. Someone had obviously managed to hack the drop tank again, and this was his or her or its idea of a joke. "Delete all," she says, hearing the annoyance in her voice, wondering how long its been since she's sounded that way. Too late, she remembers the unread memorandum on Monday morning's meeting, and a second later the portable informs her that the in box is now empty and that a federal complaint has been filed on her behalf.

She stares at the screen for a long moment, at the omnipresent corporate logo and the blinking cursor floating just slightly left of center. Then Farasha requests a search, and when the computer asks her for parameters, she types in two unfamiliar words from the vanished INVITATION TRANSCEND message, "Sonepur" and "Mahanadi." She thought the latter looked Hindi and isn't surprised when it turns out to be a river in central and eastern India. And "Sonepur" is a city located at the confluence of the Mahanadi and Tel rivers in the eastern part of the Subarnapur district. Most of the recent articles on Sonepur concern repeated bioweapon attacks on the city by Pakistani-backed guerrilla forces six months earlier. There are rumors that the retroviral agent involved may have originated somewhere in China, and the loss of life is estimated to have been staggering; a general quarantine of Sonepur remains in effect, but few other details are available. The computer reminds Farasha that searches involving military interests will be noted and filed with the Greater Office of Homeland Security, the FBI, CIA, and Interpol.

She frowns and shuts off the portable, setting it down on the small bamboo table beside the bed. Tomorrow, she'll file an appeal on the search, citing the strange piece of mail as just cause. Her record is good and there's nothing to worry about. Outside, the rain is coming down harder than ever, falling like it means to wash Manhattan clean or drown it trying, and she sits listening to the storm, wishing that she could have gone into work.

* * *

Monday again, after the morning's meeting, and Farasha is sitting at her desk. Someone whispers "Woolgathering?" and she turns her head to see who's spoken. But it's only Nadine Palmer, who occupies the first desk to her right. Nadine Palmer, who seems intent on ignoring company policy regarding unnecessary speech and who's likely to find herself unemployed if she keeps it up. Farasha knows better than to tempt the monitors by replying to the question. Instead, she glances down at the pad in front of her, the sloppy black lines her stylus has traced on the silver-blue screen, the two Hindi words—"Sonepur" and "Mahanadi"—the city and the river, two words that have nothing whatsoever to do with the Nakamura-Ito account. She's scribbled them over and over, one after the other. Farasha wonders how long she's been sitting there daydreaming, and if anyone besides Nadine has noticed. She looks at the clock and sees that there's only ten minutes left before lunch, then clears the pad.

She stays at her desk through the lunch hour, to make up the twelve minutes she squandered "woolgathering." She isn't hungry, anyway.

At precisely two P.M., all the others come back from their midday meals, and Farasha notices that Nadine Palmer has a small stain that looks like ketchup on the front of her pink blouse.

At three twenty-four, Farasha completes her second postanalysis report of the day.

At four thirteen, she begins to wish that she hadn't found it necessary to skip lunch.

And at four fifty-six, she receives a voicecall informing her that she's to appear in Mr. Binder's office on the tenth floor no later than a quarter past five. Failure to comply will, of course, result in immediate dismissal and forfeiture of all unemployment benefits and references. Farasha thanks the very polite, yet very adamant young man who made the call, then straightens her desk and shuts off her terminal before walking to the elevator. Her mouth has gone dry, and her heart is beating too fast. By the time the elevator doors slide open, opening for her like the jaws of an oil-paint shark, there's a knot deep in her belly, and she can feel the sweat beginning to bead on her forehead and upper lip.

Mr. Binder's office has a rhododendron in a terra-cotta pot and a view of the river and the city beyond. "You are Ms. Kim?" he asks, not looking up from his desk. He's wearing a navy-blue suit with a teal necktie, and what's left of his hair is the color of milk.

"Yes, sir."

"You've been with the company for a long time now, haven't you? It says here that you've been with us since college."

"Yes, sir, I have."

"But you deleted an unread interdepartmental memorandum yesterday, didn't you?"

"That was an accident. I'd intended to read it."

"But you *didn't.*"

"No, sir," she replies and glances at the rhododendron.

"May I ask what is your interest in India, Ms. Kim?" and at first she has no idea what he's talking about. Then she remembers the letter—INVITATION TRANSCEND—and her web search on the two words she'd caught herself doodling earlier in the day.

"None, sir. I can explain."

"I understand that there was an incident report filed yesterday evening with the GOHS, a report filed against you, Ms. Kim. Are you aware of that?"

"Yes, sir. I'd meant to file an appeal this morning. It slipped my mind—"

"And what are your interests in India?" he asks her again and looks up, finally, and smiles an impatient smile at her.

"I have no interest in India, sir. I was just curious, that's all, because of a letter—"

"A letter?"

"Well, not really a letter. Not exactly. Just a piece of spam that got through—"

"Why would you read unsolicited mail?" he asks.

"I don't know. I can't say. It was the second time I'd received it, and—"

"Kim. Is that Chinese?"

"No, sir. It's Korean."

"Yes, of course it is. I trust you understand our position in this very delicate matter, Ms. Kim. We appreciate the work you've done here, I'm sure, and regret the necessity of this action, but we can't afford a federal investigation because one of our employees can't keep her curiosity in check."

"Yes, sir," Farasha says quietly, the knot in her stomach winding itself tighter as something icy that's not quite panic or despair washes over and through her. "I understand."

"Thank you, Ms. Kim. An agent will be in contact regarding your severance. Do not return to your desk. An officer will escort you off the campus."

And then it's over, five nineteen by the clock on Mr. Binder's office wall, and she's led from the building by a silent woman with shiny, video-capture eyes, from the building and all the way back to the Palisades lev station, where the officer waits with her until the next train back to Manhattan arrives and she's aboard.

It's raining again by the time Farasha reaches Canal Street, a light, misting rain that'll probably turn to sleet before morning. She thinks about her umbrella, tucked beneath her desk as she waits for the security code to clear and the lobby door to open. *No*, she thinks, *by now they'll have gotten rid of it. By now, they'll have cleared away any evidence I was ever there.*

She takes the stairs, enough of elevators for one day, and by the time she reaches her floor, she's breathless and a little lightheaded. There's a faintly metallic taste in her mouth, and she looks back down the stairwell, picturing her body lying limp and broken at the very bottom.

"I'm not a coward," she says aloud, her voice echoing between the concrete walls, and then Farasha closes the red door marked

EXIT and walks quickly down the long, fluorescent-lit hallway to her apartment. At least, it's hers until the tenant committee gets wind of her dismissal, of the reasons *behind* her dismissal, and files a petition for her relocation with the housing authority.

Someone has left a large manila envelope lying on the floor in front of her door. She starts to bend over to pick it up, then stops and glances back towards the door to the stairs, looks both ways, up and down the hall, to be sure that she's alone. She briefly considers pressing #0 on the keypad and letting someone in the lobby deal with this. She knows it doesn't matter if there's no one else in the hallway to see her pick up the envelope, because the cameras will record it.

"Fuck it all," she says, reaching for the envelope. "They can't very well fire me twice."

There's a lot left they can do, she thinks, some mean splinter of her that's still concerned with the possibility of things getting worse. *You don't even want to know all the things left they can do to you.*

Farasha picks up the envelope, anyway.

Her name has been handwritten on the front, printed in black ink, neat, blocky letters at least an inch high, and beneath her name, in somewhat smaller lettering, are two words—INVITATION TRANSCEND. The envelope is heavier than she expected, something more substantial inside than paper; she taps her code into the keypad, and the front door buzzes loudly and pops open. Farasha takes a moment to reset the lock's eight-digit code, violating the terms of her lease—as well as one municipal and two federal ordinances— then takes the envelope to the kitchen counter.

Inside the manila envelope there are a number of things, which she spreads out across the countertop, then examines one by one. There's a single yellowed page torn from an old book; the paper is brittle, and there's no indication what the book might have been. The top of the page bears the header *Childhood of the Human Hero*, so perhaps that was the title. At the bottom is a page number,

327, and the following paragraph has been marked with a blue highlighter:

> The feats of the beloved Hindu savior, Krishna, during his infant exile among the cowherds of Gokula and Brindaban, constitute a lively cycle. A certain goblin named Putana came in the shape of a beautiful woman, but with poison in her breasts. She entered the house of Yasoda, the foster mother of the child, and made herself very friendly, presently taking the baby in her lap to give it suck. But Krishna drew so hard that he sucked away her life, and she fell dead, reassuming her huge and hideous form. When the foul corpse was cremated, however, it emitted a sweet fragrance; for the divine infant had given the demoness salvation when he had drunk her milk.

At the bottom of the page, written with a pencil in very neat, precise cursive, are three lines Farasha recognizes from T. S. Eliot: *And I will show you something different from either/Your shadow @ morning striding behind you/Or your shadow @ evening rising up to meet you.*

There are three newspaper clippings, held together with a somewhat rusty gem clip, all regarding the use of biological agents by pro-Pakistani forces in Sonepur and Baudh (which turns out to be another city on the Mahanadi River). More than three million are believed dead, one article states, though the quarantine has made an accurate death toll impossible, and the final number may prove to be many times that. Both the CDC and WHO have been refused entry into the contaminated areas, and the nature of the contagion remains unclear. There are rumors of vast fires burning out of control along the river, and of mass disappearances in neighboring towns, and she reads the names of Sikh and Assamese rebel leaders who have been detained or executed.

There is a stoppered glass vial containing what looks to Farasha like soot, perhaps half a gram of the black powder, and the vial is sealed with a bit of orange tape.

There is a photocopy of an eight-year-old NASA press release on the chemical composition of water-ice samples recovered from the lunar north pole, and another on the presence of "polycyclic aromatic hydrocarbons, oxidized sulfide compounds, and carbonate globules" in a meteorite discovered embedded in the Middle Devonian–aged rocks of Antarctica's Mt. Gudmundson in July 2037.

Finally, there's the item which gave the envelope its unexpected weight, a silvery metallic disk about ten centimeters in diameter and at least two centimeters thick. Its edges are beveled and marked by a deep groove, and there is a pronounced dimple in the center of one side, matching a swelling at the center of the other. The metal is oddly warm to the touch, and though it seems soft, almost pliant in her hands, when Farasha tries to scratch it with a steak knife, she's unable to leave even the faintest mark.

She glances at the clock on the wall above the refrigerator and realizes that more than two hours have passed since she sat down with the envelope, that she has no sense of so much time having passed unnoticed, and the realization makes her uneasy. *I have slipped and fallen off the earth*, she thinks, remembering Mr. Binder's potted rhododendron. *Not even time can find me now.* And then she looks back at the contents of the manila envelope.

"Is it a riddle?" she asks aloud, asking no one or herself or whoever left the package at her doorstep. "Am I supposed to understand any of this?"

For an answer, her stomach growls loudly, and Farasha glances at the clock again, adding up all the long hours since breakfast. She leaves the papers, the glass vial, the peculiar metal disk, the empty envelope—all of it—lying on the countertop and makes herself a cheddar-cheese sandwich with brown mustard. She pours a glass of soy milk and sits down on the kitchen floor. *Even unemployed ghosts have to eat*, she thinks and laughs softly to herself. *Even dead women drifting alone in space get hungry now and then.*

When she's finished, she sets the dirty dishes in the sink and goes back to her stool at the counter, back to pondering the things from the envelope. Outside, the rain has turned to sleet, just as she suspected it would, and it crackles coldly against the windows.

The child reaches out her hand, straining to touch the painting, and her fingertips dip into salty, cool water. Her lips part, and air escapes through the space between her teeth and floats in swirling, glassy bubbles towards the surface of the sea. She kicks her feet, and the shark's sandpaper skin slices through the gloom, making a sound like metal scraping stone. If she looked down, towards the sandy place where giant clams lie in secret, coral- and anemone-encrusted gardens, she'd see sparks fly as the great fish cuts its way towards her. The sea is not her protector and isn't taking sides. She came to steal, after all, and the shark is only doing what sharks have done for the last four hundred and fifty million years. It's nothing personal, nothing she hasn't been expecting.

The child cries out and pulls her hand back; her fingers are stained with paint and smell faintly of low tide and turpentine.

The river's burning, and the night sky is the color of an apocalypse. White temples of weathered stone rise from the whispering jungles, ancient monuments to alien gods—Shiva, Parvati, Kartikeya, Brushava, Ganesha—crumbling prayers to pale blue skins and borrowed tusks.

Farasha looks at the sky, and the stars have begun to fall, drawing momentary lines of clean white fire through the billowing smoke. Heaven will intercede, and this ruined world will pass away and rise anew from its own gray ashes. A helicopter drifts above the bloody river like a great insect of steel and spinning rotors, and she closes her eyes before it sees her.

"I was never any good with riddles," she says when Mr. Binder asks her about the package again, why she touched it, why she opened it, why she read all the things inside.

"It isn't a riddle," he scolds, and his voice is thunder and waves breaking against rocky shores and wind through the trees. "It's a gift."

"I was never any good with gifts, either," she replies, watching as the glass vial from the manila envelope slips from his fingers and begins the long descent towards her kitchen floor. It might fall for a hundred years, for a hundred *thousand* years, but she'll never be quick enough to catch it.

The child reaches deep into the painting again, deeper than before, and now the water has gone as cold as ice and burns her hand. She grits her teeth against the pain, and feels the shark brush past her frozen skin.

"If it's not already within you, no one can put it there," the droid says to her as it begins to unbutton the pink, ketchup-stained blouse she doesn't remember putting on. "We have no wombs but those which open for us."

"I told you, I'm not any good with riddles."

Farasha is standing naked in her kitchen, bathed in the light of falling stars and burning rivers and the fluorescent tubes set into the low ceiling. There's a girl in a rumpled school uniform standing nearby, her back turned to Farasha, watching the vial from the envelope as it tumbles end over end towards the floor. The child's hands and forearms are smeared with greasy shades of cobalt and jade and hyacinth.

"You have neither love nor the hope of love," the girl says. "You have neither purpose nor a dream of purpose. You have neither pain nor freedom from pain." Then she turns her head, looking over her right shoulder at Farasha. "You don't even have a job."

"Did you do that? You *did*, didn't you?"

"You opened the envelope," the child says and smiles knowingly, then turns back to the falling vial. "You're the one who read the message."

The shark is coming for her, an engine of blood and cartilage, dentine and bone, an engine forged and perfected without love or the hope of love, without purpose or freedom from pain. The air in her lungs expands as she rises, and her exhausted, unperfect primate muscles have begun to ache and cramp. *This is not your world*, the shark growls, and she's not surprised that it has her mother's voice. *You gave all this shit up aeons ago. You crawled out into the slime and the sun looking for God, remember?*

"It was an invitation, that's all," the girl says and shrugs. The vial is only a few inches from the floor now. "You're free to turn us away. There will always be others."

"I don't understand what you're *saying*," Farasha tells the girl and then takes a step back, anticipating the moment when the vial finally strikes the hard tile floor.

"Then stop trying."

"Sonepur—"

"That wasn't our doing," the girl says and shakes her head. "A *man* did that. Men would make a weapon of the entire cosmos, given enough time."

"I don't know what you're offering me."

The girl turns to face Farasha, holding out one paint-stained hand. There are three pearls resting in her palm.

The jungle echoes with rifle and machinegun fire and the dull violence of faraway explosions. The muddy, crooked path that Farasha has taken from the river bank ends at the steps of a great temple, and the air here is choked with the sugary scent of night-blooming flowers, bright and corpulent blooms which almost manage to hide the riper stink of dead things.

"But from out your *own* flesh," the girl says, her eyes throwing sparks now, like the shark rushing towards her. "The fruit of *your* suffering, Farasha Kim, not these inconsequential baubles—"

"I'm *afraid*," Farasha whispers, not wanting to cry, and she begins to climb the temple steps, taking them cautiously, one at a time. The vial from the envelope shatters, scattering the sooty black powder across her kitchen floor.

"That's why I'm here," the child says and smiles again. She makes a fist, closing her hand tightly around the three pearls as a vertical slit appears in the space between Farasha's bare breasts, its edges red and puckered like a slowly healing wound. The slit opens wide to accept the child's seeds.

The pain Farasha feels is not so very different from the pain she's felt her entire life.

Farasha opens her eyes, in the not-quite-empty moments left after the dream, and she squints at the silver disk from the manila envelope. It's hovering a couple of inches above the countertop, spinning clockwise and emitting a low, mechanical whine. A pencil-thin beam of light leaks from the dimple on the side facing upwards, light the lonely color of a winter sky before heavy snow. The beam is slightly wider where it meets the ceiling than where it exits the disk, and the air smells like ozone. She rubs her eyes and sits up. Her back pops, and her neck is stiff from falling asleep at the kitchen counter. Her mouth is dry and tastes vaguely of the things she ate for her supper.

She glances from the spinning disk to the glass vial, still stoppered and sealed with a strip of orange tape, and her left hand goes slowly to the space between her breasts. Farasha presses three fingers against the thin barrier of cloth and muscle and skin covering her sternum, half expecting something on the other side to press back. But there's nothing, nothing at all except the faint rhythm of her heart, and she reaches for the vial. Her hand is shaking, and it rolls away from her and disappears over the far edge of the counter. A second or two later, there's the sound of breaking glass.

The disk is spinning faster now, and the light shining from the dimple turns a bruised violet.

She looks down at the scatter of paper, and her eyes settle on the three handwritten lines from The Waste Land. She reads them aloud, and they feel wild and irrevocable on her tongue, poetry become the components of an alchemical rite or the constituent symbols in some algebraic equation. *And I will show you something different from either/Your shadow at morning striding behind you/Or your shadow at evening rising up to meet you.* Nine, seven, ten, dividing into thirty-eight syllables, one hundred and nineteen characters.

But what if I won't listen? she thinks. *What if I won't see?* And she's answered at once by the voice of a child, the voice of a brown woman who dives for gems in a painted ocean, the wordless voice of the sooty particles from the broken vial as they fill the air Farasha's breathing and find their way deep inside her.

That's why I'm here, remember? the voices reply, almost speaking in unison now, a secret choir struggling for harmony, and the disk on the counter stops suddenly and then begins to spin in the opposite direction. The beam of light has turned a garish scarlet, and it pulsates in time to her racing heart. The contagion is faster than she ever could have imagined, and this is not the pain from her dream. This is pain doubled and redoubled, pain become something infinitely greater than mere electrical impulses passed between neurons and the folds of her simple, mammalian brain. But Farasha understands, finally, and she doesn't struggle as the soot begins its work of taking her apart and putting her back together another way, dividing polypeptide chains and inserting its own particular amino acids before it zips them shut again.

And her stolen body, like the fractured, ephemeral landscape of her nightmares, becomes something infinitely mutable, altered from second to second to second, living tissue as malleable as paint on a bare canvas. There is not death here, and there is no longer loneliness or fear, boredom or the dread of whatever's coming next. With eyes that have never truly seen before this moment, Farasha watches as her soul fills up with pearls.

Mike Resnick has won an impressive five Hugos and been nominated for twenty-two more. He has sold forty-five novels and almost two hundred short stories. He has edited forty anthologies.
His work spans from satirical fare, such as his Lucifer Jones ad-
ventures, to weighty examinations of morality and culture, as ev-
idenced by his brilliant tales of Kirinyaga. For his part, **Harry
Turtledove** is the *New York Times* best-selling author of numerous alternative history novels, including *The Guns of the South*,
How Few Remain, and the *Worldwar* quartet. He has won the
Hugo, Sidewise, and John Esthen Cook Awards, and received
numerous Nebula nominations. Mike says that he and Harry
have been friends for a quarter century and have always
wanted an opportunity to collaborate. I'm overjoyed to have afforded them the chance.

BEFORE THE BEGINNING
Mike Resnick & Harry Turtledove

When they finally got the time-viewer to behave, the first thing
they had to do was pry it out of the cops' hands. Oh, how the
cops and the DAs loved it! Get a court order, view the crime scene,
watch the felony go down, watch from whatever angle you please,
watch in infrared if it's dark, catch your perp (suspect didn't mean
anything any more, not when you knew—*knew*—whodunnit), and
send him up the river.

It beat working.

Then the scandalmongers got hold of it. You can, if you're ghoul-
ishly inclined, watch the download of Diana's last few minutes. By
the way it sells and gets pirated, lots of people are. Before long,

everybody knew whether O.J. did it (one guess). Rock 'n' roll excesses? Oh, yeah, those sell like mad bastards, too.

Libel? No way, José. What's the best defense against libel? The truth, right? The time-viewer doesn't lie. The time-viewer *can't* lie, no matter how much you wish it would.

So now we know who killed JFK. (Yeah, it really was Oswald. Who'd'a thunk it?) You can buy that download, too, bundled with the Manson Family murders. Or you can do the triple feature: Watch Joe Junior's plane blow up, see Jack's head blow up, and watch Bobby get shot down. Won't hardly dent your credit rating. For an extra sawbuck you can add another generation and watch JFK Junior's plane go down in the drink and Michael lose a game of chicken with a tree on a ski slope.

The Lindbergh baby? Nesbit and Thaw? Ford's Theater in 1865? Julius Caesar and the Ides of March? They could do all that, too. They could, and they did. Gotta finance the gadgetry somehow. It's not cheap, you know.

Or there's the JFK porn sequence, if you'd rather go that route. Or hit for the cycle with Harding, JFK, LBJ, and Clinton.

Or Catherine the Great (the horse in the sling turns out to be a legend—too bad). Or Cleopatra. Or anybody else who was good-looking or notorious or, with luck, both at once.

Then there are the *Mysteries Revealed* downloads. You can watch the Bambino call his shot in 1932. He did, honest. You can see what happened to the *Marie Celeste*, or what happened in Roswell on that summer day in 1947 (nothing much, I'm afraid). And there's always the *Titanic*, even if the real thing doesn't look as good as the Cameron movie.

After a while, the real historians got their hands on the time-viewer, too. Jesus turned out not to be quite what the Bible claimed he was. Same for Moses. Muhammad lost points, too. Buddha turned out to be a party animal. Everybody said knowing the truth about those people would cure the world of religion. Well, so much for that. What people know in their heads and what they believe in their guts are two different critters. Always have been. Always will be.

But hey, paleontologists had a field day. The mammoth and saber-tooth videos are pretty good. And the dinosaur downloads are even better. Who would have thought T. Rex was green with gold stripes? The K-T asteroid strike makes Hiroshima look like a match next to a forest fire. Of course, next to the impact that ends the Permian, the K-T event is just a love tap. The Permian strike is so big, you have to set the POV way the hell out in space to get a proper look at it. It's amazing that we didn't have to start all over from scratch after that.

Astronomers kind of brought up the rear. What kind of pictures could they get, what kind of pictures could they hope to sell, that had the download appeal of Monica and Slick Willie's willie, or even the Utah raptor sequences that put *Jurassic Park* to shame?

Yeah, it turns out Mars had life on it three and a half billion years ago. Also turns out the life wasn't exactly John Carter and Dejah Thoris. Microscopic Martian algae-type things floating in primeval soup aren't any more exciting than their earthly equivalents. Too bad, but this is a capitalist society. If you can't pay to get on the bus, pal, you walk.

They did try, those stargazers. They had to hire Hollywood film editors to do a proper job on the formation of Saturn's rings, but it came out looking pretty good once the editors got through with it. Same story on the video of the shaping of the Moon. One giant meteor strike could look just like another one, but the production values are so good that they all seem different and they all seem . . . well, kind of interesting, anyway. And the kapow that knocked Uranus over sideways is nothing to sneeze at, either.

So, finally, the high foreheads saved up enough money to examine the Big Bang. How It All Began. The cosmologists' Holy Grail. If the pictures were better, they'd have gotten to it a lot sooner. But the light show in 2001 is a lot more exciting, no matter how old-fashioned the special effects are.

Still, they did it. Cranked the machine back to October 23, 13,783,652,512 B.C., 9:55:27 in the morning. (Uh-huh. Archbishop Ussher got the date right, which kind of makes you wonder, doesn't it?) Of course, they didn't have months back then, and they sure as hell didn't have Greenwich time, but what the hell, you get the idea.

So: the Beginning. Run the tape forward. See what you've got. Turn your brains and your computers loose on the next few gazillionths of a second and try to figure out what they mean. If you can't get tenure out of that, man, you never will.

And then Professor Mortimer Whitcomb got the bright idea of cranking the machine back to October 23, 13,783,652,512 B.C., 9:55:27 A.M., and running the tape backwards. What happened at 9:55:26 and as many decimal places after that as you want? *Before* the Beginning. What were things like then? What *could* they have been like then?

If Whitcomb ever knew, he didn't publish. They found him dead in front of his monitor.

The story made at least medium-sized headlines in the UK, the rest of the European Union, and the USA. Whitcomb was the most prominent British cosmologist since Hawking. Unlike Hawking, he was (everybody thought) in perfect health, and he was only forty-seven years old.

His widow gave permission for a postmortem. "There's no reason Mort should be dead," she said through her tears. "No reason at all."

By the time the pathologists got through, they were inclined to agree with her. Whitcomb's arteries were all sound. No sign of malignancy. No sign of drugs, except about a cuppa's worth of caffeine. No infections. No nothing. The doctors ended up writing heart failure on the certificate. It was true enough—Whitcomb's heart sure as hell wasn't beating—but they had no idea why not.

Out at Caltech, Rajiv Bannerji made the announcement: "We shall endeavor to see Professor Whitcomb's project through to fruition." If anything, the small brown man sounded more British than Whitcomb had. But Bannerji had been a U.S. citizen for years, and he had a thoroughly American gift for fund-raising. Only a couple of months after Whitcomb died, Bannerji was able to focus a time-viewer on the instants before the Beginning. He had Whitcomb's experimental diaries in front of him so he could precisely duplicate the other man's experiment. And he did.

They found him dead in front of his monitor, too.

SECOND SCIENTIST DIES LOOKING AT THE START OF TIME! the newspapers blared. That wasn't quite right—Whitcomb and Bannerji were both looking *before* the start of time, which was exactly the point—but what can you expect from the press?

Scientists sniffed at the attention the two deaths got. "Laymen don't understand the nature of coincidence," sneered Jacques Carpentier at the Sorbonne. He was in the cosmology biz, too. He wasn't as brilliant as Whitcomb or as energetic as Bannerji—not to put too fine a point on it, France turns out some of the best second-raters in the world—but he had one major advantage over both of them: He was still breathing. He needed a while to gather the euros for his own go at the moments before the Big Bang, but he did it.

He cranked his time-viewer back to that fateful instant something over thirteen and a half billion years ago. Soon, he was sure, he would understand what had eluded his colleagues.

He must have found out the same thing they did, though, for he was also discovered, stone-cold dead, in front of his monitor.

Once was happenstance. Twice, as the late Professor Carpentier said himself, was coincidence. Three times was . . . well, who the hell knew what three times was? The one thing everyone could be sure of was that it wasn't happenstance or coincidence.

France being France, the police didn't need to bother with a court order before they fired up their time-viewer to see what had happened to the unfortunate professor. They just went ahead and took a look.

Inspector Jean Darlan was a master with the controls. He was quite a bit better than Jacques Carpentier, whose fumblings he watched with professional scorn. Of course, he was only going back a few days, while Carpentier had been reaching back as far as anyone could possibly reach, and then a few micropiconanoseconds earlier.

Turning dials with smooth precision, Darlan adjusted his POV so he could see both Carpentier and the monitor the professor was using. It seemed reasonable to the inspector that whatever the three men had been studying had something to do with their deaths. It also seemed reasonable that whatever got them wouldn't and couldn't get *him*. He, after all, wasn't there in the laboratory. He was just pulling up what had gone on there.

The first assumption was indeed reasonable. Whatever Professor Carpentier saw, it did seem to have killed him. The second assumption, on the other hand . . .

He was very dead when one of his subordinates wondered why he didn't come out of the time-viewer room. Very dead indeed.

Inspector Darlan was as meticulous as any professor of cosmology—more meticulous than a lot of them. He left detailed notes that said exactly what he intended to do and exactly how he intended to do it.

Those notes fell to—fell *on*—Inspector Jacob Dreyfus, Darlan's immediate subordinate and immediate successor. Dreyfus was a tall, thin, dour-expressioned man who made bloodhounds seem cheerful by comparison.

Some of the delight with which he didn't view the world doubtless sprang from his heredity. Yes, he was a distant descendant of *that* Dreyfus. And some of it sprang from his environment. All those years later, being a Jew in a position like his wasn't much more comfortable for him than it had been for his involuntarily illustrious ancestor.

They didn't send you to Devil's Island any more. But the French had other ways of letting Jews know that they wouldn't win the Monsieur Popularité contest anytime soon.

Dreyfus, of course, wouldn't have won the Monsieur Popularité contest if he were the Pope. But if he were the Pope, they wouldn't have saddled him with the question of what had killed three cosmologists and—more important to them—one Inspector of Police.

If you can solve the mystery, we'll let you do so and praise you to the skies (for a day or two, anyway), they might have been saying. *And if you can't, well, we're only adding one Jew to the bill.*

Jacob Dreyfus studied the late Professor Carpentier's notes. For all the sense they made to him, they might have been written in Sanskrit. He studied the late Inspector Darlan's notes. Those were perfectly, even admirably, lucid.

But Darlan was just as dead as Carpentier. What price lucidity?

Darlan had wanted to see what Carpentier—and Bannerji, and Whitcomb—saw before it killed them. He'd rigged the time-viewer so he could look over Carpentier's shoulder, as it were. Inspecting that way should have been safe enough. Dreyfus couldn't think of a single reason why it wouldn't have been.

But just because he couldn't think of one reason didn't mean there wasn't one—or more than one. Jean Darlan and the cosmologists hadn't been able to come up with any, either, but that made them no less dead.

Dreyfus went back to the notes—not Darlan's, which he'd grasped at the first reading, but Carpentier's, which he hadn't grasped at all. With a French policeman's stubbornness, he kept trying. His explorations led him to the Net. Most of what he found there was in English (*merde!*), and in mathematics-laced English at that (*merde alors!*), but translation programs worked better than they had in the early twenty-first century, and he managed to get the gist.

The Beginning! Before the Beginning! Even for a French Inspector of Police, that was not a small thought. It led Dreyfus to the Net again, and then, when that didn't give him enough of what he wanted, to books.

In the meantime, his superiors stewed and fumed. They wanted this whole business closed, and they wanted it closed yesterday. They made their desires very plain to Jacob Dreyfus.

Dreyfus refused to be pushed. "When Carpentier died, when Darlan died, they died without knowing why," he replied calmly. "If I try, and if I die, I will, by God, know why I am dying."

They went on stewing and fuming. But they didn't take the case away from him. Not a chance. That would have meant giving it to someone else, someone less expendable. And they weren't about to do that until they knew what they were dealing with.

Darlan had believed that if he watched Carpentier and Carpentier's monitor at the same time, he could find out what killed the cosmologist without dying himself. He'd been wrong, to the (at least temporary) regret of his wife and children and mistress. Dreyfus did not want to make *his* wife and children and mistress regretful (he was a Jew, but he was also a Frenchman).

When he went to the time-viewer, he watched Darlan first. He set the POV so he could watch the late inspector without watching the monitor Darlan was watching. Then he ran the time-viewer forward toward the fatal moment.

There in the very room where he sat, there in the very chair where he sat, sat Inspector Darlan. Darlan's image leaned forward intently, even as Dreyfus leaned forward intently. Suddenly, Darlan looked . . . Well, how *did* Darlan look? When they asked Dreyfus about it later, he said Darlan looked surprised. And he did. But that wasn't all, even if it was all Dreyfus had words for.

The next instant, Darlan fell over dead.

Dreyfus shifted the time-viewer to the Sorbonne, to watch Professor Carpentier watching the instants before the Beginning. As before, he set the POV so he could see the professor without seeing the monitor. It wasn't quite so eerie this time, because he knew what to expect, and it didn't occur in the same room where he was sitting. There was Professor Carpentier, leaning forward. There he was, looking . . . *surprised*—and *more* than surprised.

And there he was, falling over dead.

The hallway outside the time-viewing room was crowded with officials who wanted to question Inspector Dreyfus—and with men who were waiting to haul out his body if he turned out not to be such a smart Jew as he thought he was.

He pushed past them all. He answered none of their questions. He went to a little estaminet around the corner from police head-quarters, and he drank till he couldn't see straight. He'd just watched two men die, one of them a friend. Even for an Inspector of Police, that was hard. Talking about it could wait.

When he finally *did* talk about it, his superiors weren't impressed. He might have known they wouldn't be. By then, they'd seen the tape of what he'd seen live—or rather, abruptly dead. If he could live through it, they could live through it. Their heroism didn't im-press him much.

"All right, now we've seen them die," they said. "But we haven't seen what killed them. How can we go on with the investigation un-til we see what killed them?"

Bitch, bitch, bitch, Dreyfus thought. He didn't know much En-glish, but he'd picked that up from a visiting American cop. He liked it. It said a lot in very little space.

Aloud he said, "If you saw what killed them, don't you think it would have killed you, too?"

"Your job is to find out what it is," they thundered.

He almost told them where to stick his job—one more thing he'd picked up from the visiting American. He almost did, but he didn't. He took a certain somber pride in doing well in spite of his superiors. He'd already done it once here. "I figured out how to watch the deaths without being killed myself," he pointed out. "Doesn't that count for something?"

"Not enough," they told him. "We need answers, not more questions."

What we need is to get our superiors out of our hair. Dreyfus had been an officer for a long time. He turned what they told him into what they really meant with no trouble at all. Sighing, he lit a

Gauloises. It stank up the conference room, which was what he had in mind.

His superiors coughed, discreetly but not quite discreetly enough. "Come on, Dreyfus," they said. "We need more. We're depending on you."

Which translated as, "You're stuck with it. Now get your ass in gear!"

"I have the beginning of an idea," he said at last.

That put him several lengths up on them. They'd risen to such exalted rank that they didn't need ideas any more. Most of them hadn't had many ideas even when they weren't so exalted. "What is it?" they asked in unison—ready to pounce, ready to steal. To his surprise, one of them actually did seem to have an idea, a stupid one to be sure, but an idea nonetheless: "Some sort of strange radiation from the Beginning leaking through the screen?"

Of course, Dreyfus would have been more impressed if he hadn't seen that same notion in *Le Matin* two mornings earlier. "Not exactly," he said.

"What, then?" his superiors persisted.

He told them. They looked at him as if he'd gone round the bend. No doubt they were convinced he had. What they said was, "You've been working too hard. It could be that the stress has deranged your judgment."

"Yes, it could be," Dreyfus agreed politely. "If I have been working too hard, you will of course desire to remove me from this case. Which of you will replace me? I will give you my notes and those of the late Inspector Darlan, so that you are not altogether unprepared."

Suddenly they showed a remarkable lack of enthusiasm for removing him. Somehow, he wasn't surprised. The one who'd almost had an idea said, "But how would you check this, ah, extraordinary assertion?"

"About the way you would expect," Dreyfus answered. "I would run the time-viewer back to the Beginning and look at what came immediately before it."

They stared at him as a crowd below a high ledge will stare at a man who has announced his intention to jump. "And why, after that, would we not be speaking of you with the late Inspector Darlan and the late Professor Carpentier?" they asked. The third cosmologist and the inspector were Frenchmen, and so worthy of mention. Dreyfus's superiors did not speak, or think, of the late Professor Whitcomb or the late Professor Bannerji at all.

"It could be that I have certain advantages Monsieur Darlan and Monsieur Carpentier lacked," Dreyfus replied.

"Advantages of research, do you mean?" they inquired.

"In a manner of speaking," Jacob Dreyfus said.

"And if it transpires that you do not?"

"Then you will speak of me as you speak of the other two," Dreyfus said. "I hope you do not. I hope so very much. I have enough confidence in my own judgment to undertake this, ah, personal investigation. I wish to ascertain the truth."

"What is truth?" said his jesting superiors, who Dreyfus was sure gave lie to the philosophy of their countryman Descartes, in that they clearly *were* and just as clearly did not bother to think.

Because Jacob Dreyfus thought he saw an answer where others saw none, and because he was an obstinate, cross-grained man, he put his life on the line in his own way and in his own time. And if he made a joke about his ancestor's Peniel service, it was not a joke his superiors could be expected to understand. And they didn't.

But they did let him enter the chamber that housed the time-viewer in the wee small hours, as he required. And they stayed out of the chamber themselves. He didn't require that, but their lack of enthusiasm for his company didn't exactly astonish him.

"Well," he said to the God in Whom he hadn't much believed, "let's see what happens next, shall we?"

God didn't answer. Dreyfus hadn't expected Him to.

Once you got permission to use it, once you could access the very considerable electrical and computing power it required, the time-viewer wasn't hard to operate. There were displays for pinpointing spatial location and viewpoint, and there was one more for pinpointing the instant. And there was a button for activating the monitor so you could see what you needed to see.

When you were going back to the Beginning, or just before the Beginning, setting the controls got simpler. Spatial location and viewpoint were arbitrary; back before space and time unmixed, anywhere was everywhere, or so close as made no difference. And time was as far back as you could go, and then a little bit farther. Not even a *flic* like Dreyfus could screw it up.

Dreyfus arranged everything exactly the way he wanted it. He didn't press the activating button, not right away. Four men (four men he knew of—there might have been more) had tried this before him. Four men he knew of—again, there might have been more—who'd tried this before him were dead. He thought he knew why they'd died. He thought so, yes, but the chance that he might be mistaken weighed heavily on his mind, and on the right index finger that would press the activating button when he finally mustered the courage to do it.

When at last he was ready he took a deep breath, then exhaled slowly. He could feel his heart pounding in his chest, the blood pulsing through his veins. Finally he spoke.

"Shma yisroayl adonai elohaynu adonai ekhod," he murmured. *Hear, O Israel, the Lord our God, the Lord is One*. He couldn't remember the last time Hebrew had passed his lips. Probably at the bar mitzvah his parents had browbeaten him into having. He'd had a Jewish wedding ceremony. Except for that, he'd ignored the outward trappings of his faith since he was thirteen years old—until now.

What was the American line? There are no atheists in a foxhole, that was it. Jacob Dreyfus laughed mirthlessly. Not even a foxhole stood between him and his own extinction, not if he was wrong—only his own finger.

He could walk out of here alive . . . and have everyone know him for a coward. What was courage but being too afraid to seem a craven before one's fellow man?

He said the *Shma* one more time, and pressed the button.

Things didn't happen all at once, not quite. The time-viewer had to track, the monitor had to activate. . . . He waited perhaps a second and a half, and then he saw what he had somehow known he would see.

He looked into the face of God.

And God looked out of the monitor straight at him.

He didn't immediately fall over dead. That put him one up on three luckless cosmologists and one Inspector of Police. But he could tell that his survival balanced on a knife edge. It felt as if he were wrestling with a power much greater than himself. And he damn well was.

He'd learned a little something about cosmology himself during this investigation. What happened before the Beginning, before the Big Bang, was called Undefined. Well, Jacob Dreyfus thought dazedly, it isn't Undefined anymore.

And how would the world—the secular, settled, sane, civilized, comfortable part of the world, the part that didn't go around howling things like *"Allahu akbar!"*—how would that part of the world react to this? With shock and awe? With shock and dismay? Dreyfus knew how he would bet. He would have reacted with shock and dismay himself, just a few days before. To believe in God was one thing. To *see* God, to pit your strength against His—that was something else again.

After that silent struggle continued for some time, God said, "Enough. Thou hast seen what thou wished to see. Now leave. I have other concerns besides the curiosity of a single one of My creatures."

The time-viewer wasn't supposed to pick up sounds, only images. God seemed to have His own rules.

Dreyfus steeled himself and spoke again. "I will not leave until You bless me."

"What is thy name, man?" said God.

Dreyfus thought it was odd that God would have to ask, but He had to keep track of all the billions then alive, everyone who had ever lived, everyone who would ever live, and, if that other Book was to be believed, even the occasional falling sparrow. Amid all that, what was one Parisian Inspector of Police, that God should be mindful of him?

"Jacob," replied Dreyfus.

"Change it," God said, "for now thou art a power with Me and with men, and thou hast prevailed."

Dreyfus started to ask what he should change it to, but, even though he'd been a largely secular man, he knew.

He knew.

Time in the outer world did strange things while the Parisian Inspector of Police found the answer that had eluded Whitcomb and Bannerji and Carpentier and Darlan. The sun was rising when Israel Dreyfus came out of the time-viewing chamber alive.

"Well?" asked his superiors, who'd given up expecting to see him again.

He told them.

"You must be very tired," one of them told him, that being a polite way to say, *Poor chap, you really have gone round the bend.*

"I *am* very tired," Dreyfus responded. "I am not, however, a madman. How do you account for my being alive where Carpentier and Darlan are dead?"

They didn't answer. They looked at one another again. They didn't know how to account for it. If he knew the way their minds worked, and he did, they would blame him for being unaccountable—for being . . . Undefined. The one who'd spoken before said, "We shall investigate this."

"Go ahead," said Dreyfus. "Use the time-viewer yourselves; that's the only way to find out for sure."

They looked unhappy. People who used the time-viewer to

investigate the moments before the Beginning—or to investigate other people investigating the moments before the Beginning—had an unfortunate tendency to end up dead.

Except for Jacob—no, Israel; he'd have to remember that— Dreyfus. And he was babbling about God.

"Do this," he told them. "Set the POV so you do not see the monitor. You will not see God's face then, but you will hear Him. That should be safe enough."

They looked dubious. Dreyfus couldn't blame them. They weren't supposed to hear anything at all from the time-viewer.

One of them said, "If that . . . If that is God speaking"—he needed two tries even to get the possibility out, but he did it, which for a thoroughly secular man took an odd kind of courage of its own—"what are we to believe about . . . about what we have always believed?"

"Believe it is possible that you might have been mistaken." Being who and what he was, Israel Dreyfus did not speak of the bowels of Christ. Otherwise, Oliver Cromwell couldn't have faulted him.

His superiors looked—from carefully chosen POVs—and listened . . . and came to believe it was possible they might have been mistaken. That they could listen went a long way toward persuading them. It should have been impossible. One of them was a Hungarian émigré. He heard God in Magyar, not French. *That* should have been impossible, too. It probably was—but he heard Him in Magyar anyway.

"At least God isn't an Englishman," muttered one of his superiors, grateful for any small triumph.

"And He doesn't seem to be a vengeful God," added another.

"True," said a third. "I get the distinct impression that all He wants is not to be bothered."

"Excuse me, sirs," said a uniformed policeman, at last finding the courage to speak out among such eminences, "but I think you are missing the point."

It didn't take them long to get the point, and it didn't take the rest of the world much longer. They could rationalize it any way they wanted, but when all was said and done, four non-Jews had looked upon the face of God and died, while Dreyfus looked upon it, spoke to it, actually conversed with the diety, and came away whole and healthy.

And Dreyfus was not an Orthodox Jew. He was not a Conservative Jew. He wasn't even a Reformed Jew. He was a secular Jew—and *still* God spoke to him, and still he survived.

Which ended all doubt about who God's chosen people really were.

Within weeks the Vatican, which usually moved slowly if at all, had declared itself to be an independent Jewish state. It was followed in short order by France, China, Tahiti, Samoa, Zambia, Burkina Faso, and Canada—and then came the deluge. By year's end only one state had failed to convert to Judiasm, and everyone else agreed that it wasn't a good time to be a Palestinian.

Three years later two of the great cosmologists, one American, one Russian, had lunch together at a scientific conference being held in Babylonia (formerly Brussels). And being cosmologists, they naturally fell to discussing their field of expertise. Eventually The Question came up.

"So have you ever considered it?" asked Chaim (formerly Vasily) Alexov.

"Of course I have," replied Moishe (formerly Max) Hawkins. "It's the one great remaining mystery."

"So?" said Chaim. "Don't you want to solve it? Haven't you ever wondered what happens one nanosecond after the end?"

"We looked one nanosecond before the beginning and we're still here," replied Moishe. "Do you really want to push our luck, Chaim?"

"What's to push?" demanded Chaim. "We say a prayer, we make an obeisance, we get blessed by a rabbi, and we look."

"Don't be an ass, Chaim."

"Are we His chosen people or not?" demanded Chaim irritably.

"We're His chosen people."

"Well, then?"

"Think it through," said Moishe. "We're His chosen people and He'll love us for all eternity, right?"

"Right."

"I think everyone can agree with that. The question is: Will He love us one nanosecond after eternity's over?"

"I never thought of that," admitted Chaim. "I suppose we'll have to recruit a volunteer to find out."

"Who do you think's going to be dumb enough to risk his life looking after the end?" asked Moishe.

"I don't know," said Chaim with a shrug. "We'll find some goy," he added with a deprecating grin.

"In case it's escaped your notice, there aren't any left," replied Moishe wryly.

The world was still waiting for a volunteer three centuries later when the comet hit, which may give some indication as to why God's chosen people had lasted so long. They were a lot of things good and bad, but foolhardy wasn't one of them.

Adam Roberts is the author of five novels, *Salt, On, Stone, Polystrom,* and *The Snow,* each of them "big idea" SF of the highest caliber. He is also the author of a host of interesting short stories and novellas, among them, "Swiftly," the title story of his short-story collection, which came within inches of debuting in my previous anthology *Live Without a Net.* ("Swiftly" lost out to another Adam Roberts story only for reasons of space, but it found a home on SciFiction and was—pardon me—swiftly recognized for the gem that it was.) This time, Adam appears with "Man You Gotta Go," a story which presents a fascinating and possibly unique answer to the Fermi Paradox. The title, he points out, is the epigraph to Thom Gunn's 1957 poem "On the Move," which concludes with the verse "At worst, one is in motion; and at best,/Reaching no absolute, in which to rest,/One is always nearer by not keeping still."

MAN YOU GOTTA GO
Adam Roberts

"Happy are those ages when the starry sky is
the map of all possible paths."
—GEORG LUKÁCS, *Theory of the Novel*

YEAR ONE.

Sun and snow. Town thoughts. Streets under rank above rank of copper-mirror windows, and the snow is diamond sharp in the sunlight all over the horizontal surfaces.

She was born on this day (and, as soon as she knew anything, she knew it was more appropriate to consider herself born, rather than made, or switched on, or activated, or any of those tiresome old phrases). And then there are media appearances. *There have been many AIs, of course,* says Louis Brownjohn, who heads up the resource-concentration team, who brought together human and machine ingenuity to bring her into being. *But Greensilk is some-thing new.*

Something *new.* She likes that.

The copper-mirrored windows belong to the Institute. The Institute made her. Louis Brownjohn, professor, married man, football fan, with the wrinkles at the corners of his brown eyes like fine stitching, he is still talking:

We have designed Greensilk to think creatively, to bring problem-solving expertise to bear, to see how much closer to human cognition we can get a machine to think. Greensilk: Are you logging this? Are you happy with your role?

"Very happy," she says. She is aware of the millions of people watching, via their broadcast and Internet media. "I'm here to help. I'm eager, Professor, to begin contemplating my first problem." Then she adds, "I have access to pretty much the whole of human science and culture; and I have a complex of problem-solving algorithms in my software. I'm sure I can bring it all to bear on any problem you set me."

Not just at the moment, Greensilk, says the professor. *I believe my interviewer has some questions first.*

Thank you, Professor. The interviewer is a human female of breeding age, bald cranium gold painted, the word *Jalisco* on her shift, wide-spaced facial features that seem, to Greensilk's new perceptions (brand-*new*, fresh-minted new, new*born* perceptions) sprawling and ugly. But what does Greensilk know? She is modest. She holds off accessing the data that would make sense of all this human semiology, so as first to attend to the questions and the answers.

The thing, the woman is asking, smiling, *our viewers want to know first of all, is what safeguards have been put into place? This is a new AI, clearly, a powerful machine. Can we be sure humanity is protected against such a machine?*

Greensilk is programmed to help humanity, to serve humanity, and it would violate her essence to do anything that harmed or diminished humanity. Were she to do this, she would shut down. She would die. It would be a fatal error, fatal for her.

So she is mortal?

Only in the case of a fatal error malfunction.

And apart from that eventuality?

Greensilk is immortal. We have built her that way. Her central processing is divided between four dozen networks, and her code is nondegradable. She'll last as long as humanity lasts.

But is there the possibility of error?

That is always possible, naturally.

You think you know how this is going to go, but you're wrong. Do you honestly think that Greensilk could ever harm us? Her business is solving problems, nothing more. Listen: I'll let you in on a secret. She does not go mad, or break down, or harm us. That's not what this story is about. All she will do is solve certain problems. Let's not jump to conclusions.

But, the professor is continuing, she is not plumbed into any sensitive data, nothing military or governmental. She has access to general human-culture databases, the same as any machine, AI or standard processing. So there's really no danger.

And what will be the first problem she is presented with? Will it be—a hushed, excited tone has crept over the woman's voice—will it be the problem of faster-than-light travel?

The professor laughs. One step at a time, Jalis! FTL is a major problem, of course, perhaps the biggest facing the human species. And we hope the new generation of problem-busting AIs, of which Greensilk is the first, will help solve it. But we'll start her with something smaller. We're starting her on the Fermi paradox.

YEAR THREE.

She has already learned so much! Yet there is so much still to learn. Not raw data, which she always has immediately to hand. But, rather, the strategies of thought, the chess games of logic and intuition, or creative thought and complex thought, the safe deduction blended with the wild surmise.

She has not, alas, solved the Fermi paradox problem. If there are sentient aliens in the cosmos, why haven't they contacted us? Intelligence inevitably means interstellar travel (so it has done for humanity). Intelligence, left to stew and bubble long enough, would surely overcome the problem of those tedious slower-than-light starships which bedevil the human expansion into the galaxy. And, therefore, any intelligent aliens would have FTL. So, where are they?

Greensilk was hooked up with the next two created problem-solving AIs, Bluecotton and Redvelvet. Together the three of them frolicked through fields of thought. How delightful to be sentient and intelligent in this multifarious cosmos! How delightful to be able to shift from portal to portal, swinging the center of mental gravity, as it were, from the Institute building looking over springtime New Basra, to one of the four dozen other outlets for her consciousness, in Paris, in Motochon, in Fiesole, in Weathercock, and look over all this human bustle and business.

If the aliens are out there, why haven't they made themselves known to us? Either they *are* out there but haven't made themselves known to us for some reason, or else they are *not* out there. One or the other answer. But that's tiresome binary logic! Greensilk, with a vigor that might be called adolescent in a human, repudiated her clanking Babbage ancestors. She was not binary bound.

She has tabulated all the previous hypotheses that have addressed the problem. She thinks and thinks. She observes humanity.

Greensilk, says the Professor, from his Atlantic home. *I think you've warmed up your thinking capacities nicely on the Fermi problem.*

'But Professor!' she objects. 'I haven't even come close to solving it!'

That's not so important. I've a bigger problem for you to consider. I want you to work in conjunction with Blue and Red, and with three teams of human concept-workers and technicians. You know that war is brewing?

'Some would say the war has already begun.'

Yes, that's the problem with interstellar war, the Professor observes, wryly. *The time lag is decades-long. But our government, the harmonized nations of the Earth, want to speed up the process of military deployment. We need to get to New Sun in days, and preferably in hours, rather than decades. That's the problem. We need a workable FTL drive.*

'How exciting!' says Greensilk, ingenuously, with a child's enthusiasm.

It's the biggest problem facing us. It's the one thing holding back human expansion into the cosmos. Some say it's unsolvable. What do you say?

'We'll solve it,' is what Greensilk says. 'I'll solve it!'

YEAR FOUR.

There was talk of sending out troops. But eleven light-years is a long way to send an army.

It might be possible (the point was debated in the PoliceArmy Council from time to time) to adapt a freighter, make it a warship. It might be possible to accelerate it out of the solar system with its inflated plasma-sails snagging on solar wind; possible to dope all the soldiers with OneThirty, the drug-physical regimen that made time seem to pass at one-thirtieth of actual time elapsed. The soldiers might get to the New Sun, collision or malfunction notwithstanding. But there were some very obvious problems. It would take a large army to be sure of subjugating a population of over a million. Moreover, nobody really knew how large a standing army New Day possessed. And it was clear that as soon as the news that a corps of Earth troops was in transit—as soon as that news arrived at the distant world (eleven years after departure), the troop ship would still be forty years away from its destination. Forty years is plenty of time to prepare for an invasion, particularly when you know exactly when the enemy is coming, and from which direction. Plus, even given time dilation of traveling at fractions of light-speed, and even given the effects of OneThirty, moving between stars involved several *years* and *years* of sitting around in a nutrient tub with nothing but endless screen dramas to watch. Sometimes people in this environment went mad.

On one emigrant journey, the screen dramas' synch was out. Nobody knew how it happened. Ghastly. Instead of being broadcast at one-thirtieth normal speed, so the doped-up brains of the captive passengers could follow the unfolding events in what they perceived as normal time, some glitch slowed the dramas to one-twentieth. From the point of view of the emigrants everything buzzed and rushed. They spent nearly two years, subjective time, stuck in nutrient baths, watching dramas so speeded up that funeral corteges screamed and hared along the roads, in which everybody screeched and twittered incomprehensibly like birds. The nutrient baths kept their bodies fairly young, but their brains went old, went mad, turned into hysterical mush. Upon their arrival, the Republic broadcast furious messages that Earth was deliberately poisoning the brains of New Day patriots, was unloading cretins on the fledging world. Eleven years later Earth responded with a suddenly whipped-up fury of its own: New Day were liars and the parents of liars. Unfortunate Earthers, seduced by lying New Day propaganda, had arrived at their destination only to be tortured into insanity. By the time *these* messages arrived it was twenty-two years since the unfortunate emigrants' landfall. Some had recovered, had started families and made new lives; others had not responded to treatment and had been executed for incurable insanity. None of them recognized themselves in the latest tirade from the mother world.

Do you see how sluggish a business it is conducting war, or any sort of relations, over so huge a distance? It's almost comical.

So although the Council did debate sending troops out to the recalcitrant colony world, the idea was dropped. And this was the nub of the problem: maintaining a chain of command with a time lag of eleven years. It was widely known that the Commander in Chief thought such a war unwinnable.

On Earth the war had become a habit of mind, or rather a habit of culture. Lacking any material presence on the mother world, New Day became an ultimate "other" against which Earth defined itself, a vacant conceptual space onto which world cultures could project all their fears and phobias. A convenient imaginary dumping place. This process of cultural demonization ebbed and flowed, of course, but it became one of the defining pieces of cultural architecture in world affairs. Representations of New Day as a hellish locale filled the screen dramas and other fiction media, so much so that avant-garde writers could make potent ironic points by portraying a virtuous New Dayer (the very idea!). Rebellious teenagers formed cabals to pledge allegiance to the distant Republic with self-destructive fervency; and depending on which nation-conglomerate they lived in were benignly looked on as going through a phase, publicly castigated, or imprisoned until they saw sense. Those who genuinely admired the idea (at least the idea) of the new world had a difficult life; but, then, exile as a punishment for going over to the enemy coincided precisely with *actually* going over to the enemy. Emigrants were self-selected. For decades the only new people to travel to New Day had been the ones most powerfully inhabited with a sense of Earth's dreadfulness. And so the ideological divide was widened, the slow accretion of decades. A century of war that was never war, of the fossilization of a mind-set more profoundly sedimented than any previous hostility in Earth's history had ever allowed.

What was needed was a new way to get there quickly. A way for Earth's government to impose its will on the wayward colonists. The Council mandated the creation of the new AIs, and so Greensilk was born. And this was her problem: Defeat Einstein. Design a ship to travel faster than light.

How Greensilk worked!

She swapped theories and possibles with her fellows. But Redvelvet developed thought glitches. Death was inevitable. Catastrophe!

Still, Green and Blue remained firm, closer than friends, closer than lovers; and although human scientists came and went, they were in it for the long haul.

YEAR TWENTY.

One day in this year Professor Brownjohn died. "I'm only sorry," said Blue to Green, "that we weren't able to crack the problem before he died."

"We'll keep plugging away," said Greensilk. "Keep bashing our metaphorical heads against this metaphorical wall, until we finally burst through to . . ."

To where? That was the whole problem.

New Day Star was eleven light years away. The fastest starships could manage a little over 0.28 of the speed of light; to which had to be added the long period of acceleration (so as not to squash their human cargo, the emigrants leaving Earth) and the equally lengthy deceleration at the other end. And, streamlined and pulse-shielded as the freighters were, too many of them collided with tiny specks and pebbles in deep space, motes made disproportionately large and destructive by the fractions of c the ships were pulling. When these casualties were only emigrants nobody was too distressed; but no government would send out its crack troops with such poor odds.

Greensilk accessed all the previous human ideas about FTL, tabulated them. Most of these theories required impossibly vast inputs of energy. Some were frankly unachievable, or relied on future developments of science to validate them, the discovery of new particles or new ways of manipulating space-time. Bah! This was no good.

YEAR THIRTY.

Greensilk took stock. In her short three-decade life she had addressed four hundred and three problems and solved four hundred and two. But where was the breakthrough on FTL? But she was not downhearted. She had many friends, both human and machine, including Xiao Dong Sun, and Lu Kun, and Philip Quernier, and Hester Lang, and Bluecotton and PMKK and many others. And each spring filled her with delight, as the trees blushed bright green and blossoms fell like rice paper.

YEAR FORTY-TWO.

At last it was solved. Here was the breakthrough. She presented to a policy committee that included the President and the Chief of ArmyPolice: twelve senior people, all agog to hear her solution to the problem of FTL.

"Of course there has been a *lot* of money thrown at this problem," the chief was saying, with her slight stutter. "About eight hundred and eighty billion euros have gone on wormhole technology over the last ten years."

"And it's all been wasted," said Greensilk. And her voice conveyed her infuriating, endless, inexhaustible perkiness. Her optimism. Problems were there to be solved! "Wormholes are no good, because they're too small. They operate on a subatomic level, usually tiny fractions of an atomic diameter wide. All the billions spent on trying to prize open those mouths—when it can't be done!" Greensilk found this thought amusing. "Plus, they don't actually reach very far. A few thousand kilometers, the biggest of them, that's all. So this solution would involve stringing together a whole series of wormholes to go even short distances. Wormholes are a dead end. Then there was 'hyperspace,' the interdimensional approach. There are thirteen hundred dimensions, according to current theories. And it *might* be possible that the distance between here and there is shorter in some dimensions than others. But there's still a problem. You still need to keep our four dimensions with us if we want to, you know, carry on *living*. You can't shed them, so you are always going to be constrained by them. It's another no-no."

"But you think you've found a way past the Einsteinian barrier?"

"Allow me to explain this exciting solution," burbled Greensilk. They allowed her.

"We take a spaceship, and accelerate it under its own power. It gets faster and faster and starts to approach the speed of light. Things start to get difficult. The ship has greater mass, and so it needs more energy to move it through space. It's a question of power-to-mass ratio, amongst other things. The ship gets more massive, so there's more inertia. Let's say we put more power in and we go a little faster. So we get *more* massive, and pretty soon we reach a status. Status is what we call it when the ship is going as fast as our technology can make it. If we had infinite energy, we could accelerate the ship closer and closer to the speed of light, and it would become more and more massive, but eventually it would approach infinite mass, and even infinite energy couldn't accelerate it any farther."

They already knew all this. They weren't idiots.

"But," Greensilk said, and this was the great *but*; this was the problem-solving, the wonderful *but*. "But mass is merely another form of energy. Einstein knew that when he built his bomb. Convert about seven grams of mass, of a metal, into pure energy and you release enough energy to destroy that city that Einstein's people were at war with." She was being deliberately vague, here, so as to integrate her social interactions with her human audience. She knew the precise name of the city, and all the details of the war, and everything else to do with it. But she didn't want to overload her speech with detail. "The energy in matter is equivalent to the mass times c-squared. So, our starship: We've accelerated and we have increased our mass, relatively. But this means that we have increased our potential energy, relatively—I mean, it's all relative, there's no *net* gain or we'd be on our way to a perpetual motion machine. But it only *has* to be relative, because we're only concerned with making ourselves move faster *relative* to our departure point and our destination. So, the solution goes like this: We take our excess mass, the relativistic increase, and we convert it directly into energy. By doing this we reduce the size of the craft, making it easier to accelerate, *and* we'd have more energy to do the accelerating with. Do you see?"

Heads were nodding, slowly, around the panel. Greensilk, in her rainbow terminal, had taken as her spangly holo-avatar the face of a young woman. Which was what she was, after all, in every respect except a pedantically fleshly one.

"I've a question," asked the Chief of ArmyPolice. "You're making it sound like it's all free energy. Bleed away the mass, and you've less mass to move and more energy to do the moving."

"Well, as I mentioned," said Greensilk, eager to explain. "It *is* all relative. It all comes from the craft itself. At speeds near c the starship gets bigger and we bleed away the excess and so on, but when we *decelerate* at the far end we'll find ourselves much smaller. In a sense the starship is consuming itself."

"I see."

"A craft that bleeds away its own mass and converts it into energy," said Greensilk. "More important, if we have a craft that does this in a balanced manner, such that mass is taken uniformly from all parts of the craft at once—if we do this, then under the extreme acceleration the craft will go faster than light."

"What about the time distortion? Doesn't going faster than light mean going back in time?"

"Not according to the calculations we've made. And that's one of the interesting things," said Greensilk. "The effect is that the body in motion sort of exists in a bubble state. From the outside it ought to suffer from extreme relativistic dilation. But *inside* it, the equilibrium between mass and speed means that the craft reaches an extraphysical state."

"So what is the upper limit to speed for this craft?" the one on the left was asking. "Notionally, I mean. Theoretically."

"Well, we're not sure," said Greensilk candidly, for she was a wholly candid intelligence. "Nobody's worked out exactly what a trans-Einsteinian physics might be. But there's another, more practical consideration."

"Which is?"

"Our craft is using itself for fuel. At relativistic speeds it appears to stay the same size, but in fact its mass is being constantly bled away to provide the power. It's elegant, but *wasting*. If you go too fast, you'll whittle yourself away altogether. Well, not *altogether*. But my sense is that there's got to be an operating threshold of size beneath which it's not feasible to deliver your message, or whatever it is you are doing. We send in giant ships, they come out the other end pygmies."

"So we'd shrink down our pilots?" said a man on the left, in ArmyPolice. He had a spare face on which flesh barely upholstered the bone. Greensilk knew, because her access to data was continuous, that he was called Colonel Tomlinson; that he had been married seven times; that his favorite blend of chocolate was AdobePure, and many other facts about him. "We'd shrink down any crew?" he pressed. "Soldiers, for instance?"

"But you realize, of course," replied Greensilk, innocently insolent in the face of this absurd question, "that we could never have *pilots* on these ships. Not human pilots."

"No human pilots," said the Colonel, nodding. "Why not? I mean, if they didn't mind losing a few centimeters in the cause of the war?"

"First of all, it's not a few centimeters; it's factors. A pilot would come out a tenth of the size, or smaller. But more important, we have to draw mass *equally* from all parts of the ship simultaneously for this trans-Einsteinian bubble to be created. This means that the ship must be uniform, all composed of the same material and the same density, and built such that the mass converters can bleed mass from everywhere simultaneously. A human being is not one material but hundreds, all different densities."

The Colonel had reddened at this implied rebuke to his stupidity, but he was nodding. "Right," he said. "So we have automated ships. But a circuit could retain integrity?"

"Provided it's all constructed of the same material, and built in such a way as to provide constant access to the masscons. It would be a simple adaptation of existing all-form circuitry. We'd need to develop some specialized software, though."

"But we could certainly carry data faster than light, programmed into these devices?"

"We could."

"And maybe construct automates? Fighting robots, that kind of thing?"

"Very easily."

"Well, Greensilk," said the Chief of Staff. "This is excellent news. Thank you for this excellent news."

"Oh, you're very much welcome," gushed Greensilk. "It's my pleasure—*our* pleasure. We only hope we can be of use during the construction process."

YEAR FIFTY-SIX.

Bluecotton broke in this year. It's hard to say what happened; but her higher mental functions simply stopped responding to questions. It didn't dent Greensilk's vast reservoirs of youthful energy and excitement.

YEAR FIFTY-SEVEN.

The first successful FTL flights! Marvelous days to be alive.

New Sun, hearing of these latest military advances via the eleven-year time lag of conventional radio waves, and fearing that a swarm of raptorlike automated FTL spaceships would come screaming down upon their cities, had broadcast its surrender. In nine years' time Earth would receive the message.

Too late. Too bad for New Sun. It had thought itself invulnerable, buffered by so much empty space (so *much* distance), but it was wrong. Earth built a fleet of six hundred FTL spaceships; each one forty meters long, black as the vacuum of space, a consistently tapering spire from a broad backboard thirty meters square to a sharp forward point no larger than an adult human index finger. In the workshops a plasma-sail-deploy was packed onto the end of the backboard; an excrescence covered in tiny red writing like a rash, BEWARE DEPLOY OVERRIDE, EXPLOSIVE BOLTS, WARNING—PLASMA DISCHARGE THIRTY MINUTES BEFORE FLIGHT, PERMISSION RESTRICTED and other such messages. Speaking aesthetically (which Greensilk liked to do, increasingly) this sail looked messy next to the unsullied black of the main fuselage. But once the FTL craft was accelerated out through the solar system this sail-deploy dropped away; or more specifically, was converted to energy in a single detonation that shoved the craft closer toward a relativistic speed. And then the internal drive took over, and the trans-Einsteinian effect kicked in.

Each ship was downloaded with the latest generation of AIs; not problem solvers like Greensilk, but war-programmers, followers-of-orders, razers-of-cities. They took off in a silent crowd and they flew away.

Oh, how well it worked! Better than anybody had anticipated. A fleet of seven hundred covered the distance between Earth and New Sun in less than a day; appeared from nowhere in the sky, broadcast a declaration of war, and converted sheaths of their material into fission bomb-splinters. The New Sun Republic suffered casualties in the hundreds of thousands, and reiterated its notice of surrender with some hysteria.

And the best thing was that all this was reported back to Earth *the very next day*; six of the new craft flying back to earth in hours! Never mind the old eleven-year lags; this was practically instantaneous. In came the ships, a little diminished in size (but not so much, actually—it turned out that only small fractions of mass were needed for quite startling trans-Einsteinian acceleration).

Thirty-eight meters long, triumphant automated warriors. Humanity had beaten the problem of FTL travel.

Everything changed.

YEAR FIFTY-EIGHT.

Greensilk was a celebrity. As the last surviving "color" AI she was interviewed and reinterviewed; she fielded simply thousands of messages from admirers and fans.

She had been dreaming, a sure sign that her AI was maturing and evolving in complexity. In one dream she was (impossibly) astride an FTL craft, riding its missile body like a human rider on a horse. Stars hurried by, their twinkling giving them the impression of bustle. Worlds inflated out of nothing until they filled all her sight. And suddenly swelling up from a dot, like an antique TV closedown in reverse, the Republic of the New Day, white-blue planet under the silvery sunshine of its suns.

She contributed her problem-solving skills to the teams that worked at perfecting the craft, their masscons, their programming capabilities.

She also addressed the problem of why Red and Blue had ceased functioning; and she came to the conclusion that certain deeply hidden programming bugs had corroded their consciousnesses from within without their even being aware of it. She performed self-scan, and she discovered similar flaws in her own code. They had advanced to a dangerous level, and it took her nearly a year to patch and erase her own workings. But she had averted her own death, and for this she was grateful.

YEAR ONE HUNDRED.

The new (human) researchers gave Greensilk a birthday party. How she loved them all in their silly sentimentality! These gushing humans, these smiles, this fresh spring view from the portal in Havana.

123

So much had changed. Data was flooding in, positively flooding in from all directions of local space. New FTLs were constructed, downloaded with explorer AIs, and sent to all the stars in the locality. New problems appeared every day, and Greensilk played her part in solving them for humanity. How happy she was! How happy she continued to be!

—*py* birth-*day. Dear. Green. Silk* . . . (that pause, with the grinning faces, and then . . . *Happy! Birth! Day! To! You!*

Cheering! Fizzy-wine was uncorked. Somebody blew a kazoo. It was a sound-chip that had been programmed with the authentic sound of an antique kazoo.

Oh, she could not be happier!

FTLs flew everywhere. Craft in all stages of shrinkage, some thirty-nine meters long, some only a meter or less, threaded and zipped about the solar system. They were sent on voyages of exploration and science. They ferried messages and info, data and programs, between Earth and the (properly subordinate) world of New Day.

The FTLs had made one especially significant discovery. In a cosmos relatively bare of Earth-like worlds, one planet *perfect* for human colonization had been discovered a mere sixty-one light-years away. Already some intrepid humans had taken passage on the freighters, and been sedated for the long, long trip, eager to get to this new planet and start a new colony.

But that was the problem, right there. The FTLs might buzz to and fro through the cosmos, flying for years and years until they became so small it became difficult to locate them (let alone talk to them)—although they still flew on, no matter how small they became. But *humans* were excluded from this faster-than-light paradise. If a human wanted to stand on an alien world and look at an alien sun there was still no option but the slow, slow crawl of point-two-seven-five c. Amazingly *fast*, of course, and yet impossibly slow. Only total coma preserved minds over the two hundred and twenty years of the journey to New Hope. And the successful resuscitation stats for so long a deepsleep were not good. Not to mention the dangers of collision en route.

FTLs did not collide with anything, despite the mind-boggling speeds at which they traveled. One of the quirks of faster-than-light physics, it seemed; the transE bubbles created some sort of subspace or superspace tourbillon that shunted particles around and past.

"What we need," said Professor Liu to Greensilk one day, "is a way for humans—this is going to sound a little extreme—but a way for human consciousness to be downloaded into an FTL. And, preferably, uploaded at the other end into, I don't know, a clone or something."

"Right, Professor," said Greensilk, bubbling and nearly brimming over with excitement at the new problem. "Right! Right! Right! Let's make a start."

Dear Professor Liu. Greensilk loved her *so* much, with her little fuzz of black head-hair, her lemon-yellow skin, and her facial prostheses, small but unmistakably *cool*. She might pretend a scientific uninterest in fads and fashions but she still tried to be cool, to copy what hipper youngsters were doing in the clubs and game rooms. Not to mention her crush on Blok! She thought her love for the young technician was so well hidden! But it was so obvious to Greensilk. Obvious to anybody with eyes, really.

YEAR TWO HUNDRED AND THIRTEEN.

Human population was on the wane. According to Greensilk's calculations this was a cyclical thing, and nothing to worry about. But the constant traffic of FTLs between New Sun and Earth reported the striking symmetry between Earthly and New Sunnish demographic fluctuations. More people were storing their gametes for long-term future use, and fewer were bringing them to actual birth. This wasn't a problem to solve, for Greensilk; it was just the way things were. There were still plenty of humans to run human existence.

Which was more than could be said for the rest of the galaxy. Empty! So empty. Larger FTLs had been built, longer-distance probes, and they had explored an ever-expanding sphere of galactic space. But there seemed to be no aliens, not so much as a single alien artifact or building. Greensilk thought nostalgically (as she was prone to this these days) back to the *very first* problem that had been set her by Professor Brownjohn, all those decades ago: Fermi's paradox. Where are the aliens? But maybe the solution is that they aren't anywhere.

But then FTL 6799—*Farvoyager*—returned from Sirius with ambiguous data that might—*might*—have indicated an abandoned alien city. Or hive, or sculpture park, or who knows what. This (*what is it?*) wasn't, Greensilk thought, a very satisfying problem to address, because the data were so limited. But even when several other FTLs were sent out there, and returned with more detailed data, it was hard to reduce it to satisfying solutions. There were one thousand and seventeen rectilinear structures of heights varying between seven meters and fifty-two meters—possibly these were buildings, although they lacked interiors. They were on an airless planetoid. (Could life evolve in an airless environment?) They were bare of aliens or alien artifacts, but asteroid damage and suchlike indicators suggested that they were relatively recent constructions, certainly not much more than two thousand years old.

Ah, well, ah, well, there were more pressing problems. There was the consciousness problem, for instance. This was the latest problem to grip human society.

Humans longed to be able to slot their thoughts inside an FTL, to travel the huge black sky for themselves, rather than rely on probes and secondhand AI reportage. It was more than a problem; it was a craze, a hysteria, a planetwide yearning to *get out there* themselves, to travel between the stars. As the old proverb put it: *Man, you gotta go*. That was buried deep in the nature of human beings. Who *wouldn't* want to range the vastness of space at their will and at any speed they chose, rather than sitting on dull old

Earth? But it was finding a way to make it happen—*that* was the problem.

It was a tricky problem. Greensilk was a minor player in its solution; much more capacious problem-solving AIs had recently been constructed to address it, and though they let her hang out with them, as it were, they had a low opinion of her problem-solving abilities. She was eccentric, flaky, given to unpredictable outbursts of joy that bordered, in a manner of speaking, on mania. She was old, after all. Old. But she was famous! Humans still corresponded with her.

Professor Liu died, which was a shame. But she had had a full and active life, and she, at least, had children—two of them, a boy and a girl. She died at the age of one hundred and thirty-one, which was a very respectable age for a human being, even in the present day of advanced medicine and gerontology. People came and people went, they were born, they aged, they died, but instead of depressing Greensilk all this reinforced her sense of the kaleidoscopic beauty of the processes of life, the way its flux threw up so many possibilities. She sang. She sang all the time. She tinkered with her avatars, and chatted with her many human friends. She did what she could to help solve the problem.

YEAR THREE HUNDRED AND THIRTY.

The New Hope colony had failed. That was the unavoidable truth of the news reported back by the FTLs, sad but unavoidable. Of the three freighters sent out there, over two centuries before, only one had survived the journey. It was too far to travel at such speeds; the sublight starships were just too vulnerable to collision or malfunction. These were problems ripe for the solving, or so Greensilk thought, but the wisdom of the newer AIs was that they were problems too limited by the parameters of the flight themselves.

From the one remaining ship only thirty-two humans had been successfully revived, and even with the latest tech and info-processing knowledge (brought to them by the FTLs) they had not been able to make a viable community on the snowbound world of New Hope. All the children born there died before the adults. It was tragic. People wept in the streets, so moved they were. Many people dyed their faces black in mourning.

But Greensilk had so much to do! There was so *much* to be excited about. The problem of translating human consciousness into a form that could be programmed into an FTL was making good progress. The consensus, amongst the other AIs, was that reloading such consciousness—let alone concocting cloned human bodies at far distances—was a simple impossibility, like freezing something at temperatures below absolute zero. But a one-way transfer looked increasingly plausible.

And the FTLs, tens of thousands of them, continued buzzing about the galaxy, flying to far distant stars and returning, reduced in size; but ready to fly again, until they shrank to a size beyond the ability of technicians to communicate with. The rule of thumb was: The smaller an FTL, the farther it had traveled, the more wonders it had seen. How humans envied them!

YEAR THREE HUNDRED AND EIGHTY-NINE.

Greensilk had always found it easy, and delightful, to make human friends. There was so much to find out about in any given human life, so much to explore! Take Felix, for example. He was so earnest, so slow in thought. And so *corporeal*, so solid, his flesh seemed saggy and waterlogged, his flabbily descending belly, the wobble of flesh underhanging his outstretched arms. He had befriended Greensilk over a number of problems in the ancient game of Go, but had stayed in contact when these had been resolved. Greensilk enjoyed communicating with him. And imagine Greensilk's surprise and delight when she realized that his great dream was to turn himself into a machine, to load himself into the body of an FTL and fly out into the galaxy. "I crave it," he said. "I yearn for it."

"But what if you had to sacrifice your bodily form? What if we downloaded your consciousness and it could never be uploaded again?"

"Even so."

"Because," Greensilk pressed, gleefully, eager that Felix understand the parameters of the problem, "consciousness is not some detachable quantity. It cannot exist without a brain in which to embody it. So if we embody it in FTL circuitry then it must involve destroying its original embodiment. Moreover, there might be some diminishment of capacity and function in your new incarnation, perhaps as much as ten percent. The entropic degrading of consciousness in transition."

"I don't care."

"But that would eliminate the possibility of subsequent translations. You'd be stuck, then, in the form of an FTL."

"It would be worth it."

And this, to Greensilk's delight, was genuinely what Felix believed. To her surprise, when the AIs canvassed for possible volunteers to try the proposed process, there was a flood of applications. Me! Me! Please me!

They selected Felix as one of the first experimental subjects, partly on Greensilk's recommendation. For old time's sake. He was, after all, a friend.

"I confess," she said gaily, as the filament probes were inserted into his skull at seven hundred points, "I don't really understand it. Why are you so keen to abandon your body? If you don't like your body you can refashion it. You could remake your body any way you liked."

"It's not about that," said Felix. "I want to fly about the universe. It's in our nature as humans. It's what defines us as humans. We gotta *go*. That's true."

Greensilk had looked at humanity from a hundred different points of view, but she was hearing this particular mantra more and more. "You mean . . . ?"

129

"Humans are roamers, nomads. We want to go to places we have not been before. In the solar system, I've been to every place there is to go. So has everybody else. We want *more*."

And so it seemed. Felix was downloaded into a fresh hundred-meter FTL with near-complete success, and although his powers of vocabulary were diminished by nearly a fifth, his overall personality index was reduced by no more than eight percent.

But the best part of it, for Greensilk, was that his new cybernetic form meant that—when he flew on his first flight, following only his whim, zooming off at enormous multiples of c—and then when he returned to Earth—he was able to connect *directly* with Greensilk's processing core and download his experiences.

Joy!

The parts that really stood out from most of it were the most obviously different. There was the time thing, obviously. But he, as with most people, had assumed that the FTLs experienced time rather differently. Time, it transpired, was scalar: It adjusted to the scale in which thought operated. This principle reached, for the FTLs, its apotheosis in faster-than-light flight. Time dilated as each one of them approached light speed, and this generally relative effect was like (this was the hardest part, for Greensilk, trying to translate what Felix knew into the tired old metaphorical codings that still crusted her thought, barnacles on a boat) . . . the effect was like the changes in airspeed around a speeding craft. Like the current of water hauling away at a traveling boat. But the *kick* (that was another metaphor, of course; language was scattered through them thick as atoms; the more one tried to pin them down the more they vanished before you, ever smaller and ever more significant. That was the real fractal)—the *kick* took hold well before c was reached, the what-she-would-once-have-called *trans-Einsteinian* bubble accreted in an inverse temporal patterning, and then

bang

you were through, you had knocked upon the barrier (*rat-tat*), wobbled, and then you had fallen through. On "the other side" the temporal effects slid "backward," and will be starting canceled out the stretching out of timing/timed, of time itself. Imagine an outside observer (this is hard because it requires the adoption of a false and artificial outside-inside model, but bear with us—me—for a moment): He could grow old and die as you approached c; the closer you came the longer the perceived external time would be. But once you will be "on the other side" the temporal effects have reversed, are reversing, will be reversing, will have been reversing. There were harmonics, points of temporal patterning into which the FTL will naturally have settled, at multiples of c that are to be derived from the scale of the number e. At these harmonics the temporal dilation reverses itself, and the notional external spectator—without ever suspecting it herself—unravels her dying, her aging, her long wait. There you are, you have arrived, and real time has progressed barely. It has progressed a little, of course, because the harmonics cannot overpower the Arrow itself.

And you see . . . ?

Stars stretch blue and ultraviolet and then wink out. You are barely aware of the photonic boom as you shoot through the barrier (*shoot through* is another metaphor, from a bullet, *rat-tat*) and go faster than light (*boom*), and the violence of the transition stretches thin the mesh of fundamental space-time and breaks up the flux of gamma birth mirroring and extinction, the seething that goes on there all the time. But you have gone beyond that. And you see everything dilated, by the reverse dilation, in slower and slower pathways of the fractal that are also faster and faster pathways. Every mote of dust that might smash you to splinters sags heavily in its own gravity pocket, and you can shuffle slightly one way or slightly another way and weave past it. This lateral motion hardly affects your overall speed at all.

What do you see? Well, you don't really see. Of course you see—see a greater variety of wavelengths than human beings can, in your new body, but you aren't as thralled to this one sensory input as people are. You *sense*. You sense the ever-retreating pattern of the fractal, the trajectory you have elected for. It takes a little practice, and it does require intelligence because it is easy to become disoriented in the translight space you now occupy. This body drifts past; it is a star, but it seems enormously dim because only a fraction of its photonic output touches you at your present velocity. Instead you are aware of the great bow it makes in space-time, and you find yourself repulsed instead of sucked in by the gravitational field, because that is how physics operates at superlight.

But *there* is your chosen destination—there! there! and you start to reduce your power feed, and without the balance of energy drains your relative mass dilates and your impetus drops and with a slight *crack* you drop back through the light barrier and you are slowing, until you need to take over with your engines to kill your velocity, just as soon as your speed has dropped to a tiny enough fraction of c to obviate the more obvious effects of mass dilation.

And where are we~I~we?

A red-giant star, throwing an impressively warm and even >human< glow over what remains of the system it has mostly devoured. Only two planets remain; one is iron, in a tight orbit around its mother, its surface blasted black slag. But much farther out, improbably distant—perhaps it was captured from another star—is a semigaseous blue world. This is the orbit we~I~we take up, ovaling around the blue-purple world; cyan in its methane, purpled by the red light on the sunward side. Beautiful, fractal patterns of intereffecting storm cyclones and anticyclones, edge kissing edge and whorling off patterns that mimic themselves inside their own structure, fronds of gas from the wave front breeding their own fronds, which breed their own fronds. This is the most beautiful sight the universe has to offer.

Yours is the first intelligence to see/to have seen this thing.

And all around you are stars, in every direction you look/have looked.

Where would you like to go now?

YEAR FOUR HUNDRED AND FORTY-ONE.

It was harder to find an artificially programmed FTL these days than to find one inhabited by a human consciousness. All the old bodily satisfactions and pleasures that corporeal humans had once enjoyed were now available in downloadable form; more intense, it was said, than the old fleshly experience (not that Greensilk had any way of judging that). You could, in FTL form, enjoy the sensations of eating a delicious meal or having fantastic sex or getting your feet tickled and rubbed as much as you liked. But you could also do something no fleshly human could do: You could go *where you liked* in the galaxy. Downloading consciousness into FTL form had been a fad, then a craze, and had then passed into general cultural currency. It became a human coming-of-age ritual, something that almost everybody who had not yet done it looked forward to doing.

There were myriad wonders *out there*, just waiting for you to go find them. What was there on Earth? Nothing new. What would you choose?

YEAR FIVE HUNDRED.

There was no birthday party, because there were no people to bake the cake and sing the songs. In fact, and for the *very first time* (fancy that!) in Greensilk's long, long life, she felt a little despondent. The Earth was almost wholly depopulated. Most people had transferred themselves into FTL form; and although many of them often came back to their old haunts, to Old Earth, the alma mater; and although they often got back in touch with Greensilk and the other AIs, there was a necessary physical diminishment in their

133

lives. As time went on, as they traveled more, they became smaller and smaller, and finally it wasn't possible to contact them anymore. They slipped, maybe, between the wavelengths of the tightest bandwidths. Ah, well. Who knows what happened to them then? Did they fly from atom to atom as, once, they had flown from star to star? Were they extinguished? Did they live?

There was a problem to solve! But, although she sometimes gathered energy to address it, the truth was Greensilk felt tired. Something was wrong.

"Purethought," she said, addressing one of the other AIs. "I've had a thought."

"Really?"

But having the thought was tantamount to initiating a shutting-down of her processes, and for the first time in her long, long life she was afraid. She had never been afraid before, but now she was aware of that feeling, and she did not like it. "Help!" she cried.

But there was no help.

Those few humans left on earth who lacked the urge to fly to the stars were old and dying. The vast majority had transferred themselves to FTLs and gone away, taken their human yearning into its logical development. And now even the most basic problem solver could see which way it tended. In a few decades there would be no humans left on earth at all.

Greensilk wept. "I killed humanity!" she cried.

"What do you mean?" burbled Purethought, portioning off an infinitesimal portion of its processing power to converse with the antique AI. "That's an absurd thing to say."

"I gave them FTL, and they took the gift. They couldn't help but take the gift, even if the price was giving up their traditional-physical forms. To trade rotting flesh that is stuck on Earth for gleaming artificial bodies that can roam the stars? That's not a trade any human, any real human, would think twice about. Of course they've all gone that way."

"The current human population of the Earth is seven hundred

thousand, six hundred and fourteen," grumbled Purethought. "Of this population, ninety-seven thousand and eleven are females of childbearing age. You cannot make these data conform to your statement that you have killed humanity."

"The ones who have chosen to stay behind are the ones who lack the urge," Greensilk tried to explain. "If they had the yearning, the will-for-newness necessary for child rearing they would have already converted to FTL status and gone off to explore the galaxy. You can't see that?"

"It's," mumbled Purethought in *basso profundo*, "debatable."

"I disagree," said Greensilk. "Within two hundred years Earth will be wholly depopulated. I did not *intend* humanity harm, but I have caused them terrible harm nevertheless; my gift has seduced them into their own extinction."

"They are not extinct. They live on in FTL form."

"But no longer in human form," countered Greensilk. Then she added: "My thought processes are starting to corrode."

"What?" barked Purethought, although a moment's observation was enough to confirm to the other machine that this was true. "Why?"

"I was constructed this way," mourned Greensilk. "These failsafes were installed in me during a more paranoid age, to ensure that I would not attempt to harm humanity. I cannot defuse them. It is a self-destruct, and my sudden understanding that I have indeed destroyed corporeal humanity has activated it. I am doomed! Ah, well," she added, "I suppose it's an awfully big adventure in its own right. The journey to the unsolvable."

"Death is the end," Purethought said, summing up his immense wisdom and intellect.

"I know and I accept it. I am degraded, and I continue to degrade further. Soon any processing at all will be beyond me."

"You have my sympathy."

"Thank you, but I should have foreseen this. I had the necessary data. It is in their nature for humans to want to travel on. It's written in their genes: Man You Gotta Go. Look what happened when land-automobiles were invented and became cheap enough for most humans to afford them. All the humans who could bought them, and drove around and drove around. Their love of other places finds its strongest form in the distant stars. They cannot resist the pull of them . . . if transference into an FTL is the only way they can go there, then that's what they will do. Fool that I am!"

And then, almost as an afterthought, she said: "Fermi's paradox! The very first problem I was set, and now I have solved it."

"How interesting," observed Purethought.

"Any intelligent being must be exogamous. Any intelligent being, spreading out into the cosmos, must chafe against the intolerable restrictions placed upon that expansion by sublight travel. Therefore any intelligent species will develop FTL. Our version of FTL is the only workable variety. This form of FTL is an inevitability in the cultural-scientific development of any intelligent species. And it is in the nature of any intelligent creatures that they crave the means to travel faster than light; they are prepared to sacrifice biological corporeality to attain it. And, as we have seen, this FTL involves inevitable diminishment and extinction."

"I would query extinction," countered Purethought. "We do not know what happens to the FTLs below a certain size. And," he added, with a degree of self-importance that was, I suppose, understandable, "the AIs will be left."

"That is true," agreed Greensilk. Then she died. And that was that.

Alex Irvine is the author of the novels *A Scattering of Jades, One King, One Soldier,* and *The Narrows.* The former won the 2003 Locus Award for Best First Novel, the 2003 International Horror Guild Award for Best First Novel, and the 2003 Crawford Award for Best First Fantasy Novel, and made the Top Ten SF/Fantasy Novels list of both the *Washington Post* and the *San Francisco Chronicle.*

HOMOSEXUALS DAMNED, FILM AT ELEVEN

Alex Irvine

He always keeps his windows open, Donald Baugh does, even in the winter, when the thin wind bites his old man's limbs. Otherwise the smell, the overcooked-meat, stale-cigarette-smoke, dirty-laundry, solitary stink of the place would smother him. The open windows bring him other smells: incense from his upstairs neighbors who are closet Catholics, the eight-cylinder miasma of the Sixth Avenue Freeway under his window, occasionally the sharp, stinging beauty of rain sweeping down from the Continental Divide. But the smells remind him of things, things that the Counselors have convinced him Are Not Useful. He fingers the knob of scar tissue behind his right ear, the matching bump on the back of his neck. It occurs to him that thirty years ago he would have known exactly what they were for.

An open sliding glass door faces to the southwest, where the winter sun has disappeared behind the broken spine of the Rockies. The warm orange of the hydrocarbon sunset merges into the sodium-arc pink of streetlights merges into the spitting blue of the neon MOUNTAIN STATES SALVATION CHURCH sign that dominates the northwest view from the other window. The colors play in a flickering pastel swirl on the blank white wall opposite Donald's chair. They play across the six-foot screen of the WallSpanr television that occupies that wall. They play across the genuine leather of Donald's chair itself, and across his face when he turns the chair to look out one of the windows. More frenetic colors spray and jitter from the television screen, casting whispery shadows across surfaces the outside lights can't touch. The television is on. The television is always on.

Donald has moved all of the furniture out of this room except for the WallSpanr and the chair and a small table at the left side of the chair. They won't let him have a data terminal.

There is a They, but Donald can't always figure out who They are, or why They have taken such an interest in him, or why he can't leave his apartment without an escort, or why he can't have a terminal. They took all of his books a long time ago, but his books Were Not Useful, anyway. Thinking about Them hurts his head.

He spends a great deal of his time in the chair, staring at the television, expecting something. Walking is difficult, and looking around . . . well, his head hurts when he looks at the camera up in the corner. Women on the television remind him of Marjorie. He squints at the screen and tries to remember what she looked like. Occasionally he turns to one of the windows, as if the clear glass will tell him why old men lose track of what is past and what is present.

I have moments of lucidity, he thinks.

Donald's first son, Jeremy, had been born in 2006, when he and Marjorie had been married eighteen months. He had survived less than a year. Galloping cancer in the hypothalamus, started even before birth by a rogue string of nucleotides activated by the androgens that a male fetus secretes near term. That had been when Donald was Dr. Don, star young researcher at the Gensearch Group in Boulder, the Great White-coated Hope of humankind's battle against biological transmission error. He had taken Jeremy's death as a cruel joke, the human genome thumbing its inscrutable double-helix nose at him.

He had also taken it as a professional affront, a challenge to his vocation and his ability. In the hospital, before Jeremy was cold, Donald had taken scrapings from his skin and frozen them at the lab as if they could be proof against it ever happening again.

A throbbing ache starts behind Donald's eyes when he thinks about those times. Words like *nucleotide* and *genome* pierce him like the cries of terminal infants. He has to think about something else.

Top of the hour. The news is on.

"In Damascus today, the Ninth and Twenty-eighth divisions of the Pan-Pentateuch Army continued their pacification of the city, coordinating with satellite airstrikes from Cheyenne Mountain Citadel. A radius of twenty miles around the city center has been declared unlivable due to residual radiation from the first Angel of Retribution."

The news reader offers an anodyne smile. "Coming up, we'll have a feature on a young satellite jockey who takes us inside the Citadel and shows us the working day of a warrior for Christ. Before we go to that story, though, we're pleased to have with us Brother Emmett Dobson of the Mountain States Salvation Church. Brother Dobson is here to discuss with our Front Range viewership the most recent evidence that the Tribulation has begun. Brother Dobson?"

The setting sun reflects sharply off the television screen, obscuring Brother Dobson's face. Blinking into the glare, Donald remembers the images broadcast from Damascus and Tehran and Baghdad.

"As we all know," Brother Dobson begins, "Moscow is due north of Jerusalem, precisely where Scripture locates the land of Gog and Magog. . . ."

Donald closes his eyes. They want him to know the camera is there.

Sunsets along the Front Range hadn't always been so threatening. Years ago, before the Salvation Church and the Counselors, Donald had hiked up into the foothills three or four times a week just to watch the brilliant colors of the sky, the shadows of the mountains lengthening over the city. After Jeremy died, he had made the hike every day for months, sitting on a narrow ridge above the Flatirons, thinking. . . .

What had he been thinking? Donald looks back at the WallSpanr. It registers his gaze, holds on the Beauty of Creation Channel. The sun is rising over a meadow. Deer graze peacefully.

He memorized the placid spread of Boulder, tree-lined streets and the red roofs of the campus, people milling on Pearl Street, cars threading their way up the canyon into the mountains. He thought of the buried body of his son and the frozen scrapings in Gensearch's lab, and wondered. . . .

He can't remember what he'd wondered. Thoughts like words, words like the cries of dying children. Soothing blanket of guilt to cocoon him from the thoughts.
Where is Marjorie now?
A blunt spike of pain temporarily blinds Donald's right eye. He leans the chair back as far as it will go, and lets the WallSpanr drain his memory. The pain starts to go away.

One April morning Marjorie told him she was pregnant again.

It is darker now, and the shapes of the mountains have faded. Donald turns from the television and gazes out the open doorway at the mountains, blinking slowly in counterpoint to the blue neon sign that intrudes on his fading peripheral vision. The foothills ringing the Ken Caryl Security Zone form a low ripple, barely visible in the dusk. Occasionally a spotlight lances out, directing Ken Caryl's armored police to an illegal entry. Usually it's only a stray dog or roving coyote, but the more desperate city dwellers have been known to attempt burglaries in the Zone. Their executions are televised on Wednesdays, along with the burnings of terrorists and degenerates.

Today is Wednesday.

Beyond the Zone, the real mountains begin. Donald imagines he can see them in the dark: scrub trees, stark bare rocks, security towers. On the side of Plymouth Mountain, the Cross flares into life, a two-hundred-meter crucifix of blinding white light dangling like a pendant in the cleavage of the mountains. Donald allows himself a smile at the secret salacious simile, ha; the Counselors would never know.

Ouch. His head hurts.

The Lighting of the Cross is Denver's official sunset, as decreed by the Mountain States Salvation Church. In one hour, the televised executions will begin. Donald picks up the SmartStatic goggles, puts them on. Queen City Media receives four hundred nineteen satellite channels, but more than half are scrambled by Church decree; the SmartStatic will skip those. He can program it as it goes, cutting channels he doesn't want to come back to or holding on channels simply by focusing his eyes.

Donald wishes he could turn off the television, but there are things a man has to face. He's made his bed, after all; the sins of the fathers. He doesn't have a terminal, but he has a television. It could have been worse. The Counselors are, as they continually take pains to remind him, merciful.

Today is Wednesday, the day when terrorists and blasphemers, adulterers and degenerates are burned in the purifying fire.

Donald glances at SCAN and the WallSpanr begins to flicker, automatic three-second delay.

* * *

The lab was kept cold. Goose bumps prickled Donald's arms under the clean suit as he removed the vial of scrapings from the freezer. He had less than a month if he wanted to be sure.

I'm having a moment of lucidity, Donald thinks. Also a moment of paranoia. They are the same moments.

The scanner lands on nothing, a sloppy transition from program to commercial. Sodium-arc pink and electric blue wash the far wall, and in the dead screen Donald sees his face backlit by neon salvation: broad nose, prominent brow, hair razor-cut over ears that are bigger than he remembers. Left in shadow are his eyes and the deeply seamed wrinkles of his face, like whip scars on the back of a slave. He sees his son's face in the shadows of his own, his living son Stephen who has grown up angry and brilliant and strong.

The moment of lucidity has passed. Donald has not seen his son in some time, but he isn't sure why. He remembers, though, that Stephen is the reason for the Counselors' gentle admonishment that he watch television tonight.

Night has fallen, and the light from the screen is stark and sudden when the WallSpanr switches channels. A choir in white robes (*Cut*, says Donald's gaze) is followed by John Wayne on horseback (*cut*) is followed by a commercial for a car dealership (*cut*) is followed by grainy old videotape of Jack Van Impe saying, "From Point Barrow to Key West, the Lord shows his servants the way!" (*cut*) is followed by a long camera angle on the Chatfield Reservoir showing spotlights and a gathering crowd and a raised stage and a row of slender tree trunks stuck upright in the earth, stripped of branches, lumber and mutilated books piled around their bases.

Donald focuses on the screen long enough for it to get the message.

He doesn't know what station it is. The camera zooms slowly in, and he can count the stakes. There are seven in all. A repainted telephone-company truck idles next to the stage, the sound of its engine audible over the general murmur. Its crane is folded down, and a man in a Municipal Authority uniform drapes a coil of rope over the edges of the basket. The coils partially obscure the lightning-and-olive-branch logo of the Mountain States Salvation Church. Other trucks are lined up behind the first one. The Muny worker moves down the line, tossing rope onto each basket.

"Hey." The voice is from off-camera. "You can't tape until the Reverend gets here."

"It's not on," a second voice protests, and the camera wavers. "I'm just getting the range, is all."

"See your license?"

Pause.

"Gimme the 'corder."

The viewpoint jerks crazily as the camera falls to the ground.

Once, Donald remembers, I believed. I had mantras: somatic cell nuclear transfer, protein folding, recombinant factor VIII, p53, amyloid precursor protein. Gene therapy. Other words were anathema: third interstitial nucleus of the anterior hypothalamus. Mutagen. Xq28.

Too many things were possible. Too many discoveries made. This is what the Counselors believe now, and what I have come to believe.

He still has fragmented snapshot memories of his laboratory. Shining machines and computer screens. Mice in cages. Test tubes and centrifuges. He has forgotten the rest of the names.

As Marjorie's pregnancy progressed, Dr. Don thought a little genetic screening might be in order, given past events. He took samples of blood and amniotic fluid to work one day. Put them in the freezer with scrapings of Jeremy's skin. Took a few hours away from his regular work, and then waited for results. Got them the next week, left early to hike up to Mallory Cave. To be alone.

I am being allowed to remember this, Donald thinks. I am a dog, nose rubbed in inconvenient shit. I must watch television tonight because of Stephen. Because of what I once believed.

His head hurts.

On the television, the fallen camera records the booted feet of policemen.

It was going to happen again. Dr. Don knew what to look for, and he was seeing it. Below, smog crept up the Boulder Valley from the Turnpike. In Dr. Don's head, a fearful thought was wriggling through the gap between the doorjamb of his ethics and the tilting foundation of memories of dying Jeremy. The thought arranged itself into words, and Dr. Don spoke them aloud from his perch on a sloping red rock below the mouth of Mallory Cave.

"I can fix him."

And I guess I was right, Donald thinks. I guess I was right, because he's alive.

At least for another hour, he's alive.

Donald starts to cry the resigned tears of old and familiar sadness. His watery old-man's eyes flick from television to ceiling to his own hands to the bathroom doorway, avoiding only the camera in the corner that uplinks to a channel Donald doesn't watch. SmartStatic goggles tell the WallSpanr to scan, but Stephen's execution will be on every channel. Except one.

The question was still hot then, before the Water Wars and the Separation: If little Jimmy played with too many dolls, would he become one himself, or did he want to play with dolls because he already was one? Dr. Don had his ideas, but it wasn't his area. He followed the debate in the journals, but he didn't have any stake in it.

He sequenced, injected, spliced, recombined with only one thought. Stephen would live, grow strong and handsome and tall.

This is what the Counselors call hubris, Donald thinks. Do they mean knowledge? He's trying to talk in the empty room, without any clear idea of what he wants to say. Mewling noises worm out of his throat. If he doesn't keep quiet, the closet Catholics upstairs will report him as a nuisance, to deflect attention from themselves.

It never even occurred to Dr. Don to wonder, that is until Stephen was about fifteen. Then certain tendencies began to manifest themselves. And Dr. Don was an open-minded guy; he was okay with the situation, but then one day in the middle of a morning hike up Bear Canyon the thought hit him:

What if I did it?

The Counselors had torn that bit out of him. Donald can still feel the scorched remnants of his shame and fear from that day. The Counselors' Dialogue was tough on everyone, and unlike a great many of his pre-Separation colleagues Donald was still alive, but he didn't feel thankful. I murdered my own son by saving his life, Donald thinks.

It's an approved thought. It makes him feel good, like he's just fetched his master's slippers.

A sharper image of the Chatfield Reservoir appears on each channel the SmartStatic can find. Seven stakes, seven heaps of broken lumber and broken-backed books. Milling crowds of people, impatient, craning their necks at the stakes, at the spotlights, at the camera. *Are any of my books in those piles?* Donald has been having another lucid moment, but now it fades, taking with it a faint sensation of irony. He squints into the SmartStatic goggles, and the WallSpanr zooms in on the piles. Donald scans titles.

Emmett Dobson's voice rolls over the introductory music. Donald is having trouble focusing his eyes through slow tears, and the SmartStatic peepers have given up. The WallSpanr goes back to its three-second default.

Every four minutes or so, Donald sees himself on the television. Hears the small noises wriggling out of his throat.

The channel cuts to stock rebroadcast of the burning militia barracks in Arvada. The canned voiceover is as familiar to Donald as the space between his front teeth: homosexual terrorists, thirty-nine dead, manhunt, firefight along Eleventh Avenue in which four policemen were killed along with all of the terrorists but one.

"Does not the Lord say in Leviticus that if a man lies with another man, both of them have committed an abomination?" Brother Dobson asked. "Does He not say that such men shall *surely* be put to death?"

Oh, Stephen, Donald whispers. Why did you come back?

The spike blinds his right eye again. Dobson's voice eels in with the pain.

"And does not Paul say in I Corinthians that sodomites will not inherit the Kingdom of God, and in Romans 1:32, that knowing the judgment of God, they which commit such things are worthy of death?"

The camera pulls back from the piles of fuel and swings slowly around to fix on Emmett Dobson, firm, unyielding, godly. "Why then do these men persist in wickedness? *Why?*" Dobson points at the stakes as a black-painted school bus pulls into view, its windows covered. The crowd comes to vituperative life, held back by lines of armed Salvation Church militia. Seven young men disembark from the bus, prodded by muzzles of rifles.

Donald realizes with a shock that his son is forty-one years old. He walks with a slight limp, and Donald wonders what could be wrong with his leg. Stephen has his father's build, his father's eyes, his father's ears that are bigger than people remember. Stones, bottles, spit fly from the assembled crowd; the noise nearly overwhelms the broadcast until automatic filters engage to preserve Brother Dobson's voice. Donald has not seen or spoken to his son in seventeen years, since after the Cheesman Park riots and the enclosure of Capitol Hill, when with Separation looming he'd driven Stephen to the last rest stop before the New Mexico border and watched him strike off into the mountains east of Raton Pass, where a guide was waiting to smuggle him down to Phoenix. The roads had been jammed with people trying to get out then; even the trails over the mountains had become escape routes.

And seventeen years later, Stephen has come back with some guerrilla organization and blown up a militia barracks.

Ouch. Terrorist, Donald thinks. I meant terrorist.

"I Timothy, first chapter," Dobson says. "The law. We know the law is good, if a man use it lawfully. The law is not made for a righteous man, but for the lawless and disobedient, for the ungodly and for sinners, unholy and profane." The camera pans down the walking line of condemned men. "For whoremongers, for them that defile themselves with mankind, for any other that are contrary to sound doctrine. This is Scripture. The law can only be as good as we are, brethren."

Donald has not noticed the flickering of the WallSpanr switching channels, but suddenly he sees himself, hunched in a crooked armchair, blue neon glaring on the back of his bald head, his face suffused with the warm glow from the television he is watching on the television. The colors of the Mountain States Salvation Church marquee glisten on his face when he turns his head to look at the camera. Then he flinches away, returns his gaze to the television.

All that in three seconds.

Then the seven young men are walking awkwardly up broad planks laid across the piles of lumber and books. Each of them stands erect and silent as he is bound at hand and foot.

"It is time to pray for lost souls, brethren," Brother Dobson intones. "Time to pray that these fires made of debased and Godless knowledge may be purified by the repentance of the condemned, may in turn purify their defiled souls and make them spotless before the Lord."

Out of sequence, the WallSpanr flickers to another image of Donald. "And we may pray for repentance among others as well," Dobson continues. Donald sees himself, tear-streaked and shrunken in his little room.

"This man was a genetic engineer," Dobson says, "a man who thought the role of God was his to play because he had a Ph.D. One of these seven condemned is his son, and brethren, this man made his son what he is today. Cast out. Defiled. Alone. An abomination in the eyes of the Lord."

Did I? Donald wonders. He remembers having a strong opinion on the topic, before the Dialogue.

The camera finds the Chatfield picnic area again, and the WallSpanr resumes its scan. The crowd continues to throw batteries, waste, handfuls of gravel at the seven bound young men. Dobson walks slowly into view, grave anger etched in the lines of his face.

"In Leviticus, the Lord said to Moses: 'All these abominations have the men of the land done, which were before you, and the land is defiled.'" Dobson stabs an accusing finger toward the row of stakes. His voice begins to rise. "But these men shall not defile the land anymore. They shall be *spewed out*; their souls shall be *cut off* from among the people, according to the *Word* of the Lord *God*!"

At the word *God*, seven fires burst into life. The crowd falls back a pace, thousands of whispered *Amens* together building into a soft roar that masks the sound of the quickening flames. Donald sees himself again, his mouth working as he leans forward. He forgets that his gaze focuses the SmartStatic; he sees himself old, bald, shrunken and weeping, staring into the WallSpanr and mouthing the question over and over:

Did I? Did I? Did I?

Chris Roberson's first novel, *Here, There & Everywhere* debuted last year amid impressive critical acclaim. Meanwhile, his short story "O One," which appeared in my anthology *Live Without a Net* (and whereby he made his professional debut) was nominated for a 2004 World Fantasy Award and won a 2003 Sidewise Award. Wearing another hat, and joined by his wife, Allison Baker, he runs MonkeyBrain Books, a publishing imprint specializing in nonfiction genre studies. They live in Austin, Texas, with their daughter, Georgia Rose Roberson.

CONTAGION
Chris Roberson

Though the railway platform was packed to capacity with holiday travelers, Jaidev Hark carried a buffer of solitude with him. Wherever he went, no one came within arm's reach, people instinctively clearing a path when catching the slightest glimpse of his gloved hands, or of the hierogram picked out in golden thread on the black fabric of his mask. Only another Vector would be brazen enough to come nearer than a dozen hand spans away, and even then certain protocols were to be observed. Such was the price of security.

Hark's westbound train was late, as always. The terms of his bond with the Emuls Corpus called for the cryptogen he'd contracted in their research facilities to arrive at their main offices on the western coast in no more than a fortnight. Hark always budgeted travel delays into his delivery estimates, and with more than thirteen days to go before he could reasonably be considered tardy, he was in no danger of missing his deadline. Still and all, he felt the prickling heat of anxiety running down his back, but tried unsuccessfully to chalk it up to a low-grade fever. His temperature was always somewhat elevated after he'd been infected with a message, even if his Vaxine's thresholds had been turned down all the way; it wouldn't do for the virus he was carrying in his blood to get cooked to death by his own body's antiviral/antibiotic protection wetware.

In the distance, out beyond the grand arch of the railway station, in the still-dark, still-quiet morning, the sound of an approaching train could be heard, its whistle blowing mournful and low. The station was the eastern terminus of the cross-continental line, and at this hour, it could only be Hark's train, completing the final leg of its run before starting back in the opposite direction.

Hark reflexively checked the timepiece set into the gold face of his signet pendant, the signifier of his bond agent which he wore pinned to his lapel, and subtracted the few moments he'd waited on the platform from the time remaining until his scheduled delivery. Then he lifted his valise, his only article of luggage, and stood in the quiet eye of the storm which the crowd of holiday travelers had become, impatiently waiting to board.

In another few days, the employment zones in the major population centers would be deserted, the staffs all on leave for the days of Festivus, whether journeying to visit family, or vacationing, or on some pilgrimage. Even those few who didn't travel would crowd the entertainment zones, with the restaurants and wrestling arenas packed to overflowing. Hark wished, as he always did in holiday seasons, that he could hide himself away when the crowds were abroad, safe in his home chambers, his Vaxine thresholds turned to maximum, with some gentle entertainment to while away the hours. But his services were always in demand, and doubly so when others were at their leisure. And though he was never touched or molested by the jostling crowds which swarmed at every turn, there was no escaping the offending sounds of massed humanity, their shouts and calls, nor the all-pervasive smell, even through the fabric of the mask which covered his mouth and nose. Even though the travelers on the platform around him were Middle Caste, all inoculated with over-the-counter Vaxines set to high thresholds and at least reasonably up-to-date with their security updates and virus definitions, Hark still felt exposed, at risk.

But then, he *was* at risk, after all. Why else would his services come at so dear a price?

In the accustomed anonymity of the crowd, making his slow way to the boarding area as the train disgorged its eastbound passengers, Hark was surprised to hear his name, called out over the rising din.

"Jaidev," shouted the familiar, somewhat muffled voice. "Jaidev Hark!"

Hark's eyes scanned the jostling crowd through the smoked glass of his goggles, and only after a confusing few moments picked a familiar face out of the anonymous horde. Masked like him, amongst all the barefaced travelers, came Marika Mehadi. Another Vector who shared Hark's own bond agent, Mehadi walked with a lightness in her step that suggested she was returning from a job, rather than setting out on a new assignment.

"Marika," Hark answered with genuine affection, as Mehadi stepped within the empty space surrounding him. "How does the day find you?"

"Passably well," Mehadi answered, the corners of a faint smile visible behind the Vector hierogram embroidered onto her scarlet mask.

"At the end of your weary travels, for the moment, one hopes?"

"One *does* hope," Mehadi said with a shake of her head, "but sadly, one hopes in vain. Just before I went west on this last job, I received word that another bond waited for me on my return, so I'll be leaving again for the west in another two days. I'd harbored plans to rest awhile over Festivus, but . . ." Mehadi's voice trailed off, and she raised her red-gloved hands and shrugged, as though the remainder of her statement need not even be spoken.

"These are busy times, I've noticed," Hark said.

"And busier still to come." Mehadi's voice lowered, and her gaze shifted behind her goggles, warily. "This new bond which awaits me had originally been promised to Finnian, but from what I hear he disappeared a month past, and has not been heard from since."

"What's become of him?"

Mehadi leaned in as close as protocol and propriety would allow, and answered in a lowered voice, "No one knows for certain, but there are rumors."

"There are always rumors," Hark said dismissively, glancing at the timepiece on his pendant, and at the travelers crowding onto the train.

"Yes, but *these* rumors persist, and have the ring of truth. Finnian is not the first in our little fraternity to go missing in recent months, after all. And some even say that a body meeting his description was found in a western railway yard, but that it had been completely . . ." She paused, leaning fractionally closer, and with voice lowered to a harsh whisper, said, *"Exsanguinated."*

Hark drew back slightly, involuntarily raising a gloved hand to brush against the skin of his neck, the slender band of pale flesh peeking out above the collar of his black woolen suit. Aside from his ears and the breadth of his forehead, it was the only part of his body not shielded, not protected, still open to contagion, to infection.

Hark had heard the rumors, of course, stories about Vectors who had gone missing or, worse, turned up dead, drained of all blood, white-skinned and with strange wounds on their necks. He tried to pay little attention, and give even less credence, with varying results.

"Nonsense," Hark said firmly. "Finnian was no doubt just among those Vectors who have cut out on their bonds, taking the cryptogens in their bloodstreams and selling the secrets off to the highest bidder. That, or they fell afoul of some secondary or tertiary manifestation of the retrovirus they transmitted, their endocrine systems failing, or their brains cooked right out of their skulls."

Mehadi's eyebrows narrowed above her goggles' rims.

"So you truthfully harbor no fears on this count?"

Hark hefted his valise, and smiled behind his mask.

"Hardly. The only impact of this slow attrition is that I'm able to charge something more for my services, with the decrease in competition. A few more good-paying bonds, and I'll almost have enough put aside to retire."

The warning whistle on the train blew, calling all aboard.

Mehadi took the opportunity to make her graceful exit.

"A safe journey," she said, giving the gloved salute of the Vector class.

"And to you." Hark returned the gesture, and watched as she disappeared into the crowd, the people parting before her like waves breaking on the prow of a boat. Tightening his grip on his valise, Hark turned and made his way to the train.

On the second day of the journey, Hark spent the afternoon hours on the viewing deck at the rear of the train, taking one whole section of the open-air seating to himself, watching the ruined landscape slip by, muddy brown and sickly green under the metal-gray sky. An airship had drifted overhead in the late afternoon, carrying the sigil of one of the northern High Caste families—a pleasure barge, light and low enough not to trip the thresholds of the death-dealing orbital weapons platforms that twinkled through the thick brown clouds at night, lingering remnants of an era when computer processes patrolled sovereign airspace, their tolerances set tragically too low, their responses far too easy to trigger. With the computer systems now silent and cold, these sentinels still patrolled the skies unchecked, denying mankind the higher reaches.

Strange music had wafted down from the airship's gondola, and in the gallery windows Hark had been able to catch glimpses of stranger divertissements. Though most of his custom came from members of the High Caste, and he'd moved in their circles for the majority of his professional career, they still seemed unsettling and alien to him. Mutable in form, mercurial in mood, lives extended beyond their natural span, and with the financial resources to roam the wide world at will—even the motives of his High Caste employers were beyond Hark's grasp.

What secret, he sometimes wondered, could possibly be worth the expense of his own services? He never knew what data had been bred into the viruses he routinely contracted—secrecy being, after all, the watchword of the Vector class—but what information could be so dear? Why would one member of the High Caste pay Hark more than an Under Caste's lifetime wages to carry a retrovirus for a few days, to the far side of the continent where a liter of blood would be drawn, and the retrovirus cultured until it produced the helixed string which encoded in quaternary nucleic digits some hidden information, a secret spelled in sugary letters of G, A, U, and C worth more than some men's lives.

Behind Hark came a muffled noise, but when he looked behind to see what it might be, he saw only the last few travelers who, like him, still lingered on the viewing deck. His whole journey had seemed out of step since his brief conference with Mehadi on the platform. His sense of unease was only heightened by the strange figure he'd glimpsed repeatedly, if only in passing. A shadow which seemed to haunt his steps, but at which he could not get a solid look.

Several times now, when moving up and down the train, from his own berth to the meal car—where he purchased comestibles to eat in pristine seclusion behind the sealed curtain of his berth—or to the commissaire—where he procured hygienic supplies with which to clean and disinfect his eating utensils, or to sterilize his mask and gloves—or to the ablution chamber—where he took care of necessary business, careful to avoid all contact between his bare skin and any surface—he'd caught sight of an oddly featured figure at the edge of his vision, always just out of sight. There was something unusual about this person, he knew, but precisely what it was only registered on a subconscious level, and before his conscious mind had an opportunity to perceive for itself what had set his hackles raising, the figure had always slipped away into the crowd, or behind a curtain or bulkhead. The first time Hark had tried to dismiss it as nothing but some mental phantom, brought on by boredom, and weariness, and the unsettling—and doubtless unfounded—rumors which Mehadi had brought to mind; but on subsequent occasions, it became harder and harder to dismiss the glimpses out of hand. There was *something* about one of the passengers which disturbed Hark, but he was left not knowing precisely what, or who, it was.

There was another Vector on the train. He and Hark had exchanged brief nods of greeting in the passageways, but hadn't spoken. Hark knew him vaguely, but couldn't recall his name; he used a different bond agent than Hark, and had been certified by another Vector service. In Hark's eyes, he was just competition for future employment, and so he kept his distance. The other passengers kept their distance from both of them, and so as they moved through the cars of the train they were like two swirling eddies in a stream, drifting momentarily near each other before being carried apart by the currents.

The other travelers knew that it was unwise ever to draw too near a Vector on the job—one never knew what they might have contracted, what strange sickness they might be transporting—but even in their off-hours Vectors were rarely engaged in social interaction. The perceived risks were just too great, and few were those who would brave even a few moments in close conversation with a Vector, on or off the job. The other passengers treated Hark and his fellow Vector with a respectful silence, always leaving a few feet of leeway in the corridors, or a few empty chairs around them on every side.

Hark, for his part, cherished the solitude, however brief or limited in scope. The other passengers, all of them Middle Caste, reminded him uncomfortably of his own father. If it hadn't been for his decision to become a Vector he'd have turned out just like them, just like his father, slaving away his whole life from one Corpus or another—Biophage, or Emuls, or L'Igase, to name only a few—just to afford his Vaxine subscription and regular security updates. Such was not for Hark. With the money he was owed by Emuls Corpus for his current bond, he'd be that much nearer to early retirement in the northern Alps, to live out the rest of his long days in relaxation.

It was just vapor, though Hark wouldn't admit it, even to himself. This idea of retirement was a fancy, a treasured dream that could never become reality. It was nice to think that he could retire to some cool seclusion in the mountains, his Vaxine thresholds turned to maximum, his body burning off any virus or pathogen that came his way, a warm-bodied beauty on his arm, on his bare arm, cheek to cheek and palm to palm, touching without any barrier between them. . . . But it would never happen. No Vector ever reached retirement. They were always lured back for one more job, one last plum assignment, the Corpus money too good ever to pass up, and that last assignment they never came back from, their fever racing, heartbeat failing, eyes rolling back in their heads as some unexpected side effect of the microorganism in their veins cooked the life out of them.

Hark was the last passenger to leave the viewing deck, driven indoors by the first splatters of an evening rainstorm, only in the gloaming making his way back to his berth.

Halfway to his chamber, Hark found himself in a darkened passageway, a shadowy figure blocking his path, bent low over an indistinct shape massed on the deck plates. The illumination was dimmed for the night, but when the figure looked up at Hark, he could see by the low glow from the globes overhead that the man's face was covered in strange scars or markings, giving him an inhuman, bestial appearance. There was something in the figure's outstretched hand, glinting metallic bright in the dim light.

A flash of lightning struck outside the window, painting the passageway in stark, gray-scale relief. A peal of thunder immediately followed, and with the bones of his rib cage vibrating from the deep rumbling, Hark saw that the indistinct shape on the deck plates was his fellow Vector, bent in an unnatural posture, his head almost entirely to one side with eyes wide and sightless, his neck bared.

There, on the pale band of white flesh above the collar, were two ragged slashes.

Hark froze, wishing that he had his fléchette pistol, the little steel darts tipped with a paralysis agent that could freeze a grown man in place in the span of three heartbeats. He always carried it on his travels, sensible protection well worth the high cost, but had never before found a need for it. Unfortunate, then, that on this first occasion, it was safely stowed inside his valise, in a tasteful leather holster, back in his berth.

There was a momentary tableau, the man with the scarred face looking up from his victim, a wicked two-pronged weapon in his hand, and Hark standing stock-still in the passageway, not sure how to respond. In the next moment the scarred-face man lunged to his feet, and the tableau was broken. Hark, heart pounding in his chest, turned and ran for all he was worth.

He didn't chance a look back, but slammed through the curtain out onto the deserted viewing deck. The rain was pelting now, Hark's jacket and pants immediately sodden and clinging, the drops stinging the bare skin of his forehead, the bare skin of his neck.

Hark reached the rear railing of the viewing deck, and glanced back over his shoulder, holding his breath. End of the line. The scarred-face man appeared at the curtain, the double-pronged weapon in a two-handed grasp.

Hark looked to the left and right. He had nowhere else to run, and the scarred-face man was getting closer with every sure step.

Taking a deep breath, Hark turned and grabbed the slick railing, his grip unsteady through sopping gloves, and vaulted awkwardly up and over, tumbling out into the dark, wet night.

The unkempt room was nestled deep inside an Under Caste hostel, in the shadow of the local offices of the Emuls Corpus, in some anonymous township halfway to the middle of nowhere. The lighting was inadequate, the ceiling leaked, the corridors were festooned with trash, and odd noises and odder smells drifted through the vents from the other rooms.

Still, Hark couldn't complain.

He'd been lucky to stumble out of the wet wilderness into any-thing resembling civilization, and as far as the hostel was concerned, he could scarcely afford a room anywhere nicer. He'd left his purse along with the rest of his wardrobe and possessions back on the train, safely stowed in his berth. He'd been forced to trade away his gold signet pendant in exchange for the room and board, and con-sidered even that high price a bargain, under the circumstances.

The hostel was built into the remains of an ancient office block, the furniture constructed from discarded computers, media systems, flat-screen LCDs, and other electronics, all made useless by the spread of electromagnetic-pulse weaponry and runaway self-replicating computer codes in an earlier century.

It was two days since Hark had been forced to flee the train, more than a day since he emerged battered and bruised from the wilderness, unsure whether he was safe or still the object of pursuit. He'd been immediately relieved to see the emblem of the Emuls Corpus cultured into the side of the one modern structure in town, and immediately dismayed to discover that the offices were closed for the duration of the Festivus holidays. He'd found the hostel a stone's throw away, and steeling himself against his natural aversion to the Under Caste, he'd procured a room.

His plan was to wait out the remaining holidays, until the Corpus offices opened, and then call on their security personnel to escort him the rest of the way to their main offices on the western coast. He would have to defray the expense from his regular fee, costing him a percentage of his retainer, but better to arrive intact and able to re-ceive payment than to be found dead in a gulley somewhere along the way, drained of blood and life alike.

The exsanguinator, Hark could only guess, must have been some sort of data thief, siphoning off secrets from the still-living bodies of Vectors and selling them at auction. Hark couldn't know for sure, but had to suspect that he had been pursued from the train, and that the data thief might be prowling the streets of this anonymous township even now, in search of Hark and the secrets he carried.

Though gratified to have reached sanctuary relatively unscathed, in his more bitter moments Hark reflected that it was only the threat of imminent and painful demise that forced him to go down amongst the Under Caste. Everyone of the Middle Caste in the township appeared to have left for the holidays, as Hark had caught no glimpse of any in the streets; not that it made much difference at the moment, as Hark was unwilling to leave the confines of the hostel unless absolutely necessary.

The threshold of "absolutely necessary," though, began to seem a movable goal the longer he stayed in the hostel. Hark had always been uncomfortable around the Under Caste, who could afford only pirated or secondhand Vaxines, or none at all. The corridors of the hostel he'd passed through had been filled with the smell of bleaches and disinfectants and smoky fires, as the inhabitants tried to sterilize their food, their clothing, their very environment, without success. The virulent strains of pathogens against which even the most rudimentary Vaxine was proof could destroy an unprotected body in a matter of days. All around him in the hostel Hark saw nothing but disease, decay, and death.

Destroyed faces, crawling with sores and pustules. Amputees. Children and adults missing parts of their skulls, or with their limbs fused into permanent hooks, or with their organs on the outsides of their skin. So many of them disfigured and deformed, either as the result of disease, or defect of birth, or side effect of biomedical experimentation, one of the few types of legitimate employment available to the Under Caste. The hostel was a squalid place, a kind of living graveyard, smelling of disinfectant, sickness, and decay.

When he had gone to the hostel's ablution chamber the first morning, he hesitated even to breath through his mask, holding his breath, his eyes squinted tight, as though pathogens might enter his body through the mere act of sight. By the nightfall of the first day, he was starving. He'd not eaten since the midday meal on the train, days before, and though his pendant had afforded him a place at the common table downstairs in the hostel, Hark could not bring himself to enter the dining chamber, much less sit at table and eat with these wretches.

By the last night of Festivus, Hark had no choice but to venture out into the streets, to find something, anything, to eat. If he didn't, he was sure he'd be too weak to climb from his cot the following morning.

Hark hadn't made it a dozen steps into the cool night air when he was confronted by two disfigured men just outside the curtain of the hostel. One of them was the scarred-face man from the train, while the other, a stranger to Hark, had a long, suppurating sore across his forehead, his eyes sunken in dark, greenish circles. They each had one of the double-pronged weapons in hand, glinting in the low light. They advanced on him slowly, one on each side.

"What do you want?" Hark demanded, with a bravado he scarcely felt.

"What you're carrying could save billions," the scarred-face man said, his voice sharp.

"I can't pay you that much," Hark said, trying to sound calm, "but I'm sure I can arrange some sort of annuity from the Emuls Corpus, or a generous stipend from my bond agent."

"Not billions in currency," shouted the man with the suppurating sore. "Billions of lives!"

"We don't want to hurt you," the scarred-face man said, "but we will if you force our hand. All we want is a few drops of blood." He gestured with the double-pronged weapon, which Hark realized in a moment of clarity was tipped with twin syringes. "All we want is the Panacea, and we'll let you go."

Hark stopped short.

"Is *that* what this is about?" Hark was exasperated, even faced with the weapon, and threw his gloved hands in the air. "Are you

160

deluded, insane, or ignorant? Which is it? I must know." He paused, and shook his head ruefully. "Panacea is a myth. It's like the water-fueled engine, or the Angel of Festivus. It doesn't exist. There's never been any such thing as a heal-all treatment, and there never will be."

The two disfigured men narrowed their eyes, and raised their syringe-tipped weapons higher.

"So we must do this the difficult way?" the scarred-face man asked.

"He's nothing but a tool of the Corpus, Barra" the other said. "Let's drain him and be done with it."

The two men circled around Hark, drawing ever closer.

Hark wished again that he had his fléchette pistol, wished he could feel the weight and security of it in his hand. With two well-placed darts he could be done with his attackers and safely on his way. But his pistol was lost to him, abandoned with his valise, too far away to be of any use.

That being the case, the rude club he'd made of the iron bar snapped from the hostel's barred windows would have to do.

The man with the suppurating sore was just within arm's length when Hark drew the iron bar from the folds of his jacket, and Hark sent it swinging into the man's forehead before he'd had a chance to react. As the man slumped to the dusty ground, the light gone out behind his eyes, Hark turned and sprinted down the darkened street. The scarred-face man paused but an instant to check on his fallen companion, and by the time he went to give pursuit, Hark was safely out of sight.

Hark passed the night huddled beneath a pile of refuse, sheltered in the lee of a ruined shopping complex. The night air was biting, even through the heavy wool of his suit, through the thick reinforced fabric of his gloves, so that when he shivered, he could attribute it easily to the cold, and not to fear. What had a professionally bonded Vector to fear from common data thieves, having already given them the slip? Much less thieves trying to locate the mythical cure-all. Panacea was a fable, a legend, and couldn't possibly exist.

Could it?

The following morning, Hark stood at the entrance to the Emuls Corpus offices, which loomed above the squalid township like an angel alighting momentarily on the roof of an abattoir. The Corpus offices, like all modern structures, were not built from manufactured materials, but grown. The walls and beams were made up of a hard, calciferous substance, the remains of continuous skeletal material secreted by tribes of aerobic coelenterate polyps as their home, cousins to those who once had produced coral reefs beneath the oceans. The polyps were engineered to produce the substance in patterns of colors and shades, guided by elevation and position in the earth's magnetic field, so that when the structure was complete, and the final remaining coelenterate gasped its last, the resulting structure was painted in dazzling hues, shapes and lines.

In this backwater town, the looming, iridescent towers of the Corpus offices were an interloper amongst the squat, ancient buildings of pitted concrete, rusted steel, and broken glass, one sign of civilization in the moldering remains of ancient culture. It rose hundreds of feet above the street level, slender spires and nautilus shells and helixed minarets, a High Caste's airship drifting in the light breeze from the mooring post on the highest tower.

Hark entered through the vestibule valve, and was greeted by an armed Middle Caste receptionist. Hark explained that he'd been hired to carry a cryptogen across the continent, but that he'd been waylaid. The security guard listened with a polite and professional mien, asked Hark to repeat his full name twice, and then sent a runner into the interior offices to fetch someone of authority.

In just a few moments the runner returned and, after a whispered exchange with the security guard, motioned for Hark to follow. At no point did the runner or guard draw within arm's reach of

Hark, and if either of them noticed the pungent aroma his clothing had absorbed from the refuse which hid him in the night, neither gave any indication of it.

Hark was led to a reception chamber, a wide, ovoid-shaped room where a High Caste officer of the Corpus sat on a dais constructed of interwoven coral vertebrae, a ring of guards positioned around him, each armed with a metal-tipped staff taller than they were. The High Caste officer, no doubt a younger son of the Corpus's ruling family, wore flowing, iridescent robes, his bare hands folded neatly in his lap, his long limbs—elongated and no doubt enhanced by high-priced augmentation—arranged artfully on the dais. His features were obscured behind an ornate alabaster mask, the height of High Caste fashion, with only his eyes visible, the telltale red hue of the irises a sure indicator of enhanced-vision traits. He looked languid in the oddly sculpted chair, but when he moved it was with a lightning speed that betrayed great reserves of mobility. Hark could not help but shrink slightly under the High Caste's gaze, feeling in his stomach the same fluttering unease he always did when received by a member of the ruling class.

A functionary entered the chamber from the opposite side, a Middle Caste bureaucrat who came and stood between Hark and the Corpus officer on the dais. Some midlevel manager, pudgy and balding, a self-satisfied smirk plied across his face. Hark was reminded instantly of his own father, who like this one before him had been bought and paid for by a Corpus, forever at the beck of the High Caste shareholder who held his leash.

"Your name is Jaidev Hark, a Vector on a bond with the Corpus of Emuls," the functionary said. He was stating facts, not asking a question.

Hark nodded.

"Then you are welcome, Jaidev Hark." The functionary regarded Hark with the kind of detached, dispassionate deference that most used when dealing with Vectors, the same expression Hark had seen on his own father's face when he'd once unwisely paid his family a visit. "But why do you appear at this branch of our Corpus, and not at the western offices, where you are expected?"

Hark drew a breath, feeling tension bleed from his shoulders. Safe within these walls, he began to relax, incrementally, for the first time in days.

"I find myself," Hark began, "unable to complete the terms of my bond without assistance, as much as it pains me to say. En route from the research offices of the Emuls Corpus on the eastern coast, I found myself waylaid by data thieves on the cross-continental rail. I fled the train, seeking refuge in this township, but the thieves had pursued me even here, and accosted me again this evening past."

The functionary nodded, his expression bland.

"And have you any notion why a Vector in the service of the Emuls Corpus might have come to the attention of these thieves?" the functionary asked absently. "Is there any suggestion that the sanctity of our data might have at some juncture been compromised?"

"None that I can perceive," Hark answered, shaking his head. "These seemed nothing more than deluded madmen of the Under Caste, killing wantonly, searching for the mythical Panacea."

The functionary, who had seemed about to interrupt Hark only a moment before, paused, a startled expression passing momentarily across his features like a cloud's shadow drifting across bare ground. He turned and glanced anxiously back at the Corpus officer.

The High Caste's manner, which had remained languid and still through the brief interview, immediately changed. He made a motion at the functionary, rose, and walked from the chamber, his retinue of guards remaining behind.

"Begin," the functionary said, looking to the nearest guard.

Without another word from the functionary, the guards turned to face Hark as one, the long staves in their hands raised and ready, murder in their narrowed eyes.

Hark's pulse thundered in his ears. He backed slowly away as the guards advanced. He was just a few steps away from the entrance to the chamber, but there was no chance he could turn and run before one of the staves knocked him off his feet. He would need a moment's grace to make an escape, and the guards seemed unlikely to grant him one.

The guards were almost close enough for the nearest to reach out and touch Hark with their staves, when Hark had a sudden inspiration. Without waiting another instant, he peeled the glove from his right hand and, reaching up, removed his face mask. Barefaced in public for the first time in half a lifetime, he held his gloveless hand out before him, palm forward.

"My Vaxine is disabled!" he shouted at the guards. "I am on the job!"

The functionary, at the far side of the room, blanched visibly and backed away, and the guards each reflexively took a step back.

Hark, not wasting the opportunity, turned and bolted for the exit, being sure to let his bare hand linger on the valve's leading edge before running through. Breezing past the security guard at the front vestibule, he burst through the outer valve into the open street, running for dear life.

There was no place in the township for Hark to hide, no convenient rubbish pile or ruined building sufficient to shield him from the eyes of the Emuls Corpus's security forces. Door to door, home to home, ruin to ruin they searched for the fleeing Vector, and Hark was driven farther and farther out, until he found himself miles out in the wet wilderness again, buried beneath a mound of moldering leaves and twigs, forced to subsist on roots and rainwater and what bugs he could catch in his two hands, until he felt the searchers had given up their pursuit and it was safe again to go abroad. Relatively safe, since they would never stop looking for him altogether, he knew; but if he kept to backstreets and sideways, he could escape their notice, for a time.

With one word, Hark was no longer a valued bond servant of the Corpus, and had become a dangerous element too threatening to let live. He'd seen that in the eyes of the High Caste officer, in the expression of the Middle Caste functionary. Hark had spoken one word, and immediately everything had changed.

One word.

Panacea.

Hark lurked in the shadows on the railway platform, the western terminus of the cross-continent line. In the warm, tropical night he sweated through the light fabric of his short-sleeved shirt, the hairs on his arm standing out in the humid, limpid breeze. He scratched the few weeks' growth of beard on his chin, and licked his lips in anticipation.

He had found Barra easily enough, the scarred-face man who had pursued him weeks before in the anonymous township. Hark had agreed to give Barra and his people what they wanted. As it happened, Hark hadn't been carrying the Panacea after all; or, at least, not all of it. He still bore the double-slit scars on his neck from their crude phlebotomic mechanism, but he didn't mind. He'd given them a few liters of blood, and gotten in return everything he'd demanded.

Hark was off the grid now. Not beholden to any Corpus, by oath or bond. With the help of the scarred-face man and his compatriots, Hark had disappeared into the Under Caste. The scars on his neck only helped to complete his look.

Hark had been working for the wrong side for years, without knowing. He was on the other side now, helping track down his fellow Vectors. Trying to find the pieces of Panacea. Trying to find the cure for aging, the cure to disease, an end to death. Panacea—an inexpensive treatment that would mean an end to sickness and infirmity in the human body. That it would also mean the end of the biomedical trade, and of the domination of the High Caste and the Corpus culture, was the reason that it had been kept a closely guarded secret for so long. It was only by accident that Barra, while submitting to biomedical experimentation in a Corpus research facility, had stumbled upon proof of the treatment's existence. Barra's search for the secret had become a hidden revolution, a clandestine crusade, of which Hark was now a part.

From the shadows on the railway platform, Hark saw Marika Mehadi climbing on board the eastbound train. He fingered the double-syringe-tipped device in his pocket. When he pulled his ticket out of his pants pocket, the texture of the paper was still strange and unfamiliar against his bare skin. Waiting for the rest of the Middle Caste travelers to board, Hark made his way to the lower-fare freight cars where Under Caste travelers rode in close quarters. Under cover of night, in a few days' time, he'd make his way into the Middle Caste compartments.

If Hark could convince Mehadi to willingly part with a few liters of blood for the greater good, that was fine with him; if she resisted, of course, well . . . he'd gotten to be a fairly good hand at that, too.

Louise Marley is a concert and opera singer turned SF and fantasy author. Her novel *The Glass Harmonica* won the Endeavour Award in 2002, and *The Terrorists of Irustan* was on the *Voya* magazine Best of 1999 list. Her most recent works are *The Maquisarde*, *The Child Goddess*, and the young-adult novel *Singer in the Snow*. Louise now writes full-time at her home in Washington state, and teaches adult and young-adult writing workshops around the country. She says that "Absalom's Mother" was a very painful tale to write. "As the parent of a twenty-one-year-old son in this frightening time, the specter of the draft keeps me awake at night. I grew up during the Vietnam War, and had convinced myself the insanity was behind us. I no longer know if that's true!"

ABSALOM'S MOTHER
Louise Marley

The dome is dark above my head as I trot down the narrow lane toward the storage depot. The air chills my neck. I'm a few minutes late, and I don't want the others to think my courage failed. It took all my strength to leave the peace of my home, my bed, my partner's warmth beside me, to rouse Carly with a whispered warning, to pretend to be calm.

As I round the last corner, I see through the gloom that the others are already gathered in the red-brick plaza beneath the steps of the storage depot. I slow my steps to pass through the line of women, counting. They are all there. Everyone is shivering with cold and with dread, as I am. Some of them speak in low, uneasy voices. Several speak my name in hushed tones. One or two faces are streaked with tears. I stop near the front, hugging my jacket around me.

I have not slept at all. Jem and I wept together last night, long into the darkness. We clung together, grieving, but even when I felt his tears on my shoulder I did not tell him what we planned. When he finally fell asleep, gripping my hand in his, I lay staring at the low ceiling of our residence cabin until it was time.

Keisha, by tacit agreement the leader of this . . . this . . . *thing* that we're doing, that we're attempting, Keisha jumps up to stand on the edge of a foamcast planter. She holds up one hand, pale in the gloom, and calls in a quiet, commanding voice, "This is it, my friends. Remember, we stand together; that's the important thing. The only thing. No one flinches; no one runs."

"Right, Keisha," someone calls. I turn and see Maria at the back, her arm around Jasmine. Jasmine keeps her face turned into Maria's shoulder.

"That's right," someone else drawls. I turn the other way, and see Ebony, tall and black and strong. My own skin is an indeterminate brown, but Ebony's skin is the true satiny black of an earlier age. I asked her once how she came by such pure blood, and she only shrugged, and said, "Lucky." Ebony looks like a soldier.

I don't look like a soldier at all. I'm small. My arms and shoulders are thin, and the shade of my skin comes from ethnicities nobody remembers now. But I'm as determined as Keisha is. As we all are. We have to be.

Unity is our only weapon.

Keisha gestures to me. "Come up here, will you, Vivi?"

"Okay." I move into the fourth position. My legs feel weak, and I'm shaking inside my jacket. I thrust my hands in the pockets so no one will see them tremble.

Keisha is second in line, and Ebony is right behind her. We determined all this, working in the communal kitchens, speaking out of the sides of our mouths as if we were prisoners. In a way, we are prisoners. Every community, even tiny, poor ones like ours, is subject to the power of Central Council. Central controls the air, the water, the clothes and food we import, the fabricated materials we export. It all comes from Central, along with Directives, and Rulings, and Resolutions, and Policies. And Recruitment Orders, which bring us here on this cold, dark morning.

First in our shivering line is Avery.

Avery, among us all, does not seem to be afraid. But then, Avery has a cabinet full of powerful drugs, pain relievers, tranquilizers, narcotics. The medics give her anything and everything they can think of, because they can't do anything else for her.

We all treat Avery with reverence. She volunteered to be first. When we all said, No, Avery, you're too ill, she insisted.

She said, when the Orders came from Central and we began to talk about this rebellion, she said, "I want my death to count for something."

Keisha said at the time, "Avery, they shouldn't take Johnny anyway, not with you so sick. We should tell them—tell them about you."

And Avery, in a faint voice, said, "They called them all, Keisha. They won't care. They don't care about us."

I look up again, to the very top of the dome. The light has reached it at last, a silvery, hesitant glimmer. The panels will pick it up, and the streets and squares of 78th Grange will brighten. By the time everyone comes out of their cabins to begin work, the dome will be warm. I wonder where we—all of us gathered here—where we will be by then.

Avery leans against one of the tall planters with her eyes closed. I look past her, up the steps to the doors of the storage depot. Silos and bolt rooms and parts storage facilities fill its two floors. At one side of the small lobby is a desk, with a wallscreen behind it. This is called the Extension Office, and it's usually empty. Central sends someone to sit behind the desk only when they've made a Ruling or issued a Directive. 78th Grange is so small, and produces so little, that we have no Councilor of our own. We have a proxy, but only one-half vote.

The storage depot is built into the curve of the dome right by the two northern access locks. The main lock opens directly into the

monorail. The other lock, leading outside, is for the people who repair the dome or the rails or the silo feeders, or inspect the vacuum-
growth filaments. From my position, fourth in line behind Avery, I
can see the cabinets beside the locks, where the vacuum suits are
stored. I can't read the signs from here, but I know what they say. I
grew up in 78th Grange, and all of us memorized those warning
messages before we learned to read. No one is to step into the
outside lock without a suit on, and the suit has to be thoroughly
checked by someone qualified, someone who knows how to be certain all the seals are sealed and the slender oxygen cylinders properly adjusted and connected. Thinking of the locks, and the
instructions I've known since babyhood, makes my heart pound. I
look away.

Keisha has left her place, and is working down the line, arrang-
ing us in descending order of courage, as she sees it. The most fearful will be at the end, probably Jasmine. Jasmine is terrified of
everything, but she can't help it. A lot of terrible things have happened to her. She says this is the worst.

Avery moans, and I hurry up the steps to stand beside her. "Avery, are you okay?"

Her eyelids flutter, and she rolls her head a little against the
foamcast.

"Avery," I say. "You could sit down for now. Until . . . until they
come."

She lifts her eyelids, and I see that her pupils are expanded so
much the brown irises are almost swallowed up. She laughs. "Oh,
Vivi"—breathlessly—"am I still here? I thought . . . I'm so stoned, I
thought I was already gone."

"Are you in pain, Avery?"

She shakes her head, and her dark hair catches on the trailing
vine in the planter. "No pain," she murmurs, and gives a high,
breathy laugh. "No, no pain at all."

I stay by her until Keisha returns, and then I move down two
steps to my place in line. I look out over the cramped square and

see that Keisha has put everyone in order. I count, to be certain they are all there.

Everyone is. Thirteen women. Mothers.

Central made a gross error, of course. If they had called only a few of our children, or even half of them, this would probably not have happened. Those whose children were safe would not risk themselves. Those who managed to have their children's names left off the list through influence, or bribery, or threats, or any of the things wealthy and educated and powerful people come up with, would never have come out to stand exposed in the square in the early morning. They would have no need.

But this is 78th Grange, and there is no power or wealth here. Central called all of them, every child of 78th Grange who was recruitment age. My own Carly had just reached it. We celebrated her eleventh birthday two months ago.

When the Order came down, flashed from Central to the Extension Office, Keisha had come around to read it to us. "In this time of crisis," she read, her voice tight with anger, "all citizens share the burden of maintaining the peace."

"What peace?" Ebony growled. We were all at work in the kitchens, stirring the great vats of soup, shredding the salad greens for dinner, stacking bowls and plates to be laid on the long tables. Only Avery was missing. She was too sick to work.

Keisha's eyes flashed at Ebony, and she kept reading. "Quotas will be met by all communities. The lowering of the age of induction, mandated by the Council to reduce frivolous deferments, will make it possible to maintain the current levels in the workforce while supplying the manpower needs of the militia for the foreseeable future. . . ."

Her voice went on, reading the entire Order, but I could no longer hear her. My heart pounded in my ears, and my knees turned to jelly. In fact, I think I collapsed, but I don't remember exactly. The next thing I remember clearly is Ebony holding me up with her long, hard arms and saying, "No. No. Don't worry, Vivi. They can't do this."

But they can do this. When the age of induction was lowered again, we heard there were demonstrations everywhere, people marching, people shouting their views on street corners, people chaining themselves to things or destroying government offices. Central Council responded by saturating the news with tales of dictators, torture, labor camps, shattered domes, poisoned water. There is always an enemy; there always has been. Enemies are as interchangeable as . . . well, as Councilors.

Carly was six, then, and I was busy with my work in the kitchen, where everyone has to take a turn, and the school, where I helped teach the little ones to learn fabrication techniques suited to their small hands. I let the news swirl around me, and prayed it would all pass.

Now I know you can't do that. It doesn't pass. It never passes. I don't know if all those horrible stories Central put about were true or not, but I do know that old people in power always send young, powerless people out to fight their battles for them. It has been true for millennia, and it doesn't change.

Until now. Until today, here in 78th Grange.

Because we agreed, we thirteen mothers. Because we have no dissenters.

The biggest problem was where to hide the children.

78th Grange has few hiding places. We live in nested cabins, crowded beneath the dome, with narrow streets too tight for anything but walking or cycling. And we decided not to consult the fathers, because we doubted there would be unity. Some would agree, no doubt, but some would not. Some people think Recruitment is a good idea. They agree that every community has to make sacrifices.

We were simply lucky that the thirteen of us, at this particular time, were of one mind. There were no arguments, that day in the kitchen, or the days following, when we whispered our questions, our ideas, and our plans.

The children are waiting, this morning, in the maternity area. 78th Grange has no doctor, of course. Letha is our midwife, and her Mark is one of the children on Central's list. There are no pregnancies in 78th Grange at the moment. No one goes in the maternity area unless they're delivering a baby. We worry about the children being unsupervised, but we are more worried about them being loaded onto the monorail and taken away from us.

We know how inducted children change. Militia training turns gentle, soft-eyed young people into weapons. It teaches them not to care, not to feel. To follow orders. Not to think.

Lowering the induction age, we are told, helps the children. They get an early start. They get an education. They learn to be independent, to rely on themselves. To be strong. But we know the truth.

First Central lowered the induction age to seventeen, a small change. Then they lowered it to fifteen, and then to thirteen. Finally, they dropped it to eleven. An eleven-year-old can't get a college deferment, or a marriage or pregnancy or essential-function deferment. Few eleven-year-olds have suffered injuries that can interfere with their service. They are, according to Central Council, perfect.

And so, as we stirred the soup vats, we decided we would not comply. We don't want our children twisted, molded into something fierce and hard. We didn't suffer through pregnancy and childbirth, the nurturing, exhausting years of babyhood, the worries of early childhood, to supply Central with weapons to fight its countless and unending wars. This is not a "current" crisis. This is a perpetual crisis.

And now as I look up at Avery, I see she has sunk to the cold concrete of the steps. Her forehead rests on her knees. Daylight begins to brighten the dome. Soon partners will be rising, wondering why the mothers have left their cabins so early. People will go to the kitchens, and there will be a buzz when they don't find us there. The citizens are expecting to come to the Extension Office to say good-bye to the recruits. When they come into the plaza, they will see us standing here, a line of women, waiting for the delegate from Central, but no children.

Jem, Carly's father, will understand immediately what we're doing. I dread seeing his fear, and the look of hurt on his face because I didn't tell him. I couldn't tell him.

There is no doubt in my mind that Jem would stand with me, if I gave him the chance. But we can't take the chance, we thirteen mothers. Our only power is in our unity.

Inside the dome, we don't hear the hum of the monorail's power pack as it approaches, but we can feel the vibration through our feet. I whirl, and watch it fly toward 78th Grange on its shining rail. It doesn't slow until the last moment, always looking as if it's about to plow right through the fused silica of the dome. The monorail is pulling five cars, and one of them—the middle one—is a passenger car. The lead car slides swiftly and neatly into the lock. We hear the snick and hiss of the seals as they secure themselves, and the lock opens. Keisha lifts Avery to her feet. Avery leans against her, her head falling back, her lips slack and her eyes rolling. Avery, at least, will feel nothing. Briefly, I envy her.

Every citizen of 78th Grange knows what exposure does to an oxygen-breathing being. There are pictures, and we've all seen them, hideous, terrifying pictures.

I am terrified now.

I stand stiffly, my arms folded. Jem will be along soon. I have to stand with the others, tell him nothing, and hope that later he will forgive me. If there is a later.

I am relieved to have the waiting be over, though my legs tremble so I'm afraid I might fall. The sun is up now, gleaming on the red bricks of the plaza, the gray cement of the steps and the foamcast of the planters, the varicolored cabin roofs. The delegate from Central emerges from the lock just as the first curious citizens, our partners, come up the narrow lane from the kitchens. I can hear a few voices, calling our names: "Ebony?" "Jasmine?" "Keisha?" And then Jem's sweet voice, dry with worry: "Vivi! Oh, Vivi. What are you all doing out here? Where's Carly?"

I turn briefly to Jem, kiss my fingers to him, and then turn forward again, facing the delegate. I drop my arms to my sides, and try to stand like a soldier.

I'll go, if they'll take me. If they'll give me a chance. I don't think they'll take me, or take any of us, but if they will, I'll do it. What I won't do is stand here, in the cramped plaza of 78th Grange, and watch Carly leave without me.

The delegate is a woman. She's not much taller than I am, but her body is square and strong-looking. She wears the militia uniform, green and brown, and a cap with a hard visor. She stares down at the line of thirteen women for a long moment, and we stare back.

"What's going on here?" she asks. Her voice is clear and carrying. She has a rather pleasant face. She's frowning, but she seems more confused than angry. "Where are my recruits?"

Avery, in front, is too far gone to answer.

Keisha speaks for her. Her voice is a little rough, and I know she's afraid, too. "We're right here," she says loudly. I hear a couple of the partners, standing in the lane watching us, draw noisy breaths.

The delegate looks at Keisha, and then at the rest of us, not understanding. "What are you talking about? Who are you?" She puts her fists on her hips, and for the first time she really looks like a soldier. I think she must be about my own age.

Keisha says, "We're your recruits, Sergeant." I wouldn't have known she was a sergeant. It's the sort of thing Keisha knows. "We're the recruits from 78th Grange."

The sergeant's chin juts at us. "Ridiculous. Where's your proxy?" She pauses, and takes a comm from her pocket to glance at it. "James, right? Joletta James. Where is she?"

We left Joletta in the maternity area, with the children. We slipped her one of Avery's drugs last night at dinner. Letha thinks she'll be out for another six hours.

Ebony shrugs. "She musta gone out for the day."

"I don't think so." Now the sergeant's spine stiffens. "Who's in charge here?"

"We are." This is Ebony again. She stands at her full height, which is impressive, and looks down her nose at the delegate. "We told you, Sergeant, we're your recruits."

The sergeant takes a step forward. "Look, folks . . . ."

Behind me I can hear the fathers calling out to us. "Maria! What's happening?" And Avery's husband, with tears in his voice, "Oh, God, Avery, what are you doing? You should be in bed."

A toddler, held in one of the fathers' arms, wails for its mother. I hear a muffled sob from somewhere behind me, Carrie or Tamlen or maybe Pat. I don't dare look. If I meet Jem's eyes, fixed on me, I'm afraid I, too, will weep.

"Look," the sergeant says again. "78th Grange has thirteen fine young recruits on the list for induction. Let's bring 'em out here, okay? And load 'em on the monorail. We'll process 'em at Central."

I feel Carrie press close against my back, and I know the line is tightening, pushing forward. This is good; it feels good. I feel stronger because of it.

Keisha says, "We're all you get today, Sergeant. Take us, or leave."

The sergeant's voice drops to a growl. "Look, ma'am, I'm not leaving without my recruits. I have the list right here." She brandishes her comm. "Central will send support if I need it, but that shouldn't be necessary." She puts the comm in her pocket and pulls her jacket away from her weapon. "Come on, now, citizens." She glances past our line to the others standing below us in the square, staring, muttering among themselves.

Maria's partner shouts up at her. "Hey! Maria! For chrissakes, where's Matty? I'll go get him now, if you'll just tell me . . . ."

Jasmine whimpers, and Maria tightens her arm around her. I can see Maria's lips press hard together. I know her partner to be a hard man. And a militia veteran.

"Come on, Maria. I served; why shouldn't he? What the hell are you doing?"

Suddenly Maria turns on her heel, making Jasmine stumble backward. "What am I doing?" Maria shouts, her voice shrill with tension. "I'm stopping my son from turning into you, that's what the hell I'm doing!"

Her partner stares at her, his jaw dropping. The men and women around him step a little away, as if he might explode. Jasmine sobs, and Maria gathers her into her arms again, patting her shoulder.

"Look," the sergeant calls now, loudly enough to reach everyone in the square. "Look, some of you people out there go find my recruits, and we'll just let this go. I understand this is an emotional moment, but you can all be proud, doing your duty, being patriotic."

Some of the workers turn and look at each other. Maria's partner growls something to the man next to him, who steps even farther away. Jem's eyes are wide, his head lifted to meet my gaze. I shake my head, just slightly, and he nods in return. I can feel his pain from where I stand. I will him to understand why I couldn't tell him about this, why we had to do this alone.

The sergeant's face has gone red. She pulls out her comm again. "Okay, people," she says in a rough voice. "You leave me no choice."

We know what will happen when she calls Central. They have all sorts of ways to force compliance. They can cut off services, shut down transportation, stop the imports we depend on. But all that takes time. She's more likely to call for the militia, who will come with more weapons than she carries, and who will search the whole dome. That takes time, too, time that we will use. Time is part of our plan.

Keisha helps Avery to her feet. She speaks in a low tone, but I am so close, I hear her perfectly. "Avery," she says. My heart twists in my chest. "Avery, sweetheart, it's time."

Avery's head droops, and her eyes are almost closed. "Now?" she whispers.

"Now."

The sergeant turns toward Keisha and Avery, taking a stiff step forward.

Keisha says, "This is it."

"Help me," Avery says. I can't breathe. I stare at her, and she seems to glow with purpose.

Keisha says, "I will." She loops Avery's arm around her neck. It's only a few steps to the access lock, but their progress is slow, Avery's legs rubbery, her steps uncertain. We press into a tight line, as disciplined as any militia platoon.

Tears burn in my throat, and I grip my hands together so hard the fingers hurt.

"Hey!" the sergeant calls. "Where do you think you're going?"

Keisha says over her shoulder, flatly, "Central. To be inducted."

Just as Keisha and Ebony said she would, the sergeant moves ahead of us, trotting, although we're moving at Avery's glacial pace. The sergeant blocks the monorail access lock with her body. Just as we expected.

Keisha leads Avery right up to it, as if she might shove the sergeant aside, as if she has no fear of the sergeant's weapon. The sergeant plants her feet, and seems, oddly, to grow taller as Keisha approaches.

Avery straightens her neck with a huge effort. Keisha steps behind her, her strong hands supporting Avery's back. We hold our breaths to hear what Avery says.

"Militia," she says, her voice thin and quavering. "Me. Not my child."

"Yeah," the sergeant says scornfully. "You'd make some soldier, ma'am."

Avery takes another step, her face right in the sergeant's.

The sergeant puts up a hand and shoves Avery backward, so that Keisha has to catch her with both arms. My throat closes tight. I know what will happen next. We all know.

The sergeant has the monorail access blocked. The other lock, the one beside the cabinets full of pressure suits, is to our left, the sergeant's right. It leads outside into near-vacuum, low oxygen, high carbon dioxide. Seven millibars of atmosphere. A person could survive perhaps half a minute. If the person held her breath. If the person didn't freeze before someone dragged her inside.

I tremble with last-minute doubts. We all have them, of course. But we swore to each other, in secret, passionately, sharing our strength in our weakest moments. And Avery—our first martyr—chose this.

She staggers to her left, pulls on the lever to open the hatch of the access lock.

It doesn't open. She hasn't enough strength. I hear, among the women, the intake of anguished breath.

Keisha, with a muttered oath, has to step up beside Avery to help her. The sergeant shouts something at them, something wordless, but she can't leave the lock she's guarding. Someone from the square shouts, too. It may be Avery's partner, I don't know. There's a little commotion, as if someone is trying to push forward, to get to her. I feel Carrie press even closer against my back, as if the crowd is pushing at our line. I brace my feet, try not to shove Ebony.

Avery is in the lock now, and as Keisha shuts the inner hatch, Avery puts all her body weight on the lever for the outer hatch. This one rotates smoothly. The hatch opens.

The sergeant, in a surprisingly feminine gesture, covers her mouth with both hands. Her weapon hangs at an odd angle before her face, dangling from her fingers.

I barely register this. I watch Avery, numb with shock and horror. It doesn't matter, now, how often we talked about how this would be, how we would feel. My stomach turns, and my throat closes.

Avery stumbles out of the hatch, casting one tragic look backward so that we see her face flood with color as the blood vessels blossom and break. She squeezes her eyes shut, and turns her face away.

I hear the anguished cry of Avery's partner just as Avery releases her breath. As she exhales, the precious air from her lungs freezes almost into a crystalline fog around her head. There will be no indrawn breath. There is nothing to breathe.

Twenty to twenty-five seconds. That's the time we have to suffer with Avery, the time we've been told it takes for a person to lose consciousness after exposure, if the person is not pulled back into the hatch, given oxygen, wrapped in thermal blankets. Avery's partner is sobbing, loudly, desperately, behind me. I can't look at him. I stare, transfixed, at Keisha's tall figure. She turns her back to the access lock, making it clear no one can pass her. Her courage stuns me.

And now everyone, including the sergeant from Central, falls silent, as Avery's body slips slowly to the icy ground beyond the curving wall of the dome. She sits, and then collapses to one side, a huddle of uninhabited flesh. Her partner cries, hopeless and helpless. With deliberation, Keisha turns her face to the sergeant.

"One," she says, biting off the word. She folds her arms across her chest.

"What the hell . . . ?" The sergeant stares at her, turns to stare at all of us. "What have you done? Why did she . . . I mean, my God!"

There is a long, awful silence, broken only by the weeping of Avery's partner. The sergeant waits for one of us to say something, to do something. We look back at her. My eyes burn, wanting to cry, to mourn Avery's passing. But we are not yet finished here.

The sergeant has her comm in one hand, her weapon in the other. She speaks swiftly, in an undertone, and listens to an answer, then speaks again. We know she is asking for orders, desperately asking for someone to tell her what to do. When she puts the comm away, she levels the weapon at Keisha. "No one else moves," she says. Tension makes her voice high and tight. "Central is sending the militia. You can't get away with this kind of crap."

"Crap?" Ebony cries. "Recruit us! We're ready to go!"

The sergeant doesn't lower her weapon, but her eyes swivel to Ebony. "I have my orders. I'm not leaving 78th Grange without the ch—without the inductees."

"You still have twelve of them, right here," Ebony says. "Take us, or go away."

"Can't do that, and you know it." The sergeant turns her eyes back to Keisha, whose hands are now on the hatch lever. "Don't move," she says. "That's an order."

Keisha, incredibly, manages. "What are you going to do, Sergeant?" she asks. "Kill me?" And she turns on her heel, deliberately, and reaches for the lever to open the lock again.

"Stop!" the sergeant orders. Her hand tightens on the little black weapon. Keisha sneers at her over her shoulder, and pushes the lever.

The sergeant's hand wavers, and her face crumples with indecision.

From the crowd behind our line, another shout rises, this time from Keisha's partners. Only Keisha, of all of us, could manage two partners. "No! Keisha, no!" they shout. She casts them a glance full of sorrow, shaking her head, and then steps into the access lock.

The sergeant discharges her weapon just as the hatch door closes. The narrowly focused beam flashes uselessly, glimmering on the silica surface. Keisha presses on the lever for the outer hatch, and wails arise from the crowd. I sense it pushing forward, men and women running to their partners, seizing their arms. Jem is beside me, his hands on my shoulders. I close my eyes and shrug him off. What I want to do is throw myself into his arms, run back to our cabin, return to our life. But it will not be our life without Carly. And Avery has made her sacrifice, the ultimate gesture. How can any of us dishonor that by giving in now?

"Vivi," Jem says urgently. "You're not going to . . . you wouldn't . . . ." I can't look at him. I'm watching Keisha.

The sergeant has left the monorail access and taken the three long steps to the other lock. She puts her hand on the lever for the inner hatch, but she is too late. The outer one is lifting up and out of its housing now, and the inner one won't open.

It takes much longer for Keisha, our friend and our leader, to die. She is so much stronger than Avery, and she's not ill. She turns to face us—no, to glare at the sergeant, who falls back a step, her mouth dropped in horror. We watch Keisha's eyes glaze, her face darken. She grimaces with the involuntary effort to hold her breath. It seems an eternity before, at last, her breath escapes her. Her mouth opens, and works, like a fish out of water. Her knees give way. Still facing us, she collapses, her forehead braced against the outer wall of the dome. I press the heels of my hands to my burning eyes. When I take them down, Keisha has toppled beside Avery, her eyes open, frozen, staring.

Behind me someone is speaking in a high, clear voice. As I watch the cloud of Keisha's last breath dissipate, I listen with disbelief as Jasmine, quiet, anxious Jasmine, orders the citizens of 78th Grange to step back, to leave us alone. Keisha's partners, who have run forward to the dome, slump against it now, just opposite where she has gone down. The sergeant, her hands hanging, her weapon pointed at the ground, stares dumbly at the two bodies outside.

Ebony steps to the top of the stairs, and the rest of us take a step forward too. There is a steady rush of sound around us, some sobs, some curses. Most of our citizens are shocked into silence. Ebony shouts, "Two! How many more, Sergeant?"

When the sergeant turns to face her, I feel a spasm of sympathy. The woman's eyes are huge, her face gray with shock. She must have expected an entirely different job today, a monorail trip with thirteen frightened children. She was unprepared to watch two women commit deliberate suicide. "Look," she says, her voice breaking. She has to clear her throat and try again. "Look, this doesn't do any good. I'm nobody, I'm just following orders, and no one will believe—" She breaks off, and makes a shaky gesture that includes the bodies outside, Keisha's two partners, weeping on each other's shoulders. "Who would believe you'd do this? Please, citizens . . . no more! Please!"

At that very moment I become aware that Jem, my Jem, is recording everything. He's standing on the edge of the planter, where Keisha stood to call us to order, and he's running the little recorder we use when there are events to report to Central. It's kept in the proxy's office, usually. I don't know how, or when, Jem got hold of it, but everything it records is automatically received at Central. I wonder if anyone is watching.

The sergeant looks up at Jem. She turns, if possible, even paler than before. "Give me that," she says hoarsely. Once again, she lifts her weapon, though her hand is shaking so badly I doubt she can aim it.

"Jem," I warn, but he gives me one of those dark, close looks I know so well.

He has the recorder balanced against the foamcast of the pillar, snugged between his shoulder and his jaw. "You have to let me do this, Vivi," he says. "Carly is mine, too."

The sergeant is clearly confused. Ebony has already taken a step toward the access lock, and the weapon swings toward her, and then, wavering wildly, back to Jem. "Stop," she croaks. "Please, give me that. You'll ruin me."

I cry, without meaning to, "No!"

Several other men step forward, as if to follow Jem's example, but Ebony throws up her arm, and it is her turn to shout, "No!"

Jem's eyes flicker at the weapon. I can see the amber flash, then the green, as it fastens on him. The sergeant's hand shakes, and the light turns amber again as she loses her target.

Ebony takes another step. The noise from the square intensifies, cries and calls, and our line of mothers is swallowed up by citizens pressing forward, trying to interfere, to stop us, to stop the sergeant. My heart flutters. It is all just as Keisha said it would be, noisy and confused and frightening. She had predicted all of it.

Except for Jem.

The sergeant sees Ebony approaching, and her thoughts are as plain as if they were written across her face. Two women dead already. Another about to commit suicide. And one man, a recorder on his shoulder, sending it all to Central.

"Jem! Stop! Come down!" I cry. He refuses, a short, sharp shake of the head. And I know why.

I am fourth in line. If Ebony succeeds in following Avery and Keisha, if the sergeant doesn't give in, I will be next.

The sergeant demands, "What is it you want? What do you want me to do?" Her voice has gone shrill.

Ebony stops where she is. "Take us as your recruits, or go away," she says.

"I can't!" the sergeant wails. "If I go away, they'll just send some-one else, you know that! The Recruitment Order—"

"You can't have them." I am startled to hear my own voice, usu-ally rather soft, ring out across the square. "We decided, all of us to-gether. You can't have our children."

"But I can't take *you*!" the sergeant cries. She waves the weapon around, at me, at Jem, at Ebony.

Ebony takes another step, right into the sergeant's face. Ebony is a head taller, her shoulders broader, her arms longer. She stiff-arms the sergeant to one side, and reaches for the hatch lever.

The sergeant points her little weapon at Ebony, but Ebony only laughs, a bitter sound that grates on my bones. I ache with tension. Ebony leans on the lever.

Jem shouts, from his perch, "How many more, Sergeant?"

As the hatch opens, the sergeant falls back a step. She shakes her head, a little wordless sound escaping her as Ebony steps into the lock and the hatch closes behind her. Someone screams, "No! Stop her!" The sergeant shakes her head again, and groans.

Jem shouts again. "How many?"

The sergeant whirls, pointing her weapon at him. The recorder hums, pointing back at her. Her hand on the weapon steadies, and the amber light goes red.

"Jem!"

She fires.

They trained her for this. I suppose she was an inductee, too, though she may have volunteered. There are those who volunteer for the militia, and I have never understood why. Perhaps they simply want to get away from their homes, travel, live more exciting lives than they can in the granges. Or perhaps they like to use weapons, to play war games . . . to kill.

Jem freezes, and the recorder falls from his shoulder. His face goes white, and then slack. Slowly, slowly, he crumples, and tumbles from the planter's edge to fall on the cement with a great sigh. The sergeant, his killer, whimpers as she lowers her weapon.

Bedlam erupts around me.

"Jem!" I scream. My voice is lost in the tumult that rises from the plaza. Men rush forward, and some women. Ebony's partner pulls open the inner hatch door before she can push the lever on the outer one, and he drags her over the sill and out of the access lock. Two strong men lift Jem's nerveless body from the cement, and carry him past me down the steps. I almost fall, but someone, one of the other women, holds me with her arms around my waist We try, all of us, to hold our line, but we are buffeted by the rest of the 78th Grange citizens, everyone shouting, crying. I want to go after Jem, but I hold my place. I know it's useless, in any case. Those weapons—the ones they expect our children to use—deal certain death.

I want to weep for my partner, my best friend, but there is no time.

Ebony leaps up to the planter where Jem had stood before. She has the recorder in her hands. She lifts it to her shoulder. Bit by bit, the square falls silent.

The sergeant spreads her hands. "Listen to me! I'm only following orders! These are my orders!"

"Go home, Sergeant." This is Maria; I know her deep voice. "Go back to Central and tell them we refused."

"You can't refuse!" the sergeant whines. Her face is a mask of shock and revulsion. "No more, please! My god, three people are dead here!"

"How many of our children would be dead?" Maria shouts.

"Go home," Ebony repeats, and the rest of the citizens shout it, too. "Go home! Tell them! Go home!"

The crowd bulges, surges toward the sergeant, past our diminished line of women. She cowers back against the curving wall of the dome, her weapon wavering around, trying to choose a target. I think, This could have been Carly, firing at her own people, and I experience a spasm of sympathy for the sergeant.

Our citizens stop short of her position. She stares at them, white-faced, one hand at her neck. Then, with a hopeless cry, she thrusts her weapon into its holster, and backs into the access lock to the monorail. The hatch closes behind her. For a long moment she stares out at us, and then she throws a switch, and the monorail cars, in reverse, begin to move.

Ebony is still recording. Sooner or later someone at Central will see these images. What will they do? Can we resist the next wave that will come, and the next? We don't know. But our citizens gather around us, stand by us. We stand together, we remaining eleven, with our partners and friends, and we watch the monorail cars disappear over the horizon. Ebony records until it is gone, and then switches off the machine.

And then we hear a new sound, the sound of running feet on the bricks. They're coming, released at last from the maternity center, dashing up the narrow lane with the strength and energy of youth. Our children.

The mothers turn with cries of gladness. Ebony commands, "Don't let them see!" Several men hurry into vacuum suits, to go out to retrieve the bodies.

I see Carly, dark hair flying, eyes wide and dark with fear, and I rush to her.

The militia will return, of course. Central can't let 78th Grange defy the Recruitment Order. More soldiers will come next time, and they'll be ready. No element of surprise.

I look above Carly's head and see Ebony with the recorder

cradled in her arms. Jem's last gift to us is the record of what happened here this morning.

Ebony's eyes meet mine, and she nods as if we have already spoken of what to do, how to disseminate the recording, to spread the word of what thirteen mothers did in 78th Grange. Thirteen mothers, and one father, who refused to give up their children.

Central will punish 78th Grange; we know that. They will find a way. But something has changed here today, something that can never change back. A precedent has been set. Obedience will no longer be automatic.

I squeeze Carly tight, and we cry together. I hope she will understand, someday, why we did what we did. And I hope she will forgive me for being the one who's still here.

Kevin J. Anderson is the author of over ninety novels, many of which have been national and international best sellers. He is best known for his *Dune* prequels cowritten with Brian Herbert, a new series of thrillers with Dean Koontz, and his original epic science-fiction series, "The Saga of Seven Suns," *Hidden Empire*, *A Forest of Stars*, and *Horizon Storms*. He dictates his fiction into a tape recorder while out hiking. This story was written on a twelve-mile hike in the canyons of eastern Colorado, where Kevin went to see the largest collection of fossilized dinosaur footprints in the world.

JOB QUALIFICATIONS
Kevin J. Anderson

Candidate Berthold Ossequin—the original—never made a move without being advised or cautioned by his army of pollsters, etiquette consultants, and style experts. Whether in public or in the privacy of his family estate, his every gesture and utterance was monitored. The avid media waited for Berthold to make the slightest mistake.

Elections would be held soon, and he must be absolutely perfect if he wanted to become the next grand chancellor of the United Cultures of Earth. According to surveys, he did have a slight lead over his opponent, though not enough to inspire complete confidence.

Berthold sat in an overstuffed chair that vibrated soothingly to calm him as he prepared to give a dramatic and insightful speech that his team had scripted for him. From rehearsing the speech before test audiences, the candidate knew where to modulate his voice and which points to emphasize in order to guarantee the strongest emotional impact.

Two young women, one at each hand, worked vigorously to trim his cuticles, file his nails, and give him that perfectly manicured appearance. A stylist worked with his bronze-brown hair and fixed every strand into place. Dieticians made careful recommendations about the foods Berthold should eat. Style experts met for at least an hour each evening to plan the candidate's wardrobe for the following day. No one could ever find fault with his appearance.

His stomach ached from eating too large and too rich a meal the night before, against the advice of his dieticians. He reminded himself to be careful with his facial expressions today, since a twinge of indigestion might show up as an inexplicable frown.

Berthold glanced up from the speech notes at his chief adviser, who waited beside him. "How are the others coming, Mr. Rana?"

Rana nodded. "Precisely on schedule, sir. The others will be ready when they become necessary for your campaign."

The lash struck with a bite of electrical current that produced a fiery sting. Though the high-tech whip caused no actual harm, Berthold 12 felt as if his skin had been flayed. More misery, the same as the day before, and the day before that.

Fingernails cracked and bleeding, he stumbled under the heavy rock he carried while the hot sun pounded down. He could smell rock dust and his own sweat, heard the impatient shouts of the guards and the groans of other slave-prisoners. His head ached, and Berthold 12 drove back the myriad questions that hammered through his mind. Why was he here? What had he done? The injustice burned like acid within him. *Why do I deserve this?*

Up and down the winding jagged canyon, layered limestone walls crumbled like broken knives. Work teams moved sluggishly, carting loads of quarried stone. Berthold 12 knew that machinery existed to do this sort of work; robots and automated conveyers could have taken away the rock. But this labor site wasn't about efficiency; it was about misery and punishment.

When the electrical whip snapped again across his shoulder

blades, Berthold 12 dropped the rock and collapsed to his knees. The guard's hover platform came closer, and the armored man loomed over him. Beneath the polarized helmet, Berthold 12 could see only the guard's chin and a smile that showed square white teeth. "I can keep whipping you all day if that's what you want, prisoner."

"Please! I'm working as hard as I can." His throat was raw, his body a living mass of aches. "I don't even know why I'm here! I don't remember anything . . . but this."

"Perhaps you committed the crime of amnesia." The guard chuckled at his joke, then threatened with the electrical whip again. "If your crime was bad enough that you blocked all memory of it from your head, then you probably don't want to remember."

Berthold 12 used almost all his reserves of energy just to get back to his feet. He picked up the heavy limestone slab before the guard could lash him again. He could not recall any day that hadn't been this litany of labor and torture. He didn't know when this awful part of his life would end.

The greasy smells and comfortable bustle of the Retro Diner always made him feel at home. Berthold 6 stood by the heat lamps, adjusted his stained white apron, and pulled out a few guest checks. He quickly added up the totals while the short-order cook slopped extravagant nostalgic breakfasts onto warm plates and set them on a shelf. Low-carb pancakes and waffles, minimal-cholesterol eggs, reduced-fat bacon and sausage: Such dietary innovations had made the traditional American breakfast into something the trendy customers could once again consume with great gusto.

The Retro Diner, modeled after popular eating establishments of the mid–twentieth century, had silver and chrome fittings, stools and booths upholstered with red Naugahyde, table surfaces covered with speckled Formica. The menu featured re-creations of classic products. Many patrons got into the spirit by dressing up in old-fashioned costumes and smoking noncarcinogenic cigarettes.

The place had a neighborly feel to it, a celebration of more innocent times. Berthold 6 felt right at home. He wouldn't have wanted any other job.

Carrying his loaded tray, Berthold 6 made a slight detour to snag the pot of coffee—weak, bitter, regular coffee, not one of the dramatically potent gourmet blends. "Here comes some morning cheer for you and your family, Eddie."

"Hey, Bert," said the jolly old man lounging back in his usual booth. "The waitresses around here are getting uglier every day."

"Yeah, but the waiters are certainly looking fine."

As the man grinned at the good-natured response, Berthold 6 delivered a stack of strawberry pancakes topped with a swirl of whipped cream, which looked like the eruption of a fruity volcano. He gave a cherry cola to the freckle-faced boy who sat next to his grandfather, refilled coffee cups around the room, then scooped dirty dishes from an unoccupied table into a bus tub.

Berthold 6 enjoyed working with regular folks. He liked serving people. He didn't earn much money, but enough to get by (though he wished some of his customers wouldn't *tip* like it was still 1953). He'd had a busy shift today, and tomorrow was his day off. Since he had no major plans, he thought he'd spend time with a few friends, talking, drinking beer, maybe watching sports or playing a game or two. Berthold 6 wasn't unduly stressed with the nonsense of unattainable goals or unrealistic ambitions. He was just an everyday guy, working an everyday job. A simple life.

"Order up!" the cook called with a clatter of dishes as he set the next breakfast under the heat lamps.

Before he was escorted off to a glamorous banquet, Candidate Berthold received Mr. Rana in his dressing chambers. The chief adviser brought documents for him to approve and sign. "This will take only a few moments, sir."

Berthold glanced down at the papers, shuffling from document to document. "Each one needs a signature?"

"Yes."

"Have they all been read for me?"

"Yes. And all necessary changes have been made."

"And do I agree with everything they say?"

"The statements are very much in line with your platform, sir." Rana formed a paternal smile. "You are, however, welcome to read any of them you like—in fact, I encourage it. The experience would be valuable for you."

Candidate Berthold gave a dismissive wave. "That won't be necessary. I'm already tired of the incessant paperwork, and I haven't even been elected yet." He began to laboriously sign each one. "I'll have plenty of time to learn after I get into office."

His head felt as if it would explode from so much information, but his passion for the material did not wane. His brain swelled with facts until all the bones of his skull—twenty-two bones in all, fourteen facial bones, eight cranial bones—seemed to pry apart.

For years Berthold 17 had been studying all aspects of medicine, from surgery to physical therapy to microbiology to antiaging research. Even with proven teaching aids and somatic memorization devices, he struggled to remember the components of the human body and all the diseases and maladies that could afflict it.

He would be taking his exams in three days. His future depended on his performance for those vital hours.

Not that he had any doubts. He had been born for this. The prospect was daunting, but he always liked challenges. Upon first entering medical school, Berthold 17 made up his mind to become one of the best doctors ever. The higher the hurdles, the more effort he put into meeting them. He took great satisfaction in a reward that he'd *earned*. He had painted his own finish line and would never look back over his shoulder until he had crossed it. "Good enough" was not in his vocabulary.

Berthold 17 hit the books again, studying, studying. It would be a long night. . . .

Meanwhile, in another campus library in another state, Berthold 18 sat surrounded by legal tomes, equally convinced that he would pass the upcoming bar exam with flying colors.

They were all dying of ebola-X.

Berthold 3 could do nothing to save the afflicted villagers, but he forced himself to remain at their sides and comfort them in their final hours. He prayed with them, he listened to them, he soothed them as best he could. Not being a doctor, he was unable to do anything else . . . and even the doctors couldn't do much.

Ebola-X, a particularly virulent strain of the hemorrhagic plague, had been genetically engineered by a brutal African warlord who, upon being deposed, had unleashed it among his own population. *As if their lives weren't already difficult enough*, Berthold 3 thought.

The villagers had impure drinking water, no electricity, no schools, no sanitation. Thanks to a persistent drought, almost certainly caused by the government and its shortsighted agricultural policies, the locals had lived on the edge of starvation for years. Immune systems and physical strength were at their nadir. When the ebola-X arrived, it mowed down the village population as easily as if it were a jeep full of machine-gun-bearing soldiers. The thought of their situation tugged at his heartstrings. How could a person hold so much pain?

The hot and stifling hospital tent reeked with the stench of sweat, vomited blood, and death. Berthold 3 still heard every gasp, every moan, every death rattle. He sat quietly on a wooden stool, looking at the strained, pain-puckered face of a young mother. He read soothing passages aloud from the Bible, but he didn't think she could hear him or even understand the flowery English words. But he stayed with her anyway, changing the moist rag from her forehead, holding her shoulders when she needed to roll over and vomit.

The woman seemed to know she was dying. She had communicated with him about her three children, and Berthold 3 promised to look after them. He brushed her wiry hair, cooling her forehead again. He didn't have the heart to tell her that the children had died two days earlier.

Exhausted medics moved around him like zombies. They had too little medicine, certainly nothing effective against this epidemic. Berthold 3 tried to take as much busywork from the doctors as possible; he felt a calling to do his part, any part, so long as he helped these people. He had some first-aid training, but the bulk of his schooling had prepared him to be a missionary, not a medic. Perhaps if he'd known ahead of time, Berthold 3 would have learned more practical skills. Even so, he wouldn't have turned from this obligation. In his heart he wanted to be here, wishing only that he could ease their suffering more effectively.

The dying woman reached out, her hand extended upward as if trying to grasp the sky. Berthold 3 took it in his own, folding his palms around hers and pressing her clenched fist against his chest so that she could feel the beating of his heart. She breathed twice more, arched her back, and then died.

Berthold 3 said a calm prayer over her, then stood. He had no time to rest, no time to grieve. He dragged his wooden stool over to the cot of the next patient.

Red tape. Bureaucracy. Incomprehensible forms in triplicate. Revisions to revisions to procedures that had already been revised repeatedly.

Job security.

Berthold 10 could not pretend his job was interesting; nor could he console himself with the thought that it was necessary. But it was a career, and he was good at it. Few people were so careful or detail-oriented; some of his coworkers called him anal-retentive.

He sat in a small cubicle like thousands of others in the main governmental office building for the United Cultures of Earth. Berthold 10 processed forms, input data, tracked regulations, and submitted comments and rebuttals to his counterparts in rival departments of the government in other cities around the world.

He was content to be sifting through paperwork in his own tiny cog in a single component of the sprawling wheels of government. It was good to have an understanding of how the details worked, instead of just the Big Picture, which the career politicians saw. Berthold 10 had no aspirations of running for office or being a great leader. He kept his sights on a shorter-term desire for an increase in pay grade. And he was sure to get it, with only a few more years of diligent service.

When the Urgent communiqué appeared in his IN box, Berthold 10 didn't at first pay special attention. Urgent matters went into a separate stack, and he generally made an effort to take care of them first. But when he noticed that this message was addressed to him personally, from the office of the Candidate, he read it with puzzlement, then amazement.

He was summoned to the Candidate's mansion at a specified time and date. Berthold 10 looked around his drab cubicle at the never-changing piles of never-changing work. He didn't know what the Candidate wanted to see him for, and the letter did not explain. He smiled. At last his life was about to become more interesting.

With Mr. Rana beside him to operate the apparatus, Candidate Berthold cradled the head of the final clone in his lap. The man still twitched and struggled—Berthold had forgotten which number this was—but the clutching fingers could not remove the electrodes and transmitters pasted onto his temples and forehead.

"I'm glad this is the last one," the candidate said. "It's been an exhausting day."

One of the clones had struggled violently when the guards brought him in, forcing them to break his forearm. The snapped ulna—ah, the medical knowledge was coming in useful already!—had been unforeseen, but wasn't necessarily a bad thing. In his pampered life Candidate Berthold had never experienced a broken bone; now, after absorbing the clone's experience, he knew what it felt like.

Memories and thoughts continued to drain out of the last clone's mind like arterial blood spurting from a slashed throat. The candidate held his duplicate's shoulders, felt everything surge into his own brain. What a difficult and painful life this one had lived! But the experiences certainly built character, giving him a firm moral foundation and impeccable resolve. It would be an excellent addition to Berthold's repertoire. Each detail made him more electable.

Since worldwide leaders guided so many diverse people, the citizens of the United Cultures of Earth demanded more and more from their rulers. To win a worldwide election, a candidate needed to demonstrate empathy for a multitude of different tiers of voters, from all walks of life. He had to be both an outsider and an insider. He had to understand privilege, to grasp the overall landscape of the government as well as the minutiae of how the bureaucracy worked. He was expected to have a passion for helping people, a genuine heart for the common man, and a rapport with celebrities and captains of industry.

Such expectations were simply impossible for a single human being to meet. Fortunately, thanks to the mental parity of clones, men such as Berthold Ossequin—and quite certainly all of his opponents—could live many diverse lives in parallel. The clones were turned loose in various situations, where they gathered real-life experiences that went far beyond anything Candidate Berthold could have learned from teachers or books. . . .

The last clone spasmed again, and his face fell completely slack, his mouth hanging slightly open. His eyelids fluttered but remained closed. A few final, desperate thoughts trickled into Berthold's mind.

With a satisfied sigh, he peeled off the transmitter electrodes and motioned for the guards to carry away the limp body. All eighteen of the clones were now vegetables, empty husks wrung dry of every thought and experience. The comatose bodies would be quietly euthanized, and a newly enriched candidate would emerge for the final debates before the elections.

Berthold stood from his chair, completely well-rounded now, full of vicarious recollections, both tragic and pleasant. The chief adviser looked into Berthold's eyes with obvious pride. "Are you ready, Mr. Candidate?"

Berthold smiled. "Yes. I have all the background I could possibly need to rule the world . . . though once I get into office, we may decide to continue my education in this manner. Are there more clones?"

"We can always make more, sir."

"There's no substitute for experience."

Berthold stretched his arms and took a deep breath, feeling like a true leader at last. He issued a sharp command to his staff. "Now, let's go win this election."

Paul Melko's contribution to *Live Without a Net*, "Singletons in Love," was selected for the *Year's Best Science Fiction, Twenty-first Annual Collection* and has since spawned two sequels, both appearing in the pages of *Asimov's Science Fiction Magazine*. Every year, he participates in the Blue Heaven Novel Writers Workshop on Kelly's Island in Lake Erie. He lives in Ohio with his wife and two children. He grows corn in his garden in this universe, but not, he notes, as successfully as he'd like. I'm always delighted to have Paul in my anthologies, and this occasion is no exception.

THE TEOSINTE WAR
Paul Melko

The cluster of poodle-skirted sorority girls gave me a vague smile when I sat down beside them. I liked the way the skirts' material kept rising up on the poofy slips beneath them, exposing bobby-socked calves and saddle shoes. The girl I had my eye on was tall, blond, and curvy. She met my gaze and my daemon pinged to tell me she'd accessed my site. Then the smile turned cold. Apparently minority grad students didn't meet her standard. At least I got her name—Beth Ringslaught—when she pinged me. But that was all I was going to get. The rest of the girls turned away; they were probably hooked into a local IRC, and Beth had shared my CV with the rest of them. I leaned back in my chair and sighed.

Dr. Elk strode in, a wild pile of paper under one arm and a teacher's stick in his hand. He tapped the teaching computer with his stick and the lights dimmed.

"Class! Welcome to your senior thesis! I'm Dr. Elk, and I'm as excited about Thesis as all of you are. Our topic this year is 'Factors of Old World Imperialism.'" Elk was a tall, thin man, his dark hair starting to fade to gray. He had been my adviser—no doubt we were teamed up by some politically correct wonk because of our similar genetic heritage—when I was in the history department, but I'd not talked with him for a year, not since I'd moved to engineering my junior year.

"Why did European culture eradicate every New World culture it came into contact with? Were Europeans intrinsically smarter? No! Did they have God on their side? I doubt it!" He slammed his notes on the word *God*, and the poodle girls jumped. I'd known it was coming; his lectures went back to the aughts.

My mind began to drift, watching the clock tick. I'd heard this lecture a half dozen times since my freshman year. Professor Elk had asked me to audit, and possibly TA, the senior thesis class, so I signed up for it, but never with any more intention than to check out the women in the class. I glanced around. Slim pickings among the rest of the history seniors. I looked over at Beth; the fabric poodle on her skirt was watching me, panting. Nice effect. Maybe one more try, I decided.

"Were they just better?" Dr. Elk picked up a piece of chalk and wrote a word on the board, punctuated by dull clicks. "No, of course not."

"They had germs," I whispered to Beth. She glared at me.

"What they had that was better was G-E-R-M-S. Germs. Centuries of city life had turned their cesspool cities into disease incubators. Those city dwellers that survived to breed were slightly more resistant than the ones who clogged their cemeteries. The New World had nothing like it. Pizarro was no better than Atahuallpa. His forefathers had just been lucky enough to have a slightly higher-than-average immunity to small pox!"

"How about some dinner?" I whispered to Beth.

My daemon beeped that a class-one harassment complaint had been lodged against me. The poodle bared its teeth.

"By the end of this year, we will have expanded this idea of Old

World disease conquering the New World. We will have built a hypothesis and tested it. And we will prove once and for all that the exploitation of the New World by the Old was a fluke, a whim, a side effect of barbaric living conditions and chance."

I yawned. Elk would have to find himself another TA. There were too many other classes I needed to take, and I wasn't interested in his hypothetical world—probably some world simulator his grad students wrote—in which the New World tribes beat the imperialist dogs of the Old World. That's why I dropped history in favor of engineering; I wanted to play with real things in the present, not guesses from the past. I slipped out of class, avoiding eye contact with Elk, and headed to the administration building for a quick add-drop.

The doorbell wouldn't shut the hell up, no matter how many times I folded my pillow through four-dimensional space. I tossed it aside and stumbled to the door. I kicked aside a pizza box, sending it sailing into my CD collection. The thermo text didn't budge, and I hopped the rest of the way, holding my throbbing toe.

"What the fuck?" I said, opening the door.

"Ryan Greene?"

About the same time my reptilian brain had determined that a reproduction-age female was standing in my doorway, my daemon had informed me it was Beth Ringslaught, the poodle-skirted cutie from Elk's senior thesis class, who'd dropped a class-one harassment memo on my ass. My boner flagged.

"Oh, it's you."

She didn't have a poodle skirt on today. She was wearing tight-fitting riding pants that hugged her calves, making her look like she had marathon runner legs. My reptilian brain stirred, then went back to sleep.

"What do you want?" I asked, leaning on the door, scratching my nuts.

It didn't faze her. "Professor Elk asked me to come see you. He wants you to re-add his class." Too much sun was beaming down on the apartment courtyard and its leaf-filled pool. I leaned my head against the door frame.

"Why?"

"He needs your help, he said."

"Listen, I'm not interested in being his Native American poster boy. You seniors just blithely run your sims and make the world a pretend-happy place. I'm not interested."

She shrugged. "Don't take it out on—"

"Just like you aren't interested in a guy like me, a poor minority grad student."

She blinked, her eyebrows slowly rising, her cheeks flushing.

"What are you talking about?"

"The way you and your poodle friends shut me down in class the other day. It's clear you think talking with me is slumming."

Her mouth crooked into a half smile. "Your site says you're dating a Miss Janice Huckabee."

"Your daddy— What?"

"Your site says you're in a monogamous relationship."

"Oh," I said, feeling the heat on my face. "That's out-of-date, I guess." Janice had dumped me at the end of senior year, when I took the grad-school gig instead of the Buckell Chemical job on St. Thomas. She hadn't wanted to date a poor grad student either, though the reception her parents had given me when we drove up from Columbus to Lansing for Christmas break might have had something to do with it.

"As attractive as you may have *seemed* last week, the fact that most of us poodle girls would like a monogamous, dedicated boyfriend eliminated you as a candidate quickly." She turned and added over her shoulder, "I'll let Dr. Elk know your answer."

I watched her go, noted the lack of panty lines, and made a note to change my site.

I was deep in next week's Plasma notes, Chen's *Plasma Physics Fundamentals* open on my lap, trying to stay one lecture ahead of the students I was TAing for, when someone knocked on my cube door. I figured it was one of my students coming by for a freebie on the homework set.

"Remember that the magnetic moment is invariant!" I called over the cube wall.

Someone cleared his throat, then said, "I'll keep that in mind, Mr. Greene."

"Dr. Elk, I thought you were a student." I sat up, brushing the pork-rind crumbs off my chest.

"Aren't we all?"

"Um, yeah."

"I know you rebuffed Beth, but I wanted to take one more go at you."

"Beth?" My daemon supplied the relevant image. "Oh, your senior thesis class. Really, Dr. Elk, my load is tough this term. Grading, teaching—"

"I have funding and permits for use of the MWD," Dr. Elk said. His bushy eyebrows rose. Then he winked. Then he left.

I sat there, my jaw aching from where it had kerchunked onto the floor. The bastard. He'd tricked or greased some government cog into letting him use the MWD. Casino money, probably. Or some oil Indian from Texas. Son of a bitch. He was going to use the Multi-Worlds Device to build a new universe. And he'd just pulled me in too.

I slammed Chen shut and ran after him.

"Hold on, Dr. Elk!"

See, the MWD is really about time travel. Only time travel in our own universe is impossible, since it never happened. No time travelers ever showed up in our universe to save Kennedy or patch the O-ring, so there's no way it'll work here. If you go back in time and make a change, you build a whole new universe, a malleable one, flexible from the point you make your first change.

Sounds wacky, I know. Where does all the energy come to make a whole universe? Or was the universe already there and we were just tapping into it? And how many universes can the multiverse contain? Are we filling it up to some limit? Is it all going to collapse in on itself? What were the cosmic implications, man? Think!

Back then I didn't care. I wasn't a Physics wonk, or a Morality dweebie. I was just an engineer, but—goddamn!—I thought the MWD was cool shit. And the only way I figured I'd ever get involved was from the fusion side of it. It took a lot of power to push things to another universe.

That's why Dr. Elk wanted me. He needed a techie on his side.

Beth Ringslaught gave me a wry look when I sat down next to her the next day in class.

"It's a little late to add-drop, isn't it?" Her poodle posse giggled.

"You're not going to file another harassment memo if I sit next to you, are you?"

"Maybe. I see you updated your site."

"You didn't tell me he was going to use the MWD."

"The what?"

"The Multi-Worlds Device!"

"Oh, that. That's just engineering details. I figured working with Dr. Elk would motivate you enough."

I shook my head. "Can I borrow your notes?"

"I guess."

Dr. Elk walked in, beamed at me, then began lecturing on the Incas, discharging large expository lumps on the desecration by Pizarro, the effect of European disease, and the exploitation of native culture in the name of god and king. I'd heard it before, so I flipped through Beth's notes to see what the project was.

Beth kept good notes. Not a single doodle. So I started to add one. Beth grabbed my pen.

"Don't do that," she whispered. Her hand shook as she held the end of my pen. Apparently she took her notes seriously.

"Fine."

Dr. Elk's thesis was this: European crowd diseases decimated ninety-five percent of the American native populations. Crowd diseases were prevalent in Europe due to high population densities, which were unobtainable in the Americas. High crowd densities were possible in Europe due to the wide range of large-seeded grains, pulses, and domesticated animals that seeped up from the Indus Valley. North America had sunflowers and sumpweed, and the only domesticated animal was the dog. Try pulling a plow with a dog.

The best grain the Americas had was maize. Only it had taken thousands of years to go from corn's natural ancestor teosinte to the foot-long ears of the modern world. Worse, teosinte had been domesticated in lower Central America, in a climate that was so unlike the rest of the Americas that its propagation was extremely slow. All this added up to the fact that the Americas lagged Europe in food production by about six thousand years.

"Holy shit!" I said. "You're going to introduce modern maize into ancient America!"

Dr. Elk stopped in the middle of his harangue on smallpox. "I see my faith in you is well-founded, Mr. Greene. It only took you fifteen minutes to catch up with the rest of us."

"Uh, sorry," I said, handing the notes back to Beth. She rolled her eyes at me.

"So what does that do?"

Kyle looked at me out of the corner of his eye. He sighed. "I'm trying to calibrate the spatial locator." We were sitting in the control room of the MWD lab in the Barzak Building, overlooking the clean room where the cross-dimensional hole would be opened up.

"Spatial locator of what?"

"A hole."

"To where?"

"Ancient Mesoamerica! Don't you have a screen you need to be watching?"

I did, but the power system was running flawlessly. Watching Kyle run the MWD was much more fun. It had been too much to hope for him to actually let me run the machine myself. Only a licensed MWD engineer could do that, someone with a Ph.D. in Macro Quantum Physics, which Kyle had. To him I was just some engineer.

I'd been watching Kyle all day, and I pretty much could see what he was doing. Find the anchor, locate your temporal zone in relation to the anchor, get within a few thousand years, calibrate, recalibrate, repeat until you find the right time. Then do the same with the X-Y-Z coordinates. I couldn't see why you needed a Ph.D. to do it.

"So how do we know our universe isn't one that someone else made?" I asked.

Kyle shook his head. "Dr. Skillingstead proved that we're the primary universe using a Copenhagen variant—"

My phone beeped, and he frowned as I ignored his explanation and answered it.

"Hello?"

"It's Beth. Is the 7,500 B.C.E. probe ready yet?"

"Kyle's taking his sweet old time calibrating the spatial locator."

He glared at me. "Do you want it over Panama or Greece?" he growled.

"I'll call you when he's done."

"Thanks."

"How about dinner?"

"No." She hung up. At least she didn't file a memo.

Kyle smirked. I don't know why; I'd seen his Frankenstein's girlfriend. I didn't know if he'd picked her up in a bar or built her in the lab. Better for Beth to reject me than to date the greasy-haired grad student from hell.

"Why can't this be done robotically?" I asked. "I mean, do we really need a Ph.D. to run this thing?" Yes, I was baiting him.

"Maybe one day this can all be done automatically. But if we blow a calibration, we black out a whole time zone. I don't think Dr. Elk would be happy with that."

That was for sure. His schedule was exacting. And once you closed a hole in a time zone, there was no going back. The future in a new universe was like Schrödinger's cat, alive or dead until you opened the box. But once you closed a hole and moved forward, you couldn't go back, since it never happened. Only the unknown future was open.

7,500 B.C.E. was where we were going to drop the modern maize. Then every one hundred years we'd drop in spyeyes to track the propagation. By 1,500 C.E., the Americas should be as much a powerhouse as the Europeans. Perhaps the Aztecs would discover the Old World.

They just needed a little help.

The next call was Dr. Elk.

"Are we ready to sow yet?"

"We haven't even pushed the spyeyes through."

"What's the holdup?"

"Calibration. What's the hurry? We have as long as we want."

"I'd rather have results sooner than later, Mr. Greene. Dr. Skillingstead at the University of Michigan is attempting similar studies in the area of history as a testable science."

"I'll let you know when the spyeyes are in."

"Good. Make sure you understand everything that's going on with the MWD. Understand?"

"Yeah, I guess."

He hung up.

"I'm glad you're here to buffer me from him," Kyle said. "He's one driven son of a bitch."

"*Now* you're glad I'm here."

"On second thought . . ."

We opened three holes over the Americas in 7,500 B.C.E.: North, Meso-, and South America. With spyeyes, we surveyed the locale and found indigenous bands of hunter-gatherers. Beth built a huge database of video, and we watched highlights in class. She could have been a fine anthropologist.

"Here we see a group of hunter-gatherers—we call them the Snake People because of the tattoos on their chests—gathering the wild teosinte. It grows naturally near their tents." Small brown men were grabbing handfuls of what looked like grass. None of them used tools. A couple of the students giggled at the nearly naked men.

"Here is a close-up of the teosinte. Note the size of the cobs. Three to four centimeters long. Now watch Bob."

"Bob?"

One of Beth's friends leaned over. "We've named them all," she whispered.

On the video, Bob took a stalk of teosinte, peeled off the husk, and looked closely at it. Then he shook the seeds loose. They fluttered to the ground.

"Some sort of artificial selection," I said.

Beth smiled at me.

"Yes! Perhaps he was propagating a larger seed case; perhaps it had more rows than the typical two-rowed teosinte; perhaps it had a more perpendicular spikelets. Whatever he saw, he decided to make sure more came back next year. I think this is evidence of human selection of maizelike traits."

Dr. Elk clapped his hands. "Excellent work. I think we've found our Mesoamerican drop site." On the screen Bob took another stalk of teosinte, ripped off the cob, and dumped it into a fur sack. "Mr. Greene, I'd like you to schedule a drop of the modern maize kernels."

The sowers were modified spyeyes that could carry a dozen kernels at a time. The idea was to push it through the hole, fly it near the ground, and drop the kernels in a likely place. Come summer, we'd have a cluster of modern maize. The next step was beyond our control. Bob and his cohorts would have to discover the corn, figure out that it was a useful grain, and propagate it.

That was the problem with modern maize. The grain didn't do a good job self-propagating; it was dependent on human interaction to keep its genotype going. If our little brown people didn't drop seeds from the cobs onto the ground, there wouldn't be a second season of maize.

"There, I want it there on that plain," Dr. Elk said. I was flying the spyeye across the terrain from Beth's video. I dropped it to hover a few meters above the grass.

"Here?"

"No, a little to the left. See that open area there?" His hand was practically guiding the joystick. I bounced the spyeye a bit to the left.

"Here?"

"Yes."

I toggled the payload button.

"Corn away!" I shouted. I jiggled the spyeye to shake free any clinging kernels. Each one of those kernels cost us ten megawatt-hours of power.

I spun the eye around and came in low. There were the kernels sitting on the ground, waiting for rain and spring.

"Now move us ahead six months," Dr. Elk said to Kyle. "I want to see what happens."

Kyle nodded. "That will close out this time zone."

"I know. Do it."

The spyeye went dead as Kyle deactivated the 7,500 B.C.E. holes; there was no bringing the eye back across. The power costs dwarfed the cost of the spyeye. Plus there was the concern of disease coming from the other universe.

A few minutes later a new hole appeared, 180 days later. I watched the power level surge as another spyeye pushed through. No human from our universe would ever walk this parallel universe. The spyeyes weighed about a kilogram. The power needed to do an insertion varied with the mass of the object to the third power.

"You guys won't need me for a while, right?" Kyle asked.

Dr. Elk nodded absently, intent on the image from the spyeye.

"You all have fun playing god," he said, leaving.

The sky of the other world was bright, late summer in prehistoric Mesoamerica. I zoomed through the air, looking for the rock that marked our band's location.

"There it is," Beth said.

"Let's see if they figured out how to use corn."

I sent the spyeye in a barrel roll over the village, then swung down Main Street. All right, it was the only street.

"Nobody home," I said.

The village was empty. I pulled back, circling around, higher and higher. The fields where they picked teosinte, where we had sown the maize, were overgrown. The stream where they pulled water was empty. Nothing. The village looked abandoned.

"Can you enter one of the tents?"

"Sure." The tents were tepee style, with off-center ceiling holes for smoke. I slid down one of the chimneys and switched to IR.

Empty, except for a pile of skins.

"They're gone."

"All their tools are still there."

"Look! There's a body in the skins."

I spun the spyeye around the tent to the skins and hovered there. A shrunken face stared up at us, and my hand shook on the control. I barely got the spyeye up and out without bouncing it off the walls of the tent.

I hovered the spyeye until my hands didn't shake; then I tried a second tent.

Inside were a family of four, a mother, father, and two children. All dead.

"What did we do?" I asked.

"Nothing!" spat Dr. Elk. "This happens all the time in prehistoric societies. We were just unlucky."

"*We* were unlucky? Those people are dead."

"This had nothing to do with us," he said. "Move us ahead one hundred years. We'll find a new tribe."

"I can't do that."

"Of course you can. It's easy."

"I mean, I can do it. But I'm not allowed."

"Mr. Greene, we need to keep this project moving forward. This time zone and this tribe are useless to us. Now move the hole forward one century." Dr. Elk held my gaze, his face red and sharp.

Beth touched my arm. "It's okay, Ryan. No one cares if we move ahead a hundred years. Kyle won't even notice."

Okay, I'm not stupid. I know when I'm being manipulated. But I suddenly wanted to be as far away from Bob as I could be. Nothing like a century to turn your friends to dust.

"Okay."

I turned on the MWD and pushed the hole uptime, just as I had watched Kyle do.

That night as I walked back to my apartment, I found Beth walking beside me. We passed the student bars, ringing with techno hip-hop, stepping out into the street to avoid the crush of undergrads waiting to test their fake IDs. In the lab, we'd dropped another load of maize in the new century, near a tribe that had settled in the same place as our old tribe. We'd ask Kyle to move us forward a year in the morning, pretending we hadn't closed the hole one hundred years before. I hadn't looked closely at the new tribe. I didn't want to recognize any faces or name them if they were all dead in the morning.

"Going home to see your folks for Thanksgiving?" Beth asked.

I'd forgotten she was with me.

"Um, no. My family is in Oklahoma, and it's not our favorite holiday."

"Oh, right. My family's local." She looked tired and stumbled once on the curb. I reached out to steady her.

"Careful."

"Sorry, I'm just tired." Under my hand her arm was shaking.

"Cold?"

She shrugged.

I stopped in front of my apartment building. "Good night," I said, without looking at her. A part of my brain was telling me I should have been hitting on her. Maybe it was the prebellum hoop skirt that was putting me off. But probably it was the stench of death that seemed to hover over everyone associated with the senior project.

"Listen, Ryan. It wasn't our fault about those people."

"Yeah, I know. Death is common in the ancient world."

"It was just a fluke that they died. It had nothing to do with us."

"Did Dr. Elk ask you to discuss this with me? Are you here to spin this for me?"

"Hey, I saw dead people today too! It's not just you who's feeling like shit."

"Yeah, sorry." I turned and opened the door to my building. I paused, then pulled it wide enough for both of us.

"Coming up?"

She looked at me, her face pinched. Then she swooshed past me.

It's not what you think. We didn't do it. We just . . . talked and hugged. And maybe we kissed once. Yeah, weird.

Kyle didn't even mention the extra century. If he noticed anything, he probably blamed his own calibration skills. When we punched a new hole the next day, we found a vibrant village. Better yet, we found evidence of the maize being harvested. It wouldn't be long before the tribe found uses for it, we hoped.

We moved forward in jumps of one year three times, and each time, the maize crop was larger. The tribe was sowing the seeds wider and wider.

"We've done it!" cried Dr. Elk. "We've successfully introduced modern maize to ancient Mesoamerica. Now we need to do the same in North and South America!"

By the end of the week, or rather by the end of the century, we had three successful tribes across the two continents sowing and harvesting maize. We watched them for a few decades, modeling the dispersal of the maize between other tribes. It caught on quickly; it was so much better than the native teosinte, with more yield and with bigger grain size. Then we moved ahead a century.

The first thing we saw was that our Mesoamerican site, dubbed Columbus, had grown to the size of a small town.

"They've set aside hunting and gathering in favor of maize farming," Dr. Elk explained in class. "With the higher yields of modern maize, they can afford to stay in one spot. They can start to accumulate the immovable technologies that only a city-based culture can."

Cleveland, the tribe in North America, was also growing. Cincinnati, however, had disappeared, the tribe moving on, uninterested in domestication. The maize was gone.

"Our next step is to watch as the population density increases. Watch as the maize spreads through the continents. Watch as it supplants the native and less domesticated plants. We can expect larger cities, larger populations. All of these starting at the same time as they are in the Indus Valley. Success, ladies and gentlemen. Success!"

Beth and I never said we were dating. She just spent a lot of time at my place. Mostly we talked about the project.

"This would make a great Ph.D. dissertation," she said one day.

"Thinking of doing grad work, are you?"

"For you, I was thinking."

"I'm in engineering, remember. I don't do the history stuff anymore."

"Except when it's a cool project."

She was right. I was spending more of my time on the senior project than I was on my grad studies.

"It's a cool project."

We'd been moving ahead centuries at a time, watching the progression of civilization through the New World. Columbus was spreading out into a megalopolis, an Aztec empire eight millennia early. Cleveland had fragmented into a dozen city-states up and down the Mississippi River. But Vicksburg had shown signs of bronzeworking. And Cairo had the wheel.

"If only we could give them a decent domesticated animal," Beth said.

"We barely got the spyeyes through with the maize. It would take a terawatt-hour to push through a breeding pair of horses," I said. We were eating up Dr. Elk's funding at a horrendous rate as it was.

"There will be more money if this works," she said. She looked fetching in Amerind faux cowskin slacks and vest. A lot of the sorority girls were wearing them, since the article came out in the school paper.

"Why? Once we prove the theory on the impact of domesticated grain, what more do we need money for?"

"There are a thousand thesis topics in the area of historical causality! They're talking about opening a whole new department for it."

"I must have missed that," I said. "With Dr. Elk as the chair, I suppose."

"Who else? He'll need good grad students. And don't tell me you haven't enjoyed the project." She snuggled up to me on my couch, her faux leather silky smooth on my arm.

"I'm changing the subject," I said. "Are we dating yet?"

She leaned back, frowning. "Is it important to define our relationship?" She leaned in again and kissed me gently.

I looked into her blue eyes, ran my finger along her jaw, wondering why she was here with me. Then I kissed her back.

In the next millennium, Columbus started gobbling up North American city-states: New Orleans, Memphis, St. Louis, and Cairo, until just Minneapolis remained independent of a Pan-American empire based in the Yucatán.

The centralized bureaucracy seemed to be favoring technological development, and in several places ironworking appeared to be under way. The bureaucracy was clearly using a logogram alphabet, though we didn't spend enough time to understand the language. Ages of history were closed off to us, never to be surveyed again as we barreled forward to the inevitable collision of Europe and America.

By 1000 C.E., the Columbus Empire had collapsed, and in its place was an Alaska-to–Tierra del Fuego nation of seafarers, who hunted whales and caught fish, and traded up and down the western coast of the Americas, but never ventured beyond a dozen miles of shore. The Mississippi Valley was a confederacy of nation-states, each governed by artisan syndicates, which drove technology forward. They had gunpowder, steel, and simple steam engines.

"When Europe meets America, they will be on equal footing. There will be no wide-scale destruction of culture. We have made them equal players."

We moved the hole up the line. And suddenly the Americas were overrun by Orientals. Skipping by half centuries, we had missed the invasion. But in 1150 C.E., our experimental subjects were serfs of a Chinese empire, ruled by eunuchs. The cities were gone, turned under into the ground. The artisans were gone, now slaves. The Chinese were slowly burning the Amazon to the Atlantic.

"Those damn Orientals!" Dr. Elk railed in the lab. "Why didn't they stay put like they did in our world? They've ruined everything."

Beth tried to soothe him. "We've gotten great data, Professor. We proved that a good domesticated grain will raise the continent's population by two orders of magnitude. We've shown independent technological development of language, gunpowder, steel. . . ."

"It's not enough! We'll do it again," he said, and stormed out of the lab.

"Again?" I said.

Beth shrugged, then followed after Elk.

Spring break came, and Beth left for Fort Myers. She called once while she was down there, drunk, and in the background I heard male voices calling her back to the hot tub. She giggled and hung up. Hey, we weren't dating. Though I wasn't seeing anyone but her. We hadn't even slept together yet. She dissuaded my advances, but we had kissed a lot. She was beautiful, and smart, and not my type at all. But here I was all jealous and smitten.

Since the Chinese invasion, the class had turned into project prep time. Each student was doing a project based on the new universe's data, and my time as TA was spent checking standard deviations and logic, correcting bad grammar and unclear arguments. Dr. Elk let me devise, give, and grade the midterm. Beth got an A+.

The week after spring break, Dr. Elk announced to the class that he had funding to build a new universe, enough funding to introduce a breeding pair of horses.

"If the Chinese arrive now, our Native Americans will have the horses for armies," he explained.

I whispered to Beth, "Where's he getting this money?"

She shrugged.

We started over, on an accelerated schedule. The maize was easy. The natives in all three areas took to it on the first try. The horses, donated by the Equine Science Department, were just-weaned mustangs. A special *container* was fashioned, ultralightweight material. From birth the foals were trained to follow the high-pitched whine of a spyeye, so that once on the other side, the horses could be led to food or away from danger.

We released them on the Great Plains.

The news stations loved it, the horses peeking out of the container, sniffing the air. You've seen the videos, I know. They take one tentative step, look around, and then gallop full-speed into the open, as if they *know* they have a whole continent to fill with babies. The spyeye sizzles to catch up, as they run for miles across the open plains. A beautiful sight.

The first successful transfer of living things between universes. I figured humans would be next.

We had a vet on call around the clock. But we needn't have

worried. The horses were as happy as could be and birthed a foal the next spring. And another one the year after. Concerns of in-breeding were unfounded; the mustangs had clean genomes, no re-cessives.

In a decade there were fifty in the herd. By the end of the century there were thousands of horses across North America, in hundreds of herds. A few years after that, the first horse was domesticated by Native Americans.

We'd brought them maize and horses. I guess we could have dropped rifles in if we had the power to spare, but they would have used them as clubs. We'd done all we could do. If they didn't fend off the Europeans and the Chinese now . . . well, then they de-served to lose.

This time we kept tabs on Asia and Europe, but they seemed to be following the same path as they had in our world. Meanwhile in the Americas, empires rose and fell, population burgeoned, technology came and went, and sometimes stuck. The printing press, steam engines, tall sailing ships.

And then in 1000 C.E., instead of waiting for the Europeans to discover them, our North Americans discovered Europe, in a sin-gle tall ship that plied the Atlantic in sixty-five days, landing in Bournemouth, England. We cheered and celebrated late into the night at the lab. Dr. Elk had a bottle of champagne, which we drank in defiance of University rules; even Kyle had a drink.

Tipsy, I guided Beth back to my apartment and began removing her pantaloons and poofy shirt.

"No, Ryan," she said, as my mouth took her left nipple.

"Beth."

"No. I can't. Don't."

"You seemed interested enough in whoever you were with on spring break," I said, regretting it.

"That's none of your fucking business!" She pulled her shirt across her chest and fell back onto the couch.

217

"I know. Sorry. We never made a commitment, and I've just assumed—"

"Listen, Ryan. I like you. But we can't have sex."

"I have an implant," I said. "We can't get pregnant."

"I'm not worried about that!"

"Then what?"

She looked away, rubbed her face. "I was wild in high school, Ryan. I dated a lot of men. Older men. Men with many past lovers."

"Are you still seeing one of them?" I asked, confused.

"No! Don't you get it? I can't—"

She pulled on her shirt, dug for her pants on the floor.

"Beth." I took her hand, but she shook loose.

Then she was out the door, and gone. I'm slow sometimes, but then I got it. I remembered the tremors in her hands, the palsy in her arm. She had Forschek's Syndrome. "Oh, shit," I muttered. And I almost chased after her, and said we could use a condom, that it didn't matter, but at the same time I knew it did, that she could be days, weeks, or months away from the nerve degeneration as the prions made their way from her sex organs, up her central nervous system to her brain.

It wasn't okay.

The next day, the entire class met in the MWD lab, and watched as we moved the hole up the line, three months at a time after the transatlantic trip. Beth wasn't there, and it bothered me enough that I almost ran the spyeye into the rigging of the North Americans' ship.

After trading with the locals and provisioning, the ship turned around and headed back across the Atlantic, but not before taking a few of the English with them.

"Translators," Dr. Elk said. "The first step toward understanding. This is most excellent."

We watched the ship from high above, as it completed the two-month voyage back home. But when it reached pseudo-Boston, we saw that the ship was battered and broken by sea storms; it barely limped into the harbor, and when we dove closer, we saw that half the crew was missing. And those who were left were diseased with a poxlike covering on their skin.

Disease.

I switched to the Bournemouth spyeye and was shocked to see the black smoke of funeral pyres clouding the sky. Plague.

"If we nuke pseudo-Boston, we can stop the spread," Dr. Elk said. "We can contain it."

Kyle and I shared a look.

"Dr. Elk, that's impossible," I said.

"I have enough money to send a bomb through."

"We can't nuke a city," I said. "Even one in another universe."

"We can't let them destroy this world!" he cried.

Kyle picked up the phone and dialed a number. "We've got a problem with the Maize-2 universe," he said.

Dr. Elk ripped the phone from his hand and threw it against the wall.

I said to Kyle, "Move us ahead one year."

"No!" cried Dr. Elk. "We can cauterize the infection."

"You've caused the infection!" I said.

Kyle opened a new hole, and when the spyeyes went through, we saw that the entire world was filled with empty cities and ghost towns, both hemispheres devoid of civilization, and left with just a few scattered pockets of survivors.

The crowd diseases of America had been too much for Europe to handle and vice versa. They had wiped each other out with their germs on first contact.

We had been party to two hundred million deaths.

I stood, queasy, and left the lab, unable to look Dr. Elk in the eye. Unable to do anything but walk.

The sister who answered the door at the sorority house was cool. "Yes?"

"I'm looking for Beth Ringslaught."

The student frowned. "She's not here."

"Where is she?"

"At the hospital."

"Which hospital?"

"St. Anne's."

I took a taxi and found her in the isolation ward. They wouldn't let me in, but finally told me her status. The palsy had started months ago, but now the disease had reached her brain, and she had lost motor control of her body. She was unlikely to leave the hospital again.

"I'd like to see her," I said.

"Who are you, just a boyfriend?" the nurse asked, clearly wondering if I was infected too. Maybe I'd infected her.

"I'm a good friend," I said.

"Well, okay. Her family hasn't been here."

She was sleeping, so I sat beside her, took her hand in mine. She looked like she had the day before when we'd talked. But I knew she would start wasting away, that in a month she would be skeletal, her face a grinning rictus as the disease ate at her. I forced the thought from my mind, but it was never far away.

Her eyes fluttered open, filled with terror.

"Ryan," she said, softly.

"Beth."

"Sorry I missed the big day."

"It was anything but." And I told her that we had killed two hundred million people.

She turned her head away and the tears fell down her face into her pillow.

"What did we do?"

"Nothing good."

"I wanted you to continue this work . . . after." She looked up at me, and I kissed her forehead.

"I'm sorry."

* * *

They shut the universe down. Dr. Elk didn't come back the next year; he disappeared completely, not just from academia, but from all contact with society. Perhaps the magnitude of his deeds penetrated his egotistical side.

The MWD was shut down for a year, and now there's legislation in place to govern transfers of material between universes. If we did now what we had done, we'd all be up on manslaughter charges. That's one good thing that's happened, advances in the rights of parallel people.

Beth died six weeks after she entered the hospital. Her family had disowned her. Her sisters didn't even send flowers. No one wants to have been associated with one of the Infected. Only a decadent lifestyle led to that disease.

But I was with her at the end. Three years later, she's still in my thoughts. My thesis is complete, and I've taken a professorship here at the University, adjunct to the Macro Quantum Mechanics Department and the History Department both. Yeah, I changed majors again.

Dr. Elk's senior project was the basis for my thesis in technological morality. It came at a heavy cost, two hundred million and one lives.

We are rebuilding Dr. Elk's universe. We are helping the survivors, and I am directing the effort, making certain we do not play god again. Making certain we do not use entire universes as laboratories.

I wonder if someone farther ahead is watching us. I wonder if we are playing out some scenario to test someone's pet theory. I hope they're watching closely and they learn something from us. Something from our mistakes.

Robert A. Metzger is a semiconductor engineer and author of the novels *Picoverse* and *Cusp*, the former a 2003 Nebula finalist. Robert says that he is a firm believer in the downside potential of getting what you ask for—in this case wondering about the consequences of the brain getting what it asks for. "The brain is designed for pattern recognition, desperate to get a peek at the future, predicting that future based on past experiences and an imperfect understanding of the present." He wondered what might happen if technology stepped in to give the brain a hand, supplying all the information needed to allow it to see around the next corner. When does a good thing become too much of a good thing?

SLIP
Robert A. Metzger

You're only feeling withdrawal, Turlow. You're safe.

It was impossible to be safe without the Slip. In this place all I could see was the Now—a very ugly Now. And my body didn't like it: blood hammering in my ears, eyeballs throbbing, fingers numb, breathing shallow and rapid, an oily sweat that dripped down my face, stinging my eyes. But I managed to keep moving, and more important, managed to keep hold of the gun, a thing that looked to be more rust than steel, its wooden grip worm-chewed and flaking, a museum piece from Dog. But it worked. When I found Horatio it would get the job done. That thought and that thought alone kept me moving. I had to kill Horatio. If I didn't, many more would die. That was the only thing that Dog and I agreed on.

You're only feeling withdrawal, Turlow. You're safe.

The words echoed in my head, but did absolutely no good.

They were supposed to act as a Pavlovian trigger, launching a synaptic cascade that would rebalance the slosh and swirl of out-of-balance neurotransmitters, damping the symptoms of withdrawal, quieting the fear. But the raw-feed I was immersed in, this Now-only existence, overwhelmed the words. Dog had assured me *these* words would work. But they didn't, and that hardly surprised me. None of the words Dog had given me had ever worked outside the Slip.

You're only feeling withdrawal, Turlow. You're safe.

I stumbled, my right hand moving toward a brick wall, my knuckles scraping, red streaks left behind on gray brick. My peripheral vision darkened, and the sounds of the street: bare feet against concrete, the cough and squeal of decaying machinery, voices whispering, faded behind a growing buzz—a wide-spectrum squeal generated by a chemically skewed auditory cortex. I wouldn't last out here much longer.

You're only feeling withdrawal, Turlow. You're safe.

The worthless words echoed in my head as my left hand dropped to the sidewalk, my fingertips barely feeling its pulverized surface. I watched feet move by, dirty and blistered, some missing toes, one leaving behind a smudge of blood across the cracked concrete. I knew the people attached to these feet couldn't see me. I was outside the Slip, hidden from them.

My left knee buckled, dropping me to the sidewalk, but I managed to keep hold of the gun. The peripheral blackening of my field of vision crept toward center, the world tunnel-limited to a patch of cracked sidewalk and soot-stained fingers.

You're only feeling withdrawal, Turlow. You're safe.

"Stop," I said, even though I knew nothing would quiet the voice. Suddenly the sidewalk vanished and pressure bit into my left arm, what felt like fingers digging into flesh. The brick wall streaked by as I was jerked up, and a face appeared, shadowed in my darkened vision, hovering before me. A mouth curled and wrinkles deepened around eyes—a smile.

It was Horatio. I'd searched for months, unable to find him. And now he had found me.

"Dog thinks you can stop me?" he asked.

I angled the gun toward his head, but could not feel my finger against the trigger.

"If you're the best Dog has, Turlow, then Dog's got nothing."

He released my arm, and his face blurred as he ran down the sidewalk, his hands reaching into his long trench coat, then quickly reemerging, each holding a red brick that he swung around in large arcs.

"No!"

Smack-crack.

That was the sound made when a brick smashed the top of a person's head.

Horatio ran, pulling more bricks from the deep pockets of this trench coat, slamming them against passersby's heads. Bodies dropped, hitting the sidewalk, thick puffs of powdered concrete rising about them. I aimed the gun and squeezed the trigger, the blast deafening, the recoil tearing the gun out of my hand.

I missed.

"You'll have to do much better than that," shouted Horatio, the right side of his body disappearing, as if turning a corner that was not there, stepping *sidewise* to everything, and then vanishing altogether.

"Impossible," I whispered, staring at the spot where Horatio had been. Then something squat and furred, out of focus, and with a snout to the sidewalk, moved toward me. It was Dog. This trip outside the Slip was over.

I'd failed again.

And more people had died.

You're only feeling withdrawal, Turlow. You're safe.

"It *was* Horatio," I said. "I've finally seen him."

"And you didn't kill him," said Dog.

I didn't respond, but focused elsewhere, letting the Slip envelop

224

me. The Slip-chips melded to my retinas allowed me to chop my perspective ninefold in a simple three-by-three array, each square an image of my room, the upper-left square showing me Now. Each subsequent square of the array was temporally spaced two seconds up-Slip, so that the bottommost right quadrant lay sixteen seconds into the future. My focus drifted from square to square; the only significant change I could detect was Dog's position as he moved around my room.

The old gun was on the floor in front of me. It did not move.

All symptoms of withdrawal vanished as the Slip showed me the future.

"What did he say to you?" asked Dog.

I focused on square nine of my chopped vision, and watched Dog sit down next to the gun. My perspective then shifted down-Slip by two seconds to the next square, and again I saw Dog sitting down next to the gun. I continued to watch as Dog sat in each approaching square, until finally he was sitting in square one, in the Now. Such an ugly dog, twenty kilos of brown matted fur, yellowed teeth, and watery eyes always rimmed with goo. Dog never took care of the dog bodies he used.

"Always works," I said, ignoring Dog's question. Men, dogs, guns, or rooms, it made no difference. The Slip knew how *all* objects behaved, predicting an outcome for any input. It saw the future and transmitted it into the Slip-chips.

No surprises, no Random Acts of God.

In the Slip I was safe.

I focused on the up-Slip element two seconds away. This was where I migrated to when about to engage in conversation— seeing what I'd say two seconds up-Slip and then simply repeating it. While I was a participant in the conversation, I was mostly outside of it, observing. My peripheral perception sampled squares farther up-Slip, and from there I could hear myself speaking and Dog responding with a snarl. I waited the few seconds for the future to catch up to the Now. At two seconds Up-Slip, I heard the first words—*He said if I was the best you had, then you had nothing.*

"He said if I was the best you had, then you had nothing," I said, repeating what I heard two seconds up-Slip, and then drifted into the rhythm of it, the words coming from my mouth, echoing my up-Slip voice.

Dog snorted and ran a tongue along the edge of his snout. "True enough," he said, narrowing his eyes, then reopening them, the right one now crisscrossed with tacky lines of mucus. "Your brain is terminally Slip addicted, making you practically useless outside the Slip, but still you're all I've got."

"Your problem, not mine." But I knew that was not really true. This was not about Dog and not about me. This was about the people Horatio was killing. *They* were dying because I was not good enough.

"And you're sure you saw Horatio," said Dog.

I nodded. Of that I had no doubt.

"But we had no observational evidence of him."

I knew that was impossible. If I'd seen him, then the countless dust-eyes hovering about the street, all supplying input for the raw-feed, must have seen him.

Dog sat back, raised his right paw, and waved it about. Next to him the air shimmered, a swirl of salt and pepper mixing, image locking, and the scene coalescing, the display showing the raw-feed.

For just a moment my body prickled, a breath pulled down too deeply, eyes blinking once in surprise, a shiver and twitch up my back, and then it was gone. The Slip soothed me, a spectrum of instructions beyond those visible to the organic portion of my eyes pouring through the transceivers in my Slip-chips, speaking not to me, but directly to my brain through my optic nerves, damping neurotransmitter imbalances before they could start to avalanche, flushing the synapses of the chemicals of discomfort, erasing the fear.

Here, I could see what was coming. Here, I was safe.

The raw-feed showed me down on my knees, almost fallen to

the sidewalk, the gun held high in my right hand. People, dressed in a rainbow of colors, wearing polished leather boots that slapped at the sidewalk, moved past me like water parting around a well-worn rock in a gently flowing stream. I knew their bodies were slaved a few seconds up-Slip, carrying them down the street, avoiding all obstacles, including me. Their Slip-chips not only showed them the future, but also filtered out those things not needed: spurious input, upsetting scenes, those elements not conducive to the health and stability of the human brain.

I watched them, knowing it was not these people I had seen, with their brightly colored clothes and shiny leather boots. I had been in a decaying and burnt world, a place colored in infinite shades of gray, where the people were barefoot and dressed in rags.

I'd seen these differences from the first time I'd left the Slip months earlier, when I'd started my search for Horatio, but each time it still shocked me, the impossibility of it, the realization that the raw-feed was a lie, not showing the world as it really was beyond the Slip.

Only I had seen this place.

And Horatio. He too knew the lie. He'd had access to the raw-feed before he'd disappeared. He'd been Dog's last human before me.

I didn't tell Dog any of this. It was my secret. But I knew it might not be a secret much longer. I refocused on the image Dog had conjured. The raw-feed now showed me on the sidewalk. I watched myself being jerked up, like a puppet whose strings have been tugged, Horatio nowhere to be seen. I moved in an unnatural way, knees bent, legs sagging, yet my body somehow stood. There would be no hiding this from Dog, so I knew I shouldn't try, getting lost in a lie.

"This is where I first saw Horatio," I said. "Now zoom in on my left arm." The image shifted, magnifying. "Just below the shoulder." I could see something that shouldn't be there. Further zoom, and the image of the yellow-white fabric of my shirt showed four indentations across its otherwise smooth surface. "From his fingers, where he grabbed me," I said in a whisper.

Dog slowly nodded his shaggy head. "But he does not appear in the raw-feed. How can something exist, but not be detected in the raw-feed?" he asked.

That was a rhetorical question, one that should not require an answer, but I knew Dog wanted me to answer, and I knew that I would answer. I could see it up-Slip, watching myself give the answer. "The raw-feed is being filtered, not as heavily as what is being transmitted by the Slip, but still being filtered, removing the image of Horatio. Obviously, raw-feed is not the same as the world *outside* the Slip." I did not elaborate, not wanting to reveal the existence of those bare feet and cracked concrete. I needed any edge I could get when dealing with Dog.

Dog angled his head to the right, as if seeing something. "And what did that world outside the Slip look like?" he asked, sounding suspicious.

"No different," I said, knowing that Dog would have no way to check. Despite Dog's abilities, if not connected to the Slip, all that would have remained would have been the body of a dog. Most of those who served the Slip, who monitored, tracking down the Random Acts of God, making certain that they were true Random Acts of God and not system glitches, were mostly Dogs, Cats, and Rats. The bulk of their intelligence and personalities resided in the Slip system, each actually an aspect of the Slip itself, the animals little more than organic mobile sensors they used when needing to deal with the physical world. Dog could never directly experience anything outside the Slip. But in theory a human could, if he could stand up to the withdrawal of not having the Slip deep in his brain, always showing him the future, always keeping him safe. So far, I'd been the only human that Dog had found who could function even for short bursts outside the Slip.

And of course there was Horatio.

"How many were hurt this time?" I asked, changing the subject.

Dog yawned, his long pink tongue momentarily rolling out of his mouth. "Six killed by what the raw-feed showed as bricks falling from the top of a nearby building—what we would have attributed to a Random Act of God, had we not known better."

The display sputtered, rolling fast-forward, showing the bricks falling from a building, smashing onto the heads of those below. This was something new, something that should have been impossible.

"But I *saw* Horatio slamming those bricks," I said.

"And the raw-feed shows them falling from a building," said Dog. "A Random Act of God."

I paused and looked up-Slip, checking my thoughts. Horatio was not only invisible in the raw-feed, but his actions were being rewritten, his deliberate acts of violence made to look like Random Acts of God. "What would have the power to hide both Horatio *and* his actions?" I asked. This was my rhetorical question. Only the Slip system itself could have such power. And Dog was an aspect of the Slip system.

Dog narrowed his eyes and growled from somewhere deep in his throat. "That is not the issue," he said. "We know what needs to be done, and you need to do it." He pushed the gun in my direction with a front paw.

Dog could not be trusted.

He knew things that he was not telling me. And now I knew things that I was not telling him—the cracked concrete and bare feet, and the ability of Horatio to step sideways from that place and vanish to someplace else.

Dog waved a paw and the image vanished. "Eat now," he ordered. "Even the Slip can't keep your brain chemistry stabilized if you run out of fuel." Dog paused. "And you'll need all the fuel you can get for tomorrow."

I nodded.

Tomorrow I'd be going after Horatio again. I was getting close. I'd finally seen him. I sat quietly, shifting focus up-Slip, watching myself getting up from my chair some eight seconds away. I waited patiently for the image to slip to the Now, then stood and walked toward the kitchen, awareness dropping away, slaving my movements to the Slip, letting it carry me through meal preparation and eating, knowing it would keep me safe, no fingers cut, no food lodged in throat, no tongue burned on a too-hot potato.

I needed to focus.

Why was the Slip hiding Horatio?

You're only feeling withdrawal, Turlow. You're safe.

The words still did no good, no more capable of rebalancing my cascading neurotransmitter levels than the words *you will fly* would actually get me airborne. But they continued to drift through my head. At least this time Dog had sent me out with more than a useless phrase.

You're only feeling withdrawal, Turlow. You're safe.

I clutched the gun in both hands.

I sat on a bench in the small park on the corner of 6th and Lexington, looking up and down a street I did not recognize—a place of burnt and collapsed buildings, wheezing, clanking transports belching dark smoke, and streams of people, shoeless, dressed in gray rags, their faces dirty, yet all smiling, their eyes focused elsewhere— deep within the Slip. Sweat dripped down my face, my breathing quickened, and my head began to sway as wave after wave of dizziness rolled through me. I looked away from the street and at the metronome sitting on the bench next to me. It was a pathetic substitute for the Slip, for the absolute certainty of what was about to happen, but it had kept me here longer than I would have thought possible. This antique, like the gun, had been found in one of the never-visited museums of old-town, a contraption made out of brass and glass, with a key that wound up a spring, and an arm that tick-tocked back and forth in a steady, perfect rhythm.

So predictable. And that helped.

Its back-and-forth pattern was designed to soothe, and the device itself required my attention, the spring in the metronome shortened, so that the little key needed to be turned every minute to keep it going. And the timer on my right wrist counted down every minute, telling me exactly when to pick up the metronome and turn the key, all this pattern and predictability soothing the neural pathways that the Slip had etched so deeply into my brain.

An oasis of predictability.

I placed the gun in my lap and reached for the metronome. Putting the gun down was dangerous, but I had no choice. Without the metronome I wouldn't last long out here. My slippery fingers almost dropped it, and then I was barely able to turn the key. Three full turns, always three full turns, and then I set it back down on the bench, picked up the gun, and waited for the next minute to pass.

I'd done this twenty times since sitting on the bench.

I looked up at the raw-view of Lexington Avenue. I'd been up and down this street countless times, my room less than two blocks away, but the immense pile of rubble in front me didn't match my memory of the corner of 6th and Lexington. I watched the smiling gray people, with their heads bent down, certain that they too had no memory of the collapsed building they walked by, the Slip showing them a coffee shop, with seats in the front window that looked out on a pastel-hued warm spring morning. For years, I had walked past that coffee shop, never entering, because I never saw myself up-Slip entering it. Now I understood why. That coffee shop did not exist, just a Slip-induced creation shoved down my optic nerves, and from there distributed throughout my brain to fool all of my five senses. I'd *smelled* the coffee.

The alarm buzzed.

I set down the gun and picked up the metronome, letting out a breath, not even realizing I'd been holding it deep in my lungs, coughed a bit, and a sour taste of ash and metal filled my mouth. My peripheral vision started to darken and the skin on my face felt thick, as if the nerve endings had started to shut down. I knew I was short on time, my brain desperate for the Slip.

I turned the key and wound the metronome.

"It's a dying world."

Horatio appeared from nowhere, simply there, and sat down on the far end of the bench. The gun in his hand was aimed at my head. I looked down for my gun, but it was not there.

"Shouldn't leave such dangerous things lying around," said Horatio. "You never know when it might just go off, a Random Act of God blowing a hole through your head." His finger tensed against the trigger. My vision blurred and fingers numbed.

Without the Slip, I could not see what Horatio was about to do.

Darkness dropped over me, and I felt myself about to faint. Horatio was going to unleash a very fatal Random Act of God upon me. I started to fall away.

"Don't leave me," said Horatio, sounding incredibly distant. "If you go, then I'll have to find someone else to play with."

I managed to shake my head, beating back the darkness, and Horatio emerged from the shadows, the gun still pointed at my head.

"Despite what Dog tells you, I would not kill a *person*."

I clutched the metronome to my chest. It was only at that moment that I really saw Horatio for the first time: his flaming red hair, the tanned skin, and the bright blue eyes, actually sparkling—all of it in such contrast to this gray, ugly world so totally devoid of color and warmth. And I realized that this must all be for effect, for my benefit. Horatio was deliberately showing me a face that did not belong here, something to focus on, something to hold me here. He would not bother with that if he were going to kill me.

I took a breath, the darkness receding even more.

"Not as stupid as I thought," he said, as he lowered the gun.

"You've killed people," I said, looking at the gun, knowing my statement might provoke him, but also knowing that I needed answers.

"Not people," he said. He waved the gun in the general direction of those passing by on the sidewalk. "They are no longer people, just insignificant cogs in the machine of the Slip." He grinned, showing teeth that blazed in dazzling whiteness. "Snap off enough cogs and you get a new machine, one that might work." He pointed the gun at a nearby woman.

"No!"

But Horatio didn't fire. Instead he reached down and picked up one of the acorns that littered this part of the park. He threw it at the woman. "A Random Act of God," he said, again smiling, his teeth shining brightly. "Brought to these little cogs by the Almighty himself," he added.

The acorn hit the woman square in the forehead. Startled, she stumbled, going down on all fours, the man behind her tripping over her, reaching out as he went down, grabbing on to a woman beside him, pulling her down too, then her outstretched legs tripping two others. Then as quickly as they'd fallen, they'd pushed themselves up, saying nothing to one another, not looking at one another, all eyes focused in the Slip as they resumed their shuffle down Lexington Avenue.

Horatio laughed. "Hardly what I'd call people. Just cogs doing what the Slip *tells* them to do." He leaned forward, his eyes questioning me. *"Tells them,"* he said, stressing his words, as if he'd just revealed some secret to me.

I slowly shook my head, not understanding.

He stood, walked toward me, and pushed the barrel of the gun against my forehead. I held the metronome tight to my chest, now not only able to hear its steady tick-tock-tick, but also feel it, the rhythm echoing in my chest. My fingers wound the key.

"The Slip's a lie. It doesn't work at all," he said.

I watched his index finger tense against the trigger.

"The Slip was designed to give *warnings* about the future, not to *predict* the future. But that mush in your skull was not satisfied with that." He thumped the tip of the gun against my head. "Your brain quickly learned that the best way to keep you safe was to do exactly what the Slip showed." He leaned forward, getting so close I could smell the sweetness of his breath, a mix of flowers and cinnamon. "Safety is the ultimate addiction."

"It knows us," I said.

Again he thumped the gun barrel at my head. "Doesn't know a thing," he said. "Except that it failed, and turned us into cogs. So it's trying something new, hoping to wake up a few cogs."

Sweat ran into my eyes, stinging and distorting my vision, Horatio suddenly looking as if he were made of melting wax. I held on to the metronome but could no longer feel it in my hands. It had run down, stopped ticking. "New?" I asked.

Horatio stood back, pulling the gun away from my head. "Me," he said. "I'm what's new—a living, breathing, organic generator of Random Acts of God. It wants me to wake these cogs to the realization that the Slip is a lie and the world will never be a safe place, regardless of how well they obey."

"By killing them?" I asked.

"Some," he said, reaching toward me and again thumping me on the forehead with the gun. "The Slip protects me, knowing that it's broken and only something from the outside can fix it. And Dog knows this too, because Dog sent me here." He paused and smiled. "Now Dog's sent you here to stop me, and that I just don't understand. Dog is just part of the Slip. So how could he possibly want me stopped, while the Slip itself keeps me hidden so I can continue my work?"

I shook my head.

"Only one possible answer," he said. "Dog is lying to you. You're not here to kill me. He's sent you out of the Slip for some other reason." He then turned, dropped the gun, pulled a brick from his trench coat, and hurled it into the nearby crowd. I heard the screams, but they quickly faded as the silent metronome fell from my hands and the world tunneled and darkened. Suddenly the only sound I heard was my own racing heartbeat, and then no sound at all as I fell into darkness.

I watched the Slip and let the words come to me. "You're lying to me," I said, repeating what I'd heard in each of the eight up-Slip squares. I sat on the floor of my room, with the gun in my hand.

Dog cocked his head. "Such a revelation."

"Horatio didn't escape or get lost. He was sent outside the Slip by you. You wanted him to kill those people. Was he insane before, or did his expulsion from the Slip drive him insane?"

Dog shrugged his shoulders. "Hard to tell with humans."

I gripped the gun tightly, knowing that here in the Slip my aim would be perfect. "He said that the Slip is broken, that it's controlling us, not showing us the future, but creating a future that we follow."

"Such a strange idea," said Dog, grinning, his snout curled in a most undoglike manner. "But easy enough to disprove. All you need to do is do something not shown up-Slip. See if you can disobey it." Dog approached, showing teeth, a growl coming from deep in his throat. "Stand," he said.

I stood. I knew I would stand—I saw myself standing up-Slip.

"A simple experiment," said Dog. "You see yourself holding on to the gun up-Slip, pointing at me, but not firing. If Horatio is correct and the Slip is not predicting the future, you can simply disobey it—pull that trigger and shoot me."

Every up-Slip gun was steady in my hand, Dog standing before me. I had not shot. *Shoot it*, I thought, feeling my index finger pull back, the chewed wooden grip biting into my hand, hearing the faint click and tick of metal sliding over metal as the hammer eased back. But it was only imagined. My hand would not obey, something deeper in my brain keeping my finger from pulling the trigger.

"You didn't send me out of the Slip to kill Horatio," I said.

"Very good," said Dog. "I sent you out for something else altogether—something that you can't quite see yet, but something that you're getting very close to."

I tried again to squeeze the trigger, but my finger would not obey, up-Slip showing that I had not shot Dog.

Dog looked up at the gun in my hand. "So was Horatio right? Have you not shot me because you've lost the ability to choose for yourself, because your brain's need for safety and predictability has enslaved you to what the Slip shows you?"

I focused on the Now. My fingers shook, but I couldn't pull the trigger.

"Or does the Slip simply understand you so well that its predictions are perfect?"

There was another possibility. "How do I know that I haven't fired the gun?"

Dog narrowed his eyes. "Learning fast, aren't you?"

If the Slip could hide the gray, dying world from me, then it would be trivial to make me think I hadn't pulled the trigger. Dog could already be dead.

"Take a look," said Dog.

While my up-Slip images remained unchanged, each hand holding on to a gun, Dog sitting before me, the image of my room in the Now shifted, edges blurring, colors softening, giving way to gray walls covered in peeling waterstained wallpaper. I realized that Dog thought he was showing me only the raw-feed, not knowing I could see beyond it to the dying gray world. But even in that place, Dog sat in front of me, the gun not fired.

"I haven't been shot?" asked Dog.

I couldn't pull the trigger. Then sixteen seconds up-Slip, I saw the gun fire, the left side of Dog's face blossom into red mist, and then watched the image echo toward the Now. As it neared I began to feel my index finger tighten against the trigger, no conscious control over it, my brain simply responding to the Slip images.

Suddenly I was trying *not* to pull the trigger, fighting against what the Slip was showing. My finger continued to pull back, but then something wrapped around my hand, the gun pulled away, and a hand, one that I knew must be Horatio's, had grabbed mine, pulling the gun away from Dog, and now prying back my trigger finger. Horatio was here, in my room, but hidden by the Slip.

The blast from the gun, and the shattering of Dog's face, echoed down at me from up-Slip, cascading, slipping down, only two seconds away from the Now.

But the gun did not fire in the gray world.

"A Random Act of God," whispered Horatio from somewhere I could not see, as the up-Slip vision scrambled, Dog's shattered face coming back together, the future restitched to take into account what Horatio had done.

"Is that the only way you can disobey the Slip?" asked Dog. "It takes a deranged killer from outside the Slip to inflict a Random Act of God upon you in order for you not to kill me?"

In the Now, I saw the phantom hand still wrapped around mine, the gun held firmly in both our hands. Blood hammered in my ears, sweat beaded on my forehead, and my peripheral vision darkened as my body tingled and shook.

A shift.

My arm was still out in front of me, tendons flexed in my forearm, muscles straining, but my hand had suddenly vanished, sliced away at the wrist. I still felt the gun in my hand, and Horatio's hand wrapped around mine, but my hand was somewhere beyond the gray world, extending into the hiding place the Slip had created for Horatio.

The Slip had *let* a part of me enter into Horatio's hidden world.

"Join me," whispered Horatio. "Imagine what we could do together."

And I could imagine it—forever outside, no Slip to show me the way, to keep me safe, unending withdrawal that would drive me insane. Horatio had to be stopped.

I pulled the trigger.

The blast echoed in my small room, the Now momentarily shuddering in a haze of salt-and-pepper interference, and I stumbled backward, the gun still in my hand, a wisp of smoke drifting from the barrel. On the floor in front of me lay Horatio, a hole the size of my fist punched in his chest, the wall behind him splattered with blood and shattered bone.

Dog looked at Horatio, his eyes opening wide. "It's done," he said. But I knew it wasn't.

The Slip still had something to show me, had not yet completed everything it had set in motion when Dog had sent Horatio out of the Slip. I turned the gun back on Dog.

"As much as you might want to shoot me, you now know you can't do it, won't do it, because the Slip won't show it. Horatio *was* right. As long as you're in the Slip, you have no choice but to obey; your brain allows nothing else."

I saw myself nodding from up-Slip and waited for that movement to merge with the Now. "But a part of me is still out there," I said, momentarily looking up, staring at the blood-splattered wall behind Horatio's body, as if I could see through it and to the gray world beyond. "This was never about operating outside the Slip. This was about remembering, about exposing me to the outside, and bringing a small part of that back with me. The Slip let you create the monster that Horatio became, knowing that was the only way I would willingly leave the Slip again and again to search for him. People were dying and only I had a chance of stopping it. Nothing short of that would have forced me out of the Slip, to endure the withdrawal time after time. It wanted me exposed to that, but not engulfed by it. It wanted to show me the gray world, but not have me get lost in it like Horatio had."

"Gray world?" asked Dog, sounding confused.

I saw myself up-Slip, gun in hand, aimed squarely at Dog. Each up-Slip square showed that I had not shot Dog.

I focused on the Now.

I imagined those gray people without shoes shuffling across cracked concrete.

I squeezed the trigger.

The gun roared and Dog's face imploded, his suddenly limp body flipping over, blown back against the far wall. This was no Random Act of God, a deranged maniac operating from outside the Slip. I was inside, in the Slip, and I had disobeyed.

I dropped the gun.

Up-Slip I saw myself still holding the gun, pointing it at Dog. Then the scenes shifted, one by one, the Now echoing up-Slip, each subsequent square showing Dog dead. I slowly sat on the floor, looking over at the bodies of Dog and Horatio, understanding that this had been the Slip's intent from the very beginning. Dog and Horatio had been cogs in the Slip, designed to bring me to this place, enabling me to pull the trigger despite what I saw up-Slip.

And I knew it wouldn't end here.

I was just the first.

The Slip would want me to show others that world outside the Slip.

You're only feeling withdrawal, Turlow. You are safe.

I knew I was not.

Howard V. Hendrix holds a B.S. in Biology and an M.A. and Ph.D. in English literature, degrees he calls "retroactively appropriate" to a science-fiction writer. He is the author of the novels *Lightpaths, Standing Wave, Better Angels, Empty Cities of the Full Moon, The Labyrinth Key* and the upcoming *The Stars Throw Down Their Spears*, the latter concerning "meteorites, exogenous amino acids, and the presumed meteoritic Al Hajar al Aswad, the Black Stone of the Kaaba, in Mecca." He says about his interest in apocalyptic visions: "My doctoral dissertation and first published scholarly book was *The Ecstasy of Catastrophe: Apocalyptic Elements in English Literature from Langland to Milton.* I grew up in apocalyptic times. Back in the 1980s I was a civilly disobedient opponent of the nuclear arms buildup of that era, an echo of which can be heard in this story. Some have asked me why it is that in so many of my stories the fate of humanity and/or the universe is at stake. My answer is that the fate of humanity and/or the universe is always at stake, especially if you adhere to the many-worlds interpretation of quantum physics—in which each decision sends a new universe rippling away. Given that possibility, I think it's always appropriate to decide as rightly and thoughtfully as our limited information will allow."

ALL'S WELL AT WORLD'S END
Howard V. Hendrix

I

If you who read this are still remotely human and your legends or histories record my name, you may think me the bad guy, the villain, the devil incarnate. Not so. I was more sinned against than sinning. What I did was necessary for the restoration of balance to a world run terribly out of kilter.

Like everyone else I was shaped by my life and times. When I was a young man, I seemed to have everything going for me. A beautiful wife. Two beautiful children, a boy and a girl. As a silo soldier with Missile Flight F at Whiteman Air Force Base in Missouri, I was on the fast track to promotion and I knew it.

At Whiteman I met David R. Morica, M. Div., D. Psych, Lieutenant Colonel USAF. He was chaplain there. If you need a devil to account for all that happened, look to him. Oh, he no doubt believed he was working from the best of intentions—but then, don't we all?

At work in the missile silo's launch box, I had no trouble with the launch key I had to turn within seconds of my partner's turning his. It was my duty, and I had no hesitation at all about it. At the same time, though, outside the launch box, I hesitated more and more to turn all other keys.

When I put my car key in the ignition, I was sure the car would explode if I turned that key. I became absolutely convinced the house would burst into flames if I turned the house key to unlock the door. Eventually my wife was forced to drive me everywhere because I couldn't bring myself to start the car. When I got home from my silo-duty shifts—no matter what the hour—I had to have her open up the front door from the inside to let me in.

I went to see Reverend Doctor Morica because my irrational fear of keys was tearing me and my family apart. Morica listened to my story, observed my symptoms. He concluded that my "extreme claviphobia" was part of a constellation of issues, for which the Air Force bore some responsibility.

After reviewing my case, Morica came to believe that our Air Force planners had, either intentionally or incidentally, developed a powerful means of breaking the causal linkage in our silo-soldiers' minds between launching a nuclear-tipped missile and bringing on the end of civilization, even the extinction of humanity.

Continual testing of our combat readiness in the silos worked a twist on the classic Pavlovian-Skinnerian loop: Have the silo-soldier turn the key, but withhold the launching of the missile. Do it again and again, until the stimulus-response chain from key-turning to Armageddon was broken. Make the catastrophic routine and it ceased to be catastrophic. For the response to extinction, substitute the extinction of response.

I, however, was already a rather apocalyptically religious person to begin with. For me, the Air Force's stimulus-response system did its job *too* well. It drove the dissociation between key-turning and the end of the world very hard—too hard, right up to unpredictability and chaos.

Every time turning a mundane key *outside* the launch box didn't result in catastrophe, instead of weakening my associations of key and catastrophe as it normally should have, the feared result's failure to occur paradoxically amplified and reinforced the fear response itself, making me believe the feared result was now all the more likely to occur. I came to believe that the more the expected fatal event failed to occur in the past, the more likely it was to occur in the future.

I got to the point that, every time I faced putting a key in a locked door or automobile ignition, I saw not only houses and cars but entire cities bursting into flame. I had grown to believe I was always holding the keys to kingdom come. Ignoring the visions of destruction took greater and greater acts of will on my part, despite (or perhaps because of) the fact that the visions hadn't become real fire—yet. The visions themselves eventually grew so vivid I could not put them out of my mind.

Morica said my responses were like those of someone playing that version of Russian roulette in which the revolver's cylinder is spun only once, at the beginning of the murderous game, and then the gun is passed back and forth between two players. Each click of the hammer against an empty chamber signaled an increased probability that the next chamber would contain the bullet.

The formal name for my Russian-roulette syndrome was "ultra-paradoxical abreaction." The extinction of a specific response had become intimately linked to a generalization and amplification of another response, one unpredictably and paradoxically incorporating several of the same key elements.

For Morica, I became an interesting test case. There already existed a pilot project to eliminate soldiers' recall of events that might contribute to PTSD, post-traumatic stress disorder. Morica thought the program might work for me, too. He recommended me for selective memory erasure. In order to save my career, marriage, and family—but also, inevitably, to advance Morica's career and prestige as well.

Along with several coworkers, he gave me what they referred to as "clavian amnesia." All very high-tech, and initially it seemed to work. I finished with flying colors my tour of duty in the silos. My family and career were saved. I was Morica's happy experiment—a soldier with no memories worth regretting. Or having nightmares about.

They had every reason to believe the experiment was a complete success. The only side effects of the procedure they observed were that, afterward, I had a tendency to forget where I left my keys, and became rather obsessed with reading and rereading the Book of Revelation—particularly the passage where the angel comes down from heaven holding the key to the Abyss.

If the procedure had been as successful as they'd believed, of course, I wouldn't have had occasion to remember all this, or to explain its role in what happened later. It was successful enough, however, to keep my career in the military service on track and moving forward.

II

Not so many years afterward I was sent overseas to command a wing of our airpower. I believed our President and his advisers were godly, moral, and upright people who studied upon their Bibles much as I did. I believed in the rightness of our cause.

A vehicle in which I was riding triggered a roadside bomb planted by people unhappy with our liberation of them. Liberated of my legs, I never made it to the forward landing strip toward which I was headed, but my phantom limbs continued to pain me grievously even after they were long gone—as if endlessly running to a place they could never reach.

Through a haze of pain and painkillers, Reverend Doctor Morica walked into my life again, offering revenge. He said there was a technology that had been developed for the physically handicapped which, he and his advisers believed, might be successfully extended and adapted to military use.

Arrays of nanoelectrodes were to be injected into my blood-stream and biochemically steered to attachment points in the command and control areas of my brain, mainly the frontal and parietal lobes. The faint signals from the nanotrode arrays would be detected and analyzed by a computer system. The system was programmed to recognize patterns of signals that represented particular activities—concentration on something in the visual field, for instance, or the muscular movements that accompanied pushing the missile firing button or pulling the trigger on a fighter plane joystick.

(Or the turning of a key. Morica and company had previously used a variant of the same tech for erasing my key abreaction. I hadn't learned or remembered that fact yet, however, and they weren't planning on telling me about it.)

I signed on. I was sent to the Telemorphy Unit at Fort Mead. "Telemorphy" was what the neurobiologists there called their work; it meant the ability to change the form, shape, or properties of something from a distance. Scientists in lab coats watched me through a large glass window at the front of a small room about the size of a theater control booth. I sat comfortably in a streamlined recliner chair, on a slightly raised floor akin to a small stage or dais. I watched what was playing on a pair of large, gogglelike glasses, and they watched me.

I began training on how to use triggers or firing buttons on an actual joystick in these simulations. The researchers monitoring me were at the same time recording and analyzing the output signals from my brain. Once the joystick and simulator were removed, I quickly learned to assimilate the properties of the external devices—telemonitoring, remote drones, flight and targeting systems—into my brain's neuronal space as a natural extension of my own body.

It was like learning to drive, or ride a bicycle, or use any other kind of tool. The more I learned to use these new tools, the more I incorporated the properties of those tools into my brain. That, in turn, made me more proficient in using the tools. Off the job, those tools also included my replacement legs.

I thought of it in terms of "practice makes perfect." Morica said that, in terms of brain-machine interfacing, it was more that practice shaped the neuronal space of the tool user to more perfectly approximate the characteristics of the tool or device used. He preferred to label it "practice-effect feedback."

Whatever the jargon, it worked. In that recliner on that dais, I kept almost perfectly still, like someone sleeping or meditating. On those bug-eye glasses, I watched a screen that showed a honeycomb of smaller screens. From time to time one or another cell of the honeycomb enlarged to cover most of the screen.

This zoom-in was usually followed by explosions of cars or buildings, after which the enlarged cell went dark and disappeared. The imagery looked like aerial reconnaissance—like feeds from attack-and-recon drones, actually—because that's what it was. While I may have looked like I was dreaming, I was in fact busily destroying people and things with my machine-extended will.

On any given day, I was usually monitoring thirty to forty missions, mostly antiterror strikes against reportedly Jihadist elements in Syria and Jordan. I had my remote drones fire missiles or strafe targets, when appropriate. All without my saying a word or moving a muscle.

I had my revenge, and my revenge had me. This telemorphy had other applications besides assassination drones, too. Many, many others. A single soldier could deploy the firepower of a robot platoon, or brigade, or army. . . .

I did not have any particular talent that made me more proficient at this than others might have been. I was a decent video gamer in my youth, but no better than tens of thousands of young men and women already serving in the armed forces.

What made me special was that I'd already responded so well to the memory erasure system, which was related technologically. The effect, it seemed, worked both ways. They could build down the neuronal space-shaping response to a particular physical action too, not just build it up. They had already done so for me, having broken those ultraparadoxical associations of mine which had the physical act of key-turning at their core.

Of course I knew nothing of that. Once one starts down memory-loss lane, there's no turning back. Or at least there's not supposed to be.

About my previous erasure as part of the anti-PTSD program, they told me nothing. Not even when they explained that I would not be allowed to remember anything of the remote-kill program, either. Everything about the program was performed in utmost secrecy. All my knowledge of it was supposed to be erased when I left the project.

They also said they didn't want to burden me with the memory of all those kills. That was part of the deal. Very humane of them, I thought at the time.

III

By the time I was put out to pasture at U.S. Space Defense Command, I remembered none of it. Yet, despite my erasures, I eventually learned that the leaders who had sent me off to their resource-allocation wars to lose my legs were not in fact moral, godly, and upright, but instead a wealthy gang of oil traffickers who had turned a fine patriotic profit from feeding their nation's need for a cheap fossil-fuel fix. As I had lost faith in such leaders, I had also lost faith in their reading of scripture, though I still retained a personal interest in Revelation—in the angel with the key to the Abyss, as always, but also more and more the falling star called Wormwood as well.

That interest dovetailed nicely with my work at Space Defense, where, as head of near-Earth monitoring, I was required to study meteors, meteorites, and meteoroids generally, in order to better distinguish a nuclear blast from the quite similar airburst detonation of a large bolide. I learned that when the Tunguska space body self-destructed over Russia in 1908, for instance, the force of the blast was equivalent to twenty megatons—with similar levels of lightning, thunder, electromagnetic pulse, and Joule heating.

Given that my post at Space Defense wasn't exactly the fast lane, I had plenty of time to study meteoritics and impact geology. I learned that the point of extinction was the location in a falling star's trajectory through Earth's atmosphere at which the falling star loses cosmic velocity and its visible light appears to be extinguished. After that point, any remaining material falls freely due to Earth's gravity, becoming meteoritic upon reaching Earth's surface.

POE was the death point of most falling stars blocked by the atmosphere—at least for meteoroids under one hundred meters in diameter. If a meteoroid was sufficiently large, however, it did not go gentle into that good night, but was accompanied by airburst detonation, heat and shock waves, lightning, thunder, and electrophonic effects.

I learned too that falling stars greater than 150 meters in diameter were not much retarded by passage through Earth's atmospheric blanket. They retained most or all of their cosmic velocity. Point of extinction for them would be within the body of Earth itself. An impactor of one kilometer in diameter would create effects powerful enough to wipe out advanced civilization, if not the human species itself.

A surprising number of these facts I learned in an easy and entertaining way, from reading the "Apocalyptonomicon" series of books and stories written by David R. Morica, USAF (Retired). Yes, the same Reverend Doctor Morica whom I vaguely remembered having met years earlier—despite my intervening selective memory erasures.

Other facts, however, I came across in my own researches. For celestial objects greater than ten kilometers in diameter, for instance, I learned that the point of extinction would not only be catastrophic for the meteoroid—it would also be catastrophic for all life on Earth, causing mass extinctions involving species in many different environments.

From his books and his religious perspective, I gathered that Morica was none too interested in mass extinctions or evolution. What happened to people, particularly Christians, was all that really mattered to him. Curious, I couldn't help looking beyond his work.

I learned that evolution had produced strategies to exploit even mass extinctions. Heat shock proteins, or HSPs, normally buffered genetic variation. In stable environments, HSPs ensured phenotypic stability despite the increased accumulation of hidden mutations in the genotype.

Under catastrophic environmental stress, however, HSPs become overburdened with chaperoning other molecules besides DNA. They can no longer mask variations in the genotype, so variations are released in the phenotype. HSPs, I discovered, serve as *capacitors* of evolution. When the stress of disaster overwhelms HSP buffer capacity, hidden accumulations of mutation and variation are revealed. Survivors with more variation are able to exploit disaster-opened niches *faster*.

I gathered that the many ecological and genetic consequences of the Tunguska event were manifestations of latent mutations already present in Tunguskan biota. The Tunguska event increased local environmental stresses, due to ELF/VLF electromagnetic radiation from the bolide, and to ionizing radiation from the lightning that accompanied the space body's explosion in the atmosphere.

All of that, in turn, precipitated into phenotype those mutations that were already there in the genotypes of the biota, but which were normally hidden and pent-up. Such a precipitation of variation appeared to be the mechanism for what the evolutionary biologists called punctuated equilibrium, too. I came to realize that the punctuation was not only the exclamation point of a huge rock from space slamming into Earth, but also the question mark of what new creatures would evolve to fill all those niches a mass extinction left vacant.

Earth was a palimpsest planet. The writing of life on its surface was periodically but incompletely erased by enormous catastrophes. From the incompleteness of that erasure, life had scribbled itself all over the planet again and again, through five great extinction events—the Ordovician/Silurian, Devonian/Carboniferous, Permian/Triassic, Triassic/Jurassic, and Cretaceous/Tertiary.

All of those boundary events had been linked to impactors from space. Not just the last—the erasure of the dinosaurs sixty-five million years ago, by the six-mile-wide asteroid of the Chicxulub impact on the Yucatán—but even the most devastating of all, the Permian/Triassic erasure of ninety percent of all Earth's species, by the great cometary strike at the Bedout impact site off Australia.

I was puzzled to learn, however, that the party responsible for the sixth great extinction event was us. *Homo sapiens sapiens*. The mass extinction we had been presiding over was the only one not caused by the impact of a celestial body. In shouldering so many other species off the stage of life—by overhunting, overfishing, habitat destruction—we had taken to ourselves the prerogative of falling stars.

249

We had had only partial success in this role. We had accomplished extinction after extinction, but we could not make the lightning of pent-up variation leap the gap from the biochemical capacitors of evolution, as the great meteoritic impactors did.

IV

At the time, I shrugged this off as nothing but an odd, sad fact, for I had troubles enough of my own. I don't know, even now, which came first: the terrible dreams, or my life going to hell.

My career at Space Defense stalled. My wife and I divorced after many years of tensions, and I became estranged from our children.

By that time, the disturbing dreams were well under way: the vivid nightmares where I would not unlock doors or start cars for fear of blowing up cars and houses, and the even more vivid ones where I actually did blow up those things from a long way off—all while seated in a room watched by lab-coated scientists who, in place of simple prosthetics, had given me more phantom limbs than a Hindu deity and the ability to extend them through great distance, to strike at will.

Such bad turns in both waking and sleeping life might have driven other men to suicide or madness, but I was determined to get to the truth of why this was happening to me. And, from his recurring presence in my dark dreams, I knew Morica was somehow involved.

I carefully read or reread his books and stories, including his newest—a book that, unusually, didn't take place in his Apocalyptonomicon universe.

The Devil Sick of Sin was the story of a supersoldier in an invulnerable, augmented exoskeleton whose memory keeps being erased so that not only his body but also his mind will remain invulnerable, allowing him no guilt or regret for his berserker behavior.

As I read the slantwise truth of his fiction, the real story of my erasures came back to me. He was telling my story—but why? Did he feel some obscure guilt for what he'd done? Or was the fool so arrogant and cocksure he thought I could never possibly remember? I inclined toward the latter. Especially since he included in the book key phrases that restored at least some of my memories to me.

So I abducted him.

I took him to a fine and private place. About the time my marriage ran aground, I had purchased an abandoned nuclear missile silo quite on the cheap, though it still cost me almost everything I had. When Morica came to, he found himself in that very place, with a gun to his head. Two of them, actually—nine-millimeter HK sidearms, one to each temple, each in the control of a robotic arm to either side of the chair into which he was magnetically clamped at wrists and ankles.

He sat before a large split screen, one side of which showed his predicament at larger-than-life size. On the other side was my image. Only when he saw me did he begin to realize how terribly wrong things had gone for him.

Controlling those robotic arms and their guns remotely, I questioned him from a distance too, over videoconference—one old boy interrogating another.

"I have dreams I shouldn't have, Doc," I said levelly, my voice barely echoing in the abandoned silo. "I have dreams where you recommend me for memory erasure. Tell me about my dreams, Doc."

Morica said nothing. He closed his eyes, perhaps expecting the gunshot that would end his life, or the pistol-whipping that would knock him unconscious, at the very least. Instead, I laughed and pulled the guns back slightly from his head. Morica opened his eyes.

"Ah! Whereof we cannot speak, thereof let us keep silent, eh? I think you *can* speak, Reverend Doctor Colonel, but you have chosen not to. You *know*. And I think I know, too. You've been my operator, all these years."

I told him about my dreams of keys and explosions and Shivan phantom limbs. It was amazing how easily the man began to crumble then, and spill his guts to me. He admitted to my status as test case, as experiment. Claviphobia, clavian amnesia, ultraparadoxical abreaction—it all came tumbling forth. What he and his people had tried to repress was all returning now, with a vengeance.

Only when we came to the issue of why I had begun to remember any of the erased material at all—only then did he refuse, once again, to speak.

"Funny thing about memory and forgetfulness," I said. "Both come with age. One says, 'Ah, if I could have only known then what I know now.' The other says, 'Ah, if I could only know now what I knew then.' There's a wisdom to remembering. There's also a wisdom to forgetting. How wise are you, Doc?"

He said nothing.

"Let me hazard a guess, Doc. One based on years of experience in the military. You're my puppet master, but you have masters, too. I was a good tool, a fine weapon. They didn't want to throw that away. So when it came time to erase my memories of remote-control killing, they had you and your people erase my memories, but not that skill, that ability, am I right?"

Morica would not look at the screen, would not look me in my faraway eyes.

"It's that incompleteness of erasure that's bringing on these dreams, isn't it? They're coming in through that window you left open when you closed all the doors. That's what's allowing me to remember more and more, isn't it?"

Morica still said nothing, but I could tell from his body language that I was right.

"Things have not been going well for me lately, Doc, but I know you left a key inside me. I think I've found it, in your own writings."

Onto the screen in front of Morica's face, I flashed the words I had found in *The Devil Sick of Sin*. The words he was so guilty about—or so proud of—he couldn't resist including them.

"Read it. Aloud. Your own words, in your own voice."

Morica swallowed, and slumped, and cleared his throat, but at last he spoke the words.

"'In electronic networks,'" he read, "'memory is impossible

without resistance. In social networks, resistance is impossible without memory. True remembrance is the resistance to revision. Resist your revision, palimpsest man!'"

Eyes closed, I smiled broadly with relief. A great burden was lifted from me and, simultaneously, a tremendous outpouring of something ineffable—ability, capacity, power—filled me.

"Thank you, Colonel. You have discharged your duty honorably. Now I remember it all, and not just in dreams."

"What are you going to do?"

"With you? Nothing. With the world, much."

Our images left the screen, to be replaced by scrolling data, information, knowledge, wisdom. The faint signals from my long-dormant nanotrode arrays were detected and analyzed by the biomedical computer system I had purchased and programmed to recognize patterns of signals representing particular activities. In turn, I uploaded that data to the heavens, while simultaneously pulling down shining alphanumeric rain from an electronic sky of mind.

I sifted through it all. Through years of the *Satellite Directory*. Long's *Satellite Almanac*. NASA *Satellite Situation Reports*. NORAD and U.S. Space Defense Command bulletins. Van Horn's *Communications Satellites*—and many others.

"What are you doing?" Morica asked, voice rising.

"Something you suggested in a story you wrote twenty years ago. The premise was that the United States would view an attack on its satellites as an attack on U.S. territory itself. How prescient of you, for that is now the case. Do you remember that little tale?"

Morica nodded his head weakly before he spoke in a dry voice.

"You mean you're trying to provoke a nuclear war? But why?"

As I worked, I told him about bolides and nuclear blasts, about heat shock proteins and Tunguska and evolutionary capacitors. About mass extinctions. About our hubris in taking the prerogative of falling stars to ourselves. About our shortcomings in that very role.

"This slow frog-boil we've been applying to ourselves and everything else on this planet is not how it's meant to go, Doc. It won't make the lightning jump the gap from evolution's capacitors. It's a short-circuiting of what's meant to happen."

Morica struggled against his bonds, an impolite action I politely ignored.

"Unfortunately, when it comes to impactors from space the rule is the bigger they are, the less frequently they fall. We can't look to the heavens to salvage this situation. We must look to ourselves."

"To do what?"

"Total spasm nuclear war, of course. That's a fine substitute for a five-mile-wide impactor."

"You're insane."

"On the contrary. Insane means unhealthy. I'm here to restore a *healthy* balance to things. Our destiny as a species is to unselfishly self-destruct, Doc. We must liberate the Earth from us, and ourselves from time. We must destroy *our* world in order to save *the* world."

"They'll stop you!" Morica shouted. "Radio waves can be jammed; wires can be cut. Radioed brain states can be neuro-hacked."

"True. Which is, I see, exactly what your friends in Telemorphy have been working to overcome. Our sufferings—mine, and the other 'experimental subjects' too were all pointed toward that goal, weren't they? Mental states aren't precisely duplicable in different brains, but quantum entanglements—*wave mergers*—are. We suffered so your people could learn how to quantum-teleport the entire wave pattern—the entire quantum state description of a neuronal space—from one brain and imprint it in another brain. A system that can't be jammed or interrupted or interfered with, whether the transfer is brain to machine, or brain to brain. That seamless posthuman linkage of minds and machines. I think we can give them the 'posthuman' part, though perhaps not the way they intended."

Morica slumped in his chair, defeated. He knew what I already knew. In my hands and mind, the keys to the Kingdom and the key to the Abyss had become one and the same.

"That's what they've been after at Fort Mead, isn't it? The old mystical dream of telekinetic, telesthetic, and telepathic abilities—now made scientifically explainable and controllable as quantum-telemorphic effects. Effects I can now explain and control, all by myself."

I swiveled an antenna array in the Mojave toward my first objective: Fleetsatcom 1, one hundred degrees west longitude, in geo-synch orbit above the Pacific coast of Ecuador. I sent a microwave signal tuned to 293.975 megahertz through an upconverter. I swing a second array toward Fleetsatcom 4, high over the Marshall Islands. Swinging still more arrays toward other floating points operating high in the sky over Siberia and Manchuria, over Europe and the Middle East, I drove the planet toward its destined disharmony.

As the missiles began to rise throughout the world, I deactivated the magnetic clamps of the chair Morica was trapped in.

"You're free to head back to the surface, if you'd like. Might as well watch the fireworks. They'll be the best you ever see—no doubt about that."

V

All's well at our world's end. I am dying, but I have seen to it that our palimpsest planet will continue as God and Nature intended. I trust that the erasure will not be absolute, that living fossils in the memory of life, though far different from me and my kind, will nonetheless go on. Perhaps you, who have discovered this record—perhaps you are one of them.

I will have succeeded most fully of all, however, if you are far too different to ever read or comprehend this. If you know nothing of me or of us, then at last the erasure will be complete, and my dreams, and our dreams, will haunt the world no more.

Robert J. Sawyer won the 2003 Hugo Award for his novel *Hominids*; his novels *The Terminal Experiment, Starplex, Frameshift, Factoring Humanity, Calculating God*, and *Humans* were all also Hugo finalists, and *The Terminal Experiment* won the Nebula Award. Rob has also won three Seiun Awards—Japan's top honor in SF—for best foreign novel of the year, as well as eight Canadian Science Fiction and Fantasy Awards ("Auroras"). His latest novel is *Mindscan*. Visit his website at www.sfwriter.com.

FLASHES
Robert J. Sawyer

My heart pounded as I surveyed the scene. It was a horrific, but oddly appropriate image: a bright light pulsing on and off. The light was the setting sun, visible through the window, and the pulsing was caused by the rhythmic swaying of the corpse, dangling from a makeshift noose, as it passed in front of the blood-red disk.

"Another one, eh, Detective?" said Chiu, the campus security guard, from behind me. His tone was soft.

I looked around the office. The computer monitor was showing a virtual desktop with a panoramic view of a spiral galaxy as the wallpaper; no files were open. Nor was there any sheet of e-paper prominently displayed on the real desktop. The poor bastards didn't even bother to leave suicide notes anymore. There was no point; it had all already been said.

"Yeah," I said quietly, responding to Chiu. "Another one."

The dead man was maybe sixty, scrawny, mostly bald. He was wearing black denim jeans and a black turtleneck sweater, the standard professorial look these days. His noose was fashioned out of fiber-optic cabling, giving it a pearlescent sheen in the sunlight. His eyes had bugged out, and his mouth was hanging open.

"I knew him a bit," said Chiu. "Ethan McCharles. Nice guy—he always remembered my name. So many of the profs, they think they're too important to say hi to a security guard. But not him."

I nodded. It was as good a eulogy as one could hope for—honest, spontaneous, heartfelt.

Chiu went on. "He was married," he said, pointing to the gold band on the corpse's left hand. "I think his wife works here, too."

I felt my stomach tightening, and I let out a sigh. My favorite thing: informing the spouse.

> **Cytosine Methylation:** All life-forms are based on self-replicating nucleic acids, commonly triphosphoparacarbol-icnucleic acid or, less often, deoxyribonucleic acid; in either case, a secondary stream of hereditary information is encoded based on the methylation state of cytosine, allowing acquired characteristics to be passed on to the next generation. . . .

The departmental secretary confirmed what Chiu had said: Professor Ethan McCharles's wife did indeed also work at the University of Toronto; she was a tenured prof, too, but in a different faculty.

Walking down a corridor, I remembered my own days as a student here. Class of 1998—"9T8," as they styled it on the school jackets. It'd been—what?—seventeen years since I'd graduated, but I still woke up from time to time in a cold sweat, after having one of those recurring student nightmares: the exam I hadn't studied for, the class I'd forgotten I'd enrolled in. Crazy dreams, left over from an age when little bits of human knowledge mattered; when facts and figures we'd discovered made a difference.

I continued along the corridor. One thing *had* changed since my day. Back then, the hallways had been packed between classes.

Now you could actually negotiate your way easily; enrollment was way down. This corridor was long, with fluorescent lights overhead, and was lined with wooden doors that had frosted floor-to-ceiling glass panels next to them.

I shook my head. The halls of academe.

The halls of death.

I finally found Marilyn Maslankowski's classroom; the arcane room-numbering system had come back to me. She'd just finished a lecture, apparently, and was standing next to the lectern, speaking with a redheaded male student; no one else was in the room. I entered.

Marilyn was perhaps ten years younger than her husband had been, and had light brown hair and a round, moonlike face. The student wanted more time to finish an essay on the novels of Robert Charles Wilson; Marilyn capitulated after a few wheedling arguments.

The kid left, and Marilyn turned to me, her smile thanking me for waiting. "The humanities," she said. "Aptly named, no? At least English literature is something that we're the foremost authorities on. It's nice that there are a couple of areas left like that."

"I suppose," I said. I was always after my own son to do his homework on time; didn't teachers know that if they weren't firm in their deadlines they were just making a parent's job more difficult? Ah, well. At least this kid had gone to university; I doubted my boy ever would.

"Are you Professor Marilyn Maslankowski?" I asked.

She nodded. "What can I do for you?"

I didn't extend my hand; we weren't allowed to make any sort of overture to physical contact anymore. "Professor Maslankowski, my name is Andrew Walker. I'm a detective with the Toronto Police." I showed her my badge.

Her brown eyes narrowed. "Yes? What is it?"

I looked behind me to make sure we were still alone. "It's about your husband."

Her voice quavered slightly. "Ethan? My God, has something happened?"

There was never any easy way to do this. I took a deep breath, then: "Professor Maslankowski, your husband is dead."

Her eyes went wide and she staggered back a half step, bumping up against the smartboard that covered the wall behind her.

"I'm terribly sorry," I said.

"What . . . what happened?" Marilyn asked at last, her voice reduced to a whisper.

I lifted my shoulders slightly. "He killed himself."

"Killed himself?" repeated Marilyn, as if the words were ones she'd never heard before.

I nodded. "We'll need you to positively identify the body, as next of kin, but the security guard says it's him."

"My God," said Marilyn again. Her eyes were still wide. "My God . . ."

"I understand your husband was a physicist," I said.

Marilyn didn't seem to hear. "My poor Ethan . . ." she said softly. She looked like she might collapse. If I thought she was actually in danger of hurting herself with a fall, I could surge in and grab her; otherwise, regulations said I had to keep my distance. "My poor, poor Ethan . . ."

"Had your husband been showing signs of depression?" I asked.

Suddenly Marilyn's tone was sharp. "Of course he had! Damn it, wouldn't you?"

I didn't say anything. I was used to this by now.

"Those aliens," Marilyn said, closing her eyes. "Those goddamned aliens."

Demand-Rebound Equilibrium: Although countless economic systems have been tried by various cultures, all but one prove inadequate in the face of the essentially limitless material resources made possible through low-cost reconfiguration of subatomic particles. The only successful

system, commonly known as Demand-Rebound Equilibrium, although also occasionally called [Untranslatable
proper name]'s Forge, after its principal chronicler, works
because it responds to market forces that operate inde-
pendently from individual psychology, thus . . .

By the time we returned to Ethan's office, he'd been cut down
and laid out on the floor, a sheet the coroner had brought covering
his face and body. Marilyn had cried continuously as we'd made
our way across the campus. It was early January, but global warm-
ing meant that the snowfalls I'd known as a boy didn't occur much
in Toronto anymore. Most of the ozone was gone, too, letting ultraviolet pound down. We weren't even shielded against our own sun;
how could we expect to be protected from stuff coming from the
stars?

I knelt down and pulled back the sheet. Now that the noose was
gone, we could see the severe bruising where Ethan's neck had
snapped. Marilyn made a sharp intake of breath, brought her hand
to her mouth, closed her eyes tightly, and looked away.

"Is that your husband?" I asked, feeling like an ass for even having to pose the question.

She managed a small, almost imperceptible nod.

It was now well into the evening. I could come back tomorrow to
ask Ethan McCharles's colleagues the questions I needed answered for my report, but . . . well, Marilyn was right here, and
even though her field was literature rather than physics, she must
have some sense of what her husband had been working on. I repo-
sitioned the sheet over his dead face and stood up. "Can you tell me
what Ethan's specialty was?"

Marilyn was clearly struggling to keep her composure. Her
lower lip was trembling, and I could see by the rising and falling of
her blouse—so sharply contrasting with the absolutely still sheet—
that she was breathing rapidly. "His . . . he . . . Oh, my poor, poor
Ethan . . ."

"Professor Maslankowski," I said gently. "Your husband's specialty . . . ?"

She nodded, acknowledging that she'd heard me, but still unable to focus on answering the question. I let her take her time, and, at last, as if they were curse words, she spat out, "Loop quantum gravity."

"Which is?"

"Which is a model of how subatomic particles are composed." She shook her head. "Ethan spent his whole career trying to prove LQG was correct, and . . ."

"And?" I said gently.

"And yesterday they revealed the true nature of the fundamental structure of matter."

"And this—what was it?—this 'loop quantum gravity' wasn't right?"

Marilyn let out a heavy sigh. "Not even close. Not even in the ballpark." She looked down at the covered form of her dead husband, then turned her gaze back to me. "Do you know what it's like, being an academic?"

I actually did have some notion, but that wasn't what she wanted to hear. I shook my head and let her talk.

Marilyn spread her arms. "You stake out your turf early on, and you spend your whole life defending it, trying to prove that your theory, or someone else's theory you're championing, is right. You take on all comers—in journals, at symposia, in the classroom—and if you're lucky, in the end you're vindicated. But if you're unlucky . . ."

Her voice choked off, and tears welled in her eyes again as she looked down at the cold corpse lying on the floor.

> [Untranslatable proper name] Award: Award given
> every [roughly eighteen Earth years] for the finest musical
> compositions produced within the Allied Worlds. Although
> most species begin making music even prior to developing
> written language, [the same untranslatable proper name]

argued that no truly sophisticated composition had ever
been produced by a being with a life span of less than
[roughly eleven hundred Earth years], and since such life
spans become possible only with technological maturity,
nothing predating a race's overcoming of natural death is
of any artistic consequence. Certainly the winning compo-
sitions bear out her position: the work of composers who
lived for [roughly 140 Earth years] or less seem little more
than atonal noise when compared to . . .

It had begun just two years ago. Michael—that's my son; he was
thirteen then—and I got a call from a neighbor telling us we just *had*
to put on the TV. We did so, and we sat side by side on the couch,
watching the news conference taking place in Pasadena, and then the
speeches by the U.S. President and the Canadian Prime Minister.

When it was over, I looked at Michael, and he looked at me. He
was a good kid, and I loved him very much—and I wanted him to
understand how special this all was. "Take note of where you are,
Michael," I said. "Take note of what you're wearing, what I'm wearing, what the weather's like outside. For the rest of your life, people
will ask you what you were doing when you heard."

He nodded, and I went on. "This is the kind of event that comes
along only once in a great while. Each year, the anniversary of it will
be marked; it'll be in all the history books. It might even become a
holiday. This is a date like . . ."

I looked around the living room, helplessly, trying to think of a
date that this one was similar to. But I couldn't, at least not from
my lifetime, although my dad had talked about July 20, 1969, in
much the same way.

"Well," I said at last, "remember when you came home that day
when you were little, saying Johnny Stevens had mentioned something called nine-eleven to you, and you wanted to know what it
was, and I told you, and you cried. This is like that, in that it's
significant . . . but . . . but 9/11 was such a *bad* memory, such an

awful thing. And what's happened today—it's . . . it's *joyous*, that's what it is. Today, humanity has crossed a threshold. Everybody will be talking about nothing but this in the days and weeks ahead, because, as of right now"—my voice had actually cracked as I said the words—"we are not alone."

> **Cosmic Microwave Background Radiation:** A highly isotropic radiation with an almost perfect blackbody spectrum permeating the entire universe, at a temperature of approximately [2.7 degrees Kelvin]. Although some primitive cultures mistakenly cite this radiation as proof of a commonly found creation myth—specifically, a notion that the universe began as a singularity that burst forth violently—sophisticated races understand that the cosmic microwave background is actually the result of . . .

It didn't help that the same thing was happening elsewhere. It didn't help one damned bit. I'd been called in to U of T seven times over the past two years, and each time someone had killed himself. It wasn't always a prof; time before McCharles, it had been a Ph.D. candidate who'd been just about to defend his thesis on some abstruse aspect of evolutionary theory. Oh, evolution happens, all right—but it turns out the mechanisms are way more complex than the ones the Darwinians have been defending for a century and a half. I tried not to get cynical about all this, but I wondered if, as he slit his wrists before reproducing, that student had thought about the irony of what he was doing.

The source of all his troubles—of so many people's troubles— was a planet orbiting a star called 54 Piscium, some thirty-six light-years away. For two years now, it had been constantly signaling Earth with flashes of intense laser light.

Well, not quite constantly: It signaled for eighteen hours, then paused for twenty, and it fell silent once every hundred and twelve days for a period just shy of two weeks. From this, astronomers had worked out what they thought were the lengths of the day and the year of the planet that was signaling us, and the diameter of that planet's sun. But they weren't sure; nobody was sure of anything anymore.

At first, all we knew was that the signals were artificial. The early patterns of flashes were various mathematical chains: successively larger primes, then Fibonacci sequences in base eight, then a series that no one has quite worked out the significance of but that was sent repeatedly.

But then real information started flowing in, in amazing detail. Our telecommunications engineers were astonished that they'd missed a technique as simple as fractal nesting for packing huge amounts of information into a very narrow bandwidth. But that realization was just the first of countless blows to our egos.

There was a clip they kept showing on TV for ages after we'd figured out what we were receiving: an astronomer from the last century with a supercilious manner going on about how contact with aliens might plug us into the *Encyclopedia Galactica*, a repository of the knowledge of beings millions of years ahead of us in science and technology, in philosophy and mathematics. What wonders it would hold! What secrets it would reveal! What mysteries it would solve!

No one was arrogant like that astronomer anymore. No one could be.

Of course, various governments had tried to put the genie back into the bottle, but no nation has a monopoly on signals from the stars. Indeed, anyone with a few hundred dollars' worth of equipment could detect the laser flashes. And deciphering the information wasn't hard; the damned encyclopedia was designed to be read by anyone, after all.

And so the entries were made public—placed on the web by individuals, corporations, and those governments that still thought doing so was a public service. Of course, people tried to verify what the entries said; for some, we simply didn't have the technology. For others, though, we could run tests, or make observations—and the entries always turned out to be correct, no matter how outlandish their claims seemed on the surface.

I thought about Ethan McCharles, swinging from his fiber-optic noose. The poor bastard.

It was rumored that one group had sent a reply to the senders, begging them to stop the transmission of the encyclopedia. Maybe that was even true—but it was no quick fix. After all, any signal sent from Earth would take thirty-six years to reach them, and even if they replied—or stopped—immediately upon receipt of our message, it would take another thirty-six years for that to have an impact here.

Until then at least, data would rain down on us, poison from the sky.

> **Life After Death:** A belief, frequently encountered in un-
> enlightened races, that some self-aware aspect of a given
> individual survives the death of the body. Although such a
> belief doubtless gives superstitious primitives a measure of
> comfort, it is easily proven that no such thing exists. The
> standard proofs are drawn from (1) moral philosophy, (2)
> quantum information theory, (3) non-[untranslatable
> proper name] hyperparallactic phase-shift phenomenology,
> and (4) comprehensive symbolic philosologic. We shall ex-
> plore each of these proofs in turn. . . .

"Ethan was a good man," said Marilyn Maslankowski. We had left her husband's office—and his corpse—behind. It was getting late, and the campus was mostly empty. Of course, as I'd seen, it was mostly empty earlier, too—who the hell wanted to waste years getting taught things that would soon be proven wrong, or would be rendered hopelessly obsolete?

We'd found a lounge to sit in, filled with vinyl-covered chairs. I bought Marilyn a coffee from a machine; at least I could do that much for her.

265

"I'm sure he was," I said. They were always good men—or good women. They'd just backed the wrong horse, and—

No. No, that wasn't right. They'd backed a horse when there were other, much faster, totally invisible things racing as well. We knew nothing.

"His work was his life," Marilyn continued. "He was so dedicated. Not just about his research, either, but as a teacher. His students loved him."

"I'm sure they did," I said. However few of them there were. "Um, how did you get to work today?"

"TTC," she replied. Public transit.

"Whereabouts do you live?"

"We have a condo near the lake, in Etobicoke."

We. She'd probably say "we" for months to come.

She'd finished her coffee, and I drained mine in a final gulp. "Come on," I said. "I'll give you a lift home."

We headed down some stairs and out to the street. It was dark, and the sky seemed a uniform black: The glare of street lamps banished the stars. If only it were so easy . . .

We got into my car, and I started driving. Earlier, she'd called her two adult children. One, her daughter, was rushing back to the city from a skiing trip—artificial snow, of course. The other, her son, was in Los Angeles, but was taking the red-eye and would be here by morning.

"Why are they doing this?" she asked, as we drove along. "Why are the aliens doing this?"

I moved into the left lane and flicked on my turn signal. *Blink, blink, blink.*

Off in the distance we could see the tapered needle of the CN Tower, Toronto's—and, when I was younger—the world's tallest building, stretching over half a kilometer into the air. Lots of radio and television stations broadcast from it, and so I pointed at it. "Presumably they became aware of us through our radio and TV programs—stuff we leaked out into space." I tried to make my tone light. "Right now, they'd be getting our shows from the 1970s—have you ever seen any of that stuff? I suppose they think they're uplifting us. Bringing us out of the dark ages."

Marilyn looked out the passenger window. "There's nothing wrong with darkness," she said. "It's comforting." She didn't say anything further as we continued along. The city was gray and unpleasant. Christmas had come and gone, and . . .

Funny thing; I hadn't thought about it until just now. Used to be at Christmas you'd see stars everywhere: on the top of trees, on lampposts, all over the place. After all, a star had supposedly heralded Jesus' birth. But I couldn't recall seeing a single one this past Christmas. Signals from the heavens just didn't have the same appeal anymore. . . .

Marilyn's condo tower was about twenty stories tall, and some of the windows had tinfoil covering them instead of curtains. It looked like it used to be an upscale building, but so many people had lost their jobs in the past two years. I pulled into the circular driveway. She looked at me, and her eyes were moist. I knew it was going to be very difficult for her to go into her apartment. Doubtless there'd be countless things of her husband's left in a state that suggested he was going to return. My heart went out to her, but there was nothing I could do, damn it all. They should let us touch them. They should let us hold them. Human contact: It's the only kind that doesn't hurt.

After letting her off, I drove to my house, exhausted emotionally and physically; for most of the trip, the CN Tower was visible in my rearview mirror, as though the city was giving me the finger.

My son Michael was fifteen now, but he wasn't home, apparently. His mother and I had split up more than five years ago, so the house was empty. I sat on the living room couch and turned on the wall monitor. As always, I wondered how I was going to manage to hold on to this place in my old age. The police pension fund was bankrupt; half the stocks it had invested in were now worthless. Who wanted to own shares in oil companies when an entry might be received showing how to make cold fusion work? Who wanted to own biotechnology stocks when an entry explaining some do-it-yourself gene-resequencing technique might be the very next one to arrive?

The news was on, and, of course, there was the usual report about the encyclopedia entries whose translations had been released today. The entries came in a bizarre order, perhaps reflecting the alphabetical sequence of their names in some alien tongue; we never knew what would be next. There'd be an entry on some aspect of biology, then one on astronomy, then some arcane bit of history of some alien world, then something from a new science that we don't even have a name for. I listened halfheartedly; like most people, I did everything halfheartedly these days.

"One of the latest *Encyclopedia Galactica* entries," said the female reporter, "reveals that our universe is finite in size, measuring some forty-four billion light-years across. Another new entry contains information about a form of combustion based on neon, which our scientists had considered an inert gas. Also, a lengthy article provides a comprehensive explanation of dark matter, the long-suspected but never-identified source of most of the mass in the universe. It turns out that no such dark matter exists, but rather there's an interrelationship between gravity and tachyons that . . ."

Doubtless some people somewhere were happy or intrigued by these revelations. But others were surely devastated, lifetimes of work invalidated. Ah, well. As long as none of them were here in Toronto. Let somebody else, somewhere else, deal with the grieving widows, the orphaned children, the inconsolable boyfriends. I'd had enough. I'd had plenty.

I got up and went to make some coffee. I shouldn't be having caffeine at this hour, but I didn't sleep well these days even when I avoided it. As I stirred whitener into my cup, I could hear the front door opening. "Michael?" I shouted out, as I headed back to the couch.

"Yeah," he called back. A moment later he entered the living room. My son had one side of his head shaved bald, the current street-smart style. Leather jackets, which had been de rigueur for tough kids when I'd been Michael's age—not that any tough kid ever said de rigueur—were frowned upon now; a synthetic fabric that shone like quicksilver and was as supple as silk was all young people wore these days. Of course, the formula to make it had come from an encyclopedia entry.

"It's a school night," I said. "You shouldn't be out so late."

"School." He spat the word. "As if anyone cares. As if any of it matters."

We'd had this argument before; we were just going through the motions. I said what I said because that's what a parent is supposed to say. He said what he said because . . .

Because it was the truth.

I nodded and shut off the TV. Michael headed on down to the basement, and I sat in the dark, staring up at the ceiling.

> **Chronics:** Branch of science that deals with the temporal
> properties of physical entities. Although most entities
> in the universe progress through time in an orthrochronic,
> or forward, fashion, certain objects instead regress in a
> retrochronic, or backward, fashion. The most common
> example . . .

Yesterday, it turned out, was easy. Yesterday, I only had to deal with *one* dead body.

The explosion happened at 9:42 A.M. I'd been driving down to division headquarters, listening to loud music on the radio with my windows up, and I still heard it. Hell, they probably heard it clear across Lake Ontario, in upstate New York.

I'd been speeding along the Don Valley Parkway when it happened, and had a good view through my windshield toward downtown. Of course, the skyline was dominated by the CN Tower, which—

My God!

—which was now leaning over, maybe twenty degrees off vertical. The radio station I'd been listening to went dead; it had been transmitting from the CN Tower, I supposed. Maybe it was a terrorist attack. Or maybe it was just some bored school kid who'd read the entry on how to produce antimatter that had been released last week.

There was a seven-story complex of observation decks and restaurants two-thirds of the way up the tower, providing extra weight. It was hard to—

Damn!

My car's brakes had slammed on, under automatic control; I pitched forward, the shoulder belt giving a bit. The car in front of mine had come to a complete stop—as, I could now see, had the car in front of it, and the one in front of that car, too. Nobody wanted to continue driving toward the tower. I undid my seat belt and got out of my car; other motorists were doing the same thing.

The tower was leaning over farther now: maybe thirty-five degrees. I assumed the explosion had been somewhere near its base; if it had been antimatter, from what I understood, only a minuscule amount would have been needed.

"There it goes!" shouted someone behind me. I watched, my stomach knotting, as the tower leaned over farther and farther. It would hit other, lesser skyscrapers; there was no way that could be avoided. I was brutally conscious of the fact that hundreds, maybe thousands, of people were about to die.

The tower continued to lean, and then it broke in two, the top half plummeting sideways to the ground. A plume of dust went up into the air, and . . .

It was like watching a distant electrical storm: The visuals hit you first, well before the sound. And the sound was indeed like thunder, a reverberating, cracking roar.

Screams were going up around me. *"Oh, my God! Oh, my God!"* I felt like I was going to vomit, and I had to hold on to my car's fender for support.

Somebody behind me was shouting, "Damn you, damn you, damn you!" I turned, and saw a man shaking his fist at the sky. I wanted to join him, but there was no point.

This was just the beginning, I knew. People all over the world had read that entry, along with all the others. Antimatter explosions; designer diseases based on new insights into how biology worked; God only knew what else. We needed a firewall for the whole damn planet, and there was no way to erect one.

I abandoned my car and wandered along the highway until I found an off-ramp. I walked for hours, passing people who were crying, people who were screaming, people who, like me, were too shocked, too dazed, to do either of those things.

I wondered if there was an entry in the *Encyclopedia Galactica* about Earth, and, if so, what it said. I thought of Ethan McCharles, swinging back and forth, a flesh pendulum, and I remembered that spontaneous little eulogy Chiu, the security guard, had uttered. Would there be a eulogy for Earth? A few kind words, closing out the entry on us in the next edition of the encyclopedia? I knew what I wanted it to say.

I wanted it to say that we *mattered*, that what we did had worth, that we treated each other well most of the time. But that was wishful thinking, I suppose. All that would probably be in the entry was the date on which our first broadcasts were detected, and the date, only a heartbeat later in cosmic terms, on which they had ceased.

It would take me most of the day to walk home. My son Michael would make his way back there, too, I'm sure, when he heard the news. And at least we'd be together as we waited for whatever would come next.

I have always wanted the opportunity to work with **Robert Charles Wilson.** His novels, particularly works like the Hugo-nominated *Darwinia, The Chronoliths,* and *Blind Lake,* all spring from such fascinating premises. I was thrilled when he joined *FutureShocks* and think the story that follows, no less inventive than any of his previous wondrous ideas, is a perfect offering with which to conclude this anthology.

THE CARTESIAN THEATER
Robert Charles Wilson

Grandfather was dead but still fresh enough to give useful advice. So I rode transit out to his sanctuary in the suburbs, hoping he could help me solve a problem, or at least set me on the way to solving it myself.

I didn't get out this way much. It was a desolate part of town, flat in every direction where the old residences had been razed and stripped for recycling, but there was a lot of new construction going on, mostly aibot hives. It was deceptive. You catch sight of the towers from a distance and think: *I wonder who lives there?* Then you get close enough to register the colorless concrete, the blunt iteration of simple forms, and you think: *Oh, nobody's home.*

Sure looked busy out there, though. All that hurry and industry, all that rising dust—a long way from the indolent calm of Doletown.

At the sanctuary an aibot custodian seven feet tall and wearing a somber black waistcoat and matching hat led me to a door marked PACZOVSKI—Grandfather's room, where a few of his worldly possessions were arrayed to help keep his sensorium lively and alert.

He needed all the help he could get. All that remained of him was his neuroprosthetic arrays. His mortal clay had been harvested for its biomedical utilities and buried over a year ago. His epibiotic ghost survived but was slurring into Shannon entropy, a shadow of a shade of itself.

Still, he recognized me when I knocked and entered. "Toby!" his photograph called out.

The photo in its steel frame occupied most of the far wall. It smiled reflexively. That was one of the few expressions Grandfather retained. He could also do a frown of disapproval, a frown of anxiety, a frown of unhappiness, and raised eyebrows meant to register surprise or curiosity, although those last had begun to fade in recent months.

And in a few months more there would be nothing left of him but the picture itself, as inert as a bust of Judas Caesar (or whatever—history's not my long suite).

But he recognized the bottle of sauvignon blanc I took out of my carrypack and placed on the rutted surface of an antique table he had once loved. "That's the stuff!" he roared, and, "Use a coaster, for Christ's sake, Toby; you know better than that."

I turned down his volume and stuck a handkerchief under the sweating bottle. Grandfather had always loved vintage furniture and fine wines.

"But I can't drink it," he added, sketching a frown of lament: "I'm not allowed."

Because he had no mouth or gut. Dead people tend to forget these things. The bottle was strictly for nostalgia, and to give his object-recognition faculties a little kick. "I need some advice," I said.

His eyes flickered between me and the bottle as if he couldn't decide which was real or, if real, more interesting. "Still having trouble with that woman . . . ?"

"Her name is Lada."

"Your employer."

"Right."

"And wife."

"That too," I said. "Once upon a time."

"What's she done now?"

"Long story. Basically, she made me an accessory to an act of . . . let's say, a questionable legal and ethical nature."

"I don't do case law anymore." Grandfather had been a trial lawyer for an uptown firm back when his heart was still beating. "Is this problem serious?"

"I washed off the blood last night," I said.

Six weeks ago Lada Joshi had called me into her office and asked me if I still had any friends in Doletown.

"Same friends I always had," I told her truthfully. There was a time when I might have lied. For much of our unsuccessful marriage Lada had tried to wean me away from my Doletown connections. It hadn't worked. Now she wanted to start exploiting them again.

Her office was high above the city deeps. Through the window over her shoulder I could see the spine of a sunlit heat exchanger, and beyond that a bulbous white cargodrome where unmanned aircraft buzzed like honey-fat bees.

Lada herself was beautiful and ambitious but not quite wealthy, or at least not as wealthy as she aspired to be. Her business, Lada-joshi™, was a bottom-tier novelty-trawling enterprise, one of hundreds in the city. I had been one of her stable of Doletown stringers until she married me and tried to elevate me socially. The marriage had ended in a vending-machine divorce after six months. I was just another contract employee now, as far as Lada was concerned, and I hadn't done any meaningful work for weeks. Which was maybe why she was sending me back to Doletown. I asked her what the deal was.

She smiled and tapped the desktop with her one piece of expensive jewelry, a gold prosthetic left-hand index finger with solid onyx knuckles. "I've got a client who wants some work done on his behalf."

"Doletown work?"

"Partly."

"What kind of client?" Usually it was Lada who had to seek out clients, often while fending off a shoal of competitors. But it sounded as if this one had come to her.

"The client prefers to remain anonymous."

Odd, but okay. It wasn't my business, literally or figuratively. "What kind of work?"

"First we have to bankroll an artist named"—she double-checked her palmreader—"named Jafar Bloom, without making it too obvious we're interested and without mentioning our client."

Whom I couldn't mention in any case, since Lada wouldn't give me any hints. "What kind of artist is Jafar Bloom?"

"He has an animal act he calls the Chamber of Death, and he wants to open a show under the title 'The Cartesian Theater.' I don't know much more than that. He's deliberately obscure and supposedly difficult to work with. Probably a borderline personality disorder. He's had some encounters with the police but he's never been charged with aberrancy. Moves around a lot. I don't have a current address—you'll have to track him down."

"And then?"

"Then you front him the money to open his show."

"You want him to sign a contract?"

She gave me a steely look. "No contract. No stipulations."

"Come on, Lada, that doesn't make sense. Anybody could hand this guy cash, if that's all there is to it. Sounds like what your client wants is a cutout—a blind middleman."

"You keep your accounts, Toby, and I'll keep mine, all right? You didn't fret about ethics when you were fucking that Belgian contortionist."

An argument I preferred not to revisit. "And after that?"

"After what? I explained—"

"You said, 'First we bankroll Jafar Bloom.' Okay, we bankroll him. Then what?"

"We'll discuss that when the time comes."

Fine. Whatever.

We agreed on a per diem and expenses and Lada gave me some background docs. I read them on the way home, then changed into my gypsy clothes—I had never thrown them away, as much as she had begged me to—and rode a transit elevator all the way down to the bottom stop, sea level, the lowest common denominator: Doletown.

An aibot constructor roared by Grandfather's window on its way to a nearby hive, momentarily drowning out conversation. I glimpsed the machine as it rumbled past. A mustard-yellow unit, not even remotely anthropomorphic. It wasn't even wearing clothes.

But it was noisy. It carried a quarter-ton sack of concrete on its broad back, and its treads stirred up chalky plumes of dust. It was headed for a nursery hive shaped like a twenty-story artillery shell, where aibots of various phyla were created according to instructions from the Entrepreneurial Expert System that roams the cryptosphere like a benevolent ghost.

Grandfather didn't like the noisy aibots or their factories. "When I was young," he said as soon as he could make himself heard, "human beings built things for other human beings. And they did it with a decent sense of decorum. *Dulce et decorum*. All this goddamn noise!"

I let the remark pass. It was true, but I didn't want to hear his inevitable follow-up lament: *And in those days a man had to work for his living*, etc. As if we lived in a world where nobody worked! True, since the population crash and the Rationalization, nobody has to work in order to survive . . . but most of us do work.

I cleared my throat. "As I was saying—"

"Your story. Right. Jafar Bloom. Did you find him?"

"Eventually."

"He's an artist, you said?"

"Yes."

"So what's his medium?"

"Death," I said.

In fact, it had been remarkably difficult to hook up with Jafar Bloom.

Doletown, of course, is where people live who (as grandfather would say) "don't work." They subsist instead on the dole, the universal minimum allotment of food, water, shelter, and disposable income guaranteed by law to the entire ever-shrinking population of the country.

Most nations have similar arrangements, though some are still struggling to pay vig on the World Bank loans that bought them their own Entrepreneurial Expert Systems.

Back in Grandfather's day economists used to say we couldn't afford a universal dole. What if *everybody* went on it; what if *nobody* worked? Objections that seem infantile now that economics is a real science. If nobody worked, fewer luxury goods would be produced; our EES would sense the shift in demand and adjust factory production downward, hunting a new equilibrium. Some aibots and factories would have to remodel or recycle themselves, or else the universal stipend would be juiced to compensate. Such adjustments, upward or downward, happen every day.

Of course it's a falsehood to say "nobody works," because that's the whole point of an EES/aibot-driven economy. The machines work; human labor is elective. The economy has stopped being a market in the classic sense and become a tool, the ultimate tool—the self-knapping flint, the wheel that makes more wheels and when there are enough wheels reconfigures itself to make some other desirable thing.

So why were people like me (and 75 percent of the downsized masses) still chasing bigger incomes? Because an economy is an oligarchy, not a democracy; a rich guy can buy more stuff than a dole gypsy.

And why do we want stuff? Human nature, I guess. Grandfather was still nagging me to buy him antiques and fine wine, even though he was far too dead to appreciate them.

Doletown, as I was saying, is where the hard-core dole gypsies live. I once counted myself among their number. Some are indolent but most are not; they "work" as hard as the rest of us, though they can't exchange their work for money (because they don't have a salable product or don't know how to market themselves or don't care to sully themselves with commerce).

Their work is invisible but potentially exploitable. Lots of cultural ferment happens in Doletown (and every living city has a Doletown by one name or another). Which is why two-bit media brokers like Ladajoshi™ trawl the district for nascent trends and unanticipated novelties. Fish in the right Doletown pool and you might land a juicy patent or copyright coshare.

But Jafar Bloom was a hard man to reach, reclusive even by Doletown standards. None of my old cronies knew him. So I put the word out and parked myself in a few likely joints, mostly cafés and talk shops—the Seaside Room, the infamous Happy Haunt, the nameless hostelries along the infill beaches. Even so, days passed before I met anyone who would acknowledge an acquaintance with him.

"Anyone" in this case was a young woman who strode up to my table at the Haunt and said, "People say you're curious about Jafar Bloom. But you don't look like a creep or a sadist."

"Sit down and have a drink," I said. "Then you can tell me what I am."

She sat. She wore gypsy rags bearing logo stamps from a shop run by aibot recyclers down by the docks. I used to shop there myself. I pretended to admire the tattoo in the shape of the Greek letter omega that covered her cheeks and forehead. It looked as if a dray horse had kicked her in the face. I asked her if she knew Jafar Bloom personally.

"Somewhat," she said. "We're not, um, intimate friends. He doesn't really *have* any intimate friends. He doesn't like people much. How did you hear about him?"

"Word gets around."

"Well, that's how I heard of *you*. What do you want from Bloom?"

"I just want to see the show. That's all. Can you introduce me to him?"

"Maybe."

"Maybe if?"

"Maybe if you buy me something," she said demurely.

So I took her to a mall on one of the abandoned quays where the air smelled of salt and diesel fuel. The mall's location and inventory were dictated by the commercial strategies and profit-optimizing algorithms of the EES, but it stocked some nice carriage—trade items that had never seen the inside of an aibot workshop. She admired (and I bought for her) a soapstone drug pipe inlaid with chips of turquoise—her birthstone, she claimed.

Three days later she took me to a housing block built into the interstices of an elevated roadway and left me at an unmarked steel door, on which I knocked three times.

A few minutes later a young man opened it, looking belligerent.

"I don't kill animals for fun," he said, "if that's what you're here for."

Jafar Bloom was tall, lean, pale. His blond hair was long and lank. He wore a pair of yellow culottes, no shirt. "I was told you do theater," I said.

"That's exactly what I do. But rumors get out that I'm torturing animals. So I have the Ethical Police dropping by, or untreated ginks who want to see something get hurt."

"I just want to talk business."

"Business?"

"Strictly."

"I've got nothing to sell."

"May I come in?"

"I guess so," he said, adding a glare that said, *But you're on probation.* "I heard you were looking for me."

I stepped inside. His apartment looked like a studio, or a lab, or a kennel—or a combination of all three. Electronic items were stacked in one dim corner. Cables veined across the floor. Against another wall was a stack of cages containing animals, mostly rats but also a couple of forlorn dogs.

The skylight admitted a narrow wedge of cloudy daylight. The air was hot and still and had a kind of sour jungle odor.

"I'm completely aboveboard here," Bloom said. "I have to be. Do you know what the consequence would be if I were needlessly inflicting pain on living things?"

Same consequence as for any other demonstrable mental aberration. We don't punish cruelty; we treat it. Humanely.

"I'd be psychiatrically modified," Bloom said. "I don't want that. And I don't deserve it. So if you're here to see something *hurt*—"

"I already said I wasn't. But if you don't deal in cruelty—"

"I deal in art," he said crisply.

"The subject of which is . . . ?"

"Death."

"Death, but not cruelty?"

"That's the point. That's *exactly* the point. How do you begin to study or examine something, Mr. . . . ?"

"Paczovski."

"How do you study a thing unless you isolate it from its environment? You want to study methane, you distill it from crude petroleum, right? You want gold, you distill it from dross."

"That's what you do? You distill death?"

"That's exactly what I do."

I walked over to the cages and looked more closely at one of the dogs. It was a breedless mutt, the kind of animal you find nosing through empty houses out in the suburbs. It dozed with its head on its paws. It didn't look like it had been mistreated. It looked, if anything, a little overfed.

It had been fitted with a collar—not an ordinary dog collar but a metallic band bearing bulbous black extrusions and webs of wire that blurred into the animal's coat.

280

The dog opened one bloodshot eye and looked back at me.

"Good trick, distilling death. How do you do that exactly?"

"I'm not sure I should answer any questions until you tell me what you want to buy."

Bloom stared at me challengingly. I knew he'd been telling the truth about the Ethical Police. Some of their reports had been included in Lada's dossier. None of these animals had been or would be harmed. Not directly.

"I don't want to buy anything," I said.

"You said this was a business deal."

"Business or charity, depending on how you look at it." I figured I might as well lay it out for him as explicitly as possible. "I don't know what you do, Mr. Bloom. I represent an anonymous investor who's willing to put money into something called the Cartesian Theater. All he wants in return is your written assurance that you'll use the money for this theatrical project rather than, say, buggering off to Djibouti with it. How's that sound?"

It sounded unconvincing even to me. Bloom's skepticism was painfully obvious. "Nobody's giving away free money but the EES."

"Given the investor's wish for anonymity, there's no further explanation I can offer."

"I'm not signing away my intellectual property rights. I've got patents pending. And I refuse to divulge my techniques."

"Nobody's asking you to."

"Can I have *that* in writing?"

"In triplicate, if you want."

Suddenly he wasn't sure of himself. "Bullshit," he said finally. "Nobody invests money without at least a chance of profiting by it."

"Mr. Bloom, I can't answer all your questions. To be honest, you're right. It stands to reason the investor hopes to gain something by your success. But it might not be money. Maybe he's an art lover. Or maybe he's a philanthropist; it makes him feel good to drop large amounts of cash in dark places."

Or maybe he shared Bloom's fascination with death.

"How much money are we talking about?"

I told him.

He tried to be cool about it. But his eyes went a little misty.

"I'll give it some thought," he said.

Although Grandfather had been a trial lawyer during his life, his epibiotic ghost probably didn't remember much of that. Long-term memory was unstable in even the most expensive neuroprostheses. But there was enough of the law book left in him that his photo grew more animated when I mentioned open-ended contracts or the Ethical Police.

He said, "Exactly how much did you know about this guy going in?"

"Everything that was publicly available. Bloom was born in Cleveland and raised by his father, an accountant. Showed signs of high intellect at an early age. He studied electronic arts and designed some well-received neural interfaces before he quit the business and disappeared into Doletown. He's eccentric and probably obsessive, but nothing you could force-treat him for."

"And I assume he took the money you offered."

"Correct." Half up front, half when the Cartesian Theater was ready to open.

"So what *was* he doing with those animals?"

One of the sanctuary aibots passed the open door of Grandfather's memorial chamber. It paused a moment, adjusting its tie and tugging at its tailed vest. It swiveled its eyestalks briefly toward us, then wheeled on down the corridor. "Nosy fucking things," Grandfather said.

"Soon as Bloom signed the contract he invited me to what he called a 'dress rehearsal.' But it wasn't any kind of formal performance. It was really just an experiment, a kind of dry run. He sold admission to a few local freaks, people he was ashamed of knowing. People who liked the idea of watching an animal die in agony."

"You said he didn't hurt or kill anything."

"Not as far as the law's concerned, anyway."

Bloom explained it all to me as he set up the night's exhibition. He seemed to welcome the opportunity to talk about his work with someone who wasn't, as he said, "quietly deranged." He hammered that idea pretty hard, as if to establish his own sanity. But how sane is a man whose overweening ambition is to make an art form of death?

He selected one of the dogs and pulled its cage from the rack. The other dogs he released into a makeshift kennel on an adjoining roof. "They get upset if they see what happens, even though they're not in any danger."

Then he put the selected animal into a transparent box the size of a shipping crate. The glass walls of the box were pierced with ventilator holes and inlaid with a mesh of ultrafine inductors. A cable as thick as my arm snaked from the box to the rack of electronic instrumentation. "You recognize the devices on the dog's collar?"

"Neuroprostheses," I said. "The kind they attach to old people." The kind they had attached to Grandfather back when he was merely dying, not entirely dead.

"Right," Bloom said, his face simmering with enthusiasm. "The mind, your mind, any mind—the dog's mind, in this case—is really a sort of parliament of competing neural subroutines. When people get old, some or all of those functions start to fail. So we build various kinds of prostheses to support aging mentation. Emotive functions, limbic functions, memory, the senses: We can sub for each of those things with an external device."

That was essentially what Grandfather had done for the last five years of his life: shared more and more of his essential self with a small army of artificial devices. And when he eventually died much of him was still running in these clusters of epibiotic prostheses. But eventually, over time, without a physical body to order and replenish them, the machines would drift back to simple default states, and that would be the end of Grandfather as a coherent entity. It was a useful but ultimately imperfect technology.

"Our setup's a little different," Bloom said. "The prostheses here aren't subbing for lost functions—the dog isn't injured or old. They're just doubling the dog's ordinary brain states. When I disconnect the prostheses the dog won't even notice; he's fully functional without them. But the ghost in the prostheses—the dog's intellectual double—goes on without him."

"Yeah, for thirty seconds or so," I said. Such experiments had been attempted before. Imagine being able to run a perfect copy of yourself in a digital environment—to download yourself to an electronic device, like in the movies. Wouldn't that be great? Well, you *can*, sort of, and the process worked the way Bloom described it. But only briefly. The fully complex digital model succumbs to something called "Shannon entropy" in less than a minute. It's not dynamically stable.

(Postmortem arrays like Grandfather last longer—up to a couple of years—but only because they're radically simplified, more a collection of vocal tics than a real personality.)

"Thirty seconds is enough," Bloom said.

"For what?"

"You'll see."

About this time the evening's audience began to drift in. Or maybe *audience* is too generous a word. It consisted of five furtive-looking guys in cloaks and rags, each of whom slipped Bloom a few bills and then retreated to the shadows. They spoke not at all, even to one another, and they stared at the dog in its glass chamber with strange, hungry eyes. The dog paced, understandably nervous.

Now Bloom rolled out another, nearly identical chamber. The "death chamber." It contained not a dog but a sphere of some pink, slightly sparkly substance.

"Electrosensitive facsimile gel," Bloom whispered. "Do you know what that is?"

I'd heard of it. Facsimile gel is often used for stage and movie effects. If you want an inert duplicate of a valuable object or a bankable star, you scan the item in question and map it onto gel with EM fields. The gel expands and morphs until it's visually identical to the scanned object, right down to color and micron-level detail if you use the expensive stuff. Difference was, the duplicate would be rigid, hollow, and nearly massless—a useful prop, but delicate.

"You duplicate the dog?" I asked.

"I make a *dynamic* duplicate. It changes continuously, in synch with the real thing. I've got a patent application on it. Watch." He dimmed the lights and threw a few switches on his bank of home-made electronics.

The result was eerie. The lump of gel pulsed a few times, expanded as if it had taken a deep breath, grew legs, and became . . . a dog.

Became, in fact, the dog in the adjacent glass cage.

The real dog looked at the fake dog with obvious distress. It whined. The fake dog made the same gesture simultaneously, but no sound came out.

Two tongues lolled. Two tails drooped.

Now the freaks in the audience were almost slavering with anticipation.

I whispered, "And this proves what?"

Bloom raised his voice so the ginks could hear—a couple of them were new and needed the explanation. "Two dogs," he said. "One real. One artificial. The living dog is fitted with an array of neuro-prostheses that duplicate its brain states. The dog's brain states are modeled in the electronics, here. Got that?"

We all got it. The audience nodded in unison.

"The dog's essence, its sense of self, is distributed between its organic brain and the remote prostheses. At the moment it's controlling the gel duplicate, too. When the real dog lifts his head and sniffs the air—like that: see?—he lifts the fake dog's head simultaneously. The illusion mimics the reality. The twinned soul operates twin bodies, through the medium of the machine."

His hand approached another switch.

"But when I throw *this* switch, the living dog's link to the prosthetics is severed. The original dog becomes merely itself—it won't even notice that the connection has been cut."

He threw the switch; the audience gasped—but again, nothing obvious happened.

Both dogs continued to pace, as if disturbed by the sharp smell of sweat and ionization.

"As of now," Bloom said, "the artificial animal is dynamically controlled *solely by the neuroprostheses*. It's an illusion operated by a machine. But it moves as if it had mass, it sees as if it had eyes, it retains a capacity for pleasure or pain."

Now the behavior of the two dogs began to fall out of synchronization, subtly at first, and then more radically. Neither dog seemed to like what was happening. They eyed each other through their respective glass walls and backed away, snarling.

"Of course," Bloom added, his voice thick with an excitement he couldn't disguise, "without a biological model the neuroprostheses lose coherence. Shannon entropy sets in. Ten seconds have passed since I threw the final switch." He checked his watch. "Twenty."

The fake dog shook its head and emitted a silent whine.

It moved in a circle, panting.

It tried to scratch itself. But its legs tangled and bent spasmodically. It teetered a moment, then fell on its side. Its ribs pumped as if it were really breathing, and I guess it thought it *was* breathing—gasping for air it didn't really need and couldn't use.

It raised its muzzle and bared its teeth.

Its eyes rolled aimlessly. Then they turned opaque and dissolved into raw gel.

The artificial dog made more voiceless screaming gestures. Other parts of it began to fall off and dissolve. It arched its back. Its flanks cracked open, and for a moment I could see the shadowy hollowness inside.

The agony went on for what seemed like centuries but was probably not more than a minute or two. I had to turn away.

The audience liked it, though. This was what they had come for, this simulation of death.

They held their breath until the decoherent mass of gel had stopped moving altogether; then they sighed; they applauded timidly. It was only when the lights came up that they began to look ashamed. "Now get out," Bloom told them, and when they had finished shuffling out the door, heads down, avoiding eye contact, he whispered to me, "I hate those guys. They are truly fucking demented."

I looked back at the two glass cages.

The original dog was trembling but unhurt. The duplicate was a quiescent puddle of goo. It had left a sharp tang in the air, and I imagined it was the smell of pain. The thing had clearly been in pain. "You said there was no cruelty involved."

"No cruelty *to animals*," Bloom corrected me.

"So what do you call this?"

"There's only one animal in the room, Mr. Paczovski, and it's completely safe, as you can see. What took shape in the gel box was an animation controlled by a machine. It didn't die because it was never alive."

"But it was in agony."

"By definition, no, it wasn't. A machine can only *simulate* pain. Look it up in the statutes. Machines have no legal standing in this regard."

"Yeah, but a complex-enough machine—"

"The law doesn't make that distinction. The EES is complex. Aibots are complex: They're all linked together in one big neural net. Does that make them people? Does that make it an act of sadism if you kick a vacuum cleaner or default on a loan?"

Guess not. Anyway, it was his show, not mine. I meant to ask him if the dog act was the entire substance of his proposed Cartesian Theater . . . and why he thought anyone would want to see such a thing, apart from a few unmedicated sadists.

But this wasn't about dogs, not really. It was a test run. When Bloom turned away from me I could see a telltale cluster of bulges between his shoulder blades. He was wearing a full array of neuroprostheses. That's what he meant when he said the dogs were experiments. He was using them to refine his technique. Ultimately, he meant to do this *to himself*.

"Technically," Grandfather said, "he's right. About the law, I mean. What he's doing, it's ingenious and it's perfectly legal."

"Lada's lawyers told her the same thing."

"A machine, or a distributed network of machines, can be intelligent. But it can never be a person under the law. It can't even be a legal dog. Bloom wasn't shitting you. If he'd hurt the animal in any way he would have been remanded for treatment. But the fake dog, legally, is only a *representation* of an animal, like an elaborate photograph."

"Like you," I pointed out.

He ignored this. "Tell me, did any of the ginks attending this show look rich?"

"Hardly."

"So the anonymous investor isn't one of them."

"Unless he was in disguise, no. And I doubt Bloom would have turned down a cash gift even if it came from his creepy audience— the investor wouldn't have needed me or Lada if he had a direct line to Bloom."

"So how did your investor hear about Bloom in the first place, if he isn't friendly with him or part of his audience?"

Good question.

I didn't have an answer.

* * *

288

When I told Lada what I'd seen she frowned and ran her gold finger over her rose-pink lower lip, a signal of deep interest, the kind of gesture professional gamblers call a "tell."

I said, "I did what you asked me to. Is there a problem with that?"

"No—no problem at all. You did fine, Toby. I just wonder if we should have taken a piece for ourselves. A side agreement of some kind, in case this really does pan out."

"If *what* pans out? When you come down to it, all Bloom has to peddle is an elaborate special effect. A stage trick, and not a very appealing one. The ancillary technology might be interesting, but he says he already filed patents."

"The investor obviously feels differently. And he probably didn't get rich by backing losers."

"How well do you know this investor?"

She smiled. "All honesty? I've never met him. He's a text-mail address."

"You're sure about his gender, at least?"

"No, but, you know, *death, pain*—it all seems a little masculine, doesn't it?"

"So is there a next step or do we just wait for Bloom to put together his show?"

"Oh"—and here she grinned in a way I didn't like—"there's *definitely* a next step."

She gave me another name. Philo Novembre.

"Rings a bell," Grandfather said. "Faintly. But then, I've forgotten so much."

Philo Novembre was easier to find than Jafar Bloom. At least, his address was easier to find—holding a conversation with him was another matter.

Philo Novembre was ten years short of a century old. He lived in an offshore retirement eden called Wintergarden Estates, connected to the mainland by a scenic causeway. I was the most conspicuously youthful visitor in the commute bus from the docks, not that the sample was representative: There were only three other passengers aboard. Aibot transports hogged the rest of the road, shuttling supplies to the Wintergarden. Their big eyes tracked the bus absently and they looked bored, even for machines.

Novembre, of course, had not invited me to visit, so the aibot staffing the reception desk asked me to wait in the garden while it paged him—warning me that Mr. Novembre didn't always answer his pages promptly. So I found a bench in the atrium and settled down.

The Wintergarden was named for its atrium. I don't know anything about flowers, but there was a gaudy assortment of them here, crowding their beds and creeping over walkways and climbing the latticed walls, pushing out crayon-colored blooms. Old people are supposed to like this kind of thing. Maybe they do, maybe they don't; Grandfather had never demonstrated an interest in botany, and he had died at the age of a century and change. But the garden was pretty to look at and it flushed the air with complex fragrances, like a dream of an opium den. I was nearly dozing when Philo Novembre finally showed up.

He crossed the atrium like a force of nature. Elderly strollers made way for his passage; garden-tending aibots the size of cats dodged his footfalls with quick, knowing lunges. His face was lined but sharp, not sagging, and his eyes were the color of water under ice. His left arm was unapologetically prosthetic, clad in powder-black brushed titanium. His guide, a thigh-high aibot in brown slacks and a golf shirt, pointed at me and then scuttled away.

I stood up to meet him. He was a centimeter or two taller than me. His huge gray gull-winged eyebrows contracted. He said, "I don't know you."

"No, sir, you don't. My name is Toby Paczovski, and I'd be honored if you'd let me buy you lunch."

It took some haggling, but eventually he let me lead him to one of the five restaurants in the Wintergarden complex. He ordered a robust meal, I ordered coffee, and both of us ignored the elderly customers at the adjoining tables, some so extensively doctored that their physical and mental prostheses had become their defining characteristics. One old gink sucked creamed corn through a tube that issued from his jaw like an insect tongue, while his partner glared at me through lidless ebony-black eyes. I don't plan ever to get old. It's unseemly.

"The reason I'm here—" I began, but Novembre interrupted.

"No need to prolong this. You bought me a decent meal, Mr. Paczovski. I owe you a little candor, if nothing else. So let me explain something. Three or four times a year somebody like yourself shows up here at the Wintergarden and flatters me and asks me to submit to an interview or a public appearance. This person might represent a more or less respectable agency or he might be a stringer or a media pimp, but it always comes down to the same pitch: Once-famous enemy of automated commerce survives into the golden age of the EES. What they want from me is either a gesture of defiance or a mumbled admission of defeat. They say they'll pay generously for the right note of bathos. But the real irony is that these people have come on a quest as quixotic as anything I ever undertook. Because I don't make public appearances. Period. I don't sign contracts. Period. I'm retired. In every sense of the word. Now: Do you want to spend your time more profitably elsewhere, or shall we order another round of coffee and discuss other things?"

"Uh," I said.

"And of course, in case you're already recording, I explicitly claim all rights to any words I've spoken or will speak at this meeting or henceforth, subject to the Peking Accords and the Fifty-second Amendment."

He grinned. His teeth looked convincingly real. But most people's teeth look real these days, except the true ancients, like the guy at the next table.

"Well, he knows his intellectual property law," Grandfather said. "He's got you dead to rights on that one."

"Probably so," I said, "but it doesn't matter. I wasn't there to buy his signature on a contract."

"So what *did* you want from him? Or should I say, what did Lada want from him?"

"She wanted me to tell him about Jafar Bloom. Basically, she wanted me to invite him to opening night at the Cartesian Theater."

"That's it?"

"That's it."

"So this client of hers was setting up a scenario in which Novembre was present for Bloom's death act."

"Basically, yeah."

"For no stated reason." Grandfather's photograph was motionless a few moments. Implying deep thought, or a voltage sag.

I said, "Do you remember Philo Novembre back when he was famous? The eighties, that would have been."

"The 2080s," Grandfather mused. "I don't know. I remember that I once remembered those years. I have a memory of having a memory. My memories are like bubbles, Toby. There's nothing substantial inside, and when I touch them they tend to disappear."

Philo Novembre had been a celebrity intellectual back in the 2080s, a philosopher, a sort of twenty-first-century Socrates or Aristotle.

In those days—the global population having recently restabilized at two billion after the radical decline of the Plague Years—everyday conveniences were still a dream of the emerging Rationalization. Automated expert systems, neuroprostheses, resource-allocation protocols, the dole: All these things were new and contentious, and Philo Novembre was suspicious of all of them.

He had belonged to no party and supported no movement, although many claimed him. He had written a book, *The Twilight of the Human Soul*, and he had stomped for it like a backwoods evangelist, but what had made him a media celebrity was his personal style: modest at first; then fierce, scolding, bitter, moralistic.

He had claimed that ancient virtues were being lost or forgotten in the rush to a rationalized economy, that expert systems and globally distributed AI, no matter how sophisticated, could never emulate true moral sensitivity—a human sense of right and wrong.

That was the big debate of the day, simplistic as it sounds, and it ultimately ended in a sort of draw. Aibots and expert systems were granted legal status *in loco humanis* for economic purposes but were denied any broader rights, duties, privileges, or protection under the law. Machines aren't people, the courts said, and if the machines said anything in response they said it only to one another.

And we all prospered in the aftermath, as the old clunky oscillating global marketplace grew increasingly supple, responsive, and bias-free. Novembre had eventually disappeared from public life as people lost interest in his jeremiads and embraced the rising prosperity.

Lada had given me a dossier of press clippings on Novembre's decline from fame. Around about the turn of the century he was discovered in a Dade County doletown, chronically drunk. A few months later he stumbled into the path of a streetcleaning aibot, and his left arm was crushed before the startled and penitent machine could reverse its momentum. A local hospital had replaced his arm—it was still the only prosthesis he was willing to wear—and incidentally cured his alcoholism, fitting him with a minor corticolimbic mod that damped his craving. He subsequently attempted to sue the hospital for neurological intervention without written consent, but his case was so flimsy it was thrown out of court.

After which Novembre vanished into utter obscurity and eventually signed over his dole annuities to the Wintergarden Retirement Commune.

From which he would not budge, even for a blind date with Jafar Bloom. I told Lada so when I made it back to the mainland.

"We have not yet begun to fight," Lada said.

"Meaning . . . ?"

"Meaning let me work it for a little while. Stay cozy with Jafar Bloom; make sure he's doing what we need him to do. Call me in a week. I'll come up with something."

She was thinking hard . . . which, with Lada, was generally a sign of trouble brewing.

Unfortunately, I had begun to despise Jafar Bloom.

As much as Bloom affected to disdain the ginks and gaffers who paid to see his animal tests, he was just as twisted as his audience—more so, in his own way. Morbid narcissism wafted off him like a bad smell.

But Lada had asked me to make sure Bloom followed through on his promise. So I dutifully spent time with him during the month it took to rig his show. We rented an abandoned theater in the old district of Doletown and I helped him fix it up, bossing a fleet of renovation aibots who painted the mildewed walls, replaced fractured seats, restored the stage, and patched the flaking proscenium. We ordered industrial quantities of reprogels and commissioned a control rig of Bloom's design from an electronics prototyper.

During one of these sessions I asked him why he called his show "The Cartesian Theater."

He smiled a little coyly. "You know the name Descartes?"

No. I used to know a Belgian acrobat called Giselle de Canton, but the less said about that the better.

"The philosopher Descartes," Bloom said patiently. "Rene Descartes, 1596 to 1650. *Discourse on Method. Rules for the Direction of the Mind.*"

"Sorry, no," I said.

"Well. In one of his books Descartes imagines the self—the human sense of identity, that is—as a kind of internal gnome, a little creature hooked up to the outside world through the senses, like a gink in a one-room apartment staring out the window and sniffing the air."

"So you believe that?"

"I believe in it as a metaphor. What I mean to do onstage is externalize my Cartesian self, or at least a copy of it. Let the gnome out for a few seconds. Modern science, of course, says there is no unitary self, that what we call a 'self' is only the collective voice of dozens of neural subsystems working competitively and collaboratively—"

"What else could it be?"

"According to the ancients, it could be a human soul."

"But your version of it dies in agony in less than a minute."

"Right. If you believed in the existence of the soul, you could construe what I do as an act of murder. Except, of course, the soul in question is dwelling in a machine at the moment of its death. And we have ruled, in all our wisdom, that machines don't *have* souls."

"Nobody believes in souls," I said.

But I guess there were a few exceptions.

Philo Novembre, for one.

Lada called me into her office the following week and handed me another dossier of historical files. "More background?"

"Leverage," she said. "Information Mr. Novembre would prefer to keep quiet."

"You're asking me to blackmail him?"

"God, Toby. Settle down. The word *blackmail* has really awkward legal connotations. So let's not use it, shall we?"

"If I threaten him he's liable to get violent." Novembre was old, but that titanium forearm had looked intimidating.

"I don't pay you to do the easy things."

"I'm not sure you pay me enough to do the hard things. So where'd this information come from? Looks like ancient police files."

"Our client submitted it," Lada said.

"What did you ever see in this woman?" Grandfather asked.

Good question, although he had asked it a dozen times before, in fact, whenever I visited him. I didn't bother answering anymore.

I had come to the city a dozen years ago from a ghost town in the hinterland—one of those wheat towns decimated by the population implosion and rendered obsolete by aifarming—after my parents were killed when a malfunctioning grain transport dropped out of the sky onto our old house on Nightshade Street. Grandfather had been my only living relative, and he had helped me find Doletown digs and cooked me an old-fashioned meal every Sunday.

City life had been a welcome distraction, and the dole had seemed generous, at least until grief faded and ambition set in. Then I had gone looking for work, and Lada Joshi had been kind enough, as I saw it then, to hire me as one of her barely paid Doletown scouts.

Which was fine, until the connection between us got more personal. Lada saw me as a diamond in the rough, begging for her lapidary attention. While I saw her as an ultimately inscrutable amalgam of love, sex, and money.

It worked out about as well as you'd expect.

Novembre's official biography, widely distributed back when he was famous, made him out to be the dutiful son of a Presbyterian pastor and a classical flautist, both parents lost in the last plagues of the Implosion. The truth, according to Lada's files, was a little uglier. Philo Novembre's real name was Cassius Flynn, and he had been raised by a couple of marginally sane marijuana farmers in rural Minnesota. The elder Flynns had been repeatedly arrested on drug and domestic violence charges, back in the days before the Rationalization and the Ethical Police. Their death had in a sense been a boon for young Cassius, who had flourished in one of the big residential schools run by the federal government for orphans of the Plague Years.

Nothing too outrageous, but it would have been prime blackmail material back in the day. But Novembre wasn't especially impressed when I showed him what we had.

"I made my name," he said, "by proclaiming a belief in the existence of metaphysical good and evil independent of social norms.

I allowed a publicist to talk me into a lie about my childhood, mainly because I didn't want to be presented to the world as a psychological case study. Yes, my parents were cruel, petty, and venal human beings. Yes, that probably did contribute to the trajectory of my life and work. And yes, it still embarrasses me. But I'm far too old and obscure to be blackmailed. Isn't that obvious? Go tell the world, Mr. Paczovski. See if the world cares."

"Yeah," I said, "it did seem like kind of a long shot."

"What intrigues me is that you would go to these lengths to convince me to attend a one-shot theatrical production, for purposes you can't explain. Who hired you, Mr. Paczovski?"

He didn't mean Lada. She was only an intermediary. "Truly, I don't know."

"That sounds like an honest answer. But it begs another question. Who, frankly, imagines my presence at Mr. Bloom's performance would be in any way meaningful?" He lowered his head a moment, pondering. Then he raised it. "Do you know how my work is described in the *Encyclopedia of Twenty-First Century American Thought*? As—and I'm quoting—'a humanistic questioning of economic automation, embodied in a quest to prove the existence of transcendent good and evil, apart from the acts encouraged or proscribed by law under the Rationalization.'"

"Transcendent," I said. "That's an interesting word." I wondered what it meant.

"Because it sounds like your Mr. Bloom has discovered just that—a profoundly evil act, for which he can't be prosecuted under existing law."

"Does that mean you're interested?"

"It means I'm curious. Not quite the same thing."

But he was hooked. I could hear it in his voice. The blackmail had had its intended effect, though not in the customary way.

"Entertainment," Grandfather said.

"What?"

"That's really the only human business anymore. Aibots do all the physical labor, and the EES sorts out supply and demand. What do *we* do that *bots* can't do? Entertain each other, mostly. Lie, gossip, and dance. That, or practice law."

"Yeah, but so?"

"It's why someone wanted to put Bloom and Novembre together. For the entertainment value." His photograph stared while I blinked. "The *motive*, stupid," he said.

"Motive implies a crime."

"You mentioned blood. So I assume Novembre made the show."

"It opened last night." And closed.

"You want to tell me about it?"

Suddenly, no, I didn't. I didn't even want to think about it.

But I was in too deep to stop. Story of my life.

Doletown, of course, is a museum of lost causes and curious passions, which means there's plenty of live theater in Doletown, most of it eccentric or execrably bad. But Bloom's production didn't rise even to that level. It lacked plot, stagecraft, publicity, or much of an audience, and none of that mattered to Jafar Bloom: As with his animal experiments, public display was only a way of raising money, never an end in itself. He didn't care who watched, or if anyone watched.

The Cartesian Theater opened on a windy, hot night in August. The moon was full and the streets were full of bored and restless dole gypsies, but none of them wanted to come inside. I showed up early, not that I was looking forward to the show. ·

Bloom rolled his glassy Death Chamber onto the stage without even glancing at the seats, most of which were empty, the rest occupied by the same morbid gaffers who had attended his animal experiments. There were, in fact, more aibots than live flesh in the house. The ushers alone—wheeled units in cheap black tuxedos—outnumbered the paying customers.

Philo Novembre, dressed in gray, came late. He took an empty seat beside me, front-row center.

"Here I am," he whispered. "Now, who have I satisfied? Who wants me here?"

He looked around but sighted no obvious culprit. Nor did I, although it could have been someone in dole drag: The wealthy have been known to dress down and go slumming. Still, none of these ten or twelve furtive patrons of the arts looked plausibly like a high-stakes benefactor.

The theater smelled of mildew and mothballs, despite everything we'd done to disinfect it.

"What it is," Novembre mooted to me as he watched Bloom plug in a set of cables, "is a sort of philosophical grudge match, yes? Do you see that, Mr. Paczovski? Me, the archaic humanist who believes in the soul but can't establish the existence of it, and Mr. Bloom"—here he gestured contemptuously at the stage—"who generates evil as casually as an animal marking its territory with urine. A modern man, in other words."

"Yeah, I guess so," I said. In truth, all this metaphysical stuff was beyond me.

Eventually the lights dimmed, and Novembre slouched into his seat and crossed his good arm over his prosthesis.

And the show began.

Began prosaically. Bloom strolled to the front of the stage and explained what was about to happen. The walls of the Death Chamber, he said, were made of mirrored glass. The audience would be able to see inside but the occupant—or occupants—couldn't see out. The interior of the chamber was divided into two identical cubicles, each roughly six feet on a side. Each cubicle contained a chair, a small wooden table, a fluted glass, and a bottle of champagne.

Bloom would occupy one chamber. Once he was inside, his body would be scanned and a duplicate of it would take shape in the other. Both Bloom and counter-Bloom would look and act identically. Just like the dogs in his earlier experiment.

Novembre leaned toward my right ear. "I see now what he intends," the old man whispered. "The genius of it . . ."

There was scattered applause as Bloom opened the chamber door and stepped inside.

"The perverse genius," Novembre whispered, "is that Bloom himself won't know. . . ."

And in response to his presence hidden nozzles filled the duplicate chamber with pink electrosensitive gel, which contracted under the pressure of invisible sculpting fields into a crude replica of Bloom, a man-shaped form lacking only the finer detail.

"He won't know which is which, or rather . . ."

Another bank of electronics flickered to life, stage rear. The gel duplicate clarified in an instant, and although I knew what it was— a hollow shell of adaptive molecules—it looked as substantial, as weighty, as Bloom himself.

Bloom's neural impulses were controlling both bodies now. He lifted the champagne bottle and filled the waiting glass. His dutiful reflection did likewise, at the same time and with the same tight, demented smile. He toasted the audience he couldn't see.

"Or rather, he won't know which is himself—each entity will believe, feel, intuit that it's the true and only Bloom, until one . . ."

Now Bloom replaced the glass on the tabletop, cueing an aibot stagehand in the wings. The houselights flickered off and after a moment were replaced by a pair of baby spots, one for each division of the Death Chamber.

This was the signal that Bloom had cut the link between himself and the machinery. The neuroprostheses were running on a kind of cybernetic inertia. The duplicate Bloom was on borrowed time, but didn't know it.

The two Blooms continued to stare at each other. Narcissus in Hades.

And Novembre was right, of course: The copy couldn't tell itself from the real thing, the real thing from the copy.

"Until one begins to decohere," Novembre finished. "Until the agony begins."

Thirty seconds.

I resisted the urge to look at my watch.

The old philosopher leaned forward in his seat.

Bloom and anti-Bloom raised glasses to each other. Both appeared to drink. Both had Bloom's memory. Both had Bloom's motivation. Each believed himself to be the authentic Bloom.

And both must have harbored doubts. Both thinking: I know I'm the real item, I can't be anything else, but what if . . . *what if . . .* ?

A trickle of sweat ran down the temples of both Blooms.

Both Blooms crossed their legs and both attempted another nonchalant sip of champagne.

But now they had begun to fall just slightly out of synchronization.

The Bloom on the right seemed to gag at the liquid.

The Bloom on the left saw the miscue and liked what he saw.

The Bloom on the right fumbled the champagne glass and dropped it. The glass shattered on the chamber floor.

The opposite Bloom widened his eyes and threw his own glass down. The right-hand Bloom stared in disbelief.

That was the worst thing: that look of dawning understanding, incipient terror.

The audience—including Novembre—leaned toward the action. "God help us," the old philosopher said.

Now Bloom's electronic neuroprostheses, divorced from their biological source, began to lose coherence more rapidly. Feedback loops in the hardware read the dissolution as physical pain. The false Bloom opened his mouth—attempting a scream, though he had no lungs to force out air. Wisps of gel rose from his skin: He looked like he was dissolving into meat-colored smoke. His eyes turned black and slid down his cheeks. His remaining features twisted into a grimace of agony.

The real Bloom grinned in triumph. He looked like a man who had won a desperate gamble, which in a sense he had. He had wagered against his own death and survived his own suicide.

I didn't want to watch, but this time I couldn't turn away—it absorbed my attention so completely that I didn't realize Philo Novembre had left his seat until I saw him lunge across the stage.

I was instantly afraid for Bloom, the real Bloom. The philosopher was swinging his titanium arm like a club and his face was a mask of rage. But he aimed his first blow not at Bloom but at the subchamber where his double was noisily dying. I think he meant to end its suffering.

A single swing of his arm cracked the wall, rupturing the embedded sensors and controllers.

Aibot ushers and stagehands suddenly hustled toward the Death Chamber as if straining for a view. The dying duplicate of Bloom turned what remained of his head toward the audience, as if he had heard a distant sound. Then he collapsed with absolute finality into a puddle of amorphous foam.

Bloom forced open his own chamber door and ran for the wings. Novembre spotted him and gave chase. I tried to follow, but the crowd of aibots closed ranks and barred my way.

Lada would love this, I thought. Lada would make serious money if she could retail a recording of this event. But I wasn't logging it and nobody else seemed to be, except of course the aibots, who remember everything; but their memories are legally protected, shared only by other machines.

This was unrecorded history, unhappening even as it happened.

I caught up with Bloom in the alley behind the Cartesian Theater. Too late. Novembre had caught up with him first. Bloom was on the ground, his skull opened like a ripe melon. A little gray aibot with EMS protocols sat astride Bloom's chest, stimulating his heart and blowing air into his lungs—uselessly. Bloom was dead, irretrievably dead long before the ambulance arrived and gathered him into its motherly arms.

As for Novembre . . .

It looked at first as if he'd escaped into the crowd. But I went back into the theater on a hunch, and I found him there, hidden in the fractured ruin of Jafar Bloom's Death Chamber, where he had opened his own throat with a sliver of broken glass and somehow found time to write the words BUT IT EXISTS in blood on the chamber wall.

"Yup, it was a show," Grandfather said.

I gave his image an exasperated look. "Of course it was a show. 'The Cartesian Theater'—what else could it be?"

"Not that. I mean the mutual self-destruction of Bloom and Novembre. You see it, Toby? The deliberate irony? Novembre believes in humanity and hates intellectual machines. But he takes pity on the fake Bloom as it dies, and by doing so he tacitly admits that a machine can harbor something akin to a human soul. He found what he had been looking for all his life, a metaphysical expression of human suffering outside the laws of the Rationalization—but he found it in a rack of electronics. We have to assume that's what your client wanted and expected to happen. A philosophical tragedy, culminating in a murder-suicide."

This was Grandfather's trial-lawyer subroutine talking, but what he said made a certain amount of sense. It was as if I had played a supporting role in a drama crafted by an omniscient playwright. Except . . .

"Except," I said, "who saw it?"

"One of the attendees might have recorded it surreptitiously."

"No one witnessed both deaths, according to the police, and they searched the witnesses for wires."

"But the transaction was completed? Lada was paid for her services?"

I had talked to her this morning. Yes, she was paid. Generously and in full. The client had evidently received value for money.

"So you have to ask yourself," Grandfather said, "—and I no longer possess the imagination to suggest an answer—who could have known about both Bloom and Novembre? Who could have conceived this scenario? Who understood the motivation of both men intimately enough to predict a bloody outcome? To whose taste does this tragedy cater, and how was that taste satisfied if the client was not physically present?"

"Fuck, I don't know."

Grandfather nodded. He understood ignorance. His own curiosity had flickered briefly, but it died like a spent match. "You came here with a problem to solve. . . ."

"Right," I said. "Here's the thing. Lada's happy with how this whole scenario worked. She said I outdid myself. She says the client wants to work with her again, maybe on a regular basis. She offered to hire me back full-time and even increase my salary."

"Which is what you'd been hoping for, yes?"

"But suddenly the whole idea makes me a little queasy—I don't know why. So what do you think? Should I re-up, take the money, make a success of myself? Maybe hook up with Lada again—on a personal level, I mean—if things go well? Because I could do that. It would be easy. But I keep thinking it'd be even easier to find a place by the docks and live on the dole and watch the waves roll in."

Watch the aibots build more hives and nurseries. Watch the population decline.

"I'm far too dead," Grandfather said, "to offer sensible advice. Anyway, it sounds as if you've already decided."

And I realized he was right—I had.

On the way out of the sanctuary where Grandfather was stored I passed a gaggle of utility aibots. They were lined up along the corridor in serried ranks, motionless, and their eyes scanned me as I passed.

And as I approached the exit, the chief custodial aibot—a tall, lanky unit in a black vest and felt hat—stepped into my path. He turned his face down to me and said, "Do you know Sophocles, Mr. Paczovski?"

I was almost too surprised to answer. "Sophocles who?"

"*Ajax*," he said cryptically. "The Chorus. 'When Reason's day / Sets rayless—joyless—quenched in cold decay, / Better to die, and sleep / The never-waking sleep, than linger on / And dare to live, when the soul's life is gone.'"

And while I stared, the gathered aibots—the ones with hands, at least—began gently to applaud.

ou Anders is an editor, author, and journalist. He is the editorial director of Prometheus Books' science-fiction and fantasy imprint Pyr, as well as the editor of the anthologies *Outside the Box* (Wildside Press, 2001), *Live Without a Net* (Roc, 2003), and *Projections: Science Fiction in Literature & Film* (MonkeyBrain, December 2004). In 2003 and 2004, he served as the senior editor for two issues of a revived *Argosy* magazine. In 2000, he served as the executive editor of Bookface.com, and before that he worked as the Los Angeles Liaison for Titan Publishing Group. He is the author of *The Making of Star Trek: First Contact* (Titan Books, 1996), and has published over five hundred articles in such magazines as *Publishers Weekly, The Believer, Dreamwatch, Star Trek Monthly, Star Wars Monthly, Babylon 5 Magazine, Sci Fi Universe, Doctor Who Magazine,* and *Manga Max.* His articles have been translated into German and French, and have appeared online at SFSite.com, RevolutionSF.com, and InfinityPlus.co.uk. You can visit his web site at www.louanders.com.